Penguin Books

The Penguin World Or

Brian Aldiss lives in the semi-c...... ...ife and two children.
He is fond of travelling and has attended science fiction symposia as
far afield as Tokyo and Rio de Janeiro. His non-science fiction includes
a travel book on Yugoslavia and the best-selling saga of Horatio
Stubbs; two novels in this series have appeared, *The Hand-Reared Boy*
and *A Soldier Erect*. He has also written a history of science fiction,
Billion Year Spree, *Frankenstein Unbound* and *The Eighty-Minute Hour*.
His more recent publications include *Brothers of the Head*, *Last Orders*,
Decade: the 1960s (edited with H. Harrison), *A Rude Awakening*, *Life
in the West*, *Moreau's Other Island* and the *Helliconia* series.

Sam J. Lundwall is an author, editor, critic, translator and publisher.
His forte is satire and his best-known books include *King Kong Blues*,
Alice's World, *No Time for Heroes* and *Bernhard the Conqueror*. Born
in 1941 in Sweden, he has been instrumental in creating the current
Swedish science-fiction boom. He started his own publishing house,
Delta, in 1973.

The Penguin
World Omnibus
of Science Fiction

An anthology edited by Brian Aldiss
and Sam J. Lundwall

Penguin Books

Penguin Books Ltd, Harmondsworth, Middlesex, England
Viking Penguin Inc., 40 West 23rd Street, New York, New York 10010, U.S.A.
Penguin Books Australia Ltd, Ringwood, Victoria, Australia
Penguin Books Canada Limited, 2801 John Street, Markham, Ontario, Canada L3R 1B4
Penguin Books (N.Z.) Ltd, 182–190 Wairau Road, Auckland 10, New Zealand

First published by Penguin Books 1986
This collection copyright © Brian Aldiss and Sam J. Lundwall, 1986
All rights reserved

Pages 7–10 constitute an extension of the copyright page.

Made and printed in Great Britain by
Richard Clay (The Chaucer Press) Ltd, Bungay, Suffolk
Filmset in Monophoto Times

Contents

Acknowledgements

'The Mirror Image of the Earth' by Zheng Wenguang, copyright © Zheng Wenguang, 1980. Translated by Sun Liang.

'The New Prehistory' by René Rebetez-Cortes, copyright © René Rebetez-Cortes, 1972. Translated by Damon Knight.

'Rising Sun' by Péter Lengyel, copyright © Péter Lengyel, 1982. Translated by Oliver A. I. Botar.

'The Lens' by Annemarie van Ewyck, first published in *Kingkong Magazine*. Copyright © Annemarie van Ewyck, 1977. Translation copyright © 1984.

'Progenitor' by Philippe Curval, copyright © Philippe Curval, 1980. First published in *Le livre d'or de la SF*. Translated by Scott Baker.

'The Cage' by Bertram Chandler, copyright 1957 by Fantasy House Inc. Reprinted by permission of the E. J. Carnell Literary Agency.

Foreword

KRSTO A. MAŽURANIĆ

Take a good SF story, any good SF story: it is fun; it is aesthetically and intellectually pleasing; it makes the mosaic of the reader's awareness of the complex concept of human destiny richer by one more tiny piece of marble. In short, it is an invaluable experience.

Does it matter in which language the good SF story has been written? Does it *really matter at all*, as long as it is a *good SF story*?

Why, of course it does! The language makes all the difference in the world. *Have you* read any good SF stories written in Hungarian, Serbo-Croatian, Hebrew, etc. lately? Probably not, unless it just so happens that one of these languages is your mother tongue. And it is not for lack of good SF stories in those languages. At least, I suspect it isn't; I wouldn't know: I've never read a good SF story in Hungarian, Hebrew, etc. Or any kind of story, for that matter. It's simply that I can't read the languages. I depend on translations. There are next to none of those.

SF literature in the world is a sort of a honeycomblike archipelago of languages with a network of one-way, valve-like shipping routes among the islands. One great big island only exports; a very few maintain a shaky, lopsided balance; the majority, for all practical purposes, only import. The tiny trickle of export among the latter is sporadic, lamentably insignificant. Their home produce generally remains nothing more than locally enjoyed goodies, curiosities all but lost on the racks full of imported wordage – admittedly often good, but that is beside the point here.

This state of affairs is quite understandable in that the publishing business is exactly that: a business. Business causes the valving effect. What percentage is there in delving through reams of mediocre writing in a strange language in order to fish out possible gems? Take your pick instead where the ready-made, known quality is abundant. Why go looking for a good Romantic opera in Yugoslavia or Spain? Take Verdi!

Obviously some sort of interface is needed to provide the means of penetrating the language barriers between the islands; some method of pinpointing exportable stories in import-only languages; some literary Laker to offer a way to bypass the usual, or even to establish alternative shipping routes. Such an interface has been found and put to very good use – and has resulted in this volume of S F stories.

The young urchin among associations, called World S F, on the very day of its maturity pulls a surprise out of science fiction's hat: the first truly international collection of S F stories: each from a different country, each representative of its country's S F output. No need now to understand Italian, Dutch, etc., to be able to read good stories written in those languages. Just lean back in your armchair, turn the page and start enjoying the goodies in your own language.

Samobor, November 1985

Introduction

BRIAN ALDISS

Since science fiction is not only a charivari of distant suns and planets, let's talk about this planet for a moment.

Our planet is full of languages, all of which sound like strange noises to a majority of the global population. This is true of Chinese, of English, of Russian and any other language we care to name. In New Guinea alone, several hundred dialects are spoken.

This tendency to use language as a barrier rather than a means of communication will surely strike the ultra-civilized Rigelians as odd, when they arrive to carry out their hundred-year survey of our backward planet. But the uncomfortable instinct of humans to isolate themselves into small groups or societies survives, despite all the pressures on us to become more international and to reshuffle ourselves into larger groupings (generally ideological).

'There goes a foreigner – heave half a brick at him,' went the caption to a notorious joke in *Punch* (*c.* 1890). The joke was too painfully near the truth regarding xenophobic English attitudes at the time to be funny. In the present-day world it has become rather important that we do not heave half-bricks, or anything more formidable, at each other. One way of doing this seems to be to follow an age-old tradition – to squat down on our hunkers and talk to each other. Perhaps to tell each other tales. To laugh together.

A human language is not like a machine language, just as we are not machines. A human language is an orchestra; it has many instruments, many tunes to play. Information is by no means all it can convey – indeed, when it comes to conveying information, the languages of mathematics and machines are more precise than human language with all its enticing ambiguities. Human language conveys a variety of signals. There are right and wrong times for firing off these signals. We can promise, threaten, coax, curse, delight, pray, lie, confess, order, supplicate, lecture or merely waffle. Our language contains the means for expressing either barbarities or the gentlest endearments. Language can be as various as we are.

> In the room the women come and go
> Talking of Michelangelo.

T. S. Eliot does not tell us what the women revealed regarding Michelangelo, but we may suppose that there were decided undertones in what they had to say. Language also consists of what is unsaid, of a network of hidden assumptions.

There is a hidden assumption behind this anthology. The assumption might be expressed as follows: there's a way of talking about 'the future' which tells us something about our present. It is an assumption widely held by the members of World SF, who seek within their discipline a common language. The language is a various one but it shares a firm conviction that the era of the half-brick is over.

World SF was founded in Dublin in 1976. A conference of science fiction professionals was held at the Burlington Hotel by Harry Harrison, with devoted help from the rest of the Harrison family, who had then settled near Dublin. Harrison is one of the most internationally minded of writers. As far as I can recall, the idea for World SF was his. He was aided and abetted by like-minded men, including Frederik Pohl from the U.S.A., Peter Kucka from Hungary, Eremi Parnov from the Soviet Union, Sam Lundwall from Sweden, Pierre Barbet from France, Charlotte Franke from West Germany, me from Britain and so on.

Harrison, as Chairman of the conference, had this to say in his introduction to the conference brochure:

The organizers of this conference feel that there is no one true kind of science fiction, and hope that the members of this conference will echo this view. Our strength is that we are international now, a literature for all mankind . . . I hope – I know – that we will have our differences of opinion during this conference; it can be no other way. But we are united in one way: by our presence here, a presence that is a statement. Science fiction *is*. It is alive and well in many countries . . .

By the end of the conference, we had founded World SF. Our ambition was to demonstrate that we could overcome national differences and reach towards what we had in common, the various language we call science fiction. By meeting and talking in each other's countries, we hoped to come to a better understanding, to enlighten ourselves, and to enlighten the general public. In a short while, most of the countries of Europe had joined us – some of the most active include Italy and Poland.

In the short decade of our existence, we have met in several countries and our numbers have grown. We still welcome anyone from any country who has a professional interest in any kind of science fiction whatever.

When Frederik Pohl was President of World SF, he most usefully instituted the Karel Awards (named after the Czech writer Karel Capek) for translation. Translation is an essential part of SF. It is the medium whereby the message travels from one nation to another – though it must be said that English has become the international language of SF as it is of air traffic.

A Karel is a decorative little object. It represents a slender robot sitting on top of a globe, reading a book. Perhaps in order to represent the fragility of our organization's finances, it is executed in glass.

This anthology represents the fulfilment of another of our ambitions: to put together a collection of science fiction stories from all over the world and present it in one book. The result is as interesting and provoking as might be expected. Here is the language of story, conveying a variety of signals in a medley of modes, from illustrated lectures to complex parables, from ironies to fantasies, from adventures to idylls.

Most of the stories contain within them indications of their national origins. I cannot see how it could be otherwise. And the manner of telling throws light on something of the conditions of the country from which they have emerged. From Japan, a delightful legend with anthropological overtones; from China, a cautionary tale, stressing cooperation and the pains of a recent past. From the U.S.S.R. a story which practically launched S F in Russia, according to some reports. From Ghana, a piece of pleasant optimism written as a class exercise. Heavy responsibility, a joyride: the future offers us both options, and more.

Into some of these stories we may read subtle political comment. Others are purely blossoms of fancy – sometimes of erotic fancy, as when we are invited to have our progenital plucked out. Overall, the collection exhibits a quality which I would describe as level-headedness.

Most science fiction originates in the U.S.A. There it is read most, written most, published most, studied most. It is most influential perhaps because – like the Hollywood film – it has proved itself a good commercial export. American S F is gaudy, exciting and generally apocalyptic in tone: the world or the galaxy is to be saved or won or destroyed. The galaxy has become their oyster.

The stories in this collection represent a more level-headed view of the universe. Here, we find an upsurge of torture-yourself books; there, a clever computer crime; elsewhere, another mysterious way of life. But the world is not about to be destroyed yet again. It is not about to be saved yet again. It endures. It continues. A bit of trouble in a laboratory, a priest killed, a number of lunatics disappearing ... but nothing worse than today's newspaper headlines. This is science fiction for survivors. I like it.

A word on how the selection was made. World S F has no power. We wish only to continue writing and travelling and making ourselves at home in each other's countries. Each country looks after its own. Sam Lundwall and I have considered only those stories which were submitted to us by the various national groups (the two exceptions were in the cases of Ghana and Australia). The stories you read here were selected less by us than by committees in their countries of origin. Sam Lundwall did all the hard work of getting permissions and so on. That's what Presidents are for.

The Half-wit of Xeenemuende

JOSEF NESVADBA

The first year in school they sent him back home because he was inattentive, forgetful, scatter-brained and always fighting – he had even thrown an inkwell at his teacher. It was a clear case of oligophrenia and the doctors offered no hope. And yet the wife of Habicht the engineer loved this child of hers above all. She discovered that he had a head for figures, and before the war began she had engaged a governess for him, an elderly lady who took care of him all day. The half-wit's name was Bruno.

A cousin of mine who was sent to work in Xeenemuende during the war told me all about him. My cousin lodged with a seventy-year-old teacher who was to take the place of the strict governess at the Habichts', after she had been killed in a mysterious air-raid on 4 October. Up to then Xeenemuende had never been touched by the Allied bombers. There did not seem to be any important objectives there, either. There was only the underground factory, and nobody knew what was being made there. In the early hours of the morning of 4 October one small light-calibre bomb made a direct hit on the house where Bruno's governess lived, and killed nobody else but her, because the old lady lived alone. At the local command they swore there hadn't been an enemy plane within miles. They talked about long-range artillery fire. Why the British long-range artillery at Dover should bother to fire at Bruno's governess's house nobody had the faintest idea.

The old teacher was glad to accept Mrs Habicht's offer. He earned a bit by coaching, because his pension was too small to allow him to buy anything on the black market, even potatoes.

They didn't tell him the boy was a half-wit though. He didn't find out until the first day they spent together. Bruno was fifteen, with the face of a six-year-old and some of the habits of a toddler. During his first lesson he made a dive for a fly and swallowed it without turning a hair; he pushed his fountain pen up his nose and poured the ersatz coffee his mother had made for the teacher over the poor man's trousers. The latter of course got up and wanted to leave the house at once. The desperate mother spent a long time persuading him to stay; she raised his salary and offered to give him a hot supper every evening if only he would take her son on. And as if he wanted to ingratiate himself with the teacher all of a sudden, Bruno stood to attention and recited in a loud voice the multiplication tables, division tables, and square roots.

'He's got a wonderful head for figures,' said Mrs Habicht. 'He can remember anything. He knows the Xeenemuende telephone directory off by heart.' And Bruno promptly recited the first sixty names and addresses and telephone numbers. But he had no head for grammar, he was hopeless at history, and he couldn't read the simplest sentence. And he was fifteen, if you please. The unfortunate teacher always counted the minutes to suppertime; never in all his life had lessons seemed so long, and never before had he felt so reluctant to go and teach his pupils.

About a month later he caught sight of Bruno fighting a gang of younger children in the street. He was attacking a couple of eight-year-olds, tripping them up and then kicking them when they were down.

'Bruno!' he shouted from a way off, but he couldn't run because he had trouble with his breathing, and so it was the butcher's wife who dealt with Bruno because she had seen the whole thing from her shop. She grabbed the boy by the collar – she was a muscular woman – and just lifted him over the fence into the Habichts' garden. Then she took the other children indoors and washed their grazes for them.

'He's always doing things like that,' she explained to the horrified teacher. 'An idiot, that's what he is. Ought to be in a Home. If his father wasn't such a big bug they'd have taken him away long ago. Everybody's surprised at you going there at all.'

It was a particularly good supper at the Habichts' that evening, though, and he could even taste a hint of real coffee in the ersatz. Even Bruno was behaving quietly, only staring sulkily at one spot in the corner of the room. And so the old man could not bring himself to give notice.

That night the whole town was roused by another catastrophe. The butcher's shop opposite the Habichts' was destroyed the very same way as the governess's house had been: by a small-calibre bomb or an artillery shell. The missile must have passed in through the window, and exploded inside the room, demolishing it. The shop was burned down.

Next day Bruno was smiling all through his lesson. The teacher began to feel uneasy.

'Who looks after your boy all day?' he carefully approached Mrs Habicht at suppertime.

'Nobody. He's awfully good. He spends all his time on the verandah at the back of the house. His father put together a little workshop for him to potter about in.'

'I'd like to see that.'

'No!' the boy blurted out in a low, furious voice, and his face darkened.

'He doesn't let anybody else go in there,' his mother explained. 'That's his kingdom,' and she winked conspiratorially at the teacher. 'I've watched him through the keyhole sometimes,' she went on as she conducted the old man to the gate. 'All day long he just plays about with a set of boy's tools and some stuff my husband brought home from the factory for him. It's just harmless play.'

'Are you so sure?' the man replied as he looked across the road at the burned-out butcher's shop. 'You never can tell with children like that. He's not well, you know. He really ought to be in an institution . . .'

That made Mrs Habicht really angry; so he had gone over to the side of the neighbours who hated Bruno!

'Oh, no, not at all. I'm really quite fond of him. I'm sorry for him. But still, I think he'd be happier in a Home.'

'Never!' Mrs Habicht stamped her foot with fury. 'Never as long as I live!'

And so the teacher decided to have a look at Bruno's laboratory for himself next day. He went straight round to the verandah at the back of the house. The boy hadn't locked himself in. He'd got a little kitten tied up there and was torturing it with faradic current. The creature was half-dead when the teacher rescued it. Bruno did not want to give it up and they fought each other for it in silence, broken only by the boy's unintelligible grunts. The old man's heart began to pain him. There was only one thing to do. He aimed a blow at the boy's head. Bruno dived into a corner and stared at him with hatred.

'Krumme!' he spluttered. 'You Krumme!' Now Bruno's governess had been Miss Krumme. The tutor's name was Brettschneider, and the boy knew that very well. The old man felt a strange horror creeping over him. He did not even begin lessons that day. Avoiding Mrs Habicht, he went to see her husband at the works.

He was led along endless underground passages, with two armed men preceding him and two behind. It was like being in an anthill that was larger than life. The engineer listened to him impatiently.

'I know the boy has been responsible for a lot of trouble. He's a mischievous lad. But I really can't imagine how he could have had anything to do with either of the tragedies.'

'Well, we'll see,' said the teacher. 'Nothing is going to make me sleep at home tonight. You can keep watch with me in the garden if you like.' He lived in a little house near the station.

'You must excuse me. I've other things to think about. More important things . . .' Mr Habicht refused the suggestion.

First thing in the morning he came dashing along, though. In the course of the night the teacher's house had been destroyed by a small projectile which exploded by his bedside.

Hidden in the garden the teacher had seen quite clearly the fiery ballistic curve of the missile, which was no bigger than his hand and had left a trail of smoke behind it.

'I'm going to the Commander at once,' he told Habicht. 'Do you want to come with me?'

At that time the Commander was Major von Schwarz, and the factory was also under his surveillance. They were admitted to his presence.

'An extraordinary story. Quite incredible. And you admit it's possible?' the Major turned to Mr Habicht. 'Do you really think your son can have had anything to do with these catastrophes?'

The engineer stammered and turned first red and then white, and did not know what to say until the Major roared at him.

'I must confess, Major von Schwarz,' he said at last, 'that about a month ago I took the plans of our new secret weapon home, the Vergeltungswaffe zwei. We had so much work in the designing office that I couldn't cope with it. The boy may have got to see the papers, somehow. He can remember a lot of things. He's quite clever at some things, too. Nobody can be sure what's really going on in that head of his ...'

These words decided the elderly teacher's fate. He had unwittingly stumbled on a secret – the nature of what was being produced in the underground factory. And then, the engineer's son was now more valuable to the authorities than the man who had informed on him. The teacher disappeared into a concentration camp. That was what saved his life in the end.

'That means the boy's a genius,' said von Schwarz, as he drove round to see Bruno, accompanied by Habicht and the regimental cook.

'He's a half-wit,' said the father, 'we've got a doctor's certificate to prove it.'

'Hasn't it dawned on that blockhead of yours what your boy has managed to do? You and a dozen more like you are still not capable of guiding our rockets to a definite target. You don't know how to aim them. And here's a fifteen-year-old boy who can hit a target – a window – from a distance, to within fifteen inches or so. Can't you see how important it would be for us if our V2 could destroy certain targets in London instead of just falling at random?'

The engineer did not answer that.

'But I've never taken the plotting system home ...'

'Of course you haven't, because there isn't one. That's just what your boy has worked out ...'

And Major von Schwarz ordered the cook to unpack the cakes he had brought. For the first time in four years of war the man had been put to making cream for a chocolate cake, filling éclairs, spreading jam on a Victoria sandwich.

Bruno threw himself on the good things like a pig. Quite literally, pushing his nose deep into the cream and the decorated icing. The cook was thunderstruck and Mrs Habicht started lamenting that the boy would make himself sick. At last he burped contentedly and wanted to make off.

'Wait a minute,' the Major held him back with a grip of iron. 'You can have cakes like this every day if you'll tell us how you did it.'

'How he did what?' his mother answered for him. 'He hasn't done anything. He's a good boy.' The Major pushed her roughly out of the way.

'How do you aim your rockets?' he shouted in Bruno's ear. 'Tell the truth or I'll have the hide off you!' And he pulled his old riding-whip out of his jackboot. He cracked it once and Mrs Habicht fainted. Nobody bothered to revive her. The boy was staring sulkily into a corner and his over-large tongue was busy licking the crumbs of cake from round his mouth. He obviously didn't understand. He didn't resist when the Major whipped him. He just went on looking in the same direction.

At length the Major broke his whip in half. He was covered in sweat and breathing hard. He let the boy go, straightened up and yelled at Habicht.

'By morning you're going to find out how the boy does it, or else the whole family'll be court-martialled. And all your relations as well,' he added as he went out at the door.

Outside, the SS men were already jumping out of their cars and taking up positions round the house. Von Schwarz was still swearing as he drove away. That night he didn't go to the Town Hall to sleep, preferring to spend the night with his soldiers. There was nobody left in his Town Hall office but his pretty secretary, brought back with him from Italy at the beginning of the war.

She was killed that night when the Town Hall was demolished by a small projectile which came through the roof this time, and burned the whole place down to its foundations.

The alarm was sounded in the barracks, the Major fastened his heavy Parabellum pistol on his belt, and was driven to the Habichts' house. 'Where is Bruno?' he asked the engineer shortly. In trembling voices the Habichts said their son had gone to bed. He was found on the verandah, with his toy railway lines, putting the last touches to another rocket on its toy launching arm.

Von Schwarz shot him from behind, with a bullet in the nape of the neck. Mrs Habicht threw herself on the officer, trying to grab his pistol. She was mad with pain, tearing her hair and rending her clothes.

'What had he done to you? Murderer!' The Major tried to explain the situation to her.

'We cannot allow anyone to kill his neighbours just because they do something to annoy him. And with modern techniques, too. He was an idiot.'

'And what are you doing? How many people have you killed in London with your rockets? Did any of those Englishmen do you any harm? You've no cause for your murders. You're idiots, all of you, every one of you ...' Von Schwarz wanted to have her arrested on the spot, but the air-raid sirens sounded.

'No,' he shouted into the phone, 'there's no need to raise the alarm. I've got rid of the source of the danger ...'

In reply incendiary bombs began falling on the residential part of the town. The Allies had discovered the secret of Xeenemuende. A quarter of the inhabitants lost their lives in that first air-raid. Habicht the engineer was among them. Some people say it was a pity. He was a wonderful engineer, they say. One of the fathers of rocket weapons. A genius.

Alter Ego

HUGO CORREA

'Here is your Alter Ego, sir. Kindly sign the receipt.'

Antonio opened the box and stepped back in amazement. There he was, arms close to the body, completely naked and motionless. If the upright position were not unnatural in a sleeper, he would have attempted to wake the android, so true to life did the color of the skin look, the little wrinkles beginning to show around the eyes, the thin lips, the high forehead. The straight hair was carefully combed, like that of its human counterpart.

He took up the control box and, following the instructions, put the android in motion. It walked slowly and naturally, with none of the grotesque movements so typical of automatons in the past. It was just as though it actually possessed bones, muscles, nerves and the organs of a living being. Antonio made it go through the elementary motions – sit, dress, light a cigarette, scratch its ear. 'If android-owners wish to enjoy them,' said the instructions manual, 'they must first study their own selves very carefully, at least as to their mimicry, gestures, gait, etc.'

Antonio, expert now at handling his double, put on the introjection helmet. For a moment his eyes blinked in the dark. But once the ocular switch was turned on he recovered the use of his eyes. The living room looked as if he were seeing it from another angle. What was it? Simply that he was beginning to see through the android's eyes. Alter Ego was standing in the middle of the room facing the door, blinking naturally. The instruments moved the synthetic eyelids simultaneously with Antonio's. The man pressed a button and the double turned. He could see himself sitting in the chair, his head hidden in the helmet, the controls on his knee. Once the audio channel was working there was no doubt that he was now in the middle of the room; he could hear the street noises and those he made when shifting his position in the armchair. And smell. How to breathe through Alter Ego. The odorophones gave him the sensation of air breathed elsewhere. He tried the voice of his duplicate self; as soon as Alter Ego opened his mouth, Antonio heard himself speaking from the middle of the room.

'How are you, Antonio? You've been born again. Don't you feel like a fish in a bowl when they've just changed the water?'

Antonio listened to his own voice with complacency. He had Alter Ego walk about the room, took him to the window and, leaning out, watched the bright city under a burning sky sprinkled with helicopters. Everything looked more beautiful than when he used his own eyes; the sky was bluer and more luminous, the skyscrapers showed gayer and brighter colors. Yes, Alter Ego was showing him the true face of things. The sensations that he received through his double made him feel suddenly at peace with humankind. In his imagination the emotions of youth revived, the memories that time had slowly erased leaving behind faint images willingly or unwittingly forgotten. But now he felt overcome by a strange courage and a desire for remembrance. He could look over his past life serenely, recall youthful thoughts, aspirations, the way he had little by little given up what he loved most in order to make a position for himself.

'Remember when you wanted to be an actor and play The Emperor Jones? How you went about for weeks with your mind on his soliloquies? How you made love to Valentina, the girl who attended dramatic school with you and encouraged you because she believed in you?'

Alter Ego spoke with a clear, resonant voice, his gestures those of a man used to the stage. He lit a cigarette, inhaled deeply, then let out a thin wisp of smoke. He stopped in front of a picture of Antonio at his desk, a satisfied smile on his face, photographs, notices, billboards all round him.

'There's nothing wrong with selling toothpaste, particularly when it's a good product and properly manufactured. After all, it even has a social function; it ensures white teeth and a pleasant breath. Did you ever think of Jones's lines to Smithers as related to your own activities: "Ain't a man's talkin' big what makes him big – long as he makes folks believe it?" You managed that as a salesman. Trouble was you never believed the big things that the great salesman Antonio said.'

Alter Ego inhaled deeply, and through the bluish cloud surveyed the man in the chair whose face was hidden by the helmet. Wonders of electronics! The papillophones gave him the taste and slight heat of the smoke.

'Smoking by remote control – what a boon for today's practical men who are anxious to do all things without committing themselves too much! You get the same enjoyment that the smoker does while you run none of the risks. It is the hedonistic principle fulfilled.'

Alter Ego opened an antique cupboard and turned to Antonio with an indefinable smile.

'A museum piece, as so many men are. Aren't most men today just museum pieces after all? To begin with, they are unable to fulfil their own aspirations. They all stop halfway. You're no exception; you wanted to be an actor, and you ended up selling toothpaste because there was more money in it. You gave up Valentina because she was humble, had no ambition. You had friends, true ones, people with whom you could talk about any number of useless things. Useless? Your new acquaintances only understand the language of finance. "Is there money in that?" they ask you when you innocently attempt to get them out of their easy chairs, showing them your inner world where your aspirations are beginning to rust, fatally, resignedly, like metal corroded by oxide. You did learn to talk like them, though. Not any better! There are no levels in that world.'

Alter Ego finished smoking, put out the cigarette with a theatrical gesture and faced Antonio, pointing at him accusingly.

'And now, will your mechanical double do what you daren't do with your own hands?'

The android stood motionless, looking at the silent helmet. A dense silence floated in the room. The glass eyes glowed. Slowly, Alter Ego turned to the open cupboard. His face hardened. He took out a pistol, examined it critically and advanced towards the man with a curious solemnity, as though walking through a temple while a ceremony is being held.

'Man is the supreme inventor. He made these weapons to kill men, and doubles to pass judgment on himself.'

After the briefest pause he added, drily:

'The cycle is closed,' and carefully aimed at the figure in the chair.

A Perfect Marriage

ANDRÉ CARNEIRO

Val-T arrived at the elevator. The reduced gravity lifted him to his bachelor apartment in a few seconds. He pressed the fourth button, already stained from use, and later on he began eating his dinner, which was a bit too hot. He felt a lack of company, someone cheerful to be at his side who would comment on what was being shown on the 3-D dinner menu along with a digestive-inducing musical background. He smiled. He turned everything off with his left hand. He leaned back, relaxing muscles still tense, and began daydreaming. He never used to do that. Even when by himself, he had a hundred and one different things to amuse himself with in his 'special-category' apartment. He was twenty-eight and was starting to think about not having a mate. He went to a drawer full of papers and he pulled out his 'extrapolated-future certificate'. He had been analyzed when he was fifteen, twenty, and twenty-five. The conclusions were final and identical. Twenty-eight would be the ideal age to marry his 'better half'. It was an expression hundreds of years old, which was perfectly appropriate now.

The following day he woke up with the same feeling. He stayed at home by himself until the afternoon since he had a flexible schedule in his obligations to the state. On the public transport he met Dab-I, an old friend he liked to talk to. Val-T told him of his feelings, 'Dab-I, it's time for me to find a mate. Maybe today I'll go on over to Central Cybernetics.'

Dab-I smiled in a strange, ironic way, 'Is it you wanting to get married, or was it the analyzer that put that idea into your head?' Dab-I was a specialist in ancient history. He intentionally used archaic words and had the strange and dangerous mania of turning his back on science, exactly repeating the old concepts of personal decision-making and experiencing the intuitive drives that had ruined the people of the twenty-first century in wars.

It was evident that Dab-I knew full well Article Three of the Law Code: 'The continuous meetings, one after the other, of the committees that make up the Central Cybernetics Institute show results and make just, perfect and final decisions.'

Dab-I knew that the few billion brain cells he had were only a few centimeters against the kilometers of transistortronics in the big computer. Even so, the new laws had abolished compulsory retraining and therein lay the results. The secret party of the Antitransistorites was disrupting society's progress.

Val-T sped through the hallways of the Cohabitation Institute with his heart beating faster. He would be undergoing tests and although the pleasant, perfect and definite surprise these would give him was a certainty (with very few exceptions), he acted like a teenager playing the sexy beau for the first time.

In Room No. 2 he reread the résumé of the process that everybody knew:

A FRUITFUL, PERMANENT AND LOVING RELATIONSHIP

1. Central Computer will conduct the tests in two hours in designated rooms.
2. After reading the texts and viewing the pictures, associations will have to be instantaneous. Taking drugs five days beforehand is prohibited; offenders will be punished in accordance with regulations.
3. The extrapolated constants of thoughts, ambitions, temperament, and capabilities are reduced to your drives and immediately transmitted to Central Institute.
4. The curves of future possibilities are reconstructed in billions of variations with the corresponding female types already selected in the first choice.
5. The matched couple will sign the cohabitation papers within ten days and will have to start living together within five days after that.

The rest of it talked about special cases and other bureaucratic provisions. Val-T followed a clerk. His time had come. He sat down in a sensing chair and they put a helmet on his head. Through the technique of hypnotically induced images, real scenes would appear in his surroundings. Emotions and thoughts would be registered on an analytic curve that would classify him with formulas that made him quite distinct and apart from billions of similar people. Central Computer would sort out from the billions of women the one who would be his perfect mate, the one who was born for him. In the old days this choice was made by a physiologically intuitive process called love, a word which even today is used, albeit unnecessarily. It is curious to note that man, throughout the centuries, was the only one to use this method of marrying, an expression still used in rural districts. After retrospective calculation, it is known that so-called intuitive love only succeeds in 0.012 per cent of the cases on the average. Now, perfect unions reach 95.43 per cent, the other 4.57 per cent being composed of physiological deformities and mental aberrations, the greater part of whom are undergoing retraining in specialized institutions.

Two and a half hours later Val-T held a picture of his 'better half' in his hands. She was exactly what he had been dreaming of (the computer knew it full well); the eyes, a certain smile on the lips, the sweet voice ... When we get something we have been seeking, ours is not to reason why. Acceptance was total as well as the anxious expectation of possessing her forever. Val-T immediately signed the request.

A-Rubi (which was her name) received the proposal message an hour later. She was twenty-two, and her opportune time had come. Strangely enough, however, she did not sign her consent right away. She thought about the subject romantically and only the next day decided what scientifically was an absurdity since our mind cannot arrive at any conclusion different from a computer that does not make mistakes. After all, this was an old problem that always existed. One of the important subjects in Central Institute was the analysis of the 'contradictions, paradoxes and illogical decisions of the female's great pineal'.

Several days later, when everything had been straightened out, they met each other for the first time. A-Rubi had traveled thousands of kilometers quietly, but when Val-T approached her on the moving sidewalk, smiling at her, her heart began to flutter.

When he embraced her, kissing her on the cheek, her legs felt weak, she wanted to be there, protected by his arms. When she had been examined by the big and incredible machine, she never thought it would find her a man like this, one who could make her heart beat so, even before knowing him better. Val-T took her by the hand and they went home. To him A-Rubi appeared to be one of those prohibited beverages that induced happiness and exultation. He was an enthusiast of progress, his apartment had more buttons and knobs than those of any of his friends. He knew a good computer could predict a sneeze a month before it happened, but there are fabulous things of science that do not concern us and do not touch us directly. But his woman was there and as the days went by, his passion increased. He brought her fresh roses from the fields outside, led her through the places of his childhood, told her of his pranks, of the plane he had built when he was eleven and had crashed after some dangerous flights during which he had placed the lives of the neighborhood children in jeopardy. A-Rubi was affectionate and understanding, but Val-T was sometimes surprised at a refusal or disagreement that made him impatient. He tried to control himself since the computer had given him exactly what he had been searching for. Consequently, his desire to answer her was part of his temperament and maybe he really needed to get nervous from time to time. He recognized the fact that A-Rubi had faults. One of them that annoyed him was the one about being completely antiscientific. It was not quite that. She took no notice of cybernetic law and the principles did not affect her. When Val-T got home in the afternoon, she had not yet pushed the dinner button. A-Rubi argued that the meals prepared with all the right ingredients had no taste. She had bought a portable stove which clashed terribly with the kitchen décor. A strong smell of food permeated everything. Val-T immediately promised to get some odor neutralizer, but A-Rubi, astonished, forbade him to do so since the joy of cooking and looking forward to a meal included inhaling its 'perfume'. She seemed to have been transplanted from an ancient world since she based her opinion on sometimes groundless convictions. Val-T never saw her request a recipe or consult with the main computer. She would come up with foolishness like 'It looks like rain tomorrow' as someone would resort to a forecast to prove exact facts. When his wife asked him to explain, Val-T felt flattered. He gave her long explanations worthy of a greater audience. He was a man of perfect reasoning and of cold logic. A-Rubi looked at him while he talked and her admiration was undeniable, her eyes shone with the pride that he was hers. Val-T, however, was extraordinarily perspicacious and perceived that the woman was admiring him and proud of the fact that he could know and say all these things. But the conclusions and usage of the bare facts hardly got through to her. They would carry on lively discussions, and she had the peculiar ability of abandoning the main topic to go veering off on tangents until Val-T even tried to escape. They would get mad at each other, and A-Rubi would yell that she hated him, that he should go and sleep with all the machines he adored.

Val-T prided himself on never losing his cool, on not saying anything that was exaggerated or that deviated from the truth. He was truly capable of doing this. His composure, nevertheless, was limited to the meaning of phrases or to the line his reasoning took. He had a high, sharp voice that imparted a relentless harshness to the simplest words. A-Rubi would fight with him valiantly but her resistance was low. Faults which Val-T pointed out to her, exposing them to cold examination, were wearing down her strength, she felt herself tormented into something insignificant and despised. She would cry in desperation but she would immediately agree with her cohabitant, and he would go to the interphone to call the doctor. Val-T accepted his woman's arguments even though he was upset. For him the difference between temperament and sickness had to be measured by the vibrations of the female's great pineal. He made a great effort to support her absurdities and could not even suggest retraining since this would precipitate a new crisis. A-Rubi would shout that the number of vibrations emitted was not important and that she was not going to let any machine change them.

This blew over. Val-T took mep-14 and they made up to each other with mutual statements of love. A-Rubi would cry on his shoulder, saying that she loved him while he felt the joy of having her in his arms, destitute and fragile, but at the same time it was hard for him to accept that she would not submit herself to 'treatment' at Central Institute, the thing that would solve everything in a simple, scientific manner.

They would go through serene periods, their life would go along wonderfully. Anything insignificant could unleash a new dispute, and Val-T had decided not to take any more mep-14 for making up. It was an artificial and unjust crutch since it would disperse all his objections with an induced happiness that extinguished disagreements, but it did not enter into their causes. Val-T tried through stern self-criticism to change his temperament, to adapt his viewpoints to those of his woman's. Central Computer, right and infallible, had chosen her from billions as the perfect mate. It was necessary to straighten out these rough edges that Val-T had not seen in any other couple; they knew couples to be generally peaceful, agreeing mutually on everything. A firm believer in transistortronic justice, he supposed that perhaps it was he who bore the most guilt in the disagreements with his woman. He tried to take a new tack, to treat her differently with and without results. The basic question he accepted the least was A-Rubi's refusal to undergo any treatment. Her antipathy toward mechanical and transistortronic machines was as great as the passion Val-T felt for her. A-Rubi assembled a small collection of antiques. There were some books printed on paper, cameras still with film in them, a radio-ring and so on. Val-T found all of these obsolete and uninteresting. He did not say that often since she would get disgusted, but he thought her stubbornness was left over from earlier times. Although they controlled themselves before strangers, sometimes they let fly with loud words. Many people recommended general retraining, the very thing that was a grave offense according to A-Rubi's archaic convictions. In compensation their raptures of love also surprised the others who agreed with each other about a good dose of mep-14 and loved each other afterwards like well-behaved students conscious of their obligations. For a man as enamored of progress and rules as Val-T, maybe it was the casual, exciting delights of love and compatibility that gave him the strength to make up with A-Rubi, to forgive her and to begin anew, full of hope. Although he could be considered a scientist next to his woman, his deep-rooted ideas explored new roads. Not rough and uninteresting as might be supposed, but with a share of unexpected interest and wild thrills with which the pioneers had opened up the jungles of Mars or had experienced the Hibenstein series in primitive rockets. After all, transistortronics had picked out the perfect mate for him. He felt her absence, her presence was exciting, and there was no obligatory regulation that recommended mep-14, a drug that obliterated annoying memories, or any other remedy outside the natural ones to guarantee the happiness of a couple. Val-T had to admit he had learned to get joy out of reading the old texts. It was exhilarating to find out what the forgotten words meant, to penetrate the drama of situations that could never happen now. His friend Dab-I found him changed, with a more 'humane' understanding of problems. Val-T did not agree, saying that was not the explanation. He continued to believe in the wisdom of a new civilization where the word 'humane' was a symbol of backwardness, partiality, criminal ambition, and so on. No aspect of 'humane' decision could be compared with mathematical truth extrapolated by Central Computer. 'Look at my union, for example,' argued Val-T, 'with all its misunderstandings we still can't straighten out. It's still perfect thanks to transistortronics. I love my woman because the sum total of her characteristics is what is most adaptable to mine compared to all the other women in the universe. Had we met each other in a 'humane', intuitive manner as in past centuries, the result would be mentally unbalanced children, sexual perfidy settled by stupid crimes.' This argument in discussions with his woman served both of them in antagonistic situations. When everything went well, he called it a sign of transistortronic wisdom that ruled the world. If they quarreled, the woman would remind him by saying that Central Computer did not know a thing and that he did not find her the ideal mate.

The scene was tense but also vibrant. Val-T gained some refinement like preferring this or that dish A-Rubi prepared him on the portable stove without consulting any table of carbohydrates or vitamins. It was true regression to empiric times when the joy of eating was subsidiary to its functional uses. The Antitransistorites, whose very infantile symbol was a broken transistor, tried to reinstill certain natural values they thought better than the infallible transistortronic decisions. Val-T considered them a group completely removed from reality, trying to revive ancient freedoms, forgetting about their disastrous results. The Antitransistorites, in addition, could give themselves the luxury of praising past liberties, the free man, and his false advantages. None of them went without the giant computer's predictions or left the moving sidewalks to go on foot. Many of the most ardent were cybernetic technicians, holding important positions in the hierarchy. Dab-I, impressed with Val-T's changes, invited him to join the party. Val-T, assuring him he would not betray him, refused. He could not agree with an idealistically misguided people who, following the paths of security and convenience the machines provided, fought against them, oblivious of the fact that it was man who had invented and perfected them to fill the gaps in our ability to choose. A-Rubi did not condemn him for this. If his way of looking at things agreed with that of the Antitransistorites, this did not mean that it was for ideological reasons. She took no notice of the party since she was innocently practicing the party's ideology.

Val-T's transformation was a good victory over his stern temperament. Shocked, his own friends noticed that A-Rubi had made him much more sympathetic and tractable. However, much of what he did or let be done to please his woman came from sensible effort and little conviction. Months passed and new arguments would erupt when anything came up for discussion, and Val-T would again ask for tests and retraining while A-Rubi accused him excessively (and she did not know how to control herself). They got into a vicious circle, and the already-forgiven accusations came back with the same force, with Val-T threatening to expose all that 'abnormality'. After a disagreement when both outdid themselves, Val-T left and on an impulse went to the Cohabitation Institute. A psychocyberneticist received him and rebuked him for not having come earlier. A re-examination and new extrapolation of the data about the couple would have to be done. The psychocyberneticist came back a little later. He was upset and it was with hesitation and in a roundabout way he explained the situation to Val-T. During the time that he had been matched with A-Rubi, they had found exactly 232 cases where there had been total sabotage of the results. An Antitransistorite party member, a positronic apprentice, had replaced a vibration corrector, destroying the defect indicator. The next day various circuits had blown and the crime was discovered. During that time the infallible giant had 232 complete mismatches. The cyberneticist handed him a certificate. With this, Central Institute would annul his union, and they would be compensated: A-Rubi would return to her distant group, and he would be submitted to a new test guaranteed to get him his true better half this time. Val-T could never have imagined a surprise like this. He went back home and told A-Rubi that their union had been a cybernetic mistake. They were not two better halves but completely different people who had not even used the empiric methods of their ancestors to meet each other. Val-T did not speak in the sharp, unpleasant voice he used in arguments. He related everything in a tired and matter-of-fact tone. A-Rubi burst into tears. Val-T got up calmly, put his arm around her shoulder and said, 'You mustn't cry, A-Rubi. After all, there's no disgrace about it. Look, the food's burning. Let's eat like we used to . . .' A-Rubi quieted down to fix a meal. They ate slowly and talked about other topics casually. Val-T looked at her red eyes, that certain smile on her lips, her pleasant voice . . . When they were getting ready for bed, they avoided looking at each other. With her head on a pillow, A-Rubi started whimpering again. Val-T pulled her to him, kissed her moist eyelids, consoled her, and they made love as they had in better days.

For lack of time, Val-T did not take the certificate explaining the mistake to Central Institute for the proper annulment. In truth it was laziness, almost intentional. The fact of knowing they were not made for each other and that they were not two better halves perfectly joined gave them an original understanding to avoid arguing. The possibility that another man he knew could be a little more of a better half to A-Rubi than he made Val-T feel jealous, a shameful emotion Central Computer had long ago buried in its circuits. A-Rubi became more fascinating and seductive since no one threatened her with the nightmare of the machines any more.

As the days passed, the squabbles returned although on a lower scale. No matter how it began, A-Rubi would wind up referring to the certificate about the mistake, properly locked up in the document drawer. She mocked its worth and dared Val-T to take it to Central Institute to annul this false union she did not believe in.

Ever since he was young, Val-T in his work had at his disposal computers for making important decisions. Limited to a dependence on the fragile convolutions of the human brain, he was slow in making decisions. Much of his balance was the result of a great strength of will, a certainty about all the decisions made; when the great pineal's vibrations exceed a certain level, they are dangerous because cold reality is not taken into account. Nevertheless, his cohabitant, who said whatever came into her head, to regret or change it later, wound up influencing him. He would let fly with some insults during heated arguments. Coming from him, the merit of these statements impressed A-Rubi. 'Everything I say,' he groaned, 'you take as my exact wish and thought. Unlike you, I don't have the right to shout stupid things and then retract them later.'

Since the topic did not come up any more, Val-T mistakenly believed his better half had forgotten or thought the certificate about the mistake they could annul the union with no longer important. One day there was a fiercer argument that was reminiscent of the violent ones of other times. A-Rubi accused him of being a coward since he did not love her and did not have the courage to get a separation. That she would get a hold of the paper and take it to Central Institute herself. Val-T, on an impulse, opened the drawer, threw the paper in her lap and told her to go right now. A-Rubi gave it back, saying she hated him, telling him to go with the paper and when he got back, he would never see her again. Val-T left with the paper. He was going to take care of this foolishness. He arrived at Central Institute, but he did not go in. He sat down in a corner of the park with a strange feeling of melancholy and loneliness. He tried to relive the times with A-Rubi, to analyze them rationally. He would undergo a new test and would then have the mate he had been dreaming of. He made himself think of her as a perfect woman, comparing her with what displeased him in A-Rubi. Val-T could not escape an annoying unrest. He could not resign himself to losing his mate. Even with her faults compared to the qualities the next one would have. Let the giant computer correct its own mistakes, but Val-T began to like the mistake and he did not want to change the present situation. In that lonely corner in the park with a pleasant sun softened by the dome, breathing filtered air purer than the sea, Val-T debated with himself over his feelings against the infallible, unquestionable transistortronic culture built up over the centuries. He stood up with a decision that gave him secret joy, the pleasure of facing the problem by himself even though the road would be rougher and the responsibilities greater. He remembered she had threatened to leave. He got on the express sidewalk in a great desire to get home faster. His elevator never seemed so slow before. When the door opened, he called his mate's name. She was in the bedroom, sprawled on the bed, an open, empty traveling bag at her side. Without a word, Val-T took the certificate about the mistake out of his pocket, tore it up with all the strength his hands could muster and tossed everything in the incinerator. Suspicious, A-Rubi looked at him with her usual uncertainty. After they embraced each other out of desperation, it would be impossible to reproduce the words of love, the exaggerated promises, the confessions made between caresses, including antiscientific blasphemies spoken (with enormous injustice) against Central Computer.

The Legend of the Paper Spaceship

TETSU YANO

Translated by Gene Van Troyer and Tomoko Oshiro

Halfway through the Pacific War, I was sent from my unit to a village in the heart of the mountains, and there I lived for some months. I still recall clearly the road leading into that village; and in the grove of bamboo trees beside the road, the endless flight of a paper airplane and a beautiful naked woman running after it. Now, long years later, I cannot shake the feeling that what she was always folding out of paper stood for no earthly airplane, but for a spaceship. Some time long ago, deep in those mountain recesses . . .

1

The paper airplane glides gracefully above the earth, and weaving between the sprouts of new bamboo, stealing over the deep-piled humus of fallen and decaying leaves, a white mist comes blowing, eddying and dancing up high on the back of a subtle breeze, moving on and on.

In the bamboo grove the flowing mist gathers in thick and brooding pools. Twilight comes quickly to this mountain valley. Like a ship sailing a sea of clouds, the paper airplane flies on and on through the mist.

> *One – a stone stairway to the sky*
> *Two – if it doesn't fly*
> *Three – if it does fly, open . . .*

A woman's voice, singing through the mist. As if pushed onward by that voice, the paper airplane lifts in never-ending flight. A naked woman owns the voice, and white in her nudity she slips quickly between the swaying bamboo of the grove.

(*Kill them! Kill them!*)

Alarm sirens wove screaming patterns around shrieking voices.

(*Kill everyone! That's an order!*)

(*Don't let any get to the ship! One's escaped!*)

(*Beamers! Fire, fire!*)

A crowd of voices resounding in this mist, but no one else can hear them. These voices echo only in the woman's head.

Tall and leafy and standing like images of charcoal gray against a pale ash background, the bamboo trees appear and disappear and reappear among the gauzy veils of the always folding rolling mist. The fallen leaves whisper as the woman's feet rustle over them. Mist streams around her like something alive as she walks, then flows apart before her to allow the dim shape of what might be a small lake to peek through.

Endworld Mere: the *uba-iri-no-numa*. After they had laughed and danced through the promises and passions of living youth, old people once came often to this place to end the misery of their old age by throwing themselves into the swamp's murky waters.

Superstition holds that Endworld Mere swarms with the spirits of the dead. To placate any of the lingering dead, therefore, these valley folk had heaped numerous mounds of stones in a small open space near the mere. This place they named the *Sai no Kawara*, the earthly shore where the journey over the Great Waters began. They gathered here once a year for memorial services, when they burnt incense and clapped hands and sent their prayers across the Wide Waters to the shore of the nether world.

No matter how many stone towers you erect on the earthly shore of the River of Three Crossings, the myths tell us that demons will destroy them. Whether physical or spectral, here too the 'demons' had been about the tireless task of destruction. In the very beginning there had probably been but a few mounds of tombstones to consecrate the unknown dead; but over the years, hundreds of stones had been heaped, and now lay scattered. Throughout most of the year, the place was now little more than a last rest stop where the infrequent person bound on the one-way trip to Endworld Mere paused for a short time before moving on. Because of its deserted silence, men and women seeking a little more excitement in life found the place ideal for secret rendezvous.

Secret meetings were often a singular concern for these simple village folk. They could think of little else but pleasure. 'Endworld Mere' is a name that suggests even the old go there with stealth, and possibly the dreadful legends surrounding the place were fabricated by anxious lovers who wished to make it a place more secure for their trystings.

Owing to these frightening stories, the village children gave the mere a wide berth. Round lichen-covered stones, rain-soaked and rotting paper dolls, creaking wooden signs with mysterious, indecipherable characters inscribed on them: for children these things all bespoke the presence of ghosts and ogres and nightmare encounters with demons.

Sometimes, however, the children would unintentionally come close enough to glimpse the dank mere, and on one such occasion they were chasing the madwoman Osen, who was flying a paper airplane.

'Say, guys! Osen's still runnin' aroun' naked!'

'*Hey*, Osen! Doncha wan' any *clothes*?'

All the children jeered Osen. For adult and child alike she is a handy plaything.

But Osen had a toy, too: a paper airplane, as thin, as sharp-pointed as a spear.

> *One, a white star*
> *Two, a red star . . .*

In the mist she sings, and dreams: the reason she flies her paper airplane, the hatred that in her burns for human beings.

Osen, whose body is ageless, steps lightly over the grass, reaches the mere where the enfeebled old cast themselves away to die. The paper airplane flies on against the mist before her. No one knows what keeps the plane flying so long. Once Osen lets go of it, the 'airplane' flies on seemingly forever. That's all there is to it . . .

A madwoman, is Osen, going about naked in summer, and in the winter wearing only one thin robe.

2

There is a traditional song that the village children sang while playing ball, of which I vaguely recall one part:

> *I'll wait if it flies,*
> *if it doesn't I won't –*
> *I alone will keep waiting here.*
> *I wonder if I'll ever climb*
> *those weed-grown stairs someday –*
> *One star far and two stars near . . .*

Naked in the summer, and in the winter she wears one thin robe.

Most adults ignored the children who jeered at Osen, but there were a few who scolded them.

'Shame on you! Stop it! You should *pity* poor Osen.'

The children just backtalked, often redoubling their jeers to the tune of a local rope-skipping song, or else throwing catcalls back and forth.

'Hey, *Gen!* Ya fall in *love* with Osen? Ya *sleep* with her last night?'

'Don't be an idiot!'

Even if adults reprimanded them like this, the kids kept up exactly the same sort of raillery. After all, everyone knew that last night, or the night before, or the night before that, at least *one* of the village men made love to Osen.

Osen: she must have been close to her forties. Some villagers claimed she was much, *much* older than that, but one look at Osen put the lie to their claims: she was youthful freshness incarnate, her body that of a woman not even twenty.

Osen: community property, harlot to all who came for it, the butt of randy male superiority. Coming to know the secrets of her body was a kind of 'rite of passage' for all the young men of the village.

Osen: the village idiot. This was the other reason why the villagers sheltered her.

Osen was the only daughter and survivor of the village's most ancient family. Among those who live deep in the mountains and still pay homage to the Wolf God, the status of a household was regarded as supremely important. That such an imbecile should be the sole survivor of so exalted a household gave everyone a limitless sense of superiority – Osen! Plaything for the village sports!

Her house stood on a knoll, from where you could look down on Endworld Mere. Perhaps it's better to say where her house was *left*, rather than stood. At the bottom of the stone stairs leading up to her door, the openwork gate to her yard didn't know whether to fall down or not. Tiles were ready to drop from the gate roof, and tangled weeds and grass overgrew the ruins of the small room where long ago a servant would hold a brazier for the gatekeeper's warmth in winter.

A step inside the gate and the stone stairs leading up were choked with moss and weeds. The curious thing was, the center of the stairway had not been worn down; rather, both sides were. Nobody ever walked in the middle, say the old stories. According to the oldest man in the village, on New Year's Eve they used to welcome in the new year and send off the old with a Shinto ritual, and in one line of the chant there was a passage about a Gate protected by the Center of a Stone Stairway built by a forgotten Brotherhood; and since no one knew the meaning of that, the old man said, people felt it best to avoid the center of *this* stone stairway whenever they passed up or down it.

The stairway climbed a short way beyond Osen's house to where the ground flattened and widened out and was covered with a profusion of black stones. An old crumbling well with a collapsing roof propped up by four posts was there. Sunk into the summit of this hill, one of the highest points in the valley, the well had never gone dry: fathoms of water always filled it. If any high mountains had been massed nearby this would have explained such vast quantities of water; but there were no such mountains, and this well defied physical law. Sinner's Hole, they called it. When the men were finished with Osen they came to this wellside to wash.

Once when a shrill group of cackling old women gathered at the well to hold yearly memorial services and pray to the Wolf God, one of them was suddenly stricken with a divination and proclaimed that if Osen were soaked in the well, her madness would abate. This cheered up those who envied Osen's great beauty, so on that day twelve years ago poor Osen was stripped to the raw before the eyes of the assembled women and dunked into the winter-frigid well water. An hour later, her body blushed a livid purple, Osen fainted and was finally hauled out. Sadly her idiocy was not cured. Story has it that the old crone who blurted the augury was drunk on the millet wine being served at the memorial service, and that afterward she fell into Endworld Mere and drowned. Because of the wine?

From then on, once someone undressed her, Osen stayed that way. If someone draped a robe over her, she kept it on. Since someone undressed her nearly every night and left her as she was in the morning, Osen most often went around naked.

Beautiful as the men might find Osen's body, others thought it best to keep the children from seeing her. Therefore, each morning a village woman came around to see that she was dressed. Osen stayed stonestill when being dressed, though sometimes she smiled happily. She went on singing her songs –

> *Folding one,* dah-dum
> *fold a second one,* tah-tum
> *a third one fold,* tra-lah!
> *Fly on, I say fly!*
> *Fly ever on to my star!*

– folding her paper airplanes while she murmured and sang. And one day soon, to the stunned amazement of the villagers and eventual focus of their great uproar, Osen's stomach began growing larger.

No one had ever stopped to think that Osen might someday be gotten with child.

The village hens got together and clucked about it, fumbling in their brains for hours to find some way to keep Osen from having the child. Finally they moved en masse to the ramshackle house where Osen lived her isolated life, and they confronted her with their will.

The idiot Osen, however, shocked everyone when for the first time in living memory she explicitly stated her *own* will: She would have this baby.

'Osen! No arguments. We're taking you to the city, and you'll see a doctor.'

'Don't be ri*dic*ulous, Osen, Why, you couldn't raise it if you had it. The poor thing would lead a pa*thetic* life!'

Large tears welled in Osen's eyes and spilled down her cheeks. None of the village women had ever seen Osen weep before.

'Osen . . . baby . . . *I want it born* . . .' said Osen. She held her swollen stomach, and the tears kept streaming down her face.

How high in spirit and firm in resolve they had come here to drag Osen away! Why it all evaporated so swiftly they would never know. Captured now by the pathos, they too could only weep.

Osen soon dried her tears, and began folding a paper airplane.

'Plane, plane, fly off!' she cried. 'Fly off to my father's home!'

The women exchanged glances. Might having a baby put an end to Osen's madness?

And then the paper airplane left Osen's hand. It flew from the parlor and out into the garden, and then came back again. When Osen stood up the airplane circled once around her and flew again into the yard. Osen followed it, singing as she gingerly stepped down the stone stairs, and her figure disappeared in the direction of the bamboo grove.

One old crone, with a gloomy, crestfallen face, took up a sheet of the paper and folded it; but when she gave the plane a toss it dipped, fell to the polished planking of the open-air hallway.

'Why does *Osen's* fly so well?' she grumbled.

Another slightly younger old woman said with a sage nod and her best knowing look, 'Even a stupid idiot can do *some* things well, you know.'

3

> *First month – red snapper!*
>   hitotsuki – tai
> *Second month – then it's shells!*
>   futatsuki – kai
> *Third, we have reserve, and*
>   mittsu – enryōde

> *Fourth – shall we offer shelter?*
>   yottsu – tomeru ka
> *If we offer shelter, well then,*
>   tomereba itcho
> *Shall we fold up Sixth Day?*
>   itsuyo kasanete muika
> *Sixth Day's star was seen –*
>   muika no hoshi wa mieta
> *Seventh Day's star was too!*
>   nanatsu no hoshi mo mieta
> *Eighth – a chalet daughter*
>   yattsu yamaga no musume
> *Ninth – left crying in her longing*
>   kokonotsu koishiku naitesoro
> *Tenth at last she settled in the small chalet!*
>   tōto yamaga ni sumitsukisoro
>   *– Rope-skipping song*

Osen kept flying her airplanes, the village men kept up their nightly visits to her bower, the village women never ceased their fretting over her delivery ... and one moonlit night a village lad came running down her stone stairs yelling: 'She's *hav*ing it! Osen's baby's on the way!'

A boy was born and they named him Emon. When he was nearly named Tomo – 'common' – because Osen was passed round and round among the village men, the old midwife quickly intervened.

'As the baby was coming out, Osen cried *"ei-mon"*,' the old woman reported. 'That's what she said. I wonder what she meant.'

'Emon. Hmmm ...' said one of the other women gathered there.

'Well, try asking.'

Addressing the new mother, the midwife said, 'Osen, which do you prefer as a name for the baby – Tomo, or Emon?'

'Emon,' Osen answered clearly.

'That's better, it's related to Osen's entry gate,' said an old woman who had memorized the chants for the Year End Rites.

'How do you mean?' a fourth woman said.

'Emon means *ei-mon*, the Guardian Gates,' said the old woman.

'I've heard that in the old days the New Year's Eve rituals were recited only here, at Osen's house. *Ei-mon* is part of the indecipherable lines . . . let's see . . . ah, yes, "You must go up the center of Heaven's Stairs, the stone stairs protected by *Ei-mon*, Emon's Gate".'

At this a fifth woman nodded.

'Yes, that's right,' she said, adding, 'It's also in one of the songs we sing at the New Year's Eve Festival. Here . . . "Emon came and died – Emon came and died – Wherever did he come from? – He came from a far-off land – Drink, eat, get high on the wine – You'll think you're flying in the sky . . ." '

'Hmmm, I see now,' said the fourth woman. 'I was thinking of the *emon* cloth one wears when they die. But a man named Emon came and died? And protects the gate? I wonder what it all means . . .'

The women took pity on Osen's child and everyone resolved to lend a hand in raising him. But . . . Emon never responded to it: he had given only that first vigorous cry of the newborn, then remained silent, and would stay so for a long time to come.

'Ah, what a shame,' one woman said. 'I expect the poor deafmute's been cursed by the Wolf God. What else for the child of an idiot?'

'We said she shouldn't have it,' another replied with a nod.

Indifferent to the sympathy of these women, Osen crooned a lullaby.

> *Escaped with Emon, who doesn't know,*
> *flow, flow . . .*

'Why, it's a Heaven Song,' one of the women said suddenly. 'She just changed the name at the beginning to Emon.'

Moved to tears by the madwoman's lullaby, the women spontaneously began to sing along.

> *Escaped with Emon, who doesn't know,*
>   shiranu Emon to nigesōro
> *flow, flow, and grow old*
>   nagare nagarete oisōro
> *all hopes dashed in this mountainous land.*
>   kono yama no chide kitai mo koware

No fuel for the Pilgrim's fires –
  abura mo nakute kōchū shimoyake
no swaying Heaven's Way.
  seikankōkō obekkanashi
Emon has died, alone so alone,
  Emon shinimoshi hitori sabishiku
wept in longing for his distant home.
  furusato koishi to nakisōro

Everyone so pitied Emon, but as he grew he in no way acknowledged their gestures of concern, and because of this everyone came to think the mother's madness circulated in her silent child's blood.

Not so. When he was awake Emon could hear everyone's voices, though they weren't voices in the usual sense. He heard them in his head. 'Voice' is a vibration passing through the air, sound spoken with a will. What Emon heard was always accompanied by *shapes*. When someone uttered the word 'mountain' the syllables *moun-tain* resounded in the air; the shape projected into Emon's mind with the word would differ depending on who spoke it, but always the hazy mirage of a mountain would appear. Listen as you will to the words *Go to the mountain*, it is only possible to distinguish five syllables. But in young Emon's case, overlapping the sound waves he could sense some one thing, a stirring, a *motion* that swept into a dim, mountainous shape.

For the *tabula rasa* mind of the infant this is an enormous burden. Emon's tiny head was always filled with pain and tremendous commotion. The minds and voices of the people around him tangled like kaleidoscopic shapes, scattering through his head like voices and images on the screen of a continuously jammed television set. It's a miracle that Emon did *not* go mad.

No one knew Emon had this ability, and men kept calling on Osen as usual. In his mind Emon soon began walking with tottering, tentative steps: along with, oh, say, Sakuzo's or Jimbei's shadowy thoughts would come crystal-clear images, and with them came meanings far beyond those attached to the spoken words.

'Hey there, Emon,' they might say. 'If you go out and play I'll give you some candy.' Or they would say something like: '*A big whale* just came swimming up the river, Emon!'

But Emon's mind was an unseen mirror reflecting what these men were really thinking. It differed only slightly with each man.

And then one day when he was five years old, Emon suddenly spoke to a village woman.

'Why does everyone want to sleep with Osen?' he asked.

Osen, he said; not *Mother*. Perhaps because he kept seeing things through the villagers' minds, Emon was unable to know Osen as anything more than just a woman.

'E-emon-boy, you can *talk*?' the woman replied, eyes wide with surprise.

Shocking. Once Emon's power of speech was known, they couldn't have the poor boy living in the same house with that common whore Osen . . . So the men hastily convened a general meeting, and it was concluded that Emon should be placed in the care of 'the General Store' – the only store in the village.

This automatically meant that Emon must mix with the children's society; but as he knew so many words and their meanings at the same time, the other children were little more than dolts in comparison and could never really be his playmates. And not to be forgotten: since he was Osen's child the other boys and girls considered him irredeemably inferior, and held him in the utmost contempt. So it was that reading books and other people's minds soon became Emon's only pleasure.

4

I once spoke to Osen while gazing into her beautiful clear eyes.

'You're pretending,' I told her. 'You're crazy like a fox, right?'

Instead of answering, Osen sang a song, the one she always sang when she flew the paper airplanes, the ballad of a mad-woman:

> *Escaped with Emon, who doesn't know,*
> *flow, flow, and grow old . . .*

The 'Heaven' Song, of course. Now, if I substitute some words based on the theory I'm trying to develop, why, what it suggests becomes something far grander:

> *Shilan and Emon fled together,*
>   Shiranu to Emon to nigesōro
> *Fly, fly, and they crashed,*
>   nagare nagarete ochisōro
> *the ship's hull dashed in this mountainous land.*
>   kono yama no chide kitai mo koware
> *No fuel – the star maps have burned,*
>   abura mo nakute kōchūzu mo yake
> *interstellar navigation is not possible.*
>   seikankōkō obotsukanashi
> *Emon has died, alone so alone,*
> *Wept in longing for his distant home.*

The last two lines of this song remain the same as in the version
recorded earlier, but all of the preceding lines have subtly changed.
For example: In line one, *shiranu* would normally be taken to
mean 'doesn't know', but in my reinterpretation it is now seen as
the Japanization of a similar-sounding alien name – *Shilan*. In the
second line, I am supposing that *oisōro* (meaning 'grow old') is a
corruption of the word *ochisōro* (meaning 'fall' or 'crash'); and I
am further assuming that *kōchū shimoyake* ('Pilgrim's fires') in
line four is a corruption of *kōchūzu mo yake* ('star charts also
burned'). In lines three, four, and five, three words have double
meanings:

> *kitai* = hope/ship's hull
> *kōchū* = pilgrim/space flight
> *seikankōkō* = heavenly way/interstellar navigation

In the above manner, line three changes its meaning from 'all hopes
dashed in this mountainous land' to *the ship's hull dashed in this
mountainous land*, and so forth.

There is more of this sort of thing . . .

Once a week an ancient truck rattled and wheezed up the steep
mountain roads on the forty-kilometer run between the village
and the town far below, bearing a load of rice sent up by the
prefectural government's wartime Office of Food Rationing. This
truck was the village's only physical contact with the outside world.
The truck always parked in front of the General Store.

Next door to the store was a small lodging house where the young men and women of the village always congregated. The master of the house was Old Lady Také, a huge figure of a woman, swarthy-skinned and well into her sixties, who was rumored to have once plied her trade in the pleasure quarters of a distant metropolis. She welcomed all the young people to her lodge.

On summer evenings the place was usually a hive of chatter and activity. Even small children managed for a short time to mingle in the company of their youthful elders, dangling their legs from the edge of the open-air hallway. Rope-skipping and the bouncing of balls passed with the dusking day, and the generations changed. Small children were shooed home and girls aged from twelve or thirteen to widows of thirty-five or thirty-six began arriving, hiding in the pooling shadows. They all came seeking the night's promise of excitement and pleasure.

It was an unwritten law that married men and women stay away from the lodge, though the nature of their children's night-play was an open secret. And how marvelously different this play was from the play in larger towns and cities: the people who gathered at Old Lady Také's lodge doused the lights and immediately explored each other's bodies. This, it must be said, was the only leisure activity they had. In the mountains, where you seldom find other diversions, this is the only amusement. The muffled laughter of young girls as hands slipped beneath their sweat-dampened robes, their coy resistance . . . And the heady fragrance that soon filled the room drew everyone on to higher delights.

Occasionally one of the local wags would amble by the lodge, and from a safe distance flash a startling light on the activities. Girls squealed, clutching frantically at their bodices, draping their drenched clothes over their thighs. In order to salvage this particular night's mood, someone asked in a loud voice:

'Say, Osato, your son's gonna be coming around here any day now, isn't he?'

'*What?*' said the widow.

'Yeah – he finally made it, I think!'

'Ho!' she laughed. 'Ho! You're being nasty, kid. He's *only* twelve . . .'

'Well, if he hasn't, he'll find out how to pretty soon,' the voice continued. 'So maybe you should ask Osen as soon as possible . . .?'

'Hmmm . . . You might be right. Maybe tomorrow. I could get him spruced up, take him on over in his best kimono . . .'

A young man's voice replying from deep within the room said, 'Naw, you're too late, Osato.'

'And just what is *that* supposed to mean?'

'For Gen-boy it's too late. He beat you to it. It's been a month already.' Laughter. 'His mother's the last to know!'

'But *he* never . . . Oh, that *boy*.'

As ever, Emon was near them all and listened to their banter. And sometimes, as everyone moved in the dark, he searched their minds.

(There'll be trouble if she gets pregnant . . .)

(Ohhh, *big*. It'll *hurt*. What should I do if I'm forced too far?)

(I wonder who took my boy to Osen's place? I *know* he didn't go alone. Yard work for that boy tomorrow, lots. I'll teach *him*. And I was waiting *so* patiently . . .)

Emon's mind-reading powers intensified among them as he roved over their thoughts night after night. He could see so clearly into their thoughts that it was like focusing on bright scenes in a collage. He was therefore all the more puzzled by his mother, Osen. She was different. Didn't the thoughts of a human being exist in the mind of an idiot? The thoughts of the villagers were like clouds drifting in the blue sky, and what they thought was so transparent. But in Osen's mind thick white mist flowed always, hiding everything.

No words, no shapes, just emotion close to fear turning there . . .

As Emon kept peering into the mist, he began to feel that Osen let the men take her so that she might escape her fear. Emon gave up the search for his mother's mind and returned to the days of his endless reading.

His prodigious appetite for books impressed the villagers.

'What a bookworm!' one of them remarked. 'That kid's *crazy* about books.'

'You're telling me,' another said. 'He read all ours, too. Imagine, from Osen, a kid who likes *books*.'

'Wonder who taught him to read . . .'

Visiting all the houses in the village, Emon would borrow books, and on the way he tried to piece together a picture of his mother's past by looking into everyone's minds. *Was Osen an idiot from the time she was born?* he wanted to know. But no one knew about Osen in any detail, and the only thoughts men entertained were for her beautiful face and body. Her body, perhaps ageless because of her imbecility, was a strangely narcotic necessity for the men.

A plaything for all the men of the village, was Osen, even for the youngest: for all who wished to know her body. Their dark lust Emon could not understand, but this emotion seemed to be all that kept the people living and moving in this lonesome place – a power that kept the village from splitting asunder.

Osen – madwoman, whore: she seized the men, and kept them from deserting the village for the enchantments of far-off cities

5

A memory from when I was stationed in the village: In front of Old Lady Také's Youth Lodge some children are skipping rope. In my thoughts I hear:

> *First month – red snapper!*
> hitotsuki – tai
> *Second month – then it's shells!*
> futatsuki – kai
> *Third, we have reserve, and*
> mittsu – enryōde
> *Fourth – shall we offer shelter?*
> yottsu – tomeru ka

The rope-skipping song I recorded earlier in this tale. A little more theory: with only a shift in syllabic division the song now seems to mean:

hitotsu	*kitai*
(one)	(ship's hull)
futatsu	*kikai*
(two)	(machines)

and with but a single change of consonants we have:

mittsu	*nenryōde*
(three)	(fuel)

Almost like a checklist . . .

Eventually the day came when Emon entered school. He was given a new uniform and school bag, purchased with money from the village Confraternity of Heaven Special Fund, which had been created long ago to provide for Osen's house and living. Emon went happily to the Extension School, which was at the far end of the village. There, in the school's library, he could read to his heart's content.

Miss Yoshimura, the schoolteacher, was an ugly woman, long years past thirty, who had given up all hope of marriage almost from the time she was old enough to seriously consider it. Skinny as a withered sapling and gifted with a face that couldn't have been funnier, yet she was a kindhearted soul, and of all those in the village she had the richest imagination and most fascinating mind. Having read so many books, she knew about much more than anyone else; and the plots of the uncountable stories she had read and remembered! They merged like twisting roots in her imagination, until they seemed to be the real world, and 'reality' a dream. Most importantly, though, where everyone else never let Emon forget his inferiority, only Miss Yoshimura cared about him as equal to the others. Emon readily became attached to her, and was with her from morning until evening.

One day the old master of the General Store came to Miss Yoshimura.

'Ma'am,' he began, 'Emon's smart as a whip, but there's gonna be trouble if he becomes, you know, grows up too early.'

'Ahm, oh, well . . .' Miss Yoshimura said, flustered.

'Since he's got Osen's blood and what not,' the old man went on assuringly, 'and watches the youngsters get together at Old Lady Také's place . . . well, if he gets like Osen, there'll be trouble. Some girl'll wind up gettin' stuffed by him, sure enough.'

Embarrassed, Miss Yoshimura said, 'Well, what do you think it best to do then?'

'Now as to that, we was thinkin' since he dotes on you so, it might be better for him to stay at your lodgin' house. Of course, the Confraternity Fund'll pay all his board.'

'All right, I don't mind at all,' said Miss Yoshimura, perhaps a bit too quickly. 'Of course, only if he *wants* to do it . . . How I *do* pity the poor child . . .'

And in her thoughts an imaginary future flashed into existence, pulsing with hope – *no I could never marry but now I have a child whom I will raise as my own and days will come when we hesitate to bathe together oh Emon yes I'll be with you as you grow to manhood* – Her face reddened at her thoughts.

Emon came to live in her house, then, and happy days and months passed. Most happily, the other children ceased to make so much fun of him. And the men never came around to sleep with Miss Yoshimura as they did with Osen.

She avoided all men. Her mind shrieked rejection, that all men were nothing more than filthy beasts. Emon quite agreed. But what went on in her mind?

As much as she must hate and avoid men, Miss Yoshimura's thoughts were as burdened as any other's by a dark spinning shadow of lust, and come the night it would often explode, like furnace-hot winds out of hell.

Squeezing little Emon and tasting pain like strange bitter wine, Miss Yoshimura would curl up tightly on the floor with sharp, stifled gasps. The entangled bodies of men and women floated hugely through her thoughts, and while she tried to drive them away with one part of her mind, another part reached greedily for something else, grabbed, embraced and caressed. Every word she knew related to sex melted throughout her mind.

Miss Yoshimura always sighed long and sadly, and delirious voices chuckled softly in her mind.

(*Oh, this will never do . . .*)

Denouements like this were quickly undone, usurped by their opposites, images flocking in her head, expanding like balloons filled with galaxies of sex words that flew to Osen's house. Miss Yoshimura fantasized herself as Osen, and grew sultry holding one of Osen's lovers. Then the lines of her dream converged on Old Lady Také's lodge, and she cried out desperately in the darkness:

'I'm a woman!'

Male and female shapes moved in the night around her . . .

She returned to her room where moonlight came in shining against her body. She moaned and hugged Emon fiercely.

'*Sensei*, you're killing me!'

At the sound of Emon's voice Miss Yoshimura momentarily regained herself – only to tumble yet again into the world of her fantasies.

(Emon, Emon, why don't you grow up . . .?)

Conviction grew in Emon's mind as the days turned: in everyone's heart, including his dear *sensei*'s, there lurked this ugly thing, this abnormal desire to possess another's body. *Why?* Emon did not realize that he saw only what he wished to see.

Everyone's desire. From desire are children born. I already know that. But who's my father?

He kept up his watch on the villagers' minds, that he might unravel that mystery, and he continued to gather what scraps of knowledge there were remaining about his mother. More and more it appeared that she had escaped into her mad world to flee something unspeakably horrible.

In the mind of the General Store's proprietor he found this:

(Osen's house . . . People say it was a ghost house in the old days, and then Osen was always cryin'. No, come to think about it, weren't it her mother? *Her* grandfather was killed or passed on. That's why she went crazy . . .)

Old Lady Také's thoughts once whispered:

(My dead grandmother used to say that they were hiding some crazy foreign man there, and he abused Osen, so they killed him, or something like that . . .)

And the murmuring thoughts of Toku the woodcutter gave forth a startling image:

(Granddad saw it. Osen's house was full of blood and everyone was dead, murdered. That household was crazy for generations, anyway. Osen's father – or was it her brother? – was terrible insane. An' in the middle a' all them hacked bodies, Osen was playing with a ball.)

Old Genji knew part of the story, too:

(Heard tell it was a *long* time ago on the hill where the house is that the fiery column fell from the sky. Since around then all the beautiful girls were born in that family, generation after generation, an' couldn't one of 'em speak. That's the legend.)

Long ago, in days forgotten, something terrible happened. Osen alone of the family survived and went mad, and became the village harlot. This was all that was clear to Emon.

6

They say that time weathers memory away: in truth the weight of years bears down on memory, compressing it into hard, jewel-like clarity. A mystery slept in that village, and sleeps there still. Over the years my thoughts have annealed around these puzzling events, but the mystery will remain forever uncovered – unless I go there and investigate in earnest.

I have tried to return many times. A year ago I came to within fifty kilometers of the village and then, for no rational reason I can summon up, I turned aside, went to another, more *amenable* place. Before embarking on these journeys I am always overcome by an unshakable reluctance, almost as if I were under a hypnotic compulsion to stay clear of the place.

Another curious fact:

In all the time I was stationed there, I recall no one else from the 'outside' ever staying in the village more than a few hours; and according to the villagers I was the first outsider to be seen at all in ten years. The only villagers who had lived outside those isolated reaches were Old Lady Také and Miss Yoshimura, who left to attend Teacher's College.

If going there I actually managed to come near the village proper, unless the military backed me I feel certain the locals would somehow block my return.

Is there something, some power at work that governs these affairs?

Such a power would have a long reach and strong, to the effect that this village of fewer than two hundred people may exist outside the administration of the Japanese government. I say this because during the Pacific War no man from that village was ever inducted into the Armed Forces.

And who might wield such power? Who mesmerized everyone? Old Lady Také, or the Teacher? And if both of them left the village under another's direction, who then is the person central to the mystery?

The madwoman, Osen?

When summer evenings come, my memories are crowded with the numerous songs the village children sang. It was so queer that everything about those songs was at complete variance with the historical roots that those villagers claimed to have: That the village had been founded centuries earlier by fugitive retainers deserting the Heike Family during their final wars with the Genji in the Heian Period, and that since that time no one had left the village. Yet none of the old stories lingering there were of Heike legends. It is almost as if the village slept in the cradle of its terraced fields, an island in the stream of history, divorced from the world.

Is something still hidden beneath the stone stairs leading up to Osen's house? 'Unknown Emon' gave up in despair and abandoned *some*thing there. A pump to send water up to the well at Sinner's Hole, or something hinted at in the children's handball song –

> *I wonder if I'll ever climb*
> *those weed-grown stairs someday?*
> *One – a stone stairway to the sky*
> *Two – if it doesn't fly,*
> *if it never flies open . . .*

When the day of flight comes, will the stairs open? Or must you open them in order to fly? – Questions, questions: it may be that the mystery of 'unknown Emon' will sleep forever in that place.

And what became of Osen's child?

After a time Emon once again attempted what he long ago had given up on – a search of his mother's mind. The strange white mist shrouding Osen's thoughts was as thick as ever.

(*Begone!*)

Emon's thoughts thundered at the mist in a shock wave of telepathic power.

Perhaps the sending of a psychic command and the discharge of its meaning in the receiver's mind can be expressed in terms of physics, vectors of force; then again, it may just be that Emon's telepathic control had improved, and he was far more adept at plucking meaning out of confused backgrounds. Whatever: with his command, the mist in Osen's mind parted as if blown aside by a wind, and Emon peered within for the first time.

Her mind was like immensities of sky. Emon dipped quickly in and out many times, snatching at the fragmented leavings of his mother's past. The quantity was small, with no connecting threads of history: everything scenes in a shattered mosaic.

There was only one coherent vision among it all. A vast machine – or a building – was disintegrating around her, and a mixture of terrible pain and pleasure blazed from her as she was held in a man's embrace.

And that was *odd*: that out of all her many encounters with all the men of the village, only this one experience had been so powerful as to burn itself indelibly into her memory.

The age and face of this man were unclear. His image was like seaweed undulating in currents at the bottom of the sea. The event had occurred on a night when the moon or some other light was shining, for his body was bathed in a glittering blue radiance. All the other men Osen had known, lost forever in the white mist that filled her mind and robbed her will, and only *this* man whom Emon had never seen existed with a force of will and fervency. Joy flooded from the memory, and with it great sorrow.

Why this should be was beyond Emon's understanding.

A vague thought stirred: *This man Osen is remembering is my father . . .*

While Emon poked tirelessly through the flotsam in the minds of his mother and the villagers, Miss Yoshimura played in a fantasy world where her curiosity focused always on Osen. It was now customary for her to hold Emon at night as they lay down to sleep, and one night her heart was so swollen with the desire to be Osen and lay with any man that it seemed ready to burst.

How could she know that Emon understood her every thought?

How could anyone realize the terrible wealth of pure *fact* that Emon had amassed about their hidden lives?

But his constant buffeting in this storm of venery took its awful toll. Excluding the smallest of children, Emon was of the unswayable opinion that all the villagers were obscene beyond the powers of any description. Especially Osen and himself – they were the worst offenders. Through the minds of the men he was constantly privy to Osen's ceaseless, wanton rut, and the pain that he was Osen's child was heavy upon him. Ever she bared her body to the men, and . . .

Emon hated her. He hated the men who came to her, and in his superlative nine-year-old mind this wretched emotion was transformed into a seething hatred for all the human race.

It was on one of his infrequent visits to his mother that he at last vented his anger, and struck an approaching man with a hurled stone.

'Drop dead, you little bastard!' the man raged. 'Don't go makin' any trouble, if you know what's good for you. Who d'ya think's keepin' you *alive!*'

Emon returned to the parlor after the man left and gazed at his silent mother's dazzling, naked body. He shook with unconcealed fury.

(I want to *kill* him! I *will* kill him! *Everybody!*)

Osen reached out to him then.

'My son, try to love them,' she murmured. 'You *must*, if you are to live . . .'

Stunned, Emon fell into her arms and clung to her. For the first time in his life he wept, unable to control the flow of tears.

Moments later Osen ended it all by releasing him and standing aimlessly, and that is when Emon began to suspect – to hope! – that her madness might only be a consummate impersonation. But it may have only been one clear moment shining through the chaos. There was no sign that the madness roiling Osen's brain had in the least abated.

Emon little cared to think deeply about the meaning of Osen's words, and his hatred toward the human race still filled his heart. But now he visited his mother far more often. It was during one of these visits, as he sat on the porch beside Osen some days or weeks later, that Emon *heard* a strange voice.

The voice did not come as sound in the air, or as a voice reaching into his mind with shapes and contexts. It was a *calling*, and it was for Emon alone – a tautness to drag him to its source, a thrown rope pulling. Unusually garbed in a neat, plain cotton robe, Osen was staring down the long valley, her mind empty as always.

'Who is it?' Emon called.

Osen turned her head to watch Emon as he scrambled to his feet and shouted the question. The vacuous expression on her face suddenly blanched, frozen for an instant in a look of dread.

'Where are you!' Emon shouted.

As if pulled up by Emon's voice, Osen got slowly to her feet and pointed to the mountains massed on the horizon.

'It's over there,' she said. 'That way . . .'

Emon hardly glanced at her as he started down the stone stairs, and then he was gone. He didn't even try to look back.

Time froze in yellow sunlight for the madwoman, and then melted again. Osen wandered blindly about, wracked with sobs, at some point arriving at the small waterwheel shack that housed the village millstone. The violence of her weeping resounded against the boards. She may have lost her capacity for thought, but she could still feel the agony of this final parting from her only child.

One of the villagers, catching sight of her trembling figure as he passed by, approached her with a broad grin, reached for her body with callused hands.

'Now, now, don't cry, Osen,' he said. 'Here, you'll feel lots better . . .'

The look she fixed him with was so hard and venom-filled, the first of its like he had ever seen from her. For a moment he felt a faint rousing of fear shake his heart, then slapped his work clothes with gusto and laughed at his own stupidity.

'Now what in hell . . .' and cursing Osen, he grabbed her, to force her to the grassy earth.

Osen slapped his hands away.

'Human *filth!*' she shouted clearly, commandingly. Her words echoed and re-echoed in the stony hollows around the water mill: 'Be gone and *die!*'

As Emon hurried far off down the road, the witless villager walked placidly into Endworld Mere, a dreamy look transfixing his face as he sank unknown beneath the dark and secret waters.

In the bamboo grove white mist danced again on the back of the air, and a white naked woman-figure ran lightly, lightly, chasing a paper airplane that flew on and on forever.

At the *Sai no Kawara*, the earthly shore where children come to bewail the passing of those who have crossed over the Great Waters, there is a weather-beaten sign of wood inscribed with characters that can only be spottily read:

It seems so easy to wait one thousand – nay, ten thousand years . . . driven mad with longing for the Star of my native home . . .

Small World

BOB SHAW

I'll do it today, Robbie thought. *I'll run across the sky today.*

He drew the bedclothes more closely around him, creating a warm cave which was precisely tailored to his small frame, and tried to go back to sleep. It was not yet morning and the house was quiet except for occasional murmurs from the refrigerator in the kitchen. Robbie found, however, that making the decision about the sky run had changed his mood, permitted the big and hazardous outside world to invade his security, and that sleep was no longer possible. He got up, went to the window and drew the curtains aside.

The three mirrors which captured sunlight had not yet been splayed out from the sides of the cylindrical space colony, and therefore it was still completely dark outside the house except for the luminance from the streetlamps. The nearby rooftops were silhouetted against the horizontal strip of blackness, unrelieved by stars, which Robbie knew as the night-time sky, but higher up he could see the glowing geometrical patterns of streets in the next valley. He stared at the jewelled rectangles and pretended he was a bird soaring above them in the night air. The game occupied his mind for only a short time – he had never seen a real bird, and his imagination was not fully able to cope with the old Earthbound concepts of 'above' and 'below'. Robbie closed the drapes, went back to bed and waited impatiently for morning . . .

'Come on, Robbie,' his mother called. 'It's time for breakfast.'

He sat up with a jerk, amazed to discover that he had, after all, been able to doze off and return to the peaceful world of dreams after the pledge he had made to himself. All the while he was washing and dressing he tried to get accustomed to the idea that this was the day on which he was going to grow up, to become a full member of the Red Hammers. His mind was still swirling with the sense of novelty and danger when he went into the bright kitchen and took his place in the breakfast alcove opposite his father and mother.

Like most colonists who had managed to settle happily on Island One, they were neat, medium-sized, unremarkable people of the sort who leave their youth behind very quickly, but are compensated with a seemingly endless span of unchanging adulthood. Mr Tullis was a crystallogenetic engineer in the zero-gravity workshops at the centre of the Island's sunward cap – an occupation which was beyond Robbie's comprehension; and Mrs Tullis was a psychologist specializing in verbal communication modes – an occupation Robbie might have understood had she ever talked to him about it. They both examined him critically as he sat down.

'What are you going to do today?' his mother said, handing him a dish of cereal.

'Nothin'.' Robbie stared down at the yellow feathers of grain, and he thought, *I'm going to run across the sky*.

'Noth*ing*,' she repeated, emphasizing the ending for Robbie's benefit. 'That doesn't sound very constructive.'

'The school holidays are too long.' Max Tullis stood up and reached for his jacket. 'I'm going to be late at the plant.'

Thea Tullis stood up with him and accompanied him to the front door while they discussed arrangements for a dinner party that evening. On her return she busied herself for a few minutes disposing of the breakfast remains and, her interest in Robbie's plans apparently having faded, disappeared without speaking into the room she used as study. Robbie toyed with his cereal, then drank the chill, malty-flavoured milk from the dish. He looked around the kitchen for a moment, suddenly reluctant to go outside and face the rest of the day, but he had discovered that when his mother was working in her study the house was lonelier than when he was the only person in it. Taking some candy from a dish on the window ledge, he opened the door and went out to the back garden.

Robbie often watched television programmes which were beamed out from Earth, and so had a fairly clear mental image of how a natural environment should look, but there was no sense of dislocation in his mind as he glanced around him on a quiet, summer morning. He had been born on Island One and saw nothing out of the ordinary about living on the inner surface of a glass-and-metal cylinder little more than two hundred metres in diameter and a kilometre in length. The colony was highly industrialized – because it manufactured many of the components for larger second-generation space habitats – but it had a residential belt supporting over a thousand families. This community, with a fourteen-year history of living in space, yielded valuable sociological data and therefore was preserved intact, even though its members could have been moved on to newer colonies.

None of Robbie's friends was visible in the row of adjoining gardens, so he emitted a sharp, triple-toned whistle, a secret signal devised by the Red Hammers, and sat down on a rustic seat to await results. Several minutes went by without an answering whistle being heard. Robbie was not particularly surprised. He had noticed that – no matter how strict the injunctions were from their leaders at night – the Hammers tended to sleep late in the morning during school holidays. On this occasion, though, he was disappointed at their tardiness because he anticipated the looks of respect from the other junior members when he announced he was taking his initiation.

He munched candy for a few minutes, then boredom began to set in and he thought about asking his mother to take him to the low-gravity park in the Island's outer cap. She had refused similar requests twice already that week, and he guessed her reply would be the same today. Dismissing the idea from his mind, he lay back in the chair and stared upwards, focusing his gaze on the houses and gardens visible 'above' him in the Blue Valley. The layout of the residential areas was identical in all three valleys, and Robbie was able to pick out the counterpart of his own family's house in the Blue Valley and – by looking back over his shoulder – in the Yellow Valley. At that time there was a temporary truce between the Red Hammers and the Yellow Knives, so Robbie's attention was concentrated on enemy territory, that inhabited by the Blue

Flashes. He had memorized the map drawn up by his own gang, and as a result was able to pick out the actual houses where the Blue Flash leaders lived.

As the minutes stretched out his boredom and restlessness increased. He stood up and gave the secret whistle again, making it louder this time. When there was no response he paced around the garden twice, making sure that no adults were watching him from windows of neighbouring houses, then slipped into the cool privacy of the shrubs at the foot of the lawn. A sense of guilty pleasure grew within him as he scooped up some of the crumbly soil with his hands and uncovered a small object wrapped in plastic film. Catapults were illegal on Island One – as were firearms and all explosive devices which might be capable of puncturing the pressure skin – but most boys knew about catapults, and some claimed the historic privilege of making them, regardless of any authority.

Robbie tested the strength of the synthetic rubber strands, enjoying the feeling of power the simple weapon gave him, and took a projectile from his pocket. There were no pebbles in the sieved and sterilized soil of the Island, but he made it a practice to collect suitably small and heavy objects. This one was a glass stopper from an old whisky decanter, almost certainly stolen, which he had bought from a girl in school. He fitted it into the catapult's leatherette cup, drew the rubber back to full stretch, and – after a final check that he was not being observed – fired it upwards in the direction of the residential area of the Blue Valley.

The glass missile glittered briefly in the sunlight, and vanished from sight.

Robbie watched its disappearance with a feeling of deep satisfaction. His pleasure was derived from the fact that he had defied, and somehow revenged himself upon, his parents and all the other adults who either ignored him or placed meaningless restrictions on his life. He also had a ten-year-old boy's faith that Providence would guide the projectile to land squarely on the roof of the gang hut used by the despicable Blue Flashes. His mind was filled with a gleeful vision of one of their full-scale meetings being thrown into panic and disorder by the thunderous impact just above their heads.

A moment later he heard an elaborate whistle coming from one of the nearby gardens and he lost all interest in the now invisible missile. He wrapped up the catapult, buried it, and ran to meet his friends.

The glass stopper which Robbie had dispatched into the sky weighed some sixty grams and had he lived on Earth it would have travelled only a short distance into the air before falling back. Island One rotated about its longitudinal axis once every twenty-one seconds, thus creating at the inner surface an apparent gravity equal to that of Earth at sea level. The gradient was on an entirely different scale to that of Earth, however – falling from maximum to zero in a distance of only a hundred metres, which was the radius of the cylindrical structure.

In the early stages of its flight the gleaming missile decelerated in much the same manner as it would have done while rising from the surface of a planet, but the forces retarding it quickly waned, allowing its ascent to be prolonged. It actually had some residual velocity when it reached the zero-gravity zone of the axis and, describing a sweeping S-curve, plunged downwards into the Blue Valley.

And, because the space colony had rotated considerably during its time of flight, the stopper landed nowhere near Robbie's notional target.

Alice Ledane was lying in a darkened room at the front of her house, hands clasped to her temples, when she heard the explosive shattering of the window which overlooked the rear patio.

She lay still for a pounding moment, rigid with shock, while her heart lurched and thudded like an engine shuddering to a halt. For what seemed a long time she was positive she was going to die, but her shallow, ultra-rapid fear-breathing gradually steadied into a more normal rhythm. She got to her feet and, leaning against the wall at intervals, went towards the back of the house. The mood of calmness and resolve she had been trying to nurture had gone, and for a moment she was afraid to open the door of the living room. When she finally did so her lips began to quiver as the remnants of her self-control dwindled away.

Shards of glass were scattered around the room like transparent petals, some of them hanging by their points from the drapes, and ornaments had been toppled from the small table which sat at the window. The surface of the table was dented, but she could see nothing of the missile which must have been thrown from the back garden. Alice gazed at the damage, knuckles pressed to her mouth, then she ran to the back door and threw it open. As she had expected, there was no sign of the children who for months had been persecuting her with such unyielding determination.

'Damn you!' she shouted. 'It isn't fair! What have I done to you? Why don't you come out in the open?'

There was a lengthy silence, disturbed only by the humming of bees in the hedgerows, then the tall figure of Mr Chuikov appeared at an upper window of the next house. Alice slammed her door, suddenly afraid of being seen, and stumbled back to the front room where she had been resting. She went to the sideboard, picked up a framed photograph of her husband, and stared at the unperturbed, smiling face.

'And damn you, Victor,' she said. 'You'd no right! No ... bloody ... *right*!'

While she was looking at the photograph, her hand made its own way into the pocket of her dressing gown and emerged holding a strip of bubbled tinfoil. Alice put the picture down and ejected a silver-and-blue capsule from the strip. She raised the tiny ovoid to her mouth, but hesitated without swallowing it. For the past week – in accordance with Dr Kinley's suggestion – she had progressively delayed the taking of the first cap by an extra hour every day. The aim, the shining goal, was to get through an entire day without any psychotropic medication at all. If that could be achieved just once there would be prospects of further successes and of finally becoming a whole woman again.

Alice rolled the capsule between her finger and thumb, and knew this was not to be her day of triumph – the children had seen to that. Harold from three doors along the block, or Jean from the house on the corner, or Carl from the next street. With the casual ruthlessness of the very young they had long ago deduced that her illness made her an easy prey, and they had declared a quiet war. Alice placed the capsule on her tongue, yielding to its promise of a few hours of peace, then an irksome thought occurred to her. While she was asleep the broken window in the living room would admit dust, insects, possibly even human intruders. There had once been a time when she could have slept contentedly in an unlocked house, but the world and all the people in it had been different then.

She took the capsule from her mouth, dropped it into her pocket, and went to fetch a waste bin. It took her fifteen minutes to gather up the larger fragments of glass, an armoury of brittle daggers, and to vacuum the carpet until it was free of gleaming splinters. The next logical step would have been to contact the maintenance department and report the damage, but she had had the telephone disconnected a year previously because its unexpected ringing had jolted her nerves too much. She had even, and quite illegally, cut the wires of the public service loudspeaker in the hall for the same reason. On this occasion it would not have taken long to get dressed and go to a phone in the shopping arcade, but Alice shrank from the idea of leaving the security of the house at such short notice. Her only option was to cover the broken window in some way until she felt strong enough to have it properly mended.

In the spare bedroom, the one Victor had used as a workshop, she found a sheet of alloy wide enough to span the window, and a quick search along the shelves produced a tube of Liqueld adhesive. She carried the materials into the living room, squeezed some adhesive on to the metal window frame and pressed the alloy into position. Within a minute it was so firmly in place that it was beyond her strength to move it. Satisfied that her defences were once again intact, Alice closed up the drapes, returned to the front room and lay down on the divan. The rolls of fat which had gathered around her body in a year of housebound inactivity had hampered her in the work she had just done and she was breathing heavily. The acrid smell of unhealthy perspiration filled the room.

'Damn you, Victor,' she said to the ceiling. 'You'd no right.'

Victor Ledane had been one of a team of five who had gone outside the sunward cap of a Model Two habitat to install a parabolic mirror which was going to be used as an auxiliary power source. The work was being done in a hurry against a completion deadline imposed by engineer-politicians back on Earth. As Alice understood it, one of the team had ignored standard procedure and had begun stripping the non-reflective coating from the dish before it was fully secured. Only a fraction of the bright metal surface had been uncovered, but when the mirror accidentally swung free of its mountings a blade of solar heat had sliced open the space suits of two men. And one of them had been Victor Ledane.

Alice and he had been living on Island One for six years at the time. Those had been good years, so absorbing that she had lost contact with her few friends back on Earth, and when the Island's community director, Les Jerome, had asked her to stay on she had readily agreed. She had known, of course, that the sociologists and psychologists were mainly interested in having a genuine space widow on tap, but with Victor gone nothing seemed very important. Obligingly, she had continued to live in the same house, had waited for the promised return of joy, and had tried not to think about the hard vacuum of space which began centimetres beneath the floor.

The trouble was . . . there had been no resurgence of joy.

Eventually she had settled for an inferior substitute, one which was dispensed in the form of silver-and-blue capsules, and now it was becoming impossible to distinguish between the two. The only way to restore her judgment would be to start living without the capsules, getting through one week at a time, but the point that Dr Kinley and the others seemed to miss was that – to begin with – it would be necessary to get through that first, endless, impossible day . . .

Alice fought to hold back the tears of frustration and despair as she realized that, on a day which had begun so disastrously, she was unlikely to hold on as late as noon before seeking relief. It came to her with a rare clarity that, for some people, the burdens of humanity were, quite simply, too great.

There was a gratifying response to Robbie's announcement.

After initial whoops of disbelief the younger members of the Red Hammers lapsed into silence, and Robbie could tell that – already – they were a little afraid of him. He made himself appear calm as Gordon Webb and the three other boys who made up the Supreme Council took him aside for a talk. Robbie went with them, occasionally glancing back at the juniors, and was thrilled to find that David, Pierre and Drew – even Gordon himself – were treating him almost as an equal. They were holding something in reserve, because he had not yet actually made the run, but Robbie was being given a strong foretaste of what it would be like to be a grown-up, and he found it a satisfying concoction. He wondered if his parents would notice a change in him when he went home for his evening meal, and if they would speculate on what had brought it about . . .

'. . . make up your mind which valley you're going to,' Gordon was saying. 'Yellow or Blue?'

Robbie forced his thoughts back to the present, and to the unfortunate necessity of having to qualify for senior status in the gang. Because of the truce with the Yellow Knives there would be less risk in going in their direction, but there would be more glory in a fleeting invasion of Blue Flash territory, and it was the glory that Robbie wanted. The glory, the respect and the recognition.

'Blue,' he said, and then, remembering a line from a television drama, 'where else?'

'Good man.' Gordon clapped him on the back. 'The Flashers are going to be sick. We'll show 'em.'

'We'd better get Robbie's challenge ready,' Drew said.

Gordon nodded. 'Are there any of the Blues watching us?'

Pierre took a small telescope from his pocket, moved out from the shade of the rhododendrons and trained the instrument on the Blue Valley residential section which was visible, at an altitude of some one hundred and twenty degrees, above a strip of sky in which the Earth and Moon could be seen sweeping by every twenty-one seconds. As the distance from where the boys stood to the heart of Blue Flash territory was less than two hundred metres for the most part, the telescope was scarcely necessary, but it was a prestigious part of the Supreme Council's equipment and was always brought into action on such occasions.

'All clear,' Pierre droned presently, and Robbie felt a thrill at being at the centre of such military efficiency.

Gordon cupped his hands around his mouth and shouted instructions to the watchful group of juniors. 'Spread out and keep away from here. Create a diversion.'

The smaller boys nodded dutifully and moved away through the neat little park in the direction of their homes. Robbie was disappointed that they would not be present to see him make his run, but he understood the wisdom of Gordon's precautions. In addition to the risk of alerting the Blue Flashes, there was the more immediate danger of attracting the attention of adults in their own valley.

He went with the Council members to David's home, which was conveniently empty because both his parents were out at work, and they spent some time preparing his challenge. This was a large sheet of paper which he decorated with crossed hammers drawn in red ink. Across the bottom of the sheet, in elaborate lettering which was meant to look like Gothic script, Robbie printed the message: SIR ROBBIE TULLIS, GENTLEMAN SOLDIER OF THE RED HAMMERS, PRESENTS HIS COMPLIMENTS. When the ink had dried, the paper was folded up and tucked into an empty pickle jar, and – as the ultimate insult to the Blue Flashes – a scrap of red cloth was tied around it.

The task was more time-consuming than Robbie had expected and had barely been completed when the day-care matron for the area arrived to give David his lunch. This was the signal for the other boys to suspend operations and disperse to their own homes. Robbie was not hungry, but he went home as usual to avoid giving the impression that anything out of the ordinary was happening. He decided to preserve an enigmatic silence during the meal and, as his mother's thoughts were occupied with her morning's work, there was virtually no conversation. The house was filled with a cool stillness which seemed as though it might go on for ever.

It was with a sense of relief that Robbie finished eating and returned to the sunlit world of comradeship and conspiracy he shared with the other boys of the neighbourhood. Gordon, David, Pierre and Drew were waiting for him in a corner of the park, and as soon as he came near he knew by the solemnity of their faces that something had happened. Pierre, the tallest of the group, was anxiously scanning the vicinity, every now and then pausing to examine some item of suspicion with his telescope.

'Ole Minty saw us,' Gordon explained to Robbie. 'I think he's following us around.'

'Does that mean I can't . . .'

'No chance!' Gordon's twelve-year-old face showed the determination which had made him leader of the Red Hammers. 'We'll wear the old scarecrow down. Come on.'

Robbie tightened his grip on his challenge, which was hidden in the pocket of his jacket, and hurried after Gordon. He was impressed by the way in which the older boy seemed absolutely unafraid of one of the gang's most powerful enemies. Mr Mintoff was the Red Valley's first and only old age pensioner. Robbie knew he must have been a brilliant man to have been allowed to emigrate to Island One in his late middle age, but now he was a solitary figure with little to do except patrol the neighbourhood and act as unofficial policeman. In spite of the fact that he appeared to be senile, and walked with the aid of an alloy stick, he had the knack of divining what was going on in the Hammers' minds and of making sudden appearances at the most inopportune times.

Under Gordon's control, the group walked to the end of Centre Street and stood in a conspicuous knot, giving every indication they were planning mischief, until they saw Mr Mintoff approaching from the direction of the park. They let him get close, then split up and made their way by separate and secret routes to the opposite end of the street, where they again assembled. A good twenty minutes passed before the stooped form of Mr Mintoff caught up with them. Just before he was within hailing distance they disappeared as before, melting into the ample shrubbery of the Red Valley, and came together at their original venue to await their pursuer. The second round of the fight had got under way.

Robbie had been certain that Ole Minty would be forced to concede defeat within the hour, but he displayed a stubborn tenacity, and it was quite late in the afternoon before they saw him give up and turn into the side avenue where he lived. They waited a while longer to establish that they were in the clear, and Robbie's heart began to pick up speed as he realized that all the preliminaries had ended, that it was time for him to make his run . . .

The sidewall of the valley was constructed of smooth, seamless alloy and had a curved overhang which was supposed to make it unclimbable. Island One was an artificial environment, however, and as such it relied on complex engineering systems to maintain its various functions. The systems were designed to be as unobtrusive as possible, and most colonists were quite unaware of them, but children have an intense, detailed awareness of their surroundings, one which often confounds adult minds. Robbie and his four companions went straight to a point where a cluster of hydraulic pipes and valves made it easy to get halfway up the wall, and where a strain monitor installed by a different team of engineers provided a useful handhold at the top. He knew that if he stopped to think about what he was doing his nerve could fail, so he scaled the wall without hesitation and quickly slid on to the outer girder, where he could not be seen by anybody in his own valley. Making sure that his challenge was secure in his pocket, he turned to climb down to the surface of glass stretching away beneath.

And the universe made ready to swallow him.

Robbie froze, his muscles locked by fear, as he looked into the vertiginous deeps of space. The vast, curved window which separated two of the Island's valleys was like a tank filled with black liquid, a medium through which darted stars, planets, the blue Earth, the Moon, seemingly miniature models of other habitats – all of them impelled by the rotation of his own world. The huge plane mirror a short distance beyond the glass did nothing to lessen the fearful visual impact – it created discontinuities, a sense of depths within depths, as bright objects appeared and disappeared at its edges. Adding to the kaleidoscope of confusion were the sweeping, brilliant visions of Island One's sister cylinder, its own mirrors splayed out, which periodically drenched Robbie with upflung showers of white light.

He shrank back from the abyss, fighting to draw breath, face contorted with shock. Something in his pocket clinked against the metal of the girder. Robbie looked down at it, saw the top of the pickle jar containing his challenge, and moaned aloud as he realized he was not free to turn back. He lowered himself to the bottom flange of the girder, stepped out on to the nearly invisible surface of the glass, and began his run across the sky.

The wall of the Blue Valley was less than a hundred metres away, but as Robbie sprinted over the void it seemed to retreat, maliciously, prolonging his ordeal. Each leap over a titanium astragal brought with it a nightmarish moment of conviction that there would be nothing to land on at the other side, and that he would fall screaming into the endless night. And as he neared the midpoint of his run Robbie encountered a new and even more disconcerting phenomenon – the sun had appeared directly beneath his feet. Its reflected light blazed upwards around Robbie, blinding him and producing a nauseating sense of dislocation. He kept on running, but he had begun to sob painfully with each breath and attacks of dizziness threatened to bring him down.

All at once, the wall of the Blue Valley was looming up in front, criss-crossed by the shadows of a lattice girder. He pulled the glass jar from his pocket, hurled it over the wall and turned to run homewards on legs which had lost all strength.

Robbie made it to the centre of the window, to the centre of the fountain of golden fire, before he collapsed. He lay on his side, eyes tight-closed, knees pulled up to his chin, his immature personality in full flight from the world beyond the womb.

'Hold on a moment, Mr Mintoff.' Les Jerome set the telephone on his desk, picked up his binoculars and went to the window. From his office high up on the outer cap of Island One he could see virtually the entire structure of the colony. The opposite cap was at the centre of his field of view, and radiating from it were the three inhabited valleys interspersed with three kilometre-long transparencies. He aimed the powerful glasses at the strip between the Red and Blue Valleys, stood perfectly still for a moment, then picked up the phone.

'I see him, Mr Mintoff,' he said. 'Right beside Frame Thirty-two. O.K., you contact his mother. And thanks for calling – we'll get the little beggar in from there in a hurry.'

Jerome replaced the telephone and depressed the intercom toggle which would let him speak to the chief of his maintenance force. 'Frank, there's a kid stuck out on the glass. Yeah, on

Transparency One just beyond Frame Thirty-two. Send somebody out to get him, and make sure a medic goes as well – the brat's going to need a shot of something to calm him down.'

Returning to the window, Jerome leaned on the ledge and stared at the strange, confined world he had grown to love in spite of all its faults and peculiarities. He had a decision to make, and it had to be done quickly. Strictly speaking, the plight of the boy out there on the glass did not constitute an emergency situation, and therefore he would not be officially justified in closing up the mirrors before the scheduled hour. All three mirrors had to be retracted at the same time, to preserve the Island's symmetrical dynamics, which meant enforcing a universal black-out – and there were many colonists who objected strenuously to that sort of thing. There would be a barrage of complaints, some of them from influential people, but Jerome was a kindly man with two children of his own, and it troubled him to think of a small boy trapped on the glass, suspended in space.

The sooner he could put a semblance of solidity beneath the boy's feet and screen him off from infinity, the better chance the young adventurer would have of emerging from his ordeal without personality scars. He picked up the rarely-used red telephone which would transmit his voice to every home, office and workshop on Island One.

'This is Community Director Jerome speaking,' he said. 'There is no cause for alarm, but we are going to close up the mirrors for a short period. The black-out will be as brief as we can possibly make it, and I repeat there is no cause for alarm. I apologize for any inconvenience that may be caused. Thank you.'

Jerome then contacted his Engineering Executive and gave the order which would bring a premature sunset to his domain.

In the darkened front room of her house, midway along the Blue Valley, Alice Ledane awoke with a start.

She had been skimming on the wavetops of consciousness for hours, sometimes dipping into restless sleep as her private struggle drained her of nervous energy, then surfacing again to feel more exhausted than ever. As was usual on a day like this, she had no idea of the time. She got to her feet, parted the drapes slightly and made the discovery that it was night outside.

Incredulously, she put her hand in the pocket of her dressing gown and found the day's first capsule still there. It was sticky to the touch. She held the tiny ovoid in the palm of her hand for a few seconds, then let it fall to the floor.

Alice went back to the divan and lay down. It was much too soon, she knew, to start congratulating herself on a victory – but if she had managed to get through one day with no outside help there was nothing to prevent her getting through the others which were to follow. Nothing insurmountable, anyway . . .

The sleep which came to her almost immediately was deep and dreamless and long-lasting, in contrast to her previous shallow dozing. It was the kind of sleep which all of life's warriors need to gird them for the morning and the bright light of the sun.

The Whore of Babylon

LEON ZELDIS

'I think it's time I took Jon to the slums,' said Father, as we were having our dessert.

Mother almost choked on the rice pudding. 'But he's still a boy!' she cried, her face turning a deep shade of red. I felt myself blushing, and hated it.

'He's old enough to learn the facts of life,' decreed Father. He went on eating his pudding methodically, as if nothing had been said.

Mother stole a glance in my direction. 'Pa, we shouldn't discuss these things in front of the boy.'

Father grunted. 'Won't do him no harm. He's got to grow some day. Grown-ups discuss these subjects, once in a while.' He hesitated a moment. 'Besides, I talked it over with the Recoff, and he's harshowed it.'

That settled it.

Mother got up and started taking the dishes to the washer. I guess she wanted to busy herself so she wouldn't have to look me in the eyes. 'What do *you* think, Jon, you want to go slumming?' She obviously had to force herself to utter the question, but she made a valiant effort to say it lightly, as if it was something she talked about all the time.

I didn't have to think very long to answer that one. The idea of going to the slums for the first time had now been in my mind for half a year, ever since two of my friends had started. 'Mike and Sasha have been there already,' I said. 'I guess this is my turn.'

'You see,' exclaimed Father in a satisfied tone, 'the boy was expecting it.'

Mother didn't reply. She only sighed and served the coffee. But I noticed her as she observed me a couple of times, when she thought I wasn't aware; she had a resigned look, like somebody who has lost something valuable, that could never be returned.

'I'll take Jon to the Red House,' added Father. 'They have the nicest girls. I remember, my father took me there, and it remained my favorite place . . . till I married you, of course,' he hastened to add, with a nod towards Mother. He leaned back on his chair, remembering. Then, he stood and slapped me on the shoulder. 'Come on, son, let's take a walk while Mother finishes the dishes.'

We walked out into the garden. The air was nippy, and the plum trees were showing the first signs of flowering. Yes, spring was approaching.

'You know, Jon,' Father carefully articulated his words. 'Women don't always appreciate that a man has certain special needs. It's unhealthy only to eat, work, play, have your son or your daughter. A man needs more. A little extra, a touch of pepper to make the dish tastier. Well, I don't want to say too much. The girls will teach you much better. You may be on edge the first time, but don't worry, that's happened to all of us. I'll be there, in another room. That's a father's privilege, and if you have a son, in due time, you'll do the same.'

I didn't say a word, though I felt a storm of fear and anticipation brewing inside.

'Don't expect too much, either,' continued Father. 'Especially at the beginning. After a while, you'll enjoy it more. When you learn to relax. Whoring is not such a simple thing as you think.' He chuckled. 'There was this girl, Rosy . . .' He stopped, gave me a flicker of a look, and shook his head, keeping his memories to himself.

We went back into the house, but as we stepped inside, Father took me by the arm and whispered: 'We'll go next Saturday, but don't tell Mother yet.'

The four intervening days till Saturday dragged on and on, without end. I couldn't concentrate on my work; even my play performance fell way down. Ever since I finished school, four years ago, I have worked in the same plant, making cellulose. Processing, of course,

is fully automatic, like everything else; still, there is lots of maintenance and supervision.

My work is blue painting. Some of the pipes are painted blue;
others have different colors. I don't know the reason. My uniform
is also blue, with socks, shoes, pants, shirt and cap, all of them
blue. I really feel happy with blue. I wouldn't know what to do if I
had to wear a different color. Funny, the red painter feels the
same about red. I don't really know other guys, because we are so
busy, you see. Always running around. Getting the paint, the
brush, the bucket. We don't keep the same bucket and brush from
one day to the next, you know. It's against R and R; something to
do with quality. Every day, you start by filling in a requisition for
a bucket. Then you get it countersigned and get your blue bucket
from the storeroom. Then you walk to the paint kitchen, which is
on the other side of the plant, the chemicals side, and get your two
liters of paint for the day; then you walk back to the perishables
storeroom, in the hardware side, and get the brush. They won't
give you a brush if you haven't got the paint, which is only logical,
and you can't get the paint if you haven't got a bucket to hold it.

Sometimes I feel really tired, and I wish I could ride with the
Tech on his buggy, watching the Robomecs doing their rounds.
But riding is not allowed. Only Techs, Supers and Execs can ride
within the plant. That is Rules and Regulations. Like the re-
sponse goes: 'R and R are made for us, the world goes round with
R and R.'

In any case, when I finish the rounds, it's time for the lunch
break. After that, I do my painting for the day, return the
equipment, get everything countersigned, change and go home.
Nobody pressures me; I work at my own pace, which is great. I
hate those places they show on the HEC sometimes, where people
are working against the clock. They look so unhappy. They all
end up on the Island, I guess. I never met anybody who worked in
a plant like that. That's lucky, because I don't think I would enjoy
meeting an Unhappy.

The last day I just didn't have it in me. I would walk around
with my bucket without actually looking for a rusty spot. I'll be
very honest. I rarely find a spot. What I do, I take a section of
blue pipe, any section at all, and paint it over. Come to think of it,

I can't remember when was the last time I actually found a rust spot. Perhaps it was only during the instruction period. No matter. As long as I'm busy, nobody tells me anything. My Sect-Super has more important things to do. I see him once, perhaps twice a month. So that last day I just walked around, and perhaps painted a few meters of pipe here and there. At the end of the day I returned my bucket, full of paint. Nobody said a thing. That's what I like about this work. As long as you are busy, it's harshow, they leave you alone.

Friday night we had the weekly party at the plant. We sat around in a big circle and chanted the news, as usual. This week we had a new cheer-caster, a pretty blonde girl with really big boobs. She was full of fun, singing each item of news in a laughing voice, and then we sang our responses while she jumped up and down, waving her arms to mark the time. She also taught us a new response: 'Getting less or getting more, I'm happier now than ever before.' We sang it over and over, maybe twenty or thirty times, having lots of fun. Then we had play period. I was so happy and excited that for a while I forgot about Saturday.

But then it was morning and it was Saturday and I felt the knot in my stomach getting all twisted up.

Father accompanied me to the barbershop. Usually, he went alone, while I was still at work. Since reaching thirty and retiring, Father likes to do his chores in the morning: buying the food, getting his shave, polishing his shoes. This time he came with me. We sat side by side in the barbershop; Moss shaved me and Clem shaved Father. Clem was upset. He told us the Happy Times squad had caught a man down in Bedloe Road shaving himself. Imagine! He had the cheek to argue with the officers that he didn't feel well and wanted to stay home that day. A likely tale! Clem snorted with indignation. How did that explain a safety razor and a supply of two dozen blades at home? The man was a degenerate, that was all. Bob Diller, who lived next door, had seen the whole thing, and had told Clem the story when he came in for his shave in the morning.

Father agreed fully with Clem's judgement. That kind of egocentric behavior was intolerable. I almost asked Father what egocentric meant, but I caught myself in time. Only little children are excused if they go and ask questions in public. Even then, the parents get a fair dose of criticism for not teaching them any better.

We went back home, and had a long lunch. Mother had entered a cooking competition, and she had to try out several new recipes. We ate too much, but it was early, so we all went to bed.

After a cup of strong coffee, to wake us up, Father said something like that we were going to visit some friends. Mother didn't say a word. I think she was blushing again, but she turned away quickly, so I cannot be sure. I was glad she didn't come to the door to see us off. We just got into Father's new Volta, the elecar he received as a present from his friends in the office when he retired.

We drove in silence while crossing the business section, all empty now, except for a few refuseniks burrowing into the piles of junk on the sidewalks. Father had explained once, in confidence, that he almost pitied the wretched creatures, although they had only themselves to blame. They had refused three consecutive job offers from the Fulfil Officer, and so they had to take the fourth one, whatever it was. That's R and R, and it's fair. No one should set himself above the law. Like one of the first responses you learn at school: 'I am free to obey, and I'm happy to be free.'

We were getting close to the waterfront. Nobody lives there any longer. Most buildings are falling apart. Nobody cares. One of these days the Beauty Officer will decide to tear down the whole area, and then lots of people will have new jobs for several years. I hope they don't choose me. I'm happy with blue paint. I don't wish to change, ever. Most people at the plant retire after their ten years, without having ever changed jobs. That's nice, it shows loyalty.

We reached a really old part of the city, right next to the rotting piers. Father explained to me that this was a place where once, many years ago, huge ships arrived from all over the world, loaded with goods that were different from those made here. The auto-copiers didn't exist then and there were actually many different things in different parts of the world. I know, it sounds crazy, but that's what Father told me.

Nowadays, only the monthly ferryboat to the Island comes here, to pick up the load of old folks and Unhappies.

The street we now entered was completely different from the

rest. It was brightly lit, with shop windows showing all kinds of strange things. There were lots of old stuff that I had never seen before. I don't know their names.

People were walking up and down the street, peering into the windows, ogling the girls that stood here and there, leaning against a doorframe, or standing under a light, acting as if they were reading. Some actually had a book in their hands. Naughty, naughty, I thought.

Father parked in an alley and we walked back into the street. Here and there, red lanterns were lit above the doorways. Music was coming down from the upper floors, and voices too, as if there were parties going on.

Finally, Father saw the place he had been looking for, on the other side of the street. As we crossed, I looked at the building. It was three stories high, built of red brick. It had tall windows and colored glass panes that showed only shadows of the people inside. The ground floor had been a shop once, but it was now boarded up. A broken sign above the windows read 'Babylon Bo . . .'

Father knocked, using a shiny brass ring hinged in the top, which made a loud, unpleasant noise. I wondered why we didn't just walk in. After all, it was an outside door, but I didn't dare embarrass Father by asking a question in the street. Somebody might overhear. I made a mental note to ask him in private, at the first opportunity.

A woman opened the door for us. She was wearing a strange kind of dress, black, with closed collar and long sleeves, ending in white cuffs. She smiled at us and motioned us to come in. I was almost sick, my heart pumping like mad, and I was worried about blushing. There was a big mirror in the room where the woman took us, and I was relieved to see that I was rather pale, not red in the face.

We sat down, Father and I, on two upholstered chairs, and waited. After a while, Father leaned towards me and whispered quietly the way it operated.

'You'll be conducted to the girl's room,' he explained. 'Don't be afraid, she's very experienced. Don't feel ashamed of anything. The girls here have seen and heard a lot. She'll tell you when your time is up, and then you come back here. I'll be waiting for you, or perhaps I'll return a couple of minutes after you. In that case, you wait for me. Harshow?'

I swallowed and nodded, unable to speak.

The room was like the Museum. Yes, I knew you'd be surprised. I did go once to the Museum, before they took Granny to the Island, the very last day. She took me by the hand and we walked through together. Old Granny had guts. But she asked me never to tell anybody what we had done. I never did. Anyway, it's nothing to be proud of, but Granny said, 'a man must have tasted everything once, so that he appreciates what he's got'.

As I said, the room we were sitting in was like the Museum, with velvet upholstery and a glass spider hanging from the middle of the ceiling, with icicles hanging from the arms. On the walls were indecent pictures, framed in gold. I sneaked a look around, and even after the dirty pictures I was shocked when I saw the books in a corner. I tried not to look in that direction.

Finally, the same woman who had opened the door returned and whispered something in Father's ear. He smiled and nodded. She then took me gently by my left arm and led me out of the room.

I could hardly walk straight. We went along a corridor, very dim, with thick carpet covering almost the entire width. At the end, we went upstairs, and then walked along another corridor, with doors on both sides, all closed. We walked slowly, she in front now, and I following her. Then we found a door that was ajar. No more than a couple of centimeters of yellowish light to show the door was unlocked. The woman pushed the door open and drew me inside, turned around and went out, closing the door tight behind her.

I stood there, undecided on what to do. A large double bed was on the left, with a nice coverlet. Then, to the right, there was a curtained window, and a desk with several books on it and two chairs. One of the chairs was empty and the other was occupied by a young girl who was looking at me with half-closed eyes. She was dark haired, with a long tress coiled on the top of her head. A lamp over the desk lighted her from behind, so that her face was almost in shadows while a halo surrounded her head.

Another lamp shone near the bed, dimmed with a yellow shade. The girl wore a thin nightgown, almost transparent; on her shoulders she wore a knitted shawl, although the room was quite warm.

'Hi,' she said, 'what's your name, hon?'

'Jon,' I said, without moving.

'Come here, Jon,' she ordered, pointing to the empty chair.

I walked across the room and sat down while looking at her. She wasn't pretty, but her eyes were special. I don't believe I ever saw such big eyes before. Looking at her from closer up, I saw she was rather old, really. Her skin was sickly pale, as if she never went into the sun. I also noticed a glass half-full of a greenish liquid close to the books. I tried not to stare.

'Well, Jon,' said the woman. 'My name is Rachel. Just relax, hon, sit back on that chair, take your time. Harshow?'

I nodded.

'Good. Now, let's see. This is your first time, I understand. Yes, you look very young. That's all right, hon, I'll take care of everything. Rachel knows.'

I waited, saying nothing.

'Good. Now, let's see.' She seemed to be rehearsing in her mind what she was going to say. 'Jon, we live in a world where everybody is happy. Right? Everybody knows what to do. Everybody knows what to expect. There are no questions left. The very act of asking a question has become repugnant, immoral, even. Like pornography used to be.'

She stopped, picked up the glass and took a long gulp without looking at me.

'Pornography, Jon, do you know what it means?'

I cursed myself. I was blushing, just as I had feared all along. But the blame wasn't mine. The damned woman kept asking questions, just like that!

'No,' I managed to grunt.

'Good. Here we are alone, Jon, you know that? You must get used, first of all, to the idea that we are really alone, isolated. We can say and do whatever we please, and nobody will ever know. I can ask you questions, and you, hon, can ask me questions, and that's all right. Here it's allowed, harshow?'

'Harshow.'

'Good. Let's see, now, to return to my question. Pornography.

It used to mean, printed or visual matter designed to stimulate erotic feelings. That was many years ago, before playing became acceptable. If you were to see now an old-time pornographic picture – yes, flat pictures was all they had, then – you would split your sides laughing. Such innocent idiocy. Of course, you couldn't know what pornography means, because for you it has no meaning at all.'

She looked at me calculatingly. 'This is where we come into the picture. The whores. We are the ones who ask questions. We incite you to ask questions of your own. We break the rules. Against the current norm. You don't know what a norm is, do you? No, of course not. Don't worry, hon, we'll have enough time to give you a good shake down before you get married and stop slumming. The slums, do you know what they are? They are the last place for freedom left in the country. Real freedom, not the kind you chant by rote. Why do they let us be? I guess, for the same reason red-light districts have always been tolerated. We allow gentlemen to give vent to their lower passions without contaminating those in their own social circle.'

I didn't know what to make of her, of this whore. I hardly understood one word in three of what she was saying.

She looked closely at me and nodded. 'Jon, hon, don't you despair. I know you don't understand what I'm saying. That's all right. Later you will understand. Later. Or perhaps not, we shall see. What we are going to do, I'm going to read from one of these books here, and then we'll discuss what I have read. Don't be ashamed. Books were once the height of respectability, but then it all changed.' She sighed. 'Now, a book is an obscene object. But here, it's all right, hon. I'm a whore, remember. I can read books. Then, after we finish, we can have a play period, if you feel like it.' She glanced at the bed.

I was nonplussed. 'What for? What's play got to do with a whore?'

'It's an ancient tradition,' she answered. 'But don't feel obliged. Harshow?'

'Harshow, Rachel,' I said, feeling more at ease.

She smiled at hearing me say her name.

'Good. Now, remember, nobody can see us or hear us. And you

must force yourself to ask me, yes, ask me questions, whenever you hear something that you don't understand. Is that clear?'

'Yes,' I replied, more firmly now. I was actually getting used to hearing her ask questions.

She picked up a book, just like that, without any pretence of modesty, and opened it at a place where she had inserted a thin strip of cardboard.

'In the beginning God created the heaven and the earth,' she started. She read on for a few moments, then stopped and looked at me expectantly.

I had to make the effort. I cleared my throat.

'God,' I said. 'What is that?'

Cost of Living

ROBERT SHECKLEY

Carrin decided that he could trace his present mood to Miller's suicide last week. But the knowledge didn't help him get rid of the vague, formless fears in the back of his mind. It was foolish. Miller's suicide didn't concern him.

But why had that fat, jovial man killed himself? Miller had had everything to live for – wife, kids, good job and all the marvellous luxuries of the age. Why had he done it?

'Good morning, dear!' Carrin's wife said as he sat down at the breakfast table.

'Morning, honey! Morning, Billy!'

His son grunted something.

You just couldn't tell about people, Carrin decided, and dialled his breakfast. The meal was gracefully prepared and served by the new Avignon Electric Autocook.

His mood persisted, annoyingly enough since Carrin wanted to be in top form this morning. It was his day off, and the Avignon Electric finance man was coming. This was an important day.

He walked to the door with his son.

'Have a good day, Billy!'

His son nodded, shifted his books and started to school without answering. Carrin wondered if something was bothering him, too. He hoped not. One worrier in the family was plenty.

'See you later, honey.' He kissed his wife as she left to go shopping.

At any rate, he thought, watching her go down the walk, she's happy. He wondered how much she'd spend at the A. E. store.

Checking his watch, he found that he had half an hour before the A. E. finance man was due. The best way to get rid of a bad mood was to drown it, he told himself, and headed for the shower.

The shower room was a glittering plastic wonder, and the sheer luxury of it eased Carrin's mind. He threw his clothes into the A. E. automatic Kleen-presser, and adjusted the shower spray to a notch above 'brisk'. The five-degrees-above-skin-temperature water beat against his thin white body. Delightful! And then a relaxing rub-dry in the A. E. Auto-towel.

Wonderful, he thought, as the towel stretched and kneaded his stringy muscles. And it should be wonderful, he reminded himself. The A. E. Auto-towel with shaving attachments had cost three hundred and thirteen dollars, plus tax.

But worth every penny of it, he decided, as the A. E. shaver came out of a corner and whisked off his rudimentary stubble. After all, what good was life if you couldn't enjoy the luxuries?

His skin tingled when he switched off the Auto-towel. He should have been feeling wonderful, but he wasn't. Miller's suicide kept nagging at his mind, destroying the peace of his day off.

Was there anything else bothering him? Certainly there was nothing wrong with the house. His papers were in order for the finance man.

'Have I forgotten something?' he asked out loud.

'The Avignon Electric finance man will be here in fifteen minutes,' his A. E. bathroom Wall-reminder whispered.

'I know that. Is there anything else?'

The Wall-reminder reeled off its memorized data – a vast amount of minutiae about watering the lawn, having the Jet-lash checked, buying lamb chops for Monday, and the like. Things he still hadn't found time for.

'All right, that's enough.' He allowed the A. E. Auto-dresser to dress him, skilfully draping a new selection of fabrics over his bony frame. A whiff of fashionable masculine perfume finished him and he went into the living-room, threading his way between the appliances that lined the walls.

A quick inspection of the dials on the wall assured him that the house was in order. The breakfast dishes had been sanitized and stacked, the house had been cleaned, dusted, polished, his wife's garments had been hung up, his son's model rocket-ships had been put back in the closet.

'Stop worrying, you hypochondriac!' he told himself angrily.

The door announced, 'Mr Pathis from Avignon Finance is here.'

Carrin started to tell the door to open, when he noticed the Automatic Bartender.

Good God, why hadn't he thought of it?

The Automatic Bartender was manufactured by Castile Motors. He had bought it in a weak moment. A. E. wouldn't think very highly of that, since they sold their own brand.

He wheeled the bartender into the kitchen, and told the door to open.

'A very good day to you, sir!' Mr Pathis said.

Pathis was a tall, imposing man, dressed in a conservative tweed drape. His eyes had the crinkled corners of a man who laughs frequently. He beamed broadly and shook Carrin's hand, looking around the crowded living-room.

'A beautiful place you have here, sir. Beautiful! As a matter of fact, I don't think I'll be overstepping the company's code to inform you that yours is the nicest interior in this section.'

Carrin felt a sudden glow of pride at that, thinking of the rows of identical houses, on this block and the next, and the one after that.

'Now then, is everything functioning properly?' Mr Pathis asked, setting his brief-case on a chair. 'Everything in order?'

'Oh, yes!' Carrin said enthusiastically. 'Avignon Electric never goes out of whack.'

'The phono all right? Changes records for the full seventeen hours?'

'It certainly does,' Carrin said. He hadn't had a chance to try out the phono, but it was a beautiful piece of furniture.

'The Solido-projector all right? Enjoying the programmes?'

'Absolutely perfect reception.' He had watched a programme just last month, and it had been startlingly lifelike.

'How about the kitchen? Auto-cook in order? Recipe-master still knocking 'em out?'

'Marvellous stuff. Simply marvellous.'

Mr Pathis went on to inquire about his refrigerator, his vacuum cleaner, his car, his helicopter, his subterranean swimming pool, and the hundreds of other items Carrin had bought from Avignon Electric.

'Everything is swell,' Carrin said, a trifle untruthfully since he hadn't unpacked every item yet. 'Just wonderful.'

'I'm so glad,' Mr Pathis said, leaning back with a sigh of relief. 'You have no idea how hard we try to satisfy our customers. If a product isn't right, back it comes, no questions asked. We believe in pleasing our customers.'

'I certainly appreciate it, Mr Pathis.'

Carrin hoped the A. E. man wouldn't ask to see the kitchen. He visualized the Castile Motors Bartender in there, like a porcupine in a dog show.

'I'm proud to say that most of the people in this neighborhood buy from us,' Mr Pathis was saying. 'We're a solid firm.'

'Was Mr Miller a customer of yours?' Carrin asked.

'That fellow who killed himself?' Pathis frowned briefly. 'He was, as a matter of fact. That amazed me, sir, absolutely amazed me. Why, just last month the fellow bought a brand-new Jet-lash from me, capable of doing three hundred and fifty miles an hour on a straight-away. He was as happy as a kid over it, and then to go and do a thing like that! Of course, the Jet-lash brought up his debt a little.'

'Of course.'

'But what did that matter? He had every luxury in the world. And then he went and hung himself.'

'Hung himself?'

'Yes,' Pathis said, the frown coming back. 'Every modern convenience in his house, and he hung himself with a piece of rope. Probably unbalanced for a long time.'

The frown slid off his face, and the customary smile replaced it. 'But enough of that! Let's talk about you!'

The smile widened as Pathis opened his brief-case. 'Now, then, your account. You owe us two hundred and three thousand dollars and twenty-nine cents, Mr Carrin, as of your last purchase. Right?'

'Right,' Carrin said, remembering the amount from his own papers. 'Here's my instalment.'

He handed Pathis an envelope, which the man checked and put in his pocket.

'Fine. Now you know, Mr Carrin, that you won't live long enough to pay us the full two hundred thousand, don't you?'

'No, I don't suppose I will,' Carrin said soberly.

He was only thirty-nine, with a full hundred years of life before him, thanks to the marvels of medical science. But at a salary of three thousand a year, he still couldn't pay it all off and have enough to support a family on at the same time.

'Of course, we would not want to deprive you of necessities. To say nothing of the terrific items that are coming out next year. Things you wouldn't want to miss, sir!'

Mr Carrin nodded. Certainly he wanted new items.

'Well, suppose we make the customary arrangement. If you will just sign over your son's earnings for the first thirty years of his adult life, we can easily arrange credit for you.'

Mr Pathis whipped the papers out of his brief-case and spread them in front of Carrin.

'If you'll just sign here, sir.'

'Well,' Carrin said, 'I'm not sure. I'd like to give the boy a start in life, not saddle him with –'

'But my dear sir,' Pathis interposed, 'this is for your son as well. He lives here, doesn't he? He has a right to enjoy the luxuries, the marvels of science.'

'Sure,' Carrin said. 'Only –'

'Why, sir, today the average man is living like a king. A hundred years ago the richest man in the world couldn't buy what any ordinary citizen possesses at present. You mustn't look upon it as a debt. It's an investment.'

'That's true,' Carrin said dubiously.

He thought about his son and his rocket-ship models, his star charts, his maps. Would it be right? he asked himself.

'What's wrong?' Pathis asked cheerfully.

'Well, I was just wondering,' Carrin said. 'Signing over my son's earnings – you don't think I'm getting in a little too deep, do you?'

'Too deep? My dear sir!' Pathis exploded into laughter. 'Do you know Mellon down the block? Well, don't say I said it, but he's already mortgaged his grandchildren's salary for their full life-expectancy. And he doesn't have half the goods he's made up his mind to own. We'll work out something for him. Service to the customer is our job and we know it well.'

Carrin wavered visibly.

'And after you're gone, sir, they'll all belong to your son.'

That was true, Carrin thought. His son would have all the marvellous things that filled the house. And after all, it was only thirty years out of a life expectancy of a hundred and fifty.

He signed with a flourish.

'Excellent!' Pathis said. 'And by the way, has your home got an A. E. Master-operator?'

It hadn't. Pathis explained that a Master-operator was new this year, a stupendous advance in scientific engineering. It was designed to take all the functions of house-cleaning and cooking, without its owner having to lift a finger.

'Instead of running around all day, pushing half a dozen different buttons, with the Master-operator, all you have to do is push *one!* A remarkable achievement!'

Since it was only five hundred and thirty-five dollars, Carrin signed for one, having it added to his son's debt.

Right's right, he thought, walking Pathis to the door. This house will be Billy's some day. His and his wife's. They certainly will want everything up-to-date.

Just one button, he thought. That *would* be a time-saver!

After Pathis left, Carrin sat back in an adjustable chair and turned on the solido. After twisting the Ezidial, he discovered that there was nothing he wanted to see. He tilted back the chair and took a nap.

The something on his mind was still bothering him.

'Hello, darling!' He awoke to find his wife was home. She kissed him on the ear. 'Look!'

She had bought an A. E. Sexitizer-négligé. He was pleasantly surprised that that was all she had bought. Usually, Leela returned from shopping laden down.

'It's lovely,' he said.

She bent over for a kiss, then giggled – a habit he knew she had picked up from the latest popular solido star. He wished she hadn't.

'Going to dial supper,' she said, and went to the kitchen. Carrin smiled, thinking that soon she would be able to dial the meals without moving out of the living-room. He settled back in his chair, and his son walked in.

'How's it going, Son?' he asked heartily.

'All right,' Billy answered listlessly.

'What'sa matter, Son?' The boy stared at his feet, not answering. 'Come on, tell Dad what's the trouble!'

Billy sat down on a packing-case and put his chin in his hands. He looked thoughtfully at his father.

'Dad, could I be a Master Repairman if I wanted to be?'

Mr Carrin smiled at the question. Billy alternated between wanting to be a Master Repairman and a rocket pilot. The repairmen were the élite. It was their job to fix the automatic repair machines. The repair machines could fix just about anything, but you couldn't have a machine fix the machine that fixed the machine. That was where the Master Repairmen came in.

But it was a highly competitive field and only a very few of the best brains were able to get their degrees. And, although the boy was bright, he didn't seem to have an engineering bent.

'It's possible, Son. Anything is possible.'

'But is it possible for me?'

'I don't know,' Carrin answered, as honestly as he could.

'Well, I don't want to be a Master Repairman anyway,' the boy said, seeing that the answer was no. 'I want to be a space pilot.'

'A space pilot, Billy?' Leela asked, coming into the room. 'But there aren't any.'

'Yes, there are,' Billy argued. 'We were told in school that the government is going to send some men to Mars.'

'They've been saying that for a hundred years,' Carrin said, 'and they still haven't got around to doing it.'

'They will this time.'

'Why would you want to go to Mars?' Leela asked, winking at Carrin. 'There are no pretty girls on Mars.'

'I'm not interested in girls. I just want to go to Mars.'

'You wouldn't like it, honey,' Leela said. 'It's a nasty old place with no air.'

'It's got some air. I'd like to go there,' the boy insisted sullenly. 'I don't like it here.'

'What's that?' Carrin asked, sitting up straight. 'Is there anything you haven't got? Anything you want?'

'No, sir. I've got everything I want.' Whenever his son called him 'sir', Carrin knew that something was wrong.

'Look, Son, when I was your age I wanted to go to Mars, too. I wanted to do romantic things. I even wanted to be a Master Repairman.'

'Then why didn't you?'

'Well, I grew up. I realized that there were more important things. First I had to pay off the debt my father had left me, and then I met your mother –'

Leela giggled.

'– and I wanted a home of my own. It'll be the same with you. You'll pay off your debt and get married, the same as the rest of us.'

Billy was silent for a while. Then he brushed his dark hair – straight, like his father's – back from his forehead and wet his lips.

'How come I have debts, sir?'

Carrin explained carefully. About the things a family needed for civilized living, and the cost of those items. How they had to be paid. How it was customary for a son to take on a part of his parent's debt, when he came of age.

Billy's silence annoyed him. It was almost as if the boy were reproaching him, after he had slaved for years to give the ungrateful whelp every luxury.

'Son,' he said harshly, 'have you studied history in school? Good! Then you know how it was in the past. Wars. How would you like to get blown up in a war?'

The boy didn't answer.

'Or how would you like to break your back for eight hours a day, doing work a machine should handle? Or be hungry all the time? Or cold, with the rain beating down on you, and no place to sleep?'

He paused for a response, got none and went on. 'You live in the most fortunate age mankind has ever known. You are surrounded by every wonder of art and science. The finest music, the greatest books and art, all at your fingertips. All you have to do is push a button.' He shifted to a kindlier tone. 'Well, what are you thinking?'

'I was just wondering how I could go to Mars,' the boy said. 'With the debt, I mean. I don't suppose I could get away from that.'

'Of course not.'

'Unless I stowed away on a rocket.'

'But you wouldn't do that.'

'No, of course not,' the boy said, but his tone lacked conviction.

'You'll stay here and marry a very nice girl,' Leela told him.

'Sure I will,' Billy said. 'Sure.' He grinned suddenly. 'I didn't mean any of that stuff about going to Mars. I really didn't.'

'I'm glad of that,' Leela answered.

'Just forget I mentioned it,' Billy said, smiling stiffly. He stood up and raced upstairs.

'Probably gone to play with his rockets,' Leela said. 'He's such a little devil.'

The Carrins ate a quiet supper, and then it was time for Mr Carrin to go to work. He was on night shift this month. He kissed his wife goodbye, climbed into his Jet-lash and roared to the factory. The automatic gates recognized him and opened. He parked and walked in.

Automatic lathes, automatic presses – everything was automatic. The factory was huge and bright, and the machines hummed softly to themselves, doing their job and doing it well.

Carrin walked to the end of the automatic washing-machine assembly line, to relieve the man there.

'Everything all right?' he asked.

'Sure,' the man said. 'Haven't had a bad one all year. These new models here have built-in voices. They don't light up like the old ones.'

Carrin sat down where the man had sat and waited for the first washing-machine to come through. His job was the soul of simplicity. He just sat there and the machines went by him. He pressed a button on them and found out if they were all right. They always were. After passing him, the washing-machines went to the packaging section.

The first one slid by on the long slide of rollers. He pressed the starting button on the side.

'Ready for the wash,' the washing-machine said.

Carrin pressed the release and let it go by.

That boy of his, Carrin thought. Would he grow up and face his responsibilities? Would he mature and take his place in society? Carrin doubted it. The boy was a born rebel. If anyone got to Mars, it would be his kid.

But the thought didn't especially disturb him.

'Ready for the wash.' Another machine went by.

Carrin remembered something about Miller. The jovial man had always been talking about the planets, always kidding about going off somewhere and roughing it. He hadn't, though. He had committed suicide.

'Ready for the wash.'

Carrin had eight hours in front of him, and he loosened his belt to prepare for it. Eight hours of pushing buttons and listening to a machine announce its readiness.

'Ready for the wash.'

He pressed the release.

'Ready for the wash.'

Carrin's mind strayed from the job, which didn't need much attention in any case. He realized now what had been bothering him.

He didn't enjoy pushing buttons.

Night Broadcast

ION HOBANA

Translated by Dan Duțescu

I opened the letterbox and took out the envelope which I had glimpsed through the narrow slit when I left home. With the eye of an old stamp collector I instantly recognized the New Zealand stamps. So the last answer had arrived – the last ring of the chain which had set out to go round the Earth more than two years before.

I climbed the stairs to the fourth floor, weighing in my hand the envelope whose colour was a strange shade of orange. I looked at it with mixed feelings, as I knew that my feverish waiting would come to an end. And suddenly I felt apprehension about the certainty which perhaps lay hidden between the thin paper walls.

I dumped my sports bag in the vestibule and walked into the sitting room which the late afternoon sun had set on fire. I took off my training suit and sat down in my armchair in front of the TV set. The orange envelope radiated a warm, enticing light. I resisted the temptation to speed up the denouement and leaning against the resilient back of the chair I shut my eyes.

So far everything had gone on in about the same way as two years before. I was returning from Herăstrău Park after a game of tennis. I was tired – the pleasant fatigue of victory. From the trolleybus I saw the windows of the Institute next to my block of flats all sparkling. I thought it was the reflection of the sun declining over the horizon. When the bus drove past the building, I found that I had been wrong – the windows were lit from inside. 'They are going to work all night again. And Emil said he would drop in –'

Emil Dobrişan had been my classmate – we shared the same form too – in our ever receding teens. At present he was a distinguished physicist, head of a section in the neighbouring Institute – a fact which did not prevent him from repairing, in his spare time, all sorts of electric and electronic apparatus. *'Mon violon d'Ingres,'* he used to say with a smile hidden under the moustache he had let grow at will, as a compensation for his bald head. And he would add, 'You can't find a repairman with a doctoral degree in the Theory of Relativity round every corner!' We saw much less of each other than we would have liked to, caught as we were in the unyielding net of daily obligations. That evening, among other things, we had planned to put my television antenna up again, sited, owing to Emil's influence, on the tall roof of the Institute and knocked down the previous day by a violent storm that had come out of the blue.

As I had to change my plans, I laboured for three hours over a ticklish text, I ate something and sat down in my armchair to watch the news. I had expected the image to be at best not very clear, but the outlines were perfectly neat, as in a tridimensional projection. Too tired to try to solve the puzzle, I dozed off before the weather report.

When I woke up, a young woman was gazing at me with her dark eyes. Her face was unnaturally white – I first blamed it on a fault of the colour system – and her eyebrows were raised towards her temples like two wings. Styled according to canons of hairdressing which were foreign to me, her hair – like a copper helmet – left her broad forehead and tiny ears uncovered.

I looked at my watch – it was well past midnight. The unknown woman went on gazing at me in silence. As a matter of fact, though her lips never moved, I had an idea that she wanted to convey something to me, some message of vital importance – whether for her or for me I could not tell. I made an effort and tore my eyes away from the hypnotic face and fixed them beyond it on a cluster of indefinite shapes. As if guessing my intention, the white oval withdrew to the upper left corner of the screen and let appear in the foreground – I hesitated to define the geometric structures that were besieging the sky. An industrial centre? Or an urban complex conceived by a demented architect? There were pyramids and cubes and spheres and spirals spinning up into the air, all made of a translucent material which I was at a loss to identify. Upon closer examination, the chaos seemed to become more orderly. The alternation of forms created a rhythm, a secret harmony, an almost musical vibration.

I had no time to assess my impressions. A scintillating diagonal sectioned the screen, isolating the geometric structures to an area above which, like an effigy, the unknown woman's face persisted. On the other side there was, for a while, only a triangular strip of sky. Then somewhere, at a distance difficult to judge owing to a lack of any reference point, a sort of greyish-blue cloud appeared, a giant roller devouring the space with terrible slowness.

I repressed my uneasiness – it was, it could only be a film transmitted by who knows what foreign station and picked up thanks to some favourable circumstances. It had happened before. I also knew something about the mechanism of incidental propagation of waves to great distances. I therefore watched with detachment how a swarm of discoidal airships rushed upon the greyish-blue horror, projecting powerful bright jets. 'Laser,' I said to myself as I expected to see the cloud torn to pieces, scattered, vanquished. The flashings however came against some invisible obstacle and ricocheted off to wayward trajectories. Some of the discs that were hit crashed in flames. The rest of the armada withdrew.

The sky, chameleon-like, had turned violet. From somewhere another disc appeared, only one, huge, hovering like a threat over a threat. A shining spot detached itself from it. The disc disappeared. The spot grew into a sphere which picked up speed as it swooped down, but was stopped by the same barrier. And after a few seconds I saw the terrible mushroom growing, as if it fed on the atoms around it. Under it, untouched, invulnerable, the cloud continued to advance. I followed it for a long time, fascinated by its ever faster horizontal fall.

On the other side of the screen the shapes were now traversed by multicoloured pulsations. I wondered if it was not the means of conveying the geometric kingdom devised by the producers of the film. At long last the diagonal line faded out. The immobile face came again to the foreground, allowing the geometric structures to be seen *through it* as they were swallowed up by the greyish-blue nightmare. The pale lips never parted even then, but the eyes were burning under the auburn eyebrows. I thought I could discern in that dull flame the despair of the end of the world.

The cloud went out of the frame. After it the pyramids and the cubes and the spirals spinning up into the air began to lose consistency, to interpenetrate, to turn into a viscous substance. I remembered I had a camera. I rushed to my desk and took it out of the drawer. I adjusted the exposure time and the lens opening with a certain amount of approximation – it was my first attempt to record a televised image. When I pressed the release button, the process of disintegration had almost come to an end. One last look like a call and the transparent face melted away. For a few moments I could still see the layer of matter covering the soil, a frozen ocean, then the screen was nothing but a grey, blind rectangle.

I waited a long time for the announcer to appear, or for the image test or some sign to confirm the hypothesis of a long-distance reception. I said to myself that the favourable circumstances had ceased to work. I rose from my armchair to turn off the TV set and I felt fatigue weigh down my shoulders. I was too excited however to think of sleep. I wrote down what I had seen, without omitting any detail, and I tried to locate the transmission by the difference between the time zones. A quick calculation ruled out Europe and the adjacent areas. In all probability the source had to be sought somewhere in the area of the Two Americas or in the Far East or in Oceania. A few dozen countries, some possessing several central stations – I felt dizzy and I went to bed.

Emil listened to me with suspicious attention. No quizzical glance over his glasses, no ambiguous comment about the poor photograph – the only 'evidence' of the existence of the night broadcast. When I came to the end of my account he asked me, after a silence which threatened to become awkward:

'And what do you intend to do?'

'Find out what film that was and by whom it was broadcast.'

He shook his head.

'It isn't that simple,' he said.

'I am stubborn enough to go the whole hog.'

'I hope there is a hog –' was his comment.

He rose to go. I stopped him with a gesture.

'Don't you think that there is one more puzzle about this story?'

He looked at me, his curiosity apparently aroused.

'A long-distance transmission – an antenna out of use –' I said.

The eminent physicist blushed like the teenager he had once been.

'You know –' he faltered, 'that prolonged experiment – I couldn't wait for you – I connected the wire to the antenna of the Institute.'

'Maybe that's how the reception can be accounted for,' I said.

'Maybe,' he agreed spiritlessly. 'Excuse me but I must – I'll be seeing you.'

He walked out, waving his hand in farewell. My bewilderment did not withstand for too long my desire to elucidate the mystery of the transmission. I began to employ my mind as to how I could get the necessary addresses quickly.

After a couple of months, when I had received a dozen negative answers, Emil dropped in once more. He had phoned me up several times; he knew how matters stood and he seemed equally tense. I devised a little diversion.

'I wonder,' I said, 'if that broadcast did not come from a far greater distance –'

'What do you mean?' he wanted to know.

His voice trembled slightly. I stopped torturing him.

'That night,' I said, 'the experiment – Did you by any chance establish a connection with another planet?'

He relaxed instantly.

'For such a wonder to happen,' he said, 'we should have had – you know what a radiotelescope looks like anyway!'

'Obviously – I don't know what's worrying you.'

He examined the books on my desk, one by one; he took a long time adjusting the knot of his tie in the mirror and, just as I was going to take him to task he turned to me.

'We may have established a connection,' he said, 'but not in space –'

'Not in space?' I repeated, failing to understand.

'The experiment aimed at opening an access to the fourth dimension,' he said.

'A journey in time!'

Emil smiled from the corner of his mouth.

'Don't stir up Wells's shadow!' he said. 'All we intended was an instrumental probing into a long gone era. To understand the method you would need to possess some knowledge in a very special field. In essence, the author of the experiment maintains that by going far enough into the future one comes upon what we call the past –'

'Rather vague –' I retorted with a certain amount of vehemence, 'and rather paradoxical! Are you sure you've got somewhere?'

'Weren't you amazed to see that it was a silent film?' he replied. He seemed to have forgotten what I had asked him.

'Probably a faulty synchronization between image and sound,' I said.

'H'm – yes –' he said. 'Anyway, that night we did not only record the readings of the measuring instruments.'

He took a cassette out of his pocket. I snatched it from his hand, introduced it in my old Gründig and pressed the playback control. For a time only the droning of the little motor could be heard. Then a multiple whistling sound ('the flying discs!') – a few brief explosions ('the laser radiations reflected on the energy screen!') – an apocalyptic roaring sound ('the nuclear bang!') – the sliding of a glacier down a rocky mountain ('the disintegration of the geometric forms!') –

'If you hadn't talked to me about the experiment,' I said in a low voice after a long pause, 'I'd have said that you'd got the sound tape of the film –'

'A possibility which cannot be ruled out before you have received all the answers,' he said.

'And what if all the answers are negative?' I asked.

He shrugged his shoulders.

'I am not able to offer you a certainty. At most a hypothesis –'

My eyes urged him to go on.

'You yourself wrote once about the mysteries of the Sanskrit texts. At that time paleoastronautics were in fashion –'

'I didn't know you were interested,' I said.

'*Homo sum*, and nothing of what belongs to a man – But I never attributed the flight ships and "atomic" wars to our extraterrestrial visitors. What seemed more plausible to me was the existence of former civilizations which disappeared as a result of natural cataclysms or –'

He stopped, as if appalled at the speculations which he would have been obliged to embark upon. I was the one to dare give it utterance.

'And you suppose that we witnessed such an annihilation, a live transmission of it – Have you any idea when the event could have taken place?'

Emil began teasing his moustache between his fingers.

'The installation has not yet been brought to perfection. But I can assure you that the theoretical reinforcement is flawless!'

I had no reason to doubt it. We heard the recording once again, then Emil took the cassette and promised me a copy of it (which I haven't received yet). He left, asking me to keep him informed as to the progress of my epistolary investigation. Which proved to be an easy task, considering the monotonous string of answers, only brightened up by a few propositions that I should also send the first part of the 'interesting scenario' for a possible collaboration –

I could delay no more the opening of the orange-coloured envelope. The film which I had given a summary of had *never* been broadcast – the adverb was underlined – in New Zealand. The circle had closed. I picked up the receiver and dialled Emil's number.

'The hypothesis seems to prove true,' he said calmly upon hearing the news.

'If your instrumental probing has not stopped halfway –'

'Halfway – Will you be more specific?' he said.

'"By going far enough into the future one comes upon what we call the past" – I'm afraid you haven't gone far enough.'

Emil was silent. Slowly I put the telephone back in the cradle. I was looking at the grey screen and I seemed to see again the dissolving face, the geometric forms turned into amorphous matter. I felt the demon of vanity circling round me – But is the future an irrevocable curse?

A Perfect Christmas Evening

KONRAD FIALKOWSKI

Leaving the shade of the trees he saw his house. Through his shirt he could feel the delicate wind sweeping down from the hills which were a peculiar shade of green.

The trees grew from the red soil and had violet flowers instead of leaves. The sun was high and it was at the height of the summer season – as it was here every December.

The road approached the house. In its red clay he could trace the fresh treads of tyres and he knew that Greg had arrived. From the porch he could smell his cigar. Greg sat at the table with a glass of beer in his hand. The carton of beer bottles lay on the floor.

'I've brought Tusker for you,' said Greg. 'The best beer for Christmas Eve. They still brew it there, near to the Equator. It warmed up on the way, but I kept it in the fridge as long as I could.'

'It's good you came.' He looked at the bald, perspiring skin of Greg's head with the first brown spots of age. Greg poured a glass of beer and gave it to him. It was warm and had the taste of Europe.

'It's damned far away from my desert here,' said Greg, 'and I don't see any girls waiting.'

'I live alone, you know . . .'

'Sure. Nothing changes here, Stef. It seems as if time has stopped for good here.' Greg played with his cigar which had gone out. 'What do you do nowadays?'

'Same as usual. Measuring of fallout. In the evenings my club . . .'

'And later on?'

'Nothing.'

'So on Christmas Eve you sit here alone, unless your old friend comes to see you.'

Stef was looking into his glass. Greg stood up.

'Before we drink the next bottle I'd like to show you something I've brought along. No, not for you. For those at the museum.'

'You dug it up?'

'Yes.'

They left the house and Greg approached his Land Rover. He opened the door and climbed in. When he brought out a box Stef saw the bones, part of a skull with fragments of teeth, all wrapped in a thin plastic net.

'He died more than one and a half million years ago,' said Greg. 'Before his death he may have passed on his genes and become an ancestor of yours or mine. It all began here. They left the forests and later became men.'

'You're looking for origins, I'm measuring fallout radiation and in between stand those one and a half million years.'

'Is that long?'

Stef shrugged his shoulders. He was not looking any longer at the bones, but over the garden shrubs and down towards the golf links descending to the valley bottom, and beyond at the red roofs of the town houses and the round satellite aerials turned towards the sky.

'Have you got anything to eat?' asked Greg.

'I'll open a tin. If I'd known you were coming, I'd have had more to eat and would also have bought you a gift.'

'From me you are getting a piece of an ancestor's bone.' He handed him a tiny grey fragment. 'It will remind you that we're back at the point from which we all began and there in the north we were merely visitors.'

Stef slipped the bone into his shirt pocket.

'O.K., I've got the gift now. It's time for Christmas dinner.'

'Instead of a Christmas tree we'll have a blossoming branch . . .'

'Forget it. It's not the same. I don't like prosthesis.'

'Really?'

'. . . at least not as a Christmas tree.'

'I'm hungry,' said Greg.

'. . . and there are twelve dishes waiting for you. You know, in the place where I grew up they used to spread hay over the table and then cover it all with a table-cloth. We always had a lot of snow there, as well as frost, and if there were no clouds in the sky children would peer out from under the porch to catch a glimpse of the first star. As soon as it appeared it was time for gifts and Christmas dinner.'

'. . . and later on our civilization riding on the beast with the registration number 666 entered into the picture and since then we've had no problems like those.'

'I think you'll like this beef with some of our local peas.'

'With beer it won't be bad,' said Greg and walked back to the house.

While Stef fried up the beef, Greg polished off two more bottles. He stood the empty ones on the table, arranging them neatly in single file – the labels marked by an elephant all pointing uniformly in the same direction.

'Merry Christmas,' he called as Stef lay heaped plates on the table. He tried raising his body, but he decided it was too complicated and gave up.

'Merry Christmas,' he repeated and stretched out his hand with the glass of beer. Stef pressed his glass against Greg's and beer splashed over onto the table.

'You won't improve the mood like that,' said Greg. Later they ate beef, peas and drank beer.

'We would have had a roast stork,' Greg said as he opened the next bottle.

'Roast stork?'

'Yes. Instead of turkey. You can buy them in the market there, cleaned or not.'

'Real storks?'

'There was nothing for them in the north so they flew down to the Equator. They came and died. However hard it is to eat, it's the meal of the season. Right now people are arriving too, more and more of them. They are coming back to the cradle, the prodigal sons . . .'

The number of elephants on Greg's side had increased.

'You are not drinking,' said Greg. 'I've been keeping these damned bottles just for you.'

'I'm going to make a call.'

'Do you still call?'

'Yes.'

'You're earning too much from those fallouts. For the price of a ticket like that you could be living here with not just one but two girls.'

'It's O.K. as it is.'

'You've become strange.'

'Not just me. Now, I'll make the call and when I come back I'll even the score. Tusker is a good beer.'

He went to his room where there was nothing but a bed, a table and a telephone on the table. He shut the door behind him, sat on the bed and carefully dialled the long twelve-digit number.

He heard the dialling tone and after it her voice:

'It's you. How kind of you to call this evening.'

'You knew I would call . . .'

'That's true. I even decided to light the candles on the Christmas tree just after your call.'

'Is it already dark outside?'

'Yes. But tonight there are no stars.'

'You know what I would like to wish you?'

'. . . to wish our being together.'

'Yes. To wish us . . .'

'One day you will come . .'

'I will.'

'You know, I had that call again.'

'And what? Did you hang up as I asked?'

'. . . not immediately. I thought it was you . . .'

'What did he say?'

'That I am not any longer . . .'

'What else?'

'That our house, our town is not any longer as well . . .'

'I have asked you so many times . . .'

'I must answer calls. They might be yours. You know, there is a lot of snow here. It fell this morning. People are digging out their cars and the branches are heavy with it.'

He heard a crack and instantly he was listening only to the close silence of the interrupted connection. He waited for the dialling tone and again dialled the twelve-digit number.

The line remained silent and after a while he heard a prerecorded voice:

'The selected number did not exist in that town. Please contact the operator.'

He made the connection and said:

'Operator, I cannot get through to my home number.'

'Perhaps there wasn't a number like that there.'

'I just had the connection. It is the authentic number.'

'Are you quite sure? You know, we do not establish any numbers which did not exist in reality. This is our rule of conduct.'

'I know, but you can easily check . . .' He gave the number and his home address.

'Wait a moment,' said the operator. 'I shall check it in the old directories, not in the computer. This way is more reliable.'

Waiting for the answer he looked through the window into the valley and at the shadows of the hills approaching him.

'I must apologize,' he heard the operator again, 'but our service covers so many of the late towns that it is not easy to find anything. But your number is sound, as well as the address. There must be a failure in our system. Obviously, this day will not be put on your bill.'

'And what about tomorrow?'

'Tomorrow it will be O.K. I hope you have a sample of the voice . . .?'

'I have,' he said recalling the day of his departure when she gave him the recorded tape.

'That is fine. In the worst case we can resynthesize. On your part no additional costs are involved. I am sure you can call your home before the New Year. And today, Merry Christmas to you.'

'So, how was it?' asked Greg when he returned. 'Have you already finished?'

'I only talked for a short while. The system malfunctioned . . . You called her up, too.'

'So you know . . .' Greg looked intently at the elephant surrounded by the letters 'Tusker' in gold. 'She didn't want to talk to me . . . not even for a short while. And I was only going to wish her a Merry Christmas.'

A Meeting in Georgestown

JON BING

Through the large windows he could see the harbour, the forest of masts, flashing metalwork of groomed yachts. Not a sound penetrated the double glazing, the room was silent, with the exception of the soft hiss from the air-conditioning system and the faint popping of ice cubes slowly melting in the glasses.

If he closed his eyes, Leon Caxton could see the strange mixture of indolence and activity that ruled the yacht harbour – see middle-aged businessmen in blazing sports shirts, see the highlights of sun lotion along brown limbs, see provisions being carried aboard, see engines being mended, see the lazy circles of birds ending in abrupt dives after a promising piece of refuse in the water between the boats.

In that way Jerry Garfield had emerged from the stream of tourists and surprised him and the recent republic of Cayman Islands. The Cayman Islands were discovered by Columbus in 1503 and were named Las Tortugas after its turtles – which still were one of the most important export articles. The islands were colonized by the British from Jamaica in the seventeenth century. And they became an independent nation in 1980, a small island state in the Caribbean Sea, a bit more than 10,000 inhabitants distributed on three low coral reefs. A sunshine country where the most important commodity was holidays for tourists.

But all countries have their small secrets. Even Cayman Islands have such secrets – which they were reluctant to make known to the powerful neighbours north of them, neither those living on the mainland of the U.S.A., nor those somewhat closer on the island of Cuba. The Caribbean Sea contained oil fields and political conflicts and possibilities, and was an important area. And though Cayman Islands were small, they were politically stable, with strong links to Britain and the western world, with quite a modern society.

And this might explain why Jerry Garfield emerged just here. Why he had entered Leon Caxton's cool front office and handed Elise a thin envelope – an envelope containing a single sheet of paper. It was produced by a matrix printer of low quality – but its implication was sufficient for Garfield to be admitted immediately to Caxton's office, for Caxton to cancel his appointments for the rest of the day, for frosty glasses of rum and lime to appear on the table, and for Caxton to sit completely silent in the much too large chair, looking out of the window and listening to the smooth voice of Garfield.

'It started fours years ago,' Garfield said. 'There were two of us. Let me not mention names, let me call my partner Tom. Tom and Jerry, you get the joke, huh?' Garfield was in no hurry. He talked as if he had just arrived at the home of a close friend with a blank day in front of him. Caxton remembered well the animated films of Tom and Jerry, but could not recall whether Jerry was the cat or the mouse.

'We started a shop for home computers while we still were at the university – home computers, pocket calculators, digital watches, video games and similar gadgets. We bought a franchise from a national chain – you know how these things are arranged: We paid a large rent to the chain, but kept the profit ourselves. It worked well enough; at least, we were able to finance our studies.

'The chain had the idea of putting in point-of-sale terminals. They thought it would be good for business to be as technically advanced as possible: most of our customers fell for that type of gimmick. You know how the POS terminals work: the sums are entered directly into the terminal which communicates with a centre for electronic funds transfers. There the codes read from the customer's magnetic card are authenticated and at the same time the account of the customer is checked. Then the money is deducted from the account of the client and added to our account.

'The whole thing worked without a hitch, but we had the idea that perhaps the system might be amended slightly to our own benefit . . .'

Actually it was quite simple.

The system was designed to make misuse by the customer difficult. Not by the shop owners. Tom and Jerry simply designed a system that not only communicated the transactions to the electronic funds transfer centre, but also stored the transactions on a small computer in the shop. As they sold home computers and similar systems, there was no lack of adequate hardware. When the customer left, the whole sale could be simulated one or more times in addition to the original transaction. All codes – and the passwords – would be authentic.

They tested the system for a few months without exploiting the possibilities. At the same time they planned ahead and postponed to the same few days, on different pretexts, the finalizing of several large contracts for personal computer systems.

They ran the simulation system for four days. For each sale, not only the profit from the original sale was credited to their account, but also the gross sum for several false sales.

Jerry was at the store and took care of the customers and ran the system. They had a temporary assistant in the shop, a girl with no knowledge of the stunt they were pulling. Tom was on the road the whole time, sleeping in different cities in the area and making withdrawals from the shop's account to keep it trimmed down to its usual balance, in order not to create undue interest at the bank and to avoid making any suspiciously large single withdrawal.

The fourth day Jerry had a call from a customer who pointed out that he had not been charged for one, but five Apple III systems. Jerry said it probably was a computer error which was easily corrected, and added that these things happened all the time. He promised to look into it and call back at once. He replaced the phone, told the girl he just wanted to check something at a downtown customer's, went through the back door and started the car which was ready to go outside. That evening he met Tom in the motel they had agreed upon in advance as a meeting place. They had been able to work for the period they had hoped and had made a net profit of approximately three million dollars. That night they drove north in Tom's new car and settled in a small town in Canada.

'Three million,' Jerry said. 'It was not much. But it turned out to be sufficient.'

Caxton was still staring through the window. The sky was evenly blue, an unreal blue colour – like the painted roof of a subterranean vault. It was too early for hurricanes, but it would have been fitting if there at the horizon had been a grey smudge – the herald of a tropic storm approaching.

'We were very clever programmers,' Jerry continued. He lifted his glass and shook it, making the half-melted ice cubes jingle faintly, but put it down once more without drinking. 'Both Tom and myself. That was actually one of our greatest disadvantages; we thought programming and solving problems so much fun that the other subjects of our studies hardly got any attention. I remember we once spent a week just playing *Adventure*, day and night, on the big computer – everything else was forgotten. Perhaps that was why,' he continued distracted, 'why we went on like we did – we wanted to earn money on our problem solving.'

At the university they had abandoned a joint thesis on the problem of compressing data stored on a disc – it was to be a specification of a utility program to be used by the system operators to 'clean up' the segments different users had allocated on disc stations. During the year they lived in the small town high up in the mountains of British Columbia Tom and Jerry finalized the program. They tested it by renting time at commercial computer bureaux. At the end of that year the program was available in three versions, written in assembler for IBM, Univac and Honeywell Bull.

They would not forget that year. Most of the time it seemed like continuous winter, with the snow piled high along the streets, people huddled inside large, thick coats, yellow lamp-light indoors, late nights with coffee and Canadian whiskey.

But the program was ready. The system was named COMPRESS

85, and they organized a small shared company to market the system. They set the price of the program quite low, hired a local attorney as director, bought a marketing campaign from a bureau, paid off all their debts, and took a plane to Los Angeles. The last of the money remaining from their first stunt was used to buy a shack at the beach. They had brought the mini-computer they had used to develop the program, wired that to a modem in the shack and waited.

It was several weeks before the phone rang for the first time. At that time they were nearly broke; they dozed in the sun at the beach, drank beer from tins and chatted up slim Californian girls.

But then the phone rang for the first time.

'We had not stopped at making a good utility program,' Jerry said and stretched his long legs. 'We had written a small, unnecessary module. Programs written in assembler are difficult to read, and we guessed the customers would be satisfied to check that the program worked as specified – not try to read the program, statement by statement.

'If they had tried, they might have disclosed what in our business is known as a "Trojan horse". Inserted into the utility program was another program. This program mainly had two functions. First, it checked the priority of the user who had called and was running the utility program. If this priority was not the top priority for the system, nothing would happen. But if the priority was the top priority, another function was initiated. This routine recorded all the codes necessary and used this to gain access to the operating system itself. Here small amendments were made, which prompted the operating system to utilize the communication functions of the computer system to call our mini-computer in California. Then the operating system transferred all key data to our computer, including all data security and authentication routines.'

Their holiday was over. They had a new, very active, period.

From the powerful and flexible terminal in California they accessed the system which had been called in through the telecommunications network. They had the necessary data to gain access to user registers. They accessed the different disc segments for the different users, read the documents, monitored the transactions, and achieved in a short time complete understanding of the system.

Regrettably the system was not very interesting. It was owned by a small service bureau in Winnipeg. There was only one interesting detail in the system – a large oil company was using it as back up for their personnel information system. Tom and Jerry designed a small monitor program, and next time the personnel information system was run (and it actually was only a test-run to check compatibility), the Trojan horse followed it back through the telecommunications link. This time it took considerably longer, and was more of a challenge to gain access to the necessary information on the computer system of the oil company.

'But I will never forget the day,' Jerry said, 'when we had the print-outs from the company's geodata systems on the seismic tests off the west coast of Alaska, including clear indications of oil fields. We knew from the news media that drilling contracts in the north were being negotiated, and that "our" company was one of those bidding. When we mailed the president of the company a registered letter with the print-out and a suggestion for payment, we did not have to worry about money any more.'

Leon Caxton rose. 'Please excuse me,' he said. 'It may be just as well to let my secretary know she may leave for the day.'

Jerry Garfield nodded and smiled. Caxton opened the door and thought for a moment that he might run, escape, tell the police about Jerry Garfield – but he knew at the same time that it was futile. He sighed and nodded:

'You may leave, Elise. Ask the switchboard to stop all calls.'

She looked at him, made as if to say something, but he just shook his head and closed the door.

'I think they actually were somewhat surprised,' Jerry Garfield continued without looking at Caxton. 'We knew the money might be the best way of tracing us. The payment order was placed in the accounting system of their own computer. We accessed the computer, routed the transaction to the Winnipeg bureau and from there to a bank on the east coast. Tom was on the spot and cashed the money the moment the transaction was completed. Very difficult to trace, I believe.'

'Where does this take us, Mr Garfield?' Caxton said. 'You are not here to enjoy my admiration for your cleverness, I take it?'

'I just wanted to impress on you the efficiency of our system,' Jerry said. 'This was more than two years ago. We do not rely on our utility program any more. Actually we have sold our interest in the company we created; our attorney probably does not really understand why he was left with the profit. We did not want too many loose ends. And so many other possibilities opened up.'

They always had been attracted to problems. Computer systems were to them a kind of riddle. Suddenly they had the key to many of these riddles in their hands. It was as if someone had collected the blueprints to all the bank vaults in the world and handed them over, and they at their leisure could figure out how to crack the vaults. And that was not the end of it – the computers combined with telecommunications made it completely unnecessary to visit the systems, they could just lean back in their chairs in another part of the country and penetrate them.

They often moved, but tried to make themselves as invisible as possible. They had sufficient funds, but did not flash their money around. They lived well, but not in luxury. They had set a limit of five years – afterwards they would go their separate ways and retire. Tom joked that he would settle down as a writer of computer games, develop *Adventure* from swords-and-sorcery to reality model. Jerry considered taking a position at a research institution.

But something came up.

'We knew many companies worked on government contracts,' Jerry said. 'In the beginning we just stayed out of government systems – we might use them as gateways to other systems, but did not exploit them otherwise. The degree of integration between private and government systems were higher than we had expected. The policy of not using government services if private organizations offered the same type of services was – from our point of view – very favourable.

'Suddenly we discovered that we had accessed a system of which we did not know the identity or purpose. This proved too much for our curiosity. But we froze when we discovered that we had penetrated one of the largest – and most secret – systems in the basement of the Pentagon.'

At once they had covered their tracks. They moved once more, and next time they accessed the system, they had at their own end a monitor system to alert them to any attempts to put a trace on their activities. They hoped their monitor was better than the tracing system at the Defense Department. They were scared for several days, but nothing happened – and they grew bolder.

From this system the path was short to the next one. Soon they had a plan of the total U.S. defence systems equal to that of the President. Perhaps superior to his, as there might be systems of which the President did not have – or did not want to have – full knowledge.

But what to do with such information? They were only interested in money, and it would be rather risky to try blackmailing the Defense Department or the CIA. And they did not want to sell the information to a foreign power.

What was left?

They tested the possibilities. They accessed a computerized navigation system for Polaris submarines. This caused an incorrect adjustment of the signals from an orbiting satellite, which led a Polaris sub into the Juan de Fuca channel on the Canadian border. As soon as the episode was reported on the news, they corrected the malfunction and trusted it would remain a mystery. But they had demonstrated the possibilities. What if they created erroneous information on activities in the airspace, information indicating a missile attack? What if they pursued the Allies' communication channels? Would they find a blank wall? Or would they be able to follow further links into neutral countries and from there into the Warsaw Pact systems?

The possibilities were rather frightening. From being a kind of modern gentleman thieves they had become politicians.

Statesmen.

*

'But what do you want from me?' Leon Caxton asked.

'We cannot do more in secret,' Jerry said. 'We need a country. The Cayman Islands have sunshine – I think Tom and I will like it here. You are a small and modern nation. You have developed your telecommunications network – we know you already, to a modest degree, have a reputation as a "data haven" for those trying to escape bothersome data protection legislation and other types of regulation.'

'We have a free country, Mr Garfield.'

'Even so – we think Cayman Islands might play a part in our new and worldwide game. We could use our knowledge to many ends, to blackmail, to commit treason, to increase world tension. But we would like to use it to *reduce* world tension, to increase the possibility of a lasting peace between the superpowers. Today, world politics is a game between a few powerful nations. We would like to put a joker into the deck, a country which might give priority to other values – which might force the superpowers to act in the interest of peace. If possible we will use our knowledge to demonstrate that there are other kinds of power than that based on weapons – computer power, control of the computer systems.'

Leon Caxton rose and walked over to the large windows. The view was the same as when Jerry Garfield walked into his office – perhaps there were less people working between the yachts. In front of the cafés and restaurants tables were moved out to the pavement – soon the early diners would gather under the umbrellas in the cool twilight to drink their iced drinks of rum and mineral water.

He thought of Tom and Jerry, two cheeky young guys. They had played with their computers, challenged dwarves and trolls and pirates in *Adventure* and escaped into safety carrying imaginary treasures. Then they grew up and found a new game, which they also won – the treasures were real totals in bank accounts.

But then they discovered a third and more powerful game, where the prize was paid in other ways and the loser risked more than his own life. This was not a fictitious cave with clever dangers – this was reality: the naked and merciless reality of world politics. Did Jerry Garfield really understand this? Could such knowledge reside behind his smoothly shaved face? Could such knowledge make such a relaxed person?

And was he himself prepared to enter his own country into such a game? Was it possible to achieve anything as an eavesdropper to the negotiations of the superpowers? Was computer power real power, or only a shadow of the power created by real weapons?

Leon Caxton passed a hand across his brow and felt the wetness in spite of the air-conditioning. He turned and met the gaze of Jerry Garfield. He realized suddenly that the eyes were serious, they also contained anxiety and . . . perhaps courage?

Victims of Time

B. SRIDHAR RAO, MD

Translated by the author

I woke up a few minutes ago with a severe headache and a sense of impending death. In the next half hour or so, I know, I am going to die. Nothing can now prevent my physical condition from deteriorating rapidly. As I am trying to write as fast as my mind can think – in an attempt to finish my story before I am finished – my breathing is becoming labored, and the pain in my chest is beginning to torture me.

I was perfectly healthy the day before yesterday. When, that day, I opened the morning newspaper and read the headlines: 'Professor Theta, who disappeared four years ago, returns,' I turned pale with fright. What shocked me was his alleged statement that in a day or two he would reverse the 'de-aging' process and thus save the human race from annihilation.

At this stage it is necessary to recapitulate Professor Theta's remarkable experiments four years ago, which had a severe repercussion in the form of de-aging, since considered the greatest scourge that had ever befallen the human race.

I first learned about Professor Theta five years ago. (At that time I was suffering from advanced heart disease and was expected to die in a year or two.) To sum up, Professor Theta was the most eccentric person ever allowed to remain outside the lunatic asylum. He was pleased to propound ridiculous theories and in support thereof to contrive and reportedly carry out preposterous experiments. One of his mad theories concerned the origin of matter and energy, based on some experiments involving a series of vacuum tubes one inside another which when left aside exploded.

According to Professor Theta nothingness or *perfect* vacuum is composed of energy and 'anti-energy' and sooner or later it splits into these integers; energy and anti-energy repel each other, and it is this force of repulsion which is responsible for the explosion of the vacuum tubes referred to above. The universe was born in two stages. First nothingness split into energy and anti-energy; in the second stage, part of the energy transformed itself into matter of the suns and planets of the cosmos. The force of repulsion between energy and universe on the one hand and anti-energy on the other is responsible for the great speed at which the universe is drifting away in space.

Nobody paid any attention to Professor Theta or his experiments until four years ago when he published a brochure on 'The Production of Anti-Atomic Energy'. In this booklet he stated that his recent experiments conclusively proved that an Anti-Atomic energy could be produced. The said anti-energy if created would radiate over the earth and above it into atmosphere and space and would nullify (convert into nothingness) the artificially tapped nuclear force as well as make impossible forever the manifestation of such force.

Within a month of the publication of this brochure, industrial and other establishments using atomic power for the production of electricity detected that the power supply had mysteriously failed. Scientists were baffled to discover that atomic reactors had suddenly gone dead and that all the potential nuclear weapons had become lifeless.

For some time every one was astounded with the remarkable effects of Professor Theta's experiments. Many were jubilant that atomic warfare became impossible because of his anti-Atomic Energy. From philosophers down to the common man, all alike paid tributes to Professor Theta (though some might not have done so wholeheartedly), and wherever he went he was accorded a hero's reception.

However, it was soon realized that all was not well; suspicions first arose when women in the second and third month of pregnancy began menstruating. Many an adolescent girl complained of cessation of menstruation and reduction in breast size.

People were horrified to hear of infants growing smaller day by day. And then there were middle-aged persons whose gray hairs were turning black.

My own condition improved remarkably. Pain in chest, engorgement of neck veins and swelling of legs all subsided. I was able to get out of bed. My appetite improved, and I started putting on weight. I felt younger by many years. I also read in newspapers that many persons who were suffering from various diseases of old age were recovering rapidly.

All the above conclusively pointed to the fact that, presumably due to Professor Theta's experiments, time was reversed and a process of de-aging had set in. Under the effect of de-aging people would grow younger and younger until they became premature babies, when they would perish from their inability to tolerate the surroundings. Meanwhile, new children would not be born, for although an ovum might get fertilized, it would not grow. In another sixty or seventy years, persons then aged seventy or less would die, whereas those seventy or more would become children; humanity would soon be wiped out. With the realization of the above mentioned facts a great panic seized the populace.

At about this time Professor Theta went underground, probably for fear of being killed by the masses who were naturally outraged at his experiments which had left humanity at the brink of destruction.

Four years went by. By and by people got accustomed to de-aging. They were mentally prepared to face doomsday. The only consolation was that death would strike them at a time when in the form of babies they would have no capacity of emotionally reacting to the event or to the thought of its approach. On the other hand, there were many like myself, who were extremely pleased with the thought of enjoying another lease of life.

When I read news of Professor Theta's putting an end to de-aging in the newspaper the day before yesterday therefore, I was scared. Once de-aging ceases (and Professor Theta is capable of doing anything) a month-old baby overnight would become a four-year-old boy, a girl of nine years would change to an adolescent of thirteen years, and so on and so forth. Those who would have died during the last four years (if time were not reversed) would suddenly be reduced to corpses in various stages of decomposition corresponding to four minus the years they would have lived in the absence of de-aging. I myself would become an unrecognizable mass of dead tissue in putrefaction for the last three years or so.

As I was scribbling the above, my condition was becoming worse and worse from one line to the next. Swelling in my legs has reappeared. Pain in the chest has increased tremendously. I feel as if I have not eaten for the last several years and as if my weight has considerably gone down. I am now breathing with great difficulty. I can see my finger tips turn bluish and sense their becoming cold.

There is no strength . . .

For a moment my heart had stopped beating, and I had lost consciousness. My head is bleeding from having struck the writing desk. My breathing has become stertorous. My heart is thudding against my chest furiously in a vain attempt to . . .

Myxomatosis Forte

BERTIL MÅRTENSSON

Holzman Medica Inc. proudly presents a breathtaking new achievement in the treatment of inflammatory pulmonary diseases.

A capsule of *Pectolind* will make your nights tranquil. Available in 5 mg, 10 mg, 15 mg capsules. Also available in 25 mg ampoules for injection.

Why fear the last throes of your death? *Mortadorm* will give you that peace of mind without inhibiting your experience of the ultimate. Ask your nurse for a 25 mg injection twelve to eighteen hours before your projected demise.

Guaranteed to be without significant side effects. A special product from our Highly Equipped Scientific Laboratories.

Jason Schytte had another look at the two specimens of copy he had produced that morning on his work-screen. They were acceptable, he decided, so no reasonable person could claim that he had lost his touch, even if it felt that way and even if Lana had left him on those very grounds.

He briefly tapped the induction loop of his desk and a steaming cup of Uppit with 5 mgs of the latest unaddictive additive Think-easy appeared in front of him.

Sipping the hot, black liquid he contemplated going home to bed. He could really use some sick-leave. All in all he had been well for four months now. Could that be why he had been going downhill recently, physically and mentally?

A lasting infection and an interesting period of convalescence should turn him into a new man. But what could he take? It wasn't easy getting ill these days.

Once the genetically grafted resistance factor R14 had been introduced, ordinary diseases were defenceless against mankind. In the current year the average human being could destroy one million typhoid bacteria before they could think of reproducing.

The immune defences of the body laughed at smallpox virus and every attempt from a native cell to turn malignant resulted in police action: it was tracked down, annihilated and replaced.

People were not immortal, only nearly. At the age of two hundred they naturally had to expect some deterioration of their heart capacity and a brittleness of the arteries.

The R14 program had been carried out by a special branch of the WHO despite criticism from some of the privileged nations. But in the rest of the world, in South America, in Asia and Africa, such affluent scruples were dismissed.

Overpopulation had remained a perennial problem, and the sterilization program needed a booster, a promise, something to draw the locals to the clinic.

Few politicians and administrators actually believed in the efficacy of the R14 factor – after all, who could seriously believe in the promise of eternal health and immunity? It had been given so many times by prophets and quacks, that the idea was entirely preposterous. But if *people* believed in it, it was all right. The political evaluation was straightforward.

It must have come as a shock to many when the R14 factor lived up to all the promises made by its Thai inventor. Suddenly the hospital waiting rooms were empty. And even if sceptics dismissed that as a statistical fluctuation, the absence of world-wide disaster when a gene bank dedicated to biological warfare sprang a leak made them shut up.

The interest in R14 suddenly became epidemic. The world changed, and for a change it changed for the better.

But Jason Schytte, employed by the Creative Marketing and Brainstorming Department at Holzman Medica Inc. didn't feel at all well, however healthy he was. There was something fundamentally wrong, and not even a free sample of an unreleased product, a grave sinus infection with kidney complications, would change that fact. He had it in his pocket, but he had never taken it.

While he was wondering if that had been an error, there was a familiar tingling sound in the air, and his boss the Marketing Director entered. There was something ominous about a personal visit. Business matters were handled using the holoterminals.

'Hello there,' he said with a nonchalance so studied that it couldn't remain unnoticed. 'How's it coming?'

'Oh, fine,' Jason lied.

'Let me see.'

His boss quickly read the short drafts Jason had prepared. 'Hmm . . .' he said and his brows darkened. 'Fine, you said?'

His eyes already proclaimed his judgement.

'I think you have done your time in this department,' he said.

Jason went cold all through.

'But . . .' he stammered.

He had expected a recommendation of sick-leave perhaps, nothing this final.

'In the last year you have only produced an idea for a perfectly idiotic campaign, and some uninspired texts and ideas for diseases that made the laboratories laugh. "Typhoid fever with a secondary swelling of the left leg." Incredible!'

'Well, that wasn't my day perhaps,' Jason said, 'but I promise, I feel that something is on the way. It has been loosening up recently.'

'I don't give a damn about your feelings,' said his boss. 'There is the employment guarantee to consider, so we can't fire you, even if we wanted to. But we can reassign you wherever it is convenient, and if you don't accept that you must go.'

And now he smiled.

'I have a suggestion,' he added.

'No, not that,' Jason said.

'There is this vacancy in the tasting department. They are presently trying out an interesting sequence of diarrhoeas. It is for the perverts, but it sells . . .'

'For old friendship's sake . . .' Jason moaned.

'Don't try that sentimental rubbish with me,' was the reply. 'It merely confirms my suspicions that you are finished. There are twenty young recruits bursting with ideas standing in line for your job. I had to be your friend when you were productive, but I never really liked you. So if you want to stay, report to the tasting division within the hour. Or you can draw three months' salary, in which case we never want to see you again.'

Suddenly Jason realized that they were serious. The company actually wanted him out. That pushed him out of his lethargic state of mind.

'You goddamned son of a whore,' he exclaimed. 'This department was built on my ideas. You took them, and you used them and they made you rich. For ten years I have poured out the contents of my head to keep your machine going. And now, in a temporary slack of creativity, you just fire me.'

'We have given you several chances,' the boss said, taken slightly aback by the vehement outburst. 'So don't you . . .'

'But even if I am through here, don't you believe this is the end of me,' Jason said hoarsely. 'You will hear from me.'

'Is that a threat?' said the other, suddenly amused.

'Call it what you like,' Jason said. 'One day you will regret this.'

Bursting with adrenalin he marched out.

At last Man faced a future of sunshine and glory. It was Paradise. At least that was the official opinion. And it was supported by some pretty good arguments.

R14 had changed the world radically. For a decennium people had lived unharassed by the once common cold, and unplagued by all the undignified infectious diseases, ulcers, arthritis, or malignant growths that had used to infest them. Their vitamin uptake was optimal, as the R14 factor automatically repaired every failing intestinal cell.

The market for special diets and health fads was lost and replaced by an upsurge of culinary enthusiasm, as people found that they could eat and drink what they liked, rather than what was supposedly good for them. But eating lost its savour after a while.

Paradise? No, not really.

Nobody admitted it, but people grew inexplicably downcast and despondent as the years went by.

After ten years a psychiatrist wrote a concerned letter to *The Times* reporting a number of unexpected suicides. The initial result was official denials, but the debate ultimately led to the publication of statistics showing that paradise was far away indeed.

A conference was called. Neurologists, psychiatrists, psychologists, sociologists and cultural anthropologists met in Santiago del Populo, to discuss *Problems of Human Wellbeing*. The convention was a stormy affair, but out of it emerged a new and remarkable truth:

Mankind was too healthy.

People were never allowed to feel poorly, and that wore them down. Imagine having to feel cheerful and healthy all the time!

Despite Moraeus and Moretti's forgotten monograph on *The Social Functions of the Common Cold*, a major function of disease had never been appraised. In its absence it became visible.

No longer could you politely dodge a party invitation that you had never wanted in the first place. No longer could you stay at home for a couple of days, reading magazines or Tolstoy: 'That was a nasty cold.'

Today everybody would know that you lied. In the old days they suspected it, if you tried the trick too often, but they couldn't be sure. Now they could, and that was the problem.

The result was a health stress problem. Unconsciously protesting against this state of affairs, people had started jumping from high buildings again, throwing themselves in front of supersonic trains or killing their families.

But some solved the problem more rationally.

A bone fracture would buy a perfectly legitimate ticket to one of the few hospitals that were still maintained. Or you could ask a friend to shoot you in the leg, accidentally of course. A certain pain was the price you had to pay for being allowed to feel healthily sorry for yourself.

The only trouble was the swiftness of the healing process, as there could be no complications, ever. But your attitude towards pain changed when you knew that you couldn't get truly hurt, unless you went in for it. Stripped of its traditional frightening qualities, pain emerged as the necessary stimulant for modern man.

'Pain,' wrote the bestselling psychologist Ruth E. Minent, 'is

quickly coming into its own as a *raison d'être*, replacing the
Oedipus complex and the libido problem of yesterday.'

There was an upsurge in torture-yourself books. Flagellation
regained its sacred place in some religions. But these were the
extremes.

It was more important that the Santiago del Populo Conference
gave a quietly astonishing recommendation to medicine that was
to change, once more, the face of culture.

Pure anger kept him going for more than an hour. He felt like a
betrayed lover, for the bitter fact was that Jason Schytte was an
artist.

In a crass time when the entertainment industry had been taken
over by skilful program houses who advertised: 'Try to distinguish
our bestsellers from those written by people!' a creative talent
could no longer subsist as a source of manuscripts to the media
and the publishing houses.

As a young man he had written some pretty good poetry, but to
support himself he had been forced to turn his creative talents to
advertisement. No computer could come up with the surprising. It
took humans to do that, and Jason had been one of the best.

But the plight of the artist has always been to be squeezed dry
and to be kicked to one side as soon as he is no longer useful. It
has always been to live with the constant demand to produce
things that are fun, effective and new. Those ideas cannot be
produced by routine. They demand inspiration. And when your
inspiration fails you, you can live for a while on a stockpile of
unused old ideas, hoping that it will come back to you, that flash,
that ease, that flow of wonder.

And if it doesn't you are finished. And the crowd will look for
new gods.

That was happening to Jason now. He should have been
prepared for it, if he had been realistic, but creative talents rarely
are. He had had his downs before, and he had relied on his basic
capacity to work himself up from the bottom. This time they had
been waiting and taken advantage of the opportunity to get rid of
him. Why?

Contemplating the deceit and iniquity of men, he entered a city train at random. It was on its way to the suburbs and that suited him fine. Perhaps, like so many artists before him, he needed a rejuvenating contact with nature.

Perhaps he had acquired some personal enemies without knowing it. A row of faces passed in front of him while he looked for a seat. At noon the trains were only half full, so he got a window seat and the faces were superimposed on a landscape of airy façades that whirled past at 300 kilometres per second.

But the faces were without hatred. They were without concern. If they didn't hate him, then what?

Then it struck him, the even worse possibility.

His particular style had gone out of fashion.

One day it would be rediscovered and he would become an object of admiration, research and imitation. At that time he would be too old to enjoy anything – if he still lived.

It was now it was happening, and now he was *out*. Perhaps it was that simple.

The insight was depressing, and he experienced the sobering after-effects of his outburst of anger.

Heavily he walked past the entrance gates, once the train had made its final stop. Two policemen looked at him, but did not intervene. In the suburban streets people hurried past, eager to get home. A man came out of a pharmacy and, loudly, blew his nose.

Out here were the large park areas where the urban population could spend its Sundays, breathing oxygen and experiencing the primitive. The landscape was planned for this purpose. Genetically modified trees with a high oxygen discharge rate per unit of leaf space provided the oxygen, and bushes and aesthetically shaped mats of grass interwove with them.

It had been discovered that natural hills must not be evened out, and rocks had been flown here and made to look as if they had stood here since the ice melted away.

Nevertheless his intuition as always told him that something was wrong. The overall planning was subtle enough to fool the eye and the intellect, but not the emotions. Sometimes, he reflected, human emotion is the supreme instrument of knowledge. There was a comfort in the thought. The only one he had.

He chose a park bench and sat there, and obviously he looked suspiciously ill, for the policemen turned and approached him to ask their standard question.

If said person could not give a satisfactory account of his situation, the law obliged them to bring that person to a Health Centre for medical examination. There, if the computer readout diagnosed a disease that could be bought without a prescription, his employer was notified and the matter was dropped. If a prescription was needed, it must be produced, or there would be a charge of buying illicit diseases. The penalty was a harsh fine, or detention at an institute for behaviour correction.

'Are you ill?' one of them said.

The other inspected him and touched his forehead with a small instrument.

'No fever,' he said.

'What are you doing here?'

Jason replied truthfully.

'I am thinking about what to do. I just got the sack.'

They looked at him. Uncomprehending. Most people had steady jobs. His was an unfortunate category.

'I see,' the left one said. 'But that no longer exists.'

'No,' said Jason, 'they call it reassignment but it amounts to pretty much the same thing.'

'O.K. But we'll be watching, so don't try any aberrant stuff.'

He nodded, and they left him.

Suddenly he breathed out. They had not searched him. If they had done that, they would have found an unmarked free sample of an unreleased sinus trouble with kidney complications in his right pocket. Diseases like that were distributed carelessly among the staffs of medical companies. But today he would have lacked the backup of his company.

The R14 factor quietly made him resume breathing, and stabilized his blood pressure.

His situation was absurd.

First he had been kicked out, and now he could be suspected of booting unlicensed diseases.

But somehow the pure absurdity of it all brought him closer to life again. He rediscovered the world. The city metropolis could be seen far off, its vast solar collectors, mirrors and funnels filling the sky like a frozen firework display.

What was to happen to him now? Must he become a case for the welfare department of the city? He had grown accustomed to a large monthly salary. If he lost it, he must accept whatever job they chose to give him, sell his posh bachelor's penthouse and move into a state-subsidized single-male hotel, probably run by a religious organization that wanted something in return for their charity.

For the first time, and seriously, he contemplated killing himself.

He was forty-three.

To spend the additional two hundred and fifty odd years as a social wreck wasn't what he had been hoping for. Perhaps nothing would be better?

Someone had joined him on the lonely park bench.

'So you got the swift kick, did ya mate?'

Jason turned his head and looked at a bum, a singularly disgusting and shabby sort of a person, an intruder.

'What do you want?' he said, very irritated and rising to leave.

'No, don't go,' said the shabby fellow. 'I dress like this to fool the law. We can speak freely, there are no bugs. I put gum into it.'

He pointed under the bench.

'Now who the hell . . .?'

'Shut up and listen. Your name is Jason Schytte and you just got kicked out. O.K.? We have been watching you, and we offer you a job.'

'What!'

'Shut up, I said. If you want it, and we think you do, go to the Boulevard Solaris Complex, section five, room nine. Got it?'

'And what is in it for me?'

The stranger smiled.

'The buck that you need. And a chance to get even perhaps. Here is the law. Give me twenty units.'

Jason hesitated.

'Don't be such an ass. Or they will take us both. It's my cover, stupid.'

The policemen were approaching.

Jason took out a bill and gave it to the bum, who kissed it, shouted crude blessings and ran away.

They ignored him.

'So you are still here,' they said to Jason.

'No, I am going now. I don't want to spend the last of my money on worthless bums.'

They laughed and he left.

When the recommendation came from the Santiago del Populo Conference a decrepit business regained its confidence. To be a doctor in the twenty-first century had been like being a mercenary in a world where all issues were settled by reference to inscrutable treaties.

It would be ideal, the conference wrote, *if people could be given at least brief periods of illness by swallowing or breathing a pharmaceutically bought culture of enhanced disease agents.*

A world of medical laboratories set upon the task.

Holzman Medica Inc. had managed to get along selling penicillin derivatives for pets. Despite the protests from upset friends of the animal kingdom, no R14 treatment had been devised for dogs, cats and horses.

But Holzman scored big after two months when they produced their first minor cold. DNA-modifications of an old A-type virus had increased its vitality. Yet it was harmless. You had to eat three capsules a day and spray it into your nose in order to get any effect.

If it caught on, it made your eyes red and it gave you a runny nose. Many experienced a slight fever. You had to stay at home for at least a day.

Everybody had to try it.

The result was a world-wide epidemic.

Jason helped launch it. His wit devised a series of classic slogans and posters, the most effective of which was the simplest, a picture of an earnest man in white who looked at people everywhere and asked 'How do you feel?' After four weeks *The Good Doctor* show opened on Broadway, and the television channels were full of him.

But the competition wasn't far behind. Someone managed to add a brief dose of rheumatic fever as a complication, and the carousel had started. DNA-sculpturing could shape a virus to give all sorts of symptoms. Light migraines became popular among women, and a market for graver diseases also developed.

The governments realized that everything had to be controlled and worked out a set of rules. You could buy a common cold without a prescription, but to get anything else you needed to see a doctor.

Jason took a train toward the Boulevard Solaris, and approached the building, although his feet were cold. It could be any sort of a trap, but he couldn't see what he had to lose now.

He hesitated in front of a mock-rosewood door. What was he doing here? Trying to get even. Yes, that was it.

As he entered someone said:

'There he is.'

It was a conference room, breathing money and influence. Some men sat smoking fat cigars.

'Sit down Jason. Are you with us?'

'That is hard to decide, since I don't know who you are.'

'Spoken with true wit,' said one of the men. 'Well, we offer you a job to market our products. You are a professional, and we think they treated you like a rat. You will make millions. What do you say?'

'It does sound tempting. And the products?'

'Diseases, of course. Advanced products. Very new.'

'Since we are new we have to find our own profile,' added one of the others.

'So?'

'OK,' he said. Then it dawned upon him that he had become involved in organized crime. Here they were, well dressed, speaking about advanced diseases. Bootlegging was the worst of crimes as it upset the social order. Besides, some colds had proven to be addictive.

'We have found a scientist to run our lab. He has some pretty strong ideas. We can tell you nothing specific, but we want you to work on the novelty of the thing.'

'I see. And the target population?'

'There will be no open advertisements. Aim for the universal.'

An enormous sum of money subdued a voice that said no. At first he couldn't see how any of this would help him to get even. Then he saw that the illicit company would provide strong competition with Holzman in certain areas.

He went home and struggled with a text to sell something that was to be sold as Myxomatosis forte.

A few nights later something worried him enough to wake him up. What? He had written a superb text that in ten lines said absolutely nothing, yet conveyed the attractiveness and superiority of the product. The power of the word. He loved it.

And he had been badly treated. He had a right to get back at them. He had a moral obligation to make them sweat and repent. So why did he feel guilty?

The text had been delivered to a courier the night before. It had been duplicated by now, probably spread already to a growing network of underground couriers that he suspected were disguised as filthy bums.

The text would be used to awaken interest, after which the product would be released in a day or so. He had been promised a sample.

He went back to sleep.

At least he tried.

In the morning he knew what was wrong.

The name of the disease.

He didn't like it. He didn't like it one bit. His anger had made him swallow their proposal and choke down any decent intuition that he might have had. The encyclopedia told him more.

Myxomatosis or rabbit fever was the name of a classic disease. It had been refined by the biological genius Louis Pasteur and given to the French farmers, who requested a way to get rid of the crop-eating rabbits. The rabbits of Europe had no immunity against a disease originating in South America. They died of blindness and thirst, unable to eat or coordinate in the final stage. But they died slowly, spreading the disease by contact. There was no cure, so domestic rabbits could never again meet wild ones. A hundred years later fifty per cent of the infected rabbits still died.

But myxomatosis was for rabbits, and who would sell a disease like that among farmers? Incredible, no, impossible. It had to be intended for people.

The R14 factor would cure anyone who bought the stuff, even if it was as distasteful as he suspected. But how soon? And besides, the organization might be blown by the police. Where would he stand then?

He also knew two things that gave him a sense of responsibility. The people he had met the other day had been businessmen, with no knowledge of medicine. They had known nothing about the symptoms of the new product. Did they know what they were handing out?

Who had produced it, who was the scientist they had talked about? He couldn't ask them. He was only supposed to know this much. Then it dawned on him how he might get information about the strange follower of Pasteur who had developed a rabbit fever for man.

'You see, old friend,' he told his colleague over the holo, 'I quit Holzman's because I got a better job as a freelance writer. I have been offered to write about diseases among animals, and as you know that isn't my field. Do you know an expert on myxomatosis?'

'You're crazy,' was the reply. 'You are also competition.'

But at noon he finally found someone.

'Myxomatosis, hey? Call Lindebarger at International Health and Pharmaceutics. Perhaps he knows.'

'Thanks a lot,' he breathed, and did.

Lindebarger was a tall, slim man in his fifties – or there about, as R14 had inhibited aging.

'Myxomatosis? Hmm. Well I remember you from the convention in Australia, so the little I know I guess I can tell you. In fact you are a bit late.'

'Huh?' said Jason.

'We had someone in the research department who had myxomatosis as his private sort of pet. He was trying to convince the management that it could be developed for man, and even that the R14 immunity could be weakened to zero.'

'And . . .' said Jason, cold sweat breaking out.

'He is a nut,' said Lindebarger. 'Everybody knows that the R14 factor is lifelong and an absolute guarantee. They realized he was a nutcase and sacked him. He is on the black list circulated among the companies. So are you, by the way, but if you can make a living writing stuff, I feel free to tell you what I know. The rest is in the books.'

'Do you know if any other company may have . . .?'

'Certainly not,' said the tall man. 'He was a nutcase. Quite alone. Who else could have gotten such an idea?'

'I see,' said Jason, his knee-joints weakening. 'Thanks a lot.'

'Well, good luck, friend. I guess you need it.'

Perhaps we all do, thought Jason.

He had found out what he needed to know. His guess had been perfect. Yes, his intuition was back. One puzzle remained.

The black market companies would recruit from those sacked by the big legal firms. They had recruited him, and they had recruited a scientist who wanted to produce a myxomatosis for people, that unhinged the R14 immunity.

Why?

He had to guess. He had to use his own case. How had he felt when they sacked him? Vindictive, full of hate. Without scruples.

Imagine that he was a scientist with a passionate interest in a problem. He wished to study it, but he was dismissed and ridiculed and finally booted out. Jason could well imagine how he would feel. The safety of R14 was so established by now that nobody could question it and be taken seriously. And how does a scientist feel if he isn't taken seriously? How does anyone feel?

So, Jason thought, he was fired, and he got in touch with people who financed a secret lab, and he told them that he could develop a rabbit fever for people and that it was going to be a big underground hit. Why? To prove that he was right. Besides, he may be a nut. He has to be.

One problem left.

Why did he name it Myxomatosis forte?

That would reveal him to the world.

But perhaps that was what he wanted. What did forte mean? It was Latin, it was medical language, it meant strong.

Jason almost crumbled.

He wants to be found, he thought. He wants everybody to know that he made it. He has produced a strain of rabbit fever that attacks people, and that in some terrible way is beyond the reach of R14. Which means that it is incurable, and that nobody will have any immunity at all. He wants someone to realize that.

I have to warn them to stop the distribution. I hope I can make it in time. The man is absolutely crazy. He will kill us all.

Schytte crashed out of his apartment and headed down in the swift elevator, alone.

He was so upset when he came out that he forgot that he had bought a limousine with part of his money. He started running towards the nearest train terminal and had been running for a few hundred metres, when he saw something that made him stop dead.

A man was walking along the pavement. He seemed unable to see and his coordination was slow and jerky.

Can the period of incubation be that short? Jason thought.

Now two policemen approached. No, he wanted to cry out. Don't!

But they took him under the arms. They touched him. Now they had it. They didn't know.

But would they believe him, if he told them the truth?

Someone had been unable to wait. They had jumped the gun, and now there was nothing that could be done.

The distribution system was running.

BCO Equipment

KARL MICHAEL ARMER

Translated by M. L. Eisenberger
and Karl Michael Armer

*EVERYTHING YOU SHOULD KNOW
ABOUT BCO EQUIPMENT.
A FREE BOOKLET FOR INTERESTED PARTIES
AND QUALIFIED OPINION-LEADERS,
PRESENTED WITH THE COMPLIMENTS OF
THE BIOTEC CORPORATION*

Dear readers and patrons of our establishment,

We are gratified by your interest in our BCO devices. This interest is easy to understand for surely there has been no other invention over the past few years that has had such a permanent effect on our world as the BCOs of the Biotec Corporation. In the following eleven short chapters we therefore wish to introduce you to our range of products and to provide you with all the relevant information concerning BCOs.

01 WHAT ACTUALLY IS A BCO?
A BCO is a human being. Or at least, it is at first sight. And even at second sight, too. However, the brain inside this human body is not organic, but electronic. In other words, a BCO is simply an extremely efficient computer hidden away inside a human exterior. This means that the positive aspects of the two components are combined in a unique manner: the attractive exterior of the human being and the vast capacity and reliability of electronics.

The scientific term for such a system is a biocybernetic organism. We have abbreviated this complicated term to the acronym BCO. (BCO is a registered trade mark of the Biotec Corporation.)

The synthesis of the two components can only be described as exceptionally fortunate. For not only does every BCO unit look just like a human being, it also behaves just like one! Later on in this brochure you will find more detailed information about how this almost unbelievable accomplishment became possible.

But let's first take a look at our range of products. It consists of seven standard types, programmed with various personality-scenarios, which means that you can select the model which satisfies your own personal needs and inclinations best. (This, however, should not deter you from collecting all the models one by one!)

Descriptions of the various types are scattered at irregular intervals throughout this booklet, in order to give you time to 'catch your breath' in between and think about whether to make a certain purchase or not. But let's have a closer look at the first standard type now.

Type A: Sandra, the Cheerful Housewife
Dear bachelors, dear singles, why invest money and emotions in marriage (not to mention all the expenses of a possible divorce), when Sandra offers you everything that a wife can possibly offer? Inexpensive and easy to run, she cooks and cleans for you, looks after the household and spoils you in every way. When you come home from work at night, your meal is on the table, everything is clean and tidy, and Sandra is ready to carry out all your further wishes.

Sandra is far superior to the most convenient of convenient marriages. Admittedly, she is not what you could call a luxury model, of course, but she makes up for it by being extremely practical and inexpensive. Her pleasant appearance, her humble and modest nature, make her one of the best household appliances you can get.

02 THE WHOLE IS MORE THAN THE SUM OF ITS PARTS, OR, THE HISTORY OF AN EPOCH-MAKING INVENTION

BCOs are a masterly achievement of the biochemical industry. Their history is inseparably linked with that of James F. Jensen, Ludwig Buchberger, Seiji Fukuda and Lee A. Martino, the founders of the Biotec Corporation. It was their combined scientific and commercial talents that made BCOs possible.

James F. Jensen was working on a research project for a big medical insurance company, testing to what extent it was possible to produce cheap artificial limbs for accident victims via biochemical methods. While engaged in this work, he discovered a successful method of cloning. Cloning leads to self-organization in human cell cultures, or, to express it in a more colloquial fashion, a complete human being can be 'bred' from a single cell. With this discovery, the age of the industrial reproductibility of man had dawned. Just as a written text could be reproduced by the printing press, music by records and tapes, works of art by silk-screen printing, optical events by film and TV, it had now become possible to make as many copies of a human being as desired, thanks to the Jensen cloning process. A tremendous step forward for science!

Another important contribution was the research work done by Ludwig Buchberger, a young scientist from Germany. Not only did he succeed in 'cracking' the human genetic code, but he also managed to manipulate it with reliable and precisely predictable results (*genetic encoding*). In this way, it was possible to program human cells with synthetic genetic information. That is to say: Jensen cloning means that we do not have to be satisfied with mere copies of existing originals but can develop completely new human types with the most fantastic abilities. The incredible possibilities offered by Buchberger's breakthrough are far from exhausted.

However, it was not possible to put Jensen's and Buchberger's prodigious achievement to commercial use, because of an international resolution prohibiting cloning worldwide. It was regarded as morally reprehensible to breed, copy or optimize human beings. The solution was to install an electronic brain instead of an organic one, and thus to build a 'walking computer'. The production of such a device was permitted, as the result was obviously not a human being, but only a machine encased in bio-matter.

The extremely complex electronic brain with which all BCOs have been equipped since then was conceived by Seiji Fukuda. He developed it from the famous chess computer *Chess Champ*, the scenario-calculator *Think Tank* and the creativity computer *A Bit of Fantasy*. Unfortunately, this critical and humorous thinker met an untimely death in a laboratory accident.

Last but not least of the group is Lee A. Martino. It was his commercial genius which made the whole thing possible. He combined the three separate discoveries of these scientists to create a single solution. He brought his profound marketing skills to bear on the problem and came up with a branded article which is now in demand all over the world. So, to a certain extent, he can claim to be the *real* father of all BCOs. By the way, he is especially fond of the following type . . .

Type B: Tommy, the Bright Little Boy

You don't need to put up with the drawbacks of real children any longer, with their screaming and uncontrollable tantrums: Biotec's Tommy is here!

He is the most perfect little boy you can imagine: a really cute little imp, just like something out of a TV series. You cannot help loving him. Always in good spirits, freckle-faced Tommy is a sharp-witted little boy, who is nevertheless well-disciplined and obedient – which means that keeping him in small, modern flats is no problem, either.

Tommy is about ten years old, the ideal age for a child, and will remain so, as his growth and development are stabilized, so that you can enjoy having him around for many years. Tommy will never have any teenage crises, and he will never grow up and leave home. No, he will always remain the ten-year-old boy who loves you with all his heart.

You will take a great fancy to this little rascal – just like many other enthusiastic parents before you. So, if you are planning a child, why not make it Tommy?

Limited-period special offer: You can now purchase Tommy together with Sandra, the cheerful housewife, in a low-price family package-deal, giving you a complete picture-book family, whose members know their place and in which you are the undisputed master of the house. No one will ride roughshod over you! A genuinely recommendable offer worth thinking about.

03 MORE DETAILS ABOUT BCO DEVICES: PHYSICAL CHARACTERISTICS

BCO devices tally in every respect with the human original. They, too, have to sleep, eat and do various other things. For obvious reasons they are of course not capable of reproduction, but otherwise they are capable of *full biological functioning in every respect*. An additional advantage, and one which cannot be overlooked, is the fact that their appearance suits the prevailing ideals of beauty in a most attractive manner.

In this connection, we would also like to get rid of the widespread misconception that all BCO units look alike. This is, of course, not true, as a random computer program ensures that certain genetic parameters like hair colour, physique, size, etc. are varied during production. Thus, so many variations are made possible that every BCO unit is in fact unique, just like every human being.

Type C: Granny, the Lovable Grandmother

What an absolute treasure our Granny is! Not one of those fragile, neurotic creatures who evoke uncomfortable associations of death and decay. Not one of those 'walking reproaches' that get on your nerves with their everlasting nagging and complaining about ingratitude and lack of consideration. Not one of those tiresome old family relics whom you can well do without and whom you have to pack off to the Senior Citizens' Home in the end.

No, Granny is quite the opposite – the picture-book grandma you've always longed for! Once you have her in your home, you never want to do without her, as she looks after the household while husband and wife are at work, cares for the children, cooks for them, supervises their homework and tells them wonderful goodnight stories before they go to sleep. At the same time she is extremely simple and modest, good-natured and patient – to put it in a nutshell: she's got her I C in the right place.

Put some of the cosiness and warmth of the good old days into your modern home. With Granny – a practical and tasteful purchase of unsurpassable nostalgic charm.

04 MORE DETAILS ABOUT BCO DEVICES: INTELLECTUAL CHARACTERISTICS

Because of its construction design, the I Q of the BCO computer is approximately 240, but this figure is reduced to a human dimension of approximately 135 by means of blocking and interference circuits.

As a result of the extremely complex, highly sophisticated

structure of the electronic part, BCO devices are, within certain limits, capable of new logical combinations, which may create the impression that they can think creatively just like human beings.

However, what makes the BCOs so 'human' in their behaviour does not derive from their making genuine decisions of their own, but results from programmed behavioural patterns (the so-called *personality scenarios*), which have been imprinted in the course of an electronically simulated process of education (the so-called *socialization input*). This leads to the incorporation of a behavioural code which automatically subjects all BCOs to the liberal values of our free society.

The tendencies to deviant behaviour which occasionally gave rise to minor problems with earlier BCO models have been completely eliminated as the result of a more sophisticated psychotechnology. The new, advanced models of the second BCO generation completely satisfy all the demands of their owners without the slightest problems. In chapter 08 you will learn more about some of the spectacular achievements of biotec's BCOs.

Type D: Robert, the Dynamic Manager
Enjoy your leisure time, indulge in your hobbies – while Robert works for you! Robert is made for a successful business career: fiercely energetic, assertive, firmly resolved to safeguard his (and your!) interests, equipped with only a minimum of emotions, showing consideration for others only when the need for it is dictated by external circumstances. In addition he has a well-groomed appearance, first-class manners, is an excellent tennis-player, a daredevil driver and highly stress-resistant. In short: your ideal representative in every job: he does the work, you reap the financial rewards!

If the incognito is maintained, Robert is also an excellent, highly presentable match for single women of all ages!

05 THE BCO DEVICE IN PRACTICE: HOW TO PUT IT INTO OPERATION
Putting the device into operation is as easy as falling off a log. You just lay your hands on the BCO unit which has been delivered to you in a deactivated state, and speak an activating sentence of any kind, e.g., 'Get up and walk!' The BCO will thereupon react with the famous friendly Biotec smile, indicating that it is ready

for action. As a result of your activating sentence, the device is normed to the frequency of your voice and will obey your orders, and yours alone, from now on.

Type E: Emmanuelle, the Cuddly Sex-Kitten
Gentlemen, gone are the days when you had to seek your pleasure in dubious establishments or on expensive trips to the Far East! Gone, too, is the constant fear of suddenly being confronted with unpleasant medical consequences ...

Emmanuelle offers you everything your heart desires (and much more) in the privacy of your home – and for you alone! Submissive and devoted, she will fulfil all your wishes with skill and imagination whenever you feel in the mood for her services. With Emmanuelle in your home, you will know what it means to feel like a real man.

This model is also very popular with progressive, open-minded couples. Maybe Emmanuelle will bring more variety and vitality into your marriage, too.

Please note: Emmanuelle is also available as a heavy-duty model for commercial use in the leisure industry etc. You will find further information on this model and other exciting models, such as Lotus Blossom, Sweet Innocence, Big Mama, Justine, Domina, Victim or Pretty Baby in the comprehensively illustrated catalogue of our associated enterprise EroTec. Write and ask for your free copy without obligation – it will surely send your thoughts running wild! (Only available to adults over 16 years.)

06 THE BCO DEVICE IN PRACTICE: HANDLING AND USE
Once activated, your BCO device will carry out, within legal limits, all your instructions with utmost efficiency. Instructions are given by verbal input. However, MASTER CONTROL gives you the possibility of a more practical, reliable and versatile type of control. MASTER CONTROL (available at little extra cost) transmits your instructions direct to the control unit of the BCO over quite considerable distances: You can choose between five MASTER CONTROL models with obedience radii of five to 500 miles.

And MASTER CONTROL offers you another very decisive advantage. In cases of danger or non-obedience (which will, of course, rarely happen) you can use MASTER CONTROL to release a submission impulse which will immediately paralyse the unit concerned for about one hour. (We are pleased to inform you at this point that one of the byproducts of our MASTER CONTROL submission switch is the so-called *neuro-club*, which has so far been successfully employed in preventative action against criminal elements, in dealing with rebellious prisoners and in breaking up unauthorized demonstrations without bloodshed.)

One final reminder: The submission impulse should only be released in genuine cases of emergency. 'Fiddling around' with this switch can lead to permanent damage to the BCO unit's system.

Type F: Super Slave, the Obedient Muscle-Man
Super Slave is young, strong and black. He is as devoted as Uncle Tom and takes the greatest delight in carrying out all your demands with his gigantic muscular body. He does not shrink from extreme physical exertion either, as he is robust and sturdy. An outstanding worker, well-suited as a bodyguard and for many other personal duties. This splendid fellow, with his tremendous endurance, never loses his good temper even in the most difficult moments.

No matter how far down you are on the professional or social ladder, there will always be someone even further down: Super Slave! Whenever you get a kick in the pants, all you have to do is to pass it on. Super Slave will make you feel big, strong and superior at last.

He will give you that prickling sensation of being the masterly type, of having complete command over others. So why continue to be satisfied with training German Shepherd dogs, if you can afford a genuine slave, who will completely submit himself to your strong will and obey every word?

Super Slave will give you that great feeling of power. And what is more important in this world, after all?

07 THE BCO DEVICE IN PRACTICE: SERVICE
The law prescribes a regular, state-controlled inspection at the local Neuro-Control-Authority for all bio-cybernetic products. The official control plate at the wrist gives you a high degree of security even with secondhand BCO devices. We recommend, in addition, a regular half-yearly inspection at our own service centers, which we maintain in over one hundred countries all over the world.

Minor medical repairs are also carried out at these centers, above all the repair of injuries sustained during use, such as broken bones, burns, contusions and cuts. Here, too, discretion is of course – as in all other matters – our guiding principle.

In the event of sudden disturbances or breakdowns you should consult a qualified program analyst. He can generally pacify refractory or over-independent units by means of a fast and inexpensive local operation.

Type G: Patrick, the Sensitive Artist
Patrick is just what you always hoped your son-in-law would be like: young, good-looking, a little shy, but charmingly so, and then again full of youthful exuberance. Patrick is an excellent, cultivated companion for your young daughter, naturally only as a temporary solution; but even the lady of the house will appreciate him as a sophisticated substitute for her overworked husband. Patrick has also proved himself to be ideally suited as private secretary to sensitive bachelors.

Patrick is not only exceptionally well-versed in all questions of contemporary lifestyle, which means that you can rely on him completely in all matters of taste, but he is also an elegant, witty conversationalist and above all a very promising artist, as he has been programmed with the latest creative techniques. He is capable of amazing artistic accomplishments, but he will occasionally surprise you with somewhat unconventional remarks or actions, which is part of the personality scenario with which he is endowed.

Patrick is one of our most complex and sophisticated models. His price is therefore quite exclusive and not within everybody's reach. Owning Patrick not only proves your cultivated sense for the very unusual, but also shows that you enjoy considerable wealth. After all, relishing the sweet taste of your neighbors' envy is among the most elegant ways of *savoir-vivre*.

08 SOME OF THE MANY ACHIEVEMENTS THAT HAVE MADE BIOTEC FAMOUS ALL OVER THE WORLD
Everybody knows them, everybody loves them: the captivating, artfully naïve paintings of Granny Goldsboro.

Or who has not caught himself tapping his feet to top hits like 'Chain Gang' or 'Alien Horror' by SUPER!SLAVE!!?

The most famous BCO model is probably Patrick de Beaulieu, winner of many literary awards, who won instant acclaim with his autobiographical cycle of poems, *From the Bottom of my Heart*. His other bestsellers which have also achieved international recognition are the ballad *The Ecstasy Program*, the metaphysical thriller mc^2 and the long picaresque novels *I Was a Teenage Golem* and *The Brand-new Adventures of Dr Faustus*.

Also well-known to quite a wide public is the 'lyrical-decadent pornography of Emmanuelle Davidoff' (quotation from a renowned news magazine). Her most famous films include *The Pain and the Mercy* (formerly titled *What Are You Doing With That Whip, Darling?*) and the secular four-hour opus *The Parameters of Passion* (not officially distributed in the U.S.A.).

These achievements, recognized all over the world, prove the high standard of Biotec products. However, we consider attempts to grant human rights to the BCO models on these grounds as unfounded and grotesquely exaggerated. See the following chapter for more information on this subject.

09 A WORD OF EXPLANATION CONCERNING THE PUBLIC DISCUSSION: ARE BCO DEVICES ACTUALLY HUMAN BEINGS?

Ridiculous as this thought may seem at first sight, it has nevertheless been heard from various sides recently.

There has been wise-cracking talk of a 'futuristic variant of slavery', of an 'arrogant commercialization of the product character of modern man', whatever that means. A well-known cultural philosopher even spoke of a 'new facet of the superman-dream' and explains: 'Even if man has not been able to raise himself to the level of superman, he has at least been able to create subhumans.'

But enough of these dubious criticisms. We have cited them in some detail here, so as not to support the impression that we are avoiding the discussion. However, we see the real facts of the matter as follows:

It is absolutely stupid to speak of slavery, because how can a machine be a slave? And a BCO is nothing but a machine, subjected to a program. A machine which is 'wrapped' in biochemical matter (i.e. a body) in order to overcome the widespread emotional prejudice against machines. Even if one defined BCOs as *synthetic people*, this term itself would also denote the fact that they are not *real* people in the proper sense of the word. It is therefore downright perverse when human rights commissions consider it their duty to protect the 'interest' of machines.

Leaving the exterior 'wrapping' aside, the fundamental question is whether an electronic brain can develop a personality or not. We say: no, it cannot. A computer cannot develop a personality – that's why we had to give it one! But even this is not a real personality, of course, but only a pre-programmed behavioural pattern. The BCO is absolutely incapable of any independent conscious process which goes beyond that pattern of behaviour, just as it is also unable to experience feelings like love or hate. (The fatal attack on Dr James F. Jensen, often quoted as proof of the BCO's capacity to experience emotions, is therefore not the expression of an individual personality structure but purely and simply a mechanical defect.)

The prevailing opinion amongst the general public and all the relevant authorities is also that a computer – be it ever so sophisticated – simply cannot develop human awareness. Let's cite a few interesting and instructive examples to underline this fact:

The Supreme Court of the United States of America turned down an action which the BCO Robert Blumenthal brought against his owner Alfred Blumenthal for alleged failure to pay commissions. The court stated the opinion that such an action was absolutely out of the question as a machine has no right to salary demands.

In a similar case the West German Federal Supreme Court in Karlsruhe (BGH judgement of 29 February 1996) handed down the decision that a BCO is 'a lifeless object of a material nature' and that therefore 'its owner has the right to be the sole usufructuary of all profits yielded by the BCO'.

An Argentinian military court in Rosario expressly refused to classify the execution of guerilla leader Patrick Cortez as such, and spoke instead of an erasure. A completely apt expression, as no one was killed here, but merely a personality storage unit erased.

But the most interesting example of all is a decision of the Catholic Church ending a controversial case which was discussed all over the world. You, too, will surely recall the BCO device Sandra O'Leary, who at the time declared she was a thinking, intelligent being with a soul and therefore asked to be baptized. Pope Pius XIV turned down this application, reasoning as follows:

'A mechanically produced intelligence does not possess a soul, as it has come into existence in an unnatural way which was not God's will. It is therefore sheer blasphemy to demand the spark of divine grace for a cold shell full of lifeless memory units. A BCO is and remains an artificially produced *thing*.'

There is nothing more to be added to this conclusion. So do not allow yourself to be disconcerted by loud-mouthed critics, but take the BCO devices for what they really are: highly sophisticated, obedient machines, whose only purpose is to serve your personal interests and to which we have given an attractive exterior design because science offers us this opportunity.

If you will permit us a proud boast, we would express it this way: BCO mechanical people represent the millionfold impressions of that great endeavour called *the humanization of serving*.

10 THE BCO PROGRAM AS MIRRORED BY INTERNATIONAL PRIZES AND DISTINCTIONS

BCO devices represent top quality at the frontiers of present-day technology. This is proved by the countless prizes which our BCOs have received over the past years. Let's recall just a few highlights:

Grand Prize for Industrial Design, Venice, Italy, 1991.
Golden Gene of the Bio-Designers Club, Venice, California, 1992.
Selection as *The Year's Most Outstanding Innovation*, Tokyo, 1990.
Promotion Prize of the Institute for Applied Social Simulation, Berlin, 1993.
Award for Worldwide Commercial Excellence, Chicago, 1994.
Conferring of the *Herman* of the Bright Future Society, Sunset Crest, Arizona, 1993.

Apart from these important scientific awards there were also a large number of more practice-oriented distinctions for special applications of individual BCO types: Emmanuelle Smythe-Jones was selected *Playmate of the Year 1995*. And Sandra, the cheerful housewife, was awarded the *Quality Seal of the Whiter-'n-white Society for Domestic Science Research*, Chicago/Los Angeles, 1993.

11 'WE HAVE CHOSEN WELL!': EXCERPTS FROM
ENTHUSIASTIC LETTERS SENT TO US BY CONTENTED
BCO OWNERS

'. . . We are so satisfied with your Tommy that we are doing our best to raise our 'real' children to resemble Tommy as far as possible!' (*Henrietta Hopkins, Tampa*)

'. . . I can only say that Emmanuelle has far exceeded my wildest expectations. Within a week I ordered a few more of these chicks.' (*Wayne 'Banana' O., Amarillo*)

'What a treat it was when Granny arrived! She was exactly what I had wanted to make my domestic bliss complete!' (*Sandra Fiori, Milwaukee*)

'We have been employing the model Patrick as a publisher's reader in our company with great success. His power of judgement concerning the literary as well as the commercial value of any manuscript is superb. At last, the long overdue automatization and rationalization in the cultural sector has now been made possible.' (*A.K., publisher, New York*)

'. . . with her quiet, modest manner, Sandra shows us what values and opportunities of self-fulfilment those feminists deprive themselves of. What a grotesque whim of fate, that it had to be a machine that reminds us of the most human virtues! Sandra is teaching us to recall the original role of woman, to recall the joys of serving within the traditional family hierarchy. Once again, many thanks for this wonderful manifestation of the good old values!' (*Dr Robert Theroux, San Clemente*)

'All I can say is: Robert is tops! I have made him manager of my snack-bar chain and he is doing his job so well that the money is really rolling in! Robert is worth more than a win in the lottery, because with him I carry off the jackpot every day!' (*Frank J. Romero, Sacramento*)

Well, we believe these quotations speak for themselves. They prove that there is no better decision than to purchase a BCO from Biotec. We can guarantee that you will never regret it!

We therefore trust that we will have the pleasure of welcoming you to the world-wide family of contented Biotec patrons in the near future. We are gratified by the interest you have shown in our range of products and are convinced that you will make the right decision.

Biotec Corporation   Berkeley – Munich – Osaka

BIOTEC –
TODAY WE CREATE
THE WORLD OF TOMORROW.

Six Matches

ARKADI AND BORIS STRUGATSKY

Translated by Leonard Stoklitsky

1

The inspector put his notebook aside. 'A queer business, Comrade Leman,' he said. 'Deep, too.'

'I disagree,' said the director of the Institute.

'Indeed?'

'Yes. It's an open and shut case.'

The director was aloof. He gazed down at the empty, sun-flooded square. Nothing was happening there and his neck ached, but he stubbornly kept his head turned towards the window. He was protesting. The director was a proud young man. He knew perfectly well what the inspector meant but he did not think the man had any right to meddle. The inspector's calm persistence irritated him. He wants to dig – that's what he wants to do, the director thought angrily. It's as clear as daylight but he just wants to dig.

The inspector sighed. 'Well, it's not open and shut to me.'

The director shrugged, then glanced at his watch and stood up. 'You must excuse me, Comrade Rybnikov. I have a seminar in five minutes. If there's nothing else I can do for you now –'

'That's quite all right, Comrade Leman. But I'd like to have a talk with that chap – the "private" laboratory assistant. Gorchinsky is his name, isn't it?'

'Yes, Gorchinsky. He's not here now. As soon as he gets back he'll drop in to see you.'

The director nodded and went out. The inspector followed him with a quizzical look. Acting uppity, eh? he said to himself. Never fear, we'll see what makes *you* tick, too.

But first he had to get to the heart of the matter. On the surface, it did look like an open and shut case. If he wanted to, Inspector Rybnikov of the Labour Protection Office could have sat down that very minute and started writing his *Report on the Case of Andrei Komlin, Head of the Physics Laboratory, Central Brain Institute*. Andrei Komlin had carried out dangerous experiments on himself and had been in hospital three days now, in a state between coma and delirium, his round, bristly head covered with strange, ring-shaped bruises. He could not speak coherently, the doctors were giving him injections to keep up his strength, and they spoke ominously of 'acute nervous exhaustion', 'damage to memory centres' and 'damage to speech and auditory centres'.

Everything about the case that might interest the Labour Protection Office was clear to the inspector. This was not a matter of malfunctioning, negligence or inexperience. Nor had there been any infringement of the safety rules – not, at any rate, in their usual meaning. And on top of it all, Komlin had experimented on himself in the deepest secrecy. No one at the Institute had known anything about the experiments, not even Alexander Gorchinsky, Komlin's 'private' laboratory assistant. Although some of the laboratory staff suspected Gorchinsky knew something.

The inspector was more than just an inspector. An old-time scientific researcher himself, his intuition told him that behind the scraps of information he had collected about Komlin's work, and behind the strange accident that had occurred there lay the story of an unusual discovery. And the more he reviewed, in his mind, the statements made by the laboratory staff the stronger grew his conviction that he was right.

Three months before the accident the laboratory had received a new instrument, a neutrino generator, a device for producing and focusing beams of neutrinos. The arrival of the neutrino generator had set off a chain of events which had escaped the notice of those whose job it was to notice such things, and which had finally led to the accident.

Komlin had very willingly turned over all work on an unfinished project to his deputy, while he and laboratory assistant Alexander

Gorchinsky had locked themselves up in the neutrino generator room and got down to what he called preparations for a series of preliminary experiments.

What they were working on had become known only two days before the accident, when Komlin (with Gorchinsky as co-author) had delivered a 'breakthrough' report on neutrino acupuncture. In the three months of his work with the generator, however, Komlin had attracted the attention of other members of the staff on three occasions.

One fine day Andrei Komlin had come to the laboratory wearing a black skull-cap on a shaven head. This, in itself, might not have made any particular impression, but an hour later Gorchinsky, pale and upset, had raced out of the neutrino room, grabbed several packets of surgical dressing from the first-aid kit and dashed back to the room, slamming the door after him. While the door was open one of the other laboratory assistants had noticed Andrei Komlin standing by the window, his clean-shaven scalp glistening. His left arm was covered with what looked like blood, and he was cradling it in his right.

Later that afternoon Komlin and Gorchinsky had quietly emerged from the neutrino room and, without a glance at anyone, walked out of the laboratory. They had both looked unhappy; Komlin's left arm was bandaged.

A month after the above occurrence a junior researcher named Vedeneyev had come across Komlin one evening in a quiet lane in Blue Park. Komlin was sitting on a bench, staring straight ahead and evidently talking to himself in a half-whisper; a large book with tattered pages lay on his knees. Vedeneyev said hullo to Komlin and sat down beside him. Komlin immediately stopped whispering and turned towards Vedeneyev, stretching his neck in a curious manner. There was something odd about Komlin's expression, and Vedeneyev had felt like bolting, but thought it would look odd, and remained seated.

'An interesting book?' he asked Komlin.

'Yes, indeed. The title is *Back-Waters*, and it's by Shih Nai-an.'

Vedeneyev, a young man who knew practically nothing about Chinese classical literature, felt more awkward than ever. All of a sudden Komlin closed the book, handed it to Vedeneyev and asked him to open it to a page at random. With a somewhat uncomfortable feeling Vedeneyev did this. Komlin glanced at the page (Vedeneyev: 'Just once, a fleeting glance'), then nodded and said, 'Follow the text.'

In his clear, ringing voice Komlin began to relate how Hu Yanchou, who attacked Ho Chen and Hsieh Pao with a whip, while Wang Ying, known as 'Short-Pawed Tiger,' and his wife, 'The Green One' . . . At this point Vedeneyev realized that Komlin was reciting the page from memory. He continued to the very bottom of the page without missing a single line or confusing a single name; it was all word for word and letter for letter.

'Did I slip up anywhere?' Komlin asked when he finished.

Vedeneyev, dumbfounded, shook his head. Komlin chuckled, took the book from him and walked off. Vedeneyev did not know what to make of it. He mentioned the incident to a few of his friends, who advised him to ask Komlin himself what it was all about. Komlin, however, reacted to his question with such unfeigned surprise that Vedeneyev hurried to change the subject.

What happened only a few hours before the accident was even more curious.

That afternoon Komlin, in higher spirits than anyone had ever seen him before, gave a display of conjuring skill. His audience consisted of Alexander Gorchinsky, unshaven, his eyes glowing with affection for his chief, and three young laboratory assistants, Lena, Dusya and Katya. The girls had stayed behind to get some instruments ready for the next day's experiments.

Komlin began by offering to hypnotize any member of the group, but no one volunteered.

'Very well,' he said. 'Now, Lena, I'll guess what you hide in your desk drawer.'

Two of his three guesses turned out to be right, at which Dusya remarked that he had peeked. Komlin protested that he had done nothing of the sort. When the girls laughed in disbelief he said he knew how to put out a flame just by looking at it. Dusya took a box of matches, walked over to a corner of the room, and lit a match. After burning for a moment the match went out. Everyone was much surprised. Komlin stood with arms folded on his chest and a frown on his face, in the pose of a professional conjurer.

'You must have the lungs of an ox!' exclaimed Dusya, who was standing at least ten paces away from Komlin.

At this Komlin suggested that someone should tie a handkerchief over his mouth. When this had been done, Dusya struck another match. It went out, just like the first one.

Dusya stared at him in wonder. 'Did you do it through your nose?'

Komlin removed the handkerchief, gave a chuckle and then, seizing Dusya round the waist, waltzed her about the room.

He showed them two more tricks. He dropped a match, but instead of falling straight down it floated to the right in a fairly wide arc ('You're blowing at it,' said Dusya uncertainly). Then he placed a tungsten filament on the table. Quivering, it wriggled to the edge of the table and fell to the floor. Everyone was amazed. Gorchinsky begged Komlin to tell them how he did it.

Komlin suddenly grew serious and said that now he would multiply in his head any big figures they named.

'Six hundred and fifty-four by two hundred and thirty-one and then by sixteen,' Katya suggested timidly.

'Write down the answer,' said Komlin in a queer, tense voice. 'Four, eight, one –' His voice dropped to a whisper as he finished rapidly: 'Seven, one, four, two. From right to left.'

He turned away (the girls were amazed at how he seemed to have shrunk and become stooped), shuffled over to the neutrino room and locked himself in. Gorchinsky watched him with a worried expression on his face, then announced that Komlin had multiplied the numbers correctly. Reading the figures from right to left the answer was 2,417,184.

The girls worked until ten o'clock, with Gorchinsky helping, although he was not of much use. Komlin remained in the neutrino room. They all left at ten, wishing Komlin goodnight through the door. The next morning Komlin was taken to the hospital.

Formally speaking, the result of Komlin's three months of work was neutrino acupuncture, a method of treatment based on irradiating the brain with neutrino beams. The method was extremely interesting, but what connection was there between neutrino acupuncture and Komlin's injured arm? Or his remarkable memory? Or the tricks with the matches and the filament, and the mental multiplication?

'He kept it all to himself,' the inspector muttered. 'Because he wasn't certain? Or was he afraid of endangering his comrades? A queer business. And deep, too.'

The videophone clicked. The secretary's face appeared on the screen. 'Excuse me, Comrade Rybnikov. Comrade Gorchinsky is here.'

'Send him in,' said the inspector.

2

The back of a large man in a checkered shirt with rolled-up sleeves filled the doorway. Over the broad shoulders rose a powerful neck topped by a head covered with thick black hair through which a small bald patch shone, or two bald patches, it seemed to the inspector. The man backed into the room. Before the inspector grasped what was going on the man in the checkered shirt said, 'After you, Iosif Petrovich,' and ushered the director in. Then he carefully closed the door, faced about unhurriedly, and made a short bow. The man with the checkered shirt and unusual manners had a short, fluffy moustache and wore a gloomy expression. This was Alexander Gorchinsky, Komlin's 'private' laboratory assistant.

The director sat down in an armchair and stared silently out the window. Gorchinsky stood facing the inspector.

'Take a seat,' said the inspector.

'Thank you,' Gorchinsky rumbled. He sat down, resting his hands on his knees, and stared at the inspector with cautious grey eyes.

'Are you Gorchinsky?' asked the inspector.

'Yes, Alexander Gorchinsky.'

'Glad to meet you. I'm Rybnikov, Inspector of the Labour Protection Office.'

'It's a pleasure,' Gorchinsky said.

'You're Komlin's "private" assistant, aren't you?'

'I wouldn't put it that way. I'm a laboratory assistant in the physics laboratory of the Central Brain Institute.'

The inspector glanced sideways at the director. Had he seen the flicker of a sarcastic smile on the director's face?

'What have you been working on the past three months?' he asked.

'Neutrino acupuncture.'

'Could you give me some details?'

'It's all in the report,' Gorchinsky said. 'The whole story.'

'Still, I'd like to hear some details from you,' the inspector insisted quietly.

For a few seconds they stared at each other. The inspector flushed angrily. Gorchinsky, his moustache twitching, screwed up his eyes.

'All right,' he rumbled, 'I can do that. We studied the action of focused neutrino beams on the grey and white matter of the brain as well as on the entire body of an experimental animal.'

Gorchinsky spoke in a monotone, rocking forward and backward slightly as he talked.

'While recording pathological and other changes in the body as a whole we measured the action potentials, the differential decrement and lability-instability curves of various tissues and also the relative quantities of neuroglobulin and neurostromin –'

The inspector leaned back in his chair in a mood of fury mingled with admiration. Just you wait, he thought. The director, now tapping his fingers on the table, continued to gaze out the window.

'– The latter, like the neurokeratin –' Gorchinsky boomed.

'What happened to your hands, Comrade Gorchinsky?' the inspector suddenly asked. He could not stand being on the defence. He liked to attack.

Gorchinsky looked down at his hands resting on the arms of the chair. They were covered with blue scars. He made a movement as if to hide his hands in his pockets, then slowly made them into huge fists.

'A monkey scratched me,' he said through clenched teeth. 'In the vivarium.'

'Were your experiments on animals only?'

'Yes, I experimented on animals only,' Gorchinsky put a slight stress on the 'I'.

The inspector took the bull by the horns. 'What happened to Komlin two months ago?'

Gorchinsky shrugged. 'I don't remember.'

'Let me refresh your memory. Komlin cut his hand. How did that happen?'

'He simply cut it, that's all,' Gorchinsky said abruptly.

'Gorchinsky!' the director said warningly.

'Ask Komlin himself.'

The inspector's widely-spaced grey eyes narrowed.

'You amaze me, Gorchinsky,' he said softly. 'You seem to think I want to drag something out of you that will harm Komlin, or harm you or others. That's not it at all. I'm not an expert on the central nervous system. My field is radio optics. I have no right to judge from my own impressions. My job here is to get to the bottom of what happened, not to make wild guesses. So there's no need to get all worked up. You ought to be ashamed of yourself.'

There was a long silence. The director suddenly realized the strength of this stubborn, middle-aged man. Gorchinsky evidently did too.

'What do you want to know?' he finally asked, staring at the floor.

'What is neutrino acupunture?'

'That's Komlin's idea,' Gorchinsky said in a tired voice. 'Irradiating certain sections of the cortex with neutrino beams results in the appearance – or rather, sharply increases the body's resistance to chemical and biological poisons. Infected and poisoned dogs recovered after two or three neutrino punctures. This is something similar to the Chinese method of treatment with needles. Hence the name acupuncture. The neutrino beam plays the role of a needle. The analogy is, of course, purely superficial.'

'How is it done?'

'Neutrinic suction devices attached to the animal's shaven skull focus the neutrino beam on a layer of grey brain matter. It's very complicated, and the hardest part of it was finding the sections and spots in the cortex that stimulate phagocytic mobilization in the required direction.'

'That's extremely interesting,' said the inspector. 'What diseases can this cure?'

'Lots of them,' said Gorchinsky after a pause. 'Komlin believes that neutrino acupuncture mobilizes forces in the body about which we know nothing. Not phagocytes and not nerve stimulation, but something far more powerful. But he has not yet . . . He says that any disease can be cured with neutrino beams – toxic conditions, heart disease, malignant tumours.'

'Cancer?'

'Yes. Burns, too. And it may even be possible to restore lost organs. The body has enormous stabilizing powers, he says, and the key to them lies in the cortex. All you have to do is to find the places in the cortex to which the beams should be directed.'

'Neutrino acupuncture,' the inspector said slowly, as though testing the sound of the words. 'Splendid, Comrade Gorchinsky,' he said more energetically. 'Thank you very much.' (Gorchinsky gave a wry smile.) 'Now tell me about Komlin. You were the first to see him, weren't you?'

'Yes. When I came to work that morning I found Komlin sitting, or rather lying, in an armchair at the table –'

'In the neutrino room?'

'That's right, in the neutrino generator room. Suction devices were attached to his skull. The generator was switched on. I thought he was dead. I summoned a doctor. That's all.'

Gorchinsky's voice shook on those last words. This was so unexpected that the inspector paused before asking his next question. The director was still tapping his fingers, his gaze fixed on the window.

'Do you know what kind of experiment Komlin was conducting?'

'No, I don't. Laboratory scales and two matchboxes stood on the table in front of him. One of the boxes was empty.'

'Matches, you say?' The inspector glanced at the director and then back at Gorchinsky. 'Matches? What have matches to do with it?'

'Yes, matches,' Gorchinsky said. 'They were lying in a heap. Some were stuck together in twos and threes. Six matches lay in one pan of the scales. There was a sheet of paper with figures on it. Komlin was weighing the matches. I checked that.'

'Matches,' muttered the inspector. 'Why did he want to do that, I wonder? Know anything about it?'

'No,' said Gorchinsky.

The inspector rubbed his chin reflectively. 'The other laboratory assistants told me about those tricks with fire and with matches. Komlin was evidently working on something else beside neutrino acupuncture. But what?'

Gorchinsky said nothing.

'He must have experimented on himself many times. His scalp is covered with traces of those suction devices of yours.'

Gorchinsky still said nothing.

'Did you ever notice that Komlin was a wizard at mental arithmetic? I mean, before he showed you those tricks.'

'No, I never noticed anything of the sort. Well, now you know as much about it as I do. Komlin experimented on himself. He tried the neutrino beam on himself. He slashed his arm with a razor and then focused a neutrino beam on it to see how the wound would heal. It didn't work that time. He was also doing something else, on the side, about which none of us knew. Not even I. I only know it's connected with neutrino irradiation. That's all.'

'Did anyone else know about it?' asked the inspector.

'No, not a soul.'

'Do you know what kind of experiments Komlin conducted without you?'

'No.'

'That's all,' said the inspector. 'You may go.'

Gorchinsky rose and, without lifting his eyes, turned towards the door. The inspector gazed at the back of his head. Yes, the man had two bald spots, just as it had seemed to him the first time.

The director still stared out of the window. A small helicopter hovered above the square. Its silvery fuselage sparkling in the sun, it turned slowly on its axis and landed. The cabin door opened. The pilot, in a grey flying suit, jumped lightly to the ground. He walked across the square to the Institute, lighting a cigarette on the way. The director recognized the inspector's helicopter. Must have gone to refuel, he said to himself.

'Could neutrino acupuncture lead to mental disturbances?' the inspector asked.

'Hardly,' replied the director. 'Komlin says it doesn't.'

The inspector leaned back in his chair and stared up at the ceiling.

'Gorchinsky won't be in any condition to work today,' said the director in a low voice. 'You shouldn't have –'

'Yes, I should have,' the inspector insisted. 'You surprise me, Comrade Leman. How many bald spots do you think a man ordinarily has? Those scars on his hands, too. A worthy pupil of Komlin's indeed.'

'They're in love with what they are doing,' said the director.

The inspector stared at the director in silence for a few seconds, his face muscles working. 'Perhaps. But it's not the right way to be in love with it. It's the old-fashioned way. And you don't love your staff the way you should, Comrade Leman. We're a rich country – the richest in the world. We provide you with all the equipment you need and as many experimental animals as you want. Experiment and investigate to your heart's content. But why do you expend researchers so light-mindedly? Who gave you permission to treat human beings that way?'

'I –'

'Why do you think you can break laws passed by the Supreme Soviet? When will an end be put to this disgraceful state of affairs?'

'But this is the first case in our Institute,' protested the director.

The inspector shook his head. 'But what about other research institutes? Or factories? Did you know that Komlin is the eighth case in the past six months? It's barbarous! Barbarous heroism! Men climb into automatic rockets, into autobathyscaphes, into atomic reactors going critical.' He forced a crooked smile. 'They're seeking the shortest way to victory over nature. And they often pay for it with their lives. Your Komlin is the eighth. Can we tolerate this?'

The director scowled. 'There are circumstances when it's inevitable. Think of the doctors who injected themselves with cholera and plague.'

'Huh – historical analogies! But times have changed altogether.'

Both were silent for a while. Twilight was falling. Vague grey shadows appeared in the far corners of the room.

The director broke the silence. 'I ordered Komlin's safe to be opened. His notes were brought to me. You'll probably find them interesting.'

'Of course,' said the inspector.

The director smiled faintly. 'There's a great deal that is – hm, specific. I've glanced through the notes, and I'm afraid you'll find them rough going. I'll take them home with me and summarize them for you, if you wish.'

The inspector was clearly pleased.

'Only don't count too much on me. Those neutrino beams – they were like a bolt from the blue to all of us. None of us had imagined anything like them. Komlin's the world pioneer in this. It may be quite beyond me.'

The director left.

Komlin's notes might help, the inspector reflected. He very much hoped they would. He visualized Komlin with those suction devices pressed to his bare scalp, weighing matches that were stuck together. This was not acupuncture but something quite new, and Komlin must have had doubts about it himself if he conducted such frightful experiments on himself in secret.

But this was a wonderful time to be living in. The fourth generation of Communists. Bold, dedicated men with never a thought for themselves. They braved the unknown with such enthusiasm that it took tremendous effort to restrain them. The human race should gain mastery over nature not by sacrificing its best sons but by using powerful machines and precise instruments. Not simply because the living could accomplish far more than the dead but because Man was the most precious thing in the world.

The inspector rose stiffly and moved towards the door. He moved unhurriedly because it was natural to him, and also because of his age and his leg.

'Those old wounds,' he muttered as he hobbled across the floor of the empty reception room, dragging his right foot.

3

Next morning, at the very hour when the doctors, still in the dark as to the reason for Komlin's illness, were overjoyed to note that their patient was recovering his speech, the inspector and the director again sat at the long bare table in the latter's office. A notebook lay open on the inspector's knees. In front of the director lay a heap of papers – Andrei Komlin's notes, diagrams, sketches and drawings.

The director spoke rapidly, at times disjointedly; his eyes, red-rimmed from a sleepless night, were fixed on a point beyond the inspector. Every now and then he halted, as if to listen in amazement to his own words. As the inspector listened, the chain of events became more and more clear to him. Here is what he learned.

Komlin had not taken up irradiation of the brain with neutrino beams by accident. The method of obtaining conveniently compact neutrino beams had been discovered only a short time before and very little was known about it. When he got the neutrino generator Komlin decided to test it at once.

He expected a great deal from his experiments. High-energy irradiation by nucleons, electrons and gamma rays disrupts the molecular and intranuclear structure of brain protein and destroys the brain. It can only produce pathological changes in the body. Experiments have confirmed this. The neutrino, an uncharged elementary particle with zero rest mass, is a different matter. Komlin calculated that the neutrino would not call forth either explosive processes or molecular reorganization. He hoped it would arouse moderate stimulation of the nuclei of brain proteins, intensify the nuclear fields and perhaps arouse in brain matter completely new power fields, hitherto unknown to science. All of Komlin's conjectures had been brilliantly confirmed.

'There's a lot in Komlin's notes I do not understand,' said the director, 'and some things I simply cannot believe. For these reasons I'll tell you only about the main points and about anything that might shed light on those mysterious tricks.

'When he began experiments with animals Komlin immediately got the promising idea of neutrino acupuncture. A monkey injured its paw, and the wound healed remarkably fast. Spots on its lungs, traces of tuberculosis, which is common in monkeys in a temperate climate, disappeared just as fast.

'Several dogs were given various types of biological poisons. The neutrino "needle" cured them very quickly. The "Komlin needle" (as Gorchinsky named the method) cured tuberculosis in monkeys dozens of times faster than the most effective antibiotics.

'In that report of his Komlin put forward a supposition that the bodies of human beings and animals possess hidden curative powers science still knows nothing about but whose existence has been revealed by the experiments in neutrino acupuncture. He outlined a detailed programme of going over from experiments on animals to experiments on human beings, starting with the simplest and safest neutrino treatment and leading up to complex and combined forms. Large teams of doctors, physiologists and psychologists were to be drawn into the experiments. But –'

The inspector was right. Komlin had been working on something else besides neutrino acupuncture. Experiments with the neutrino generator very soon showed that a remarkable mobilization of the body's curative powers was not the only result of irradiating the brain with neutrino beams. Some of the experimental animals were behaving strangely. Those cured after short-term neutrino treatment usually behaved normally, but the 'favourites', the animals on which numerous experiments of various kinds were made, amazed the two researchers. Whereas the young Gorchinsky saw only amusing or irritating tricks of nature, Komlin's intuition told him he stood on the threshold of a significant discovery.

A dog named Gene (short for Generator) began to do circus stunts no one had ever taught him. He walked on his hind legs, and even on his front legs, and 'shook hands'. Once Gorchinsky found him doing a strange thing. He was sitting on a stool, staring fixedly in front of him and rising at regular intervals to give a short bark. He did not recognize Gorchinsky and growled at him.

Komlin was amazed by the behaviour of the baboon Cora. Immediately after being irradiated Cora sat in her cage chattering at Komlin. Suddenly a shock seemed to go through her. She stared at something in the corner, growled loudly, then piteously, and started moving backwards. Neither threats nor caresses affected her. Cora ran into a corner, curled herself into a ball and sat there a whole hour, staring fixedly at something invisible, from time to time uttering a sharp howl, always a danger signal. The symptoms passed, but Komlin noticed that now Cora looked first at the ill-starred corner whenever she entered her cage.

One day Gorchinsky came running to call Komlin to the monkey room. A young baboon was sitting in a cage eating a banana. There was nothing odd about either the baboon or the banana, but the attendant and Gorchinsky both maintained they had witnessed something altogether fantastic. They had found, they said, the baboon watching with obvious interest a piece of paper that was slowly but surely moving across the floor towards it. As the baboon stretched out a paw to the paper Gorchinsky hurried to find Komlin. The attendant said the baboon had swallowed the paper. At any rate, it could not be found. An attempt to reproduce the amazing phenomenon failed.

'Here is what Komlin wrote in this connection' said the director, handing the inspector a sheet of ruled paper.

The inspector read: 'Mass hallucination? Or something new? Mass hallucination including a baboon is amazing in itself. There's something here. We won't find out anything from monkeys or dogs. Have to try it myself.'

Komlin began experimenting on himself. Gorchinsky soon learned of this and immediately followed his chief's example. They had a brief quarrel on this score. Gorchinsky finally promised not to experiment any more, while Komlin promised to try only the simplest, shortest and safest irradiations. Not until the day of the accident did Gorchinsky learn that Komlin had dropped neutrino acupuncture.

'There is really very little information in Komlin's notes about the astounding results of his experiments,' said the director. 'The notes become more and more fragmentary and disjointed. You feel Komlin cannot find words with which to describe his sensations and impressions. His deductions are unclear.'

Komlin devoted several pages torn out of a notebook to describing the remarkable memory he acquired after one of the experiments. He wrote: 'After one glance at an object I can see it in all its details when I turn away or close my eyes. After one glance at a page of a book I can read it from the "image" imprinted in my memory. I don't believe I shall ever forget several chapters from *Back-Waters* or the entire four-place table of logarithms from the first to the last figure. What enormous possibilities!'

Among the notes there were observations of a general nature.

'Memory, thought, reflexes and habits,' Komlin wrote in a firm hand, as though meditating, 'have a definite material foundation that is not yet clear to us. That is elementary. The neutrino beam seeps into that foundation and creates a new memory, new reflexes and new habits. That is what happened to the dog Gene, to Cora and to myself (mnemogenesis – the creation of a false memory).'

The last few pages, clipped together, dealt with the most interesting and amazing of all Komlin's discoveries. The director picked them up and held them above his head.

'Here,' he said solemnly, 'is the answer to your questions. This is something in the nature of an outline or rough draft of a future paper. Shall I read it?'

'Do, please,' said the inspector.

' "You cannot will yourself to wink unless the muscle is there. The nervous system plays the role of an impulse trigger, nothing more. A tiny discharge leads to the contraction of a muscle that is capable of moving tens of kilograms, of performing an enormous amount of work compared with the energy of the nervous impulse. The nervous system is the fuse in the powder-magazine, the muscle is the powder, and the contraction of the muscle is the explosion.

' "Intensification of the process of thinking intensifies the electromagnetic field arising somewhere in the cells of the brain. These are action potentials. The very fact we are able to discover this means the process of thinking affects matter. Not directly, though. When I solve a differential equation the brain field grows stronger, and the needle of the instrument that measures it moves. Isn't that a mental motor? The field is the muscle of the brain!

' "I have acquired the ability to multiply with great speed. How I do it I cannot say. I just multiply. 1,919 multiplied by 237 equals 454,803. It took me four seconds by my stop-watch to multiply that. It's wonderful but not altogether clear. The electromagnetic field grows much stronger, but what about the other fields of the brain, if they exist? The 'muscle' is developed. But how is one to control it?

' "Eureka! A tungsten filament weighing 4.732 grams. Suspended in a vacuum on a nylon thread. I simply looked at it and it deviated from the initial position by about 15 degrees. That is already something. The generator regime . . ." '

The director read off a string of figures, then interrupted to say that Gorchinsky had seen a vacuum hood with a tungsten filament, but it had later disappeared. Komlin must have taken it apart.

He continued reading:

' "The psychodynamic field, the muscle of the brain, is functioning. I don't know how I do it. There's nothing strange about not knowing. What do you have to do to bend your arm? No one can tell you. To bend my arm I bend my arm. That's all. The bicep is a very obedient muscle. Muscles have to be trained. The field of the brain also has to be taught to work. But how?

' "There is not a single thing I can lift by a 'mental effort'. I can only move things. But not as I wish. A match or a piece of paper always moves to the right. Metal moves towards me. It works best with matches. Why?

' "The psychodynamic field operates through a glass hood but not through a newspaper. To influence an object I have to see it. I put out a candle on the other side of the neutrino room.

' "I am certain the possibilities of the brain are inexhaustible. All one needs is training and a definite activization, stimulation of the protein molecules and neurons. Some day man will be able to compute better than any computer; he will be able to read and understand a whole library in a few minutes.

' "This is terribly exhausting. My head is splitting. Sometimes I can work only under constant irradiation and at the end I am sweating. I must not break down. Am working with matches today." '

On this Komlin's notes ended.

The inspector sat with his eyes closed. Komlin's idea was probably destined to yield rich fruit, he thought. That was all in the future, though. Meanwhile, Komlin was in hospital. The inspector opened his eyes, and his glance fell on the sheet of ruled paper. 'We won't find out anything from monkeys or dogs. Have to try it myself.' Perhaps Komlin was right.

No, Komlin was wrong. Wrong as wrong could be. He shouldn't have taken such a risk, at any rate, not alone. Even where neither machines nor animals (the inspector again glanced at the sheet of ruled paper) could help, man had no right to play with death. Komlin had been doing just that. And you, Professor Leman, will not remain director of the Institute because you do not understand that and appear to be filled with admiration for Komlin. I tell you, comrades, that we shall not allow you to brave fire. In this day and age we can afford to be super-cautious. You and your lives are more precious to us than the most magnificent discoveries.

Aloud the inspector said: 'We must draw up a statement of the inquiry. The cause of the accident is clear to us.'

'Yes,' said the director. 'Komlin collapsed while lifting six matches.'

The director accompanied the inspector out of the building. They emerged into the square and moved unhurriedly towards the helicopter. The director was silent and absent-minded. He found it hard to keep in step with the inspector's shuffle. Gorchinsky, dishevelled and gloomy, caught up with them just as they reached the helicopter. The inspector, who had already said goodbye to the director, climbed into the cabin with difficulty. 'Those old wounds are acting up again,' he muttered.

'Komlin's much better now,' Gorchinsky said in a low voice. 'He'll be up and about in a month from now.'

'Yes, I know,' said the inspector. With a sigh of relief he finally settled himself in his seat.

The pilot quickly climbed into his seat.

'Will you write a report?' Gorchinsky asked.

'Yes, I will,' the inspector replied.

'I see.' Gorchinsky, his moustache twitching, looked the inspector in the eye. 'I say,' he blurted out, 'are you the Rybnikov who discharged those thingamajigs in Kustanai in '68, without waiting for the automatic machines?'

'I say, Gorchinsky,' the director snapped.

'And that was when your leg was injured, wasn't it?'

'Gorchinsky, stop it, I tell you!'

The inspector did not reply. He slammed the cabin door shut and leaned back in the soft seat.

The director and Gorchinsky stood in the square, staring up at the big silver beetle as it soared above the white and rose-coloured seventeen-storey tower of the Institute and disappeared from sight in the late afternoon sky.

The Ring

GORAN HUDEC

Translated by Krsto A. Mažuranić

There was a ring at the door. I rose from the easy chair where I had been idling away the warm afternoon and reached to switch on the entrance video monitor. The portly man at the front door was a stranger to me. I went.

'Inspector Strpić,' he said.

I nodded. There was no need to give him my name; inspectors generally know the names of the people to whom they decide to pay a visit. They can also hardly expect a delighted 'Pleased to . . .' from those they do call on.

'I hope you can spare me a few moments of your time,' he went on pleasantly, 'for a short chat.'

'Gladly. I've plenty of time, and I've been expecting you,' I let him know. He arched a thin eyebrow to indicate wonder, so I added, 'Well, someone of your kind. Do step in, please.'

I tried to size the man up as I showed him into the drawing room. A couple of years or so older than myself and looking it; not yet overweight. Dressed with quiet elegance. Precise, deliberate gestures; carries an air of easy assurance in his manner. Probably a lawyer by vocation, I decided.

The inspector settled himself down in a soft easy chair and I offered him a drink. His choice added to his credit with me for he declined big-name French cognacs and Scotch whiskys, preferring instead a mild and smooth brand of *šljivovica*. He took a short sip and pursed his thin lips with satisfaction.

'You have done very well for yourself,' he said, looking with admiration at my large indoor swimming pool behind the glass partition. He was absolutely right in his observation, of course, so I nodded in approval and waved a hand at the packet of cigarettes on the table.

'You may smoke if you wish.'

He glanced at the Sherman's Turkish Rounds and shook his head, declining.

'Very well indeed.' He took another sip pensively. 'The Inland Revenue,' he went on, 'is intrigued.' He threw a ghost of a smile at me. 'So are some other Services. It is a very intriguing case, yours.' He fell silent as if to reflect. Or was it that he expected me to react?

Accommodatingly, I reacted. 'If you insist. I'm quite unfamiliar with your other cases, so I can't judge mine.'

'Is that so! All right, let me try to reconstruct. You will help me fill in some necessary details, I hope?'

'Of course. As I said, I've plenty of time.'

'I dare say.' He kept his cool. 'Well. Until 20 April last year your life had been a perfectly normal, unremarkable affair . . . if you will excuse the expression.' He did not smile. 'You went to work every day. Your salary was what could be expected for an ordinary young scientist working with an ordinary research institute.' He tossed off what was left in his tumbler. I refilled it.

'On 21 April, early in the morning, before going to work, you paid a visit to your bank to open a foreign-currency account there. Your colleagues testified later that you had spent the better part of the rest of the working day absorbed in some mysterious calculations which seemed to have made you curiously glum.' The look in his pale grey eyes became distant. 'No further remarkable behaviour on your part was discovered for the next couple of days. You simply went on living as before.'

'That is,' I prompted, 'until my bank notified me that the money had arrived.'

'Precisely.' A hint of a tremor entered his soft baritone. 'But the money arrived on that very 21 April, later in the day, in a single massive transfer of a sum large enough to put you among the richest individuals in this part of the world. On the day after the bank notified you of the transfer you retired from your job and started building this . . . this . . .' He hesitated into silence for want of the proper word.

'House,' I offered. 'I call it a house.'

'A house,' repeated the inspector bitterly. 'The word, used in this context, usually denotes a human dwelling. I am not sure if it applies in your case. One of the most powerful electronic data processors in the country as well as a most complete electronic laboratory are not commodities commonly built into a dwelling-house.'

'It's the intellectual recreation wing of the house,' I explained helpfully.

'You mean to say that you built it for your amusement?'

'Mine, and my sons'. I suppose it depends on individual tastes and means ... and times, of course. Somebody else might've arranged it differently.' I spread my ten fingers in the air, explaining, 'I prefer dabbling at computer work. So will my sons some day, judging from their early interest in it. But we've drifted off our subject, I'm afraid.'

'Yes, quite so. Let us discuss the rings.' Suddenly the look on the inspector's face was not that of a happy man. 'The rings ...' He composed his thoughts. 'The scandal burst out in the Bahamas early in May. Two ladies notorious for their taste in jewellery discovered at a party that they were sporting identical diamond rings of exquisite workmanship and ... er ... value.' He looked at the tumbler in his hand. 'Why, the gems alone ... but never mind.' His face grew stern. 'The yellow press chewed over the scandal for what it was worth for a few days; then it was discovered, to add oil to the fire, that a third ring, identical in every respect to the former two, had been on display for some time in the Leningrad Hermitage as an item of an exposition entitled "Gems Through History". The ring was there identified as the work of an unidentified Dutch –'

I suppressed my chuckle; the inspector was a troubled man as it was.

'... ah, an *unknown* Dutch craftsman probably of the early seventeenth century.' The inspector leaned forward, carefully put the half-empty tumbler on the table, and settled back folding his arms on his chest. 'The press got wind of only three rings because the fact that no less than sixty-four more rings were reported to the police subsequently was kept under tightest security by

Interpol, so as to avoid causing embarrassment to the hapless owners. All sixty-seven rings were identical, and all were delivered to the present owners on the same day, 19 April, by the person they negotiated the sale with. Payment in all sixty-seven cases was executed by cheques addressed to the same account in a certain Swiss bank.'

There was a pause. I prompted him. 'And you believe that the Swiss bank remitted the whole accumulated sum, in one great big lump, to my foreign-currency account here, on 21 April.'

'I have no need to merely believe so. It is a fact.' The inspector looked me in the eye. 'Besides, the sixty-seven buyers' descriptions of the person who sold them the rings tally perfectly. There is no doubt whatever that each of them described you. The investigation was very thorough.'

'And long, it seems. You took your time.'

The inspector sighed, leaned forward, picked the tumbler from the table, and emptied it in a gulp. He was a troubled man. I refilled it.

'There were no formal charges at all,' said the inspector softly. 'The buyers are satisfied with the purchase. The rings are obviously and beyond any doubt genuine, and quite worth every last penny that was paid for them. Which is baffling, to say the least. The rings are identical, definitely and absolutely, down to the last atom. No method of analysis known to modern science discovered any variance. Any at all!'

'Remarkable,' I intoned with no inflexion. 'Identical, you say.'

He searched my face helplessly for a moment. Then he exploded. 'It is impossible to make two absolutely identical diamond rings; *two*! ... and here we have sixty-seven of them! It is humanly impossible to make sixty-seven *absolutely identical genuine diamond rings*!' He glared at me, breathing in gasps. 'At least sixty-seven, at that!'

'Yep,' I agreed. 'Fancy that, now!'

That sobered him down. After a moment he said, 'If I may, after all?' and extracted one of the Turkish Rounds from the packet. I lit it for him.

'At least, the existence of sixty-seven rings has been established,' he retreated into officialese, 'but Interpol has reasonable cause to believe that the actual number must be greater because of the substantial discrepancy between the amount of monies transferred to your foreign-currency account from Switzerland, and the composite sum of payments as reported by the sixty-seven known buyers.' Then, as an afterthought, 'Taking the current rates of exchange into account, of course.'

'I always assumed that bank accounts were inviolate?' I matched his tone of voice.

'My dear sir!' He was on a sure footing now that our conversation left the mysterious ground of spooky puzzles.

'All right, I understand. Well, all in all, ninety-four rings were sold.'

That shattered him. 'You confess to it! You actually do!'

'Nobody bothered to ask me before. No need to sweep the facts under the carpet, is there? But do go on, you're telling me things I didn't know.'

'Well, yes. Firstly, it was established that the rings were identical.' He shook his head uneasily. 'Secondly, the subsequent investigation proved that none of the rings were on the wanted list –'

'Wanted list, Inspector? Meaning?'

'Meaning none were reported stolen or otherwise missing. In fact, we could trace no existence for any of them prior to the sale.' He frowned. 'I mean, prior to the sale negotiations.'

He stubbed out the half-smoked cigarette with quick jerks of his hand. 'Which brings us to the second unexplained puzzle. During the investigation it became apparent that you – and there is no doubt it was you,' he growled, 'had to be in sixty-seven places all over the world at the same time to be able to conduct all those negotiations. Which is impossible! In addition, we know that you spoke at least twenty-eight different languages immaculately during those negotiations! A Japanese businessman swore by his ancestors' grave that no European can speak such fluent Japanese –'

'If you can call Japanese a fluent language.'

'I call it nothing. I never got past *sayonara* myself. The worst one was that Sheikh who kept insisting that you spoke the dialect endemic to his home oasis better than he did himself.' The inspector gazed at me silently for a moment. 'The only rational explanation would be that you had a number of skilled accomplices who mimed –'

'Excuse me, but the word accomplices would imply crime, wouldn't it, Inspector? And you've no grounds for that, have you?'

'Helpers, then. Satisfied?' hissed the inspector. 'Helpers. *Assistants* – for even if you somehow contrived to be in sixty-seven places at the same time, you could not have spoken all those languages. Why, you manage to tie your tongue into a knot,' there was malice in his voice, 'every time you try not to botch the few words of the two foreign languages . . .'

He simmered down. 'Well, anyway, we managed to unearth no . . . helpers. And all buyers forcefully deny they negotiated their purchase with anybody but you.'

'Naturally. I had no helpers.'

'Impossible. It would mean that you were in sixty-seven corners of the world simultaneously on 19 April last year to deliver the rings. Or, in ninety-four corners, by your own word.' His voice hardened to steel: he got me now. 'And we traced down and accounted for every damned single second of your life on that day, from the moment you woke in the morning till you and your family arrived at your sister-in-law's in the evening, for that birthday party of hers.'

'Wedding anniversary,' I corrected him in a soft voice.

'Immaterial,' brusquely.

'But still, wrong.' I grinned and stood up. 'Somebody botched.' I waved a hand. 'But I could do with a cup of coffee. Care to join me?' I went to the espresso machine.

The inspector sighed audibly. 'Make mine short, please. With sugar.'

'Cream?'

'No, thank you.'

'Right. Won't take a minute.'

The screams and yelps and stamping noises that suddenly made any further conversation impossible were no auditory manifestation of a possibly stampeding herd of wild buffaloes through a nursery school. Soon the sounds of splashing water testified that my twins had decided it was time for their afternoon swim in the pool.

'They swim quite well, it seems,' said the inspector loudly.

'Yeah, they do, don't they?' Myself, the proud father. 'And they're only just past six, did you know that? Must be the benefit of an indoor swimming pool, I'd say.'

The inspector said nothing.

'The pool was their idea. They insisted on having a large one.'

The rich aroma of hot coffee set me into motion. Busy with cups and saucers and sugar and tiny spoons and the rest of the ritual of serving the delicacy, I asked, 'Why'd you come, Inspector?'

Startled, the inspector only said, 'What?'

'I said, why did you come to visit me? No formal charges pressed, nobody sued me, no evidence of anything criminal . . .?'

'As I said, the Internal –'

'Come off it, Inspector, earnings abroad aren't taxable here and you know it better'n I do!'

The inspector only waved an impotent hand in the air.

'A mission of forlorn hope?' I put the steaming cups on the table, sat down and leaned back in the soft cushions of the easy chair. 'Or a little freelancing stint on the side?'

The inspector took a careful sip from the cup and looked at me askance, saying nothing.

'Come, come, Inspector. You've had your fun.'

'I am not going to just pack up and leave, you know,' said the inspector softly. 'Tell me your side of the story . . . please?'

The antique pendulum clock on the wall ding-donged gently, as if to itself, five times. I threw a loving glance at it. I sipped my coffee.

The situation tickled my fancy. Might be fun watching the inspector's reaction to my story. And I can't say a rude no to a pretty please, can I?

'Well, why not?' I said. 'I'll have to tell it to someone, sooner or later. Might as well be you, Inspector.' I shrugged. 'There's little to tell, though. To begin at the beginning, everything started at my sister-in-law's wedding anniversary, I guess. At some point or other we all started weeping on one another's shoulders over the chronic shortage of money. You know; the old story of young couples burdened with small children who need to be pampered, new flats that need be furnished, new cars that need be paid for, petty ambitions in following the fashions in dress that need be sated, and all the millions of other things, everything salted with beginner's income.'

We both took a sip from our cups. The inspector took another cigarette and I lit it for him.

'Later, at home, when I lay in my bed and tried to fall asleep, deeply affected with the conversation, crazy ideas kept flashing in my mind which was soaked in alcoholic vapours. All the usual idiocies, of course, like inheriting sudden money from an unknown uncle, for example.' The inspector was smiling, his eyes unfocused. We understood each other. 'No, not me. I'm not the type to have unknown rich uncles about to die. Winning at sweepstakes? No, sir, to me it can happen only if I knew the winning number in advance. Would be nice to know winning numbers in advance, wouldn't it? But I'd need a time machine for that! Like in that George Pal film my kids loved so much. A time machine, I mused, a *time machine*, of all the crazy, childish . . .

'The next moment I realized the idea wasn't so crazy after all! I thought some more and then I jumped out of bed and rushed to the desk to do some figuring. My wife was mad as a hornet at my drunken lunacy – her own words that night – but soon I had a sheaf of papers full of calculations which proved that I could build a time machine quite easily.'

The inspector was silent. He only gazed at me and his face spoke out his dilemma: was I pulling his leg right out of its socket, or should he call the nearest psychiatric clinic at once?

'I went back to bed full of beans. I walked on air; I knew how to build the time machine, and I had a plan.'

'You had a plan.' It was not exactly a question. The inspector was either too dazed for one, or perhaps he was humouring me.

'Of course, I had a plan! It was the plan that prompted me into thinking about the time machine in the first place. A very clever plan, even if I say so myself! Shall I pour?'

'Beg your pardon?'

'I said, shall I pour? D'you wish to drink some more?'

'Oh. No, thank you.'

'You sure?'

'Please! You were saying . . .?'

'Was I? Oh, yes, I was; the plan. Very elegant, once I had a time machine. I would go forward in time – say, two hundred years – and learn Dutch. You wouldn't believe their technique! It takes no longer than five minutes to transfer the entire vocabulary, grammar, and phraseology of any language out of the computer directly into the human brain. Direct stimulation of appropriate brain centres. One can even choose a dialect of a given location and period.'

'The Sheikh . . .'

'Ah, the Sheikh! It was just a prank to shatter his haggling prowess.' I fell silent for a moment to reminisce. 'He recognized my dialect at once, and he was troubled, for he didn't recognize me.'

'Why should he . . .'

'Because they're a closely knit society there, and everyone of consequence knows everyone else. And he didn't know me. It shook him so badly he hardly tried to haggle at all. I got the most from him.'

'You got a lot.' Wistfully.

'It was a lot of ring. But to go on with my plan. After I'd learned Dutch I would go back to the seventeenth century, to Amsterdam. Spices were worth their weight in gold then. More, even. For a pint of peppercorns I would've been able to buy a diamond ring that would be worth a fortune in the twentieth century. But one single ring would be nothing, of course. Wouldn't be worth the trouble.'

'So you bought more, naturally. But they are all *identical*!'

'No wonder they're all identical. On the contrary, it would be a miracle if they weren't! You see, I was lazy. I didn't bother to go to another jeweller's. Why should I? I'd found one who was pleasant to do business with, and I liked the ring. So I simply went to him again and again, each time an hour earlier than before, and bought the very same ring. Dear old Piet! By and by he came to be like an old friend to me and it grew very difficult for me to remember that each time he saw me it was the first time for him, if you see what I mean.'

'I do not.'

'Look, he kept seeing me over and over again – *in reverse*. I visited him at five p.m. and bought the ring after I'd bought it at six p.m. the same day. He couldn't remember what was to happen an hour in his future, could he?'

'But at six p.m. he would –'

'No, he wouldn't, because at six I hadn't yet visited him at five so there wasn't anything for him to remember.' Clever chap, the inspector. 'Please, Inspector, don't quibble. Remember, you wanted me to tell you details about my plan. Shall I do that, or would you rather we started a philosophical argument about the paradoxes of time travel?'

'But you –'

'Inspector,' I pointedly looked at the Cartier on my wrist, 'we're wasting time.'

The inspector sighed painfully. 'Time,' he said.

'Oh, sorry. It was a bad pun, I'll admit.'

'Go on with your story, please. I shall be silent.'

'Right. In fact, there's little more to tell. My plan was to keep visiting Piet earlier and earlier until the ring was . . . had been? . . . no more. I mean until the ring wasn't for sale because it hadn't been finished yet. I hope Piet has put to good use the five *schepels* of peppercorns he accumulated in payment for the ninety-four rings.'

The inspector was silent; he was as good as his word. But he was the most frustrated man I'd ever seen.

'Next was the problem of selling the rings. Since they were identical, it was most important to arrange the sale in such a way that all buyers get their pieces at the same moment.' I couldn't suppress a grin. 'In their real time, naturally. As for me . . . I was to use the machine to its full capacity. You know, quick hops to the twenty-second century to learn languages, longer stops in the near past to negotiate sales. To cut a long story short, the rings are now apparently owned by people in all quarters of the globe.'

'You must have spent a good deal of time travelling, as you did, in . . . er . . . time.' He smiled sheepishly.

'It doesn't matter. I always returned to the present a second after I had left. You don't –'

'No, I mean a good deal of biological time.' Something of his old hard glint blinked in his eyes. 'Your real time in the present may have stood relatively still for you, but you spent your biological time. And you look no older –'

'How would *you* know that, Inspector?'

'I can presume –'

'You can, all you want, but a few months don't change a man that much. You're quibbling again, and you promised, remember?'

He started as if to say something, but I hurried on with my story.

'The problem of spending the money was a rather pleasant one to solve. First, a house. Imagine! Frank Lloyd Wright is dead now, but I was going to have a time machine! Young, unknown architects love jobs where they can test their budding genius freely. Furnishing the house would be even more fun: Picasso sketched furniture for his own villa; he could do it for me as well, over some *vin chaud* in a Paris *bistro*. The kitchen was a bit of a problem of its own; I wanted it from the future, but not from the time when mankind will've forgotten the classical way of preparing natural food. Early twenty-first century would do the trick.'

I hurried on to quench a possible new comment on the inspector's part. 'And that's that. With the calculations for the time machine lying all over the desk and with my mind full of the plan I've just described, I went back to bed. After a few hours' sleep I woke in the morning eager to start working on my plan in earnest. I could do nothing until I built the time machine, true, but at least I could go to my bank and open the foreign-currency account there. I did that.'

I sighed and concentrated on regarding my fingernails closely. The inspector waited for a while, also sighed, and said, 'Then you went to the institute to check your calculations.' He raised an eyebrow and listened to the conclusion of my story without a sound.

'Yes,' I said, sighing again. 'It was a very humiliating experience, I can tell you! After checking my nocturnal scribblings for a while I knew them for what they really were: a big mess of the most ridiculous nonsense I'd ever seen. A time machine, bah! Haw haw, rubbish, utter bilge. I must've been sodden drunk that night. I must've drunk gallons at my sister-in-law's.

'The next couple of days were bad. I felt depressed, not so much by the fact that I wouldn't be able to build the time machine after all, but rather by the realization that alcohol could reduce me to the utter fool I was, to believe, even for a moment, that it might be possible to build a time machine at all. My wife nearly split her sides laughing at me, and my sons gave me hell nagging me about "when we were going to fight the Morlocks." '

I threw a quick glance at the inspector. He was sitting still, listening, and was silent.

'When I received information that the money had arrived I quit my job with the institute and built the house. That's all.'

The inspector went on being very still and silent for a long time, lost in thought. He flicked a fleeting glance in my direction, tossed off the *šljivovica* in his tumbler, and was silent some more.

At last he said, 'When *did* you build the time machine, then?'

'I never did. It can't be done. Even you know, Inspector, that time machines are only a fictional conjecture.' I smiled sadly.

'Conjecture! No; you can't give me that. I won't buy it. No sir. The rings are real. The money in the bank is real. This . . . this *house* is real. How do you explain *that*?'

'I don't,' I shrugged. I looked him in the eye. 'I *needn't*. I believe there's too much explaining going on in the world today anyway. I believe people push the urge to explain everything too far these days. So I'm not trying to explain what happened to me. I'm only trying to acclimatize to my new way of living. That's all!'

'That can't be all,' the inspector almost shouted at me. 'Aren't you *curious*, man?'

'As a matter of fact, I do have a suspicion. Look at my boys; they have a marvellous childhood. They live like lords. I suspect that somewhere in the future they might've used my computer to find out how to build the time machine. They may not know it yet, but they might've done very well indeed for themselves by using the flash of my drunken genius that night to plant their cuckoo's egg into my nest. Spurred by my unwitting –'

The door to the drawing room swung open with swishing insistence.

'That devilish machine has broken down again, blast its me-chanical soul! How many *times* did I tell you – Oops! Excuse me!'

The inspector just gaped at my wife. She has a way of rushing about . . .

'Take it easy, Pet,' I said. 'Inspector, meet my dear wife, the mother of our aquatic twins, and a proud owner of a modern washing machine that breaks down time and time again.' The inspector silently bowed in confusion. 'Pet,' I hurried on, 'our guest is just about to leave. I'll see him out. Inspector . . .?'

He went.

'What did he want?' asked my wife later, sipping coffee.

'He wanted to know.'

'Ah, did he? And?'

'And nothing.' I smiled. 'I'm almost sorry for him. A nice chap; would that I had met him some other way.'

'No great loss, that's what I say.'

'All right, I agree. Good riddance.' I put an arm round her shoulder. 'This calls for a nice quiet dinner in a nice quiet res-taurant, don't you agree, Pet? I happen to know of one in Cork, in 2007. Shall we go?'

There was a twinkle of a smile in her green eyes.

'I see you were telling him a story about a time machine,' my wife chuckled, playing with a big diamond ring on her finger.

We love our future.

'Oh, Lenore!' Came the Echo

CARLOS MARÍA FEDERICI

Translated by Joe F. Randolph

1

Say not thou, What is the cause that the former days were better than these? . . .

> *The three basic laws of robotics are:*
> 1. *No robot may harm any human being, or*
>   *by its inaction let any human being*
>   *be harmed.*
> 2. *A robot must obey orders . . .*

> *Once upon a midnight dreary . . .*

> *. . . so that if two points are equal and their basic spatial intervals are too,*
> *then it is possible to choose a system of coordinates, as seen by an observer*
> *moving at a calculated speed, in which events may be simultaneous, al-*
> *though . . .*

> *Allons, enfants de la patrie,*
> *le jour de gloire est arrivé! . . .*

It was dusk. Mann Bekker, the Traditologist, had for the time being given up his desperate attempts to sort out the books and manuscripts piled up on his desk.

He shook his head. How, God in heaven, *how* to tell fact from fiction beyond a shadow of a doubt? What elements were to be used as a foundation for a hypothesis, a mere starting point? A new world was being built. The human race was again starting from square one, and square one was the holocaust on Earth. And a new history – a new life – was beginning on Rigel IV.

Bekker leaned back in his chair rubbing his swollen eyes. He sighed. How few people were concerned about what had happened! *Dios mío, que solos se quedan los muertos . . .*[1]

The Traditologist smiled. Once again his famous quotes! Was he going crazy? Or, rather, had he not gone crazy yet? This delving into long-gone voices from time-frozen languages . . . was it some way to escape reality?

Reality was the brand-new Goohrk–Neoterran diplomatic relations and, more specifically, the Marthya–Lhoun romance. *Love one another*, he told himself sarcastically, remembering another one of his quotes. One another . . . Did that include the Rigelians too?

When the few survivors of the holocaust on Earth set foot on Rigel IV three centuries ago, they founded a colony called Neoterra where they tried to keep legacies from the old culture alive. But the struggle against adverse conditions was very arduous, and they soon had to direct all their efforts to basic survival of the flesh, whose needs were always more pressing than those of the spirit . . . And then there were the natives.

There were natives on Rigel IV, an old race that only wanted to be left alone. But the colonists raised their red flag with stars, built cities and erected power plants wherever it suited their interests without taking the resident race into account. And so the spark was struck and spread. Humans understood how much it would cost to try to change the name of a world. Goohrk was Goohrk . . . even though humanity insisted on calling it Rigel IV.

. . . Now they were beginning again, Bekker told himself. The armistice had finally been concluded on mutually agreeable terms, and peace reigned. That led to even more. Diplomatic relations between the two cultures were established.

And Lhoun, the Goohrk, the Rigelian, arrived from his distant Khoamm in the other hemisphere on Neoterra, the last holdout of Earth people after the conflict. Lhoun was lodged in the mansion of Julo, the governor. Julo was Marthya's father, and Marthya – blonde-haired, alas, and emerald-eyed – twenty years old, had fallen in love with the Rigelian. Marthya and Lhoun – eyes like

---

[1] My God, how lonely are the dead!

deep wells, antennae, marble-like skin – were going to get married. And Bekker had been in love with her (madly, desperately, he now realized) since way back when!

He trembled at the warm contact.

'Guess who!' every syllable sang and laughed.

The fingers covering his eyes were no use. How could he ever be in doubt!

'Marthya . . .'

The young woman came around in front of him. Her eyes sparkled at him. It was like looking at the Old Earth the chronicles spoke of, Bekker sadly marveled. Seas, red-tinted clouds and sunsets, snow, wheat . . .

'Dad's agreed!' the girl exclaimed. 'He said yes.'

'And why not? For a political coup, I assure you that it's wonderful! His own daughter . . . What better way to show friendship?'

A charming grimace spread across Marthya's face.

'Don't be like that, Mann. Dad likes him.'

'What about you?' Bekker bit his tongue.

'I adore him!'

Color appeared in Marthya's cheeks. Bekker gritted his teeth but did not say a thing.

'The engagement party's tonight. I came to invite you.'

The shadows of night had now crept into the room. The Traditologist's lean face could not be seen very well.

'I have a lot of work . . .' he replied.

'Mann!' the young woman scolded. 'Bookworm! Do you think more of these moth-eaten papers than you do of me?'

'Heavens, no!'

She must have noticed something in his voice because her smile faded.

'It's very dark in here,' she said after a while.

'I'll turn on the light.'

'No . . . no, wait, Mann. Don't go to the trouble for me. I'm on my way out. But just tell me if I'm going to see you at the party. You're coming, aren't you?'

'I can't. I'm sorry.'

In the semidarkness Marthya was a violet-colored platinum

profile. Bekker saw her getting closer and felt the warmth of her face when it got next to his.

'Pleeeaaase!'

'Marthya.'

The young woman moved away.

'What?'

'I wish you hadn't done that.'

'Mann . . .' a long silence ensued. 'Then you . . .'

'Yes.'

'For how . . . for how long, Mann?'

'I don't remember. It seems to be quite a while.'

'Oh, Mann . . .'

'Isn't that good for a lot of laughs?'

Bekker suddenly seemed to change. As he stood up, he knocked over a pile of books, and his fingers squeezed the woman's wrist.

'Don't marry him! For the sake of what you want most . . . don't!'

Marthya got out of his clutches with gentle firmness.

'*He*'s what I want most, Mann.'

'Think about what you're doing! Think about what he *is*!'

Her eyes dominated the darkness.

'Shut up! Don't ever say that again!'

'I —'

'I love him with all my heart, and he me. The difference in race doesn't matter. I know we love each other. Don't talk to me like that again!'

The Traditologist's shoulders sagged a little.

'As you wish . . . Always as you wish, Marthya.'

The girl pressed his hand between her warm and tender ones.

'Thanks, Mann.'

A frigid breeze rustled the foliage outside. Light from the three moons penetrated the transparent ceiling. Almost at the apex, an enormous white star sparkled.

'You coming to the party, Mann?'

It was as if glass needles were piercing his very soul.

'I'll be there,' he promised.

2

The vast hall in the gubernatorial palace glittered with the colorful abundance of clothes and colored-wax mosaics. Lights burned with glaring whiteness.

Mann Bekker had eyes only for Marthya, Marthya dressed in white, gold, pink, softly radiant in the midst of that unbearable brightness that hurt one's eyes. As only she could sparkle.

And then Bekker caught sight of the Rigelian.

Just like the majority of postwar Neoterrans, he had never had a chance to see a Goohrk up close. Lhoun had his back turned to the Traditologist, next to Marthya. To Bekker he seemed to be shorter than he had imagined. He was dressed in some indefinable color, dark and flaming at the same time. The nape of his neck was chalk-white, and his hair completely black. As to the rest, Bekker told himself with acrid irony, he was not all that different from a human. Each hand had five fingers, and he walked on two legs. There were no claws or tail, after all.

The Rigelian turned around at that instant, and Bekker had a hard time keeping himself from jumping. Not because of the sight of the two antennae sticking out from the sides of that very wide forehead; he was ready for them. What he could never have imagined was the true appearance of those eyes. A gaping abyss was clearly and cruelly reflected in them. Those eyes didn't *belong* to humanity. Period.

'Marthya . . .' Mann Bekker's whole being screamed.

Those alien eyes turned to the woman . . . and stopped there.

3

It was the next day when Mann Bekker observed it for the first time.

'How you doing, Mann?' Marthya greeted him as she came in and rustled the papers on the Traditologist's desk.

'Marthya. How are you?'

He said it as a matter of course. But those very words gnawed at his brain and gave rise to the idea, vague at first, but then increasingly definite (and sinister). How *was* she?

'I just wanted to thank you for coming to the party.'

Was he imagining it, or was she really quite pale?

'You keep it quite chilly in here, Mann . . .' she smiled, but crossed her arms across her chest and shivered.

'Chilly? But the heat's up to twenty,' Bekker explained.

She sat down, the ghost of a smile her apology.

'I must be coming down with something. I haven't been feeling well since last night.'

'Oh? Why?' He felt a freeze deep down inside.

'A weak spell, I think. It'll go away.'

The question that Bekker then asked was intended to distract the young woman. Or was it prompted – he thought much later – by some vague forewarning instinct?

'What about your wedding, Marthya?'

Her beaming smile slapped him right in the face.

'Soon, Mann . . . When Fomalhaut is in opposition to Gheera, in the fiftieth galaxy. Then Lhoun'll be able to get married.'

'Why's that?'

'Because of a dogma of his religion. Marriages are permitted only during those times. Still two months from now.'

Shadows once again invaded Mann Bekker's soul.

'Don't do it,' he pleaded again.

'Mann! You promised!'

'They're *different*, Marthya. As different from us as death from life. You don't know anything about them or any details about their race! Listen to me, Marthya. Don't –'

''Bye, Mann.'

'Marthya!'

The woman went out the door. Her silhouette soon became a distant dot way down the corridor leading to the palace.

Bekker sat motionless, watching her disappear from sight. His lips moved without his noticing it.

> . . . *the rare and radiant maiden whom the angels name Lenore*

4

'They're telepathic, if you like the term,' explained Professor Phoe. 'From what we gather, their antennae enable them to send and receive thoughts over distances that would be inconceivable to us. That's how they know the movements of stars in the remotest galaxies. By the same token, they apparently communicate with each other no matter where they are and without it mattering in the slightest how many kilometers separate them. But, fortunately, it's almost certain that they can't tune in on human minds nor are their powers –'

'What about their religion?' Mann Bekker interrupted. 'Their morals?'

The old man took another puff on his antique pipe.

'It's too hard to understand ... Too alien to any of our concepts. The undeniable thing is that the Great Representative, who could be compared, in a very broad sense, and only by way of illustration, with the Pope of Old Earth, knows everything about the Goohrks thanks to his extrasensory powers. So that when one of them does something the Great Representative considers sinful, he knows it right away and metes out punishment, a type of punishment that we don't understand but that they seem to dread ...'

'I heard something about weddings,' Bekker inquired.

'Oh! The periods of Gheera–Fomalhaut opposition. Yeah. One of the most sacred dogmas of their religion ... one of the most sacrilegious sins if disobeyed.'

'What I'd like to know ...' Bekker squirmed uncomfortably in the fiber chair, trying to avoid facing the exologist's watering eyes. 'What I'd like to know is something more specific about their relationships or ... sexual practices.'

The old man blinked. He inhaled a mouthful of smoke and said through it:

'From what I have personally been able to verify, their habits are no different from ours, nor their physiology. It seems that evolution has followed a parallel path on this issue. That's why, I daresay, marriage is possible between the two races. But let me clarify that. I was speaking only from a strictly physical and sexual perspective. As far as their souls, their minds . . .' his gray head moved from side to side.

'And . . . hum . . . how about their attitudes, premarital sex . . . I mean, what rules do they follow?'

Professor Phoe bent over toward Bekker.

'That's a particularly interesting subject,' he replied. 'Their moral code is strict to the point of prohibiting the slightest physical contact between couples outside marriage. Which, in order to be valid, must be performed in periods of stellar opposition and must be blessed by the Great Representative.' The exologist placed his pipe on the table with extreme care and leaned back in the stuffed chair. His eyes stared up at the roof. 'And Rigelians are by nature so impetuous and passionate that they expend truly huge amounts of energy on self-control. I believe they can endure it only because of the sustained power of their incredible intellect.'

Then, Bekker told himself, Marthya and Lhoun . . . He has not even touched her. I'll have to be content with that; however, I feel worse than before.

Those pupils. Those bottomless pupils.

5

During the next two weeks Bekker deliberately became a workaholic to take his mind off things. He sank into a dead sea of papers and stirred into the muddy bottom in search of more questions.

And at the end of this period, he got a call.

'Bekker speaking,' he answered the phone. 'What? Marthya? Is it . . . serious? I'll be right over. Thanks for calling, Governor. I hope it's nothing to be concerned about. See you soon, sir.'

He quickly got dressed, worry plainly written on his face.

Marthya, he thought in anguish, Marthya . . .

He left his sanctum and, most unusually for him, forgot to lock up. While the moving sidewalk carried him to the mansion down one of the endless plastaluminum corridors connecting different sections of the domed city, he was constantly assailed by thoughts of a worst-case scenario.

No, no, I am exaggerating. Nothing has happened. Some un-important illness, that is all.

But when he got a look at her, he pleaded for the young woman not to notice his paleness. Good God! An ominous voice told him it was what he was afraid of . . . even if he did not know for sure what it was he was afraid of.

Marthya was lying in her bed, her cheeks as white as the sheets. Her hair was loose, her eyes very green and much bigger, or at least they seemed so to Bekker.

'Mann . . . I'm so happy to see you!' He squeezed the small hand she reached out.

God, he said to himself, while trying to smile, my God. Her life is being drained away in some strange fashion. I can't even feel the weight of her hand!

'This bout of sickness keeps me feeling tired,' she smiled. 'I've been bedridden for more than ten days. It's not so bad when my dear father keeps me company so that I don't get bored.'

'You'll get over it, Marthya. In no time at all you'll even be stronger than this . . . how did you put it? . . . bookworm.'

She laughed.

'Don't be silly, Mann! You know I didn't mean it! . . . Oh, by the way, didn't you see who's here? Come over here, my love . . .'

No, Bekker pleaded inside, not *that*.

But the Rigelian was there in a corner of the room, and now he was coming over, dominating them with his eyes of unfathomable fires in a chalk-white face, his hand extended to the one Marthya was holding out.

'How goes it, Mr Bekker?' he greeted him in very correct Neo-terran; but the roaring in the Traditologist's ears drowned out the sounds.

Bekker replied even though he could not hear his own voice.

When he got to the edge of the bed, the Rigelian did something strange. With visible effort (at least, it did not escape Bekker's notice), he stopped to cover his right hand with a fine lace glove. Then he squeezed his fiancée's pale fingers, and Bekker saw the black fire in his cavernous eyes blaze up.

And at that same instant a little of Marthya's life slipped away.

6

Seven days later, Bekker's long legs paced his cubicle.

Marthya had been visibly sinking, and he knew why. It was time he admitted it.

'It's fantastic, impossible, crazy . . .'

But he knew he was right. What could be weirder and more unusual than that extraordinary race, those eyes with jet-black fires in their depths?

'God, God, *God!*'

He looked through the roof. Stars twinkled far in the distance, seemingly unchangeable. But Bekker knew that somewhere in that infinite sky two luminous points were moving and would soon be in opposition.

'Fomalhaut, Gheera . . .'

But in the meantime . . . Meantime, Marthya and Lhoun would not be able to wed. And Bekker remembered the increasingly intense black fire.

'It's the force of his desire that's killing her. It's his dreadful mind that's . . . *eating her up.*'

And saying it out loud made him feel better. It broke the remaining restraints on his rationality.

He was not mistaken. Now he had to think about a solution.

7

He ignored the moving sidewalk. He was not in the mood for it.

His plastic footwear slapped against the metal floor in measured rhythm, his swinging arms stirred up the air in the passageway.

Already inside the gubernatorial mansion, for an instant Bekker doubted the appropriateness of trying to talk to the governor first. He gave up the idea, however, because he knew Julo's remarkable political astuteness. 'Are you out of your mind? What about interracial and intercultural relations? Have you considered the catastrophe you could cause? We're walking a tightrope, boy, and you . . . On the other hand' (and the governor's solid practical sense would take over), 'what you're suggesting is absurd . . . I think all the reading you've been doing has rattled your brain, Bekker.'

Walking with greater speed, Bekker could not help wondering to what point he really was crazy. Because one single eternity was spelled out for him – Marthya. Everything else – including international or intercultural politics – was nothing but confused eventualities with no meaning at all.

He managed to get in to see the Goohrk envoy. He was conscious of his livid color and the shakiness of his legs, but he hoped nobody else noticed.

After exchanging the ritual phrases, alone with the Rigelian, he spoke calmly, getting directly to the point.

'Marthya's dying,' he stated in a hard tone of voice, 'and I know the reason why.'

Lhoun's wide forehead went up. A dull and gloomy light flickered in his cavernous eyes.

'It's true,' he murmured painfully, 'but I can do nothing.'

Mann Bekker felt cold sweat on his temples.

'I thought so. Nor would it serve any purpose for you to go away, would it?'

The Goohrk shook his chalk-white head.

'Distance doesn't exist for our minds.'

'Your desire . . .' Bekker hinted, knowing he had lost beforehand.

'Once kindled can't be put out. There's no stopping it. You people don't understand.'

Mann Bekker played his last card, walking carefully, as though on hot coals:

'If you . . . if you satisfied your desire . . . If before the date . . . Marthya and you –'

Lhoun's face took on a grayish pale-looking cast.

'You have no idea what that would mean! You people will never be able to comprehend the horrible and unforgivable sacrilege that would involve.'

Bekker felt his muscles stiffening up. He thought part of him was made of ice and stone.

'You're mistaken,' he replied. 'I do understand.'

Something in his voice must have tipped off the Rigelian. His terrible eyes gazed right into the Traditologist's, reading what was inside him, stopping time for Bekker. It was an infinitesimal fraction of eternity, but in those few microseconds Bekker's whole life, his past ideals, the dead history he was trying to resurrect, and Marthya, Marthya, all ran through his mind. The memory of the woman blotted out all the rest and controlled his fingers, muscles and will, but he could not drown out the little voice crouching in a dark corner of his mind, shouting a desperate alarm. Something's wrong! There's a detail you didn't take into account! There's an error somewhere! But to get thoroughly familiar with the meaning of this warning, to discover what it was signalling, to consider the error, mental processes had to be gone through – reflection, reasoning – and for the Traditologist, the time for reasoning was already over.

His hand dipped into his pocket and came back out.

A crack, a violet flash, and the Goohrk collapsed.

But he could still mumble through the green blood he was vomiting:

'MARTHYA!'

And in the uncontained vehemence of the strange accent Mann Bekker could read his own sentence.

(Julo, Governor of Neoterra, soon felt a sensation of unexplainable cold. When searching for the cause, he found it in the bloodless hand his fingers were holding. He looked to the bed, the growing throbbing of his heart suffocating him.

He screamed. He screamed. He screamed.)

They all burst in en masse.

Lhoun, the Goohrk diplomat, lay in a blackish pool, his extraordinary eyes wide-open, staring, stony.

Someone was standing beside him. His shoulders drooped; his arms hung limply, an antique pistol dangling in one hand. His back would never again straighten up.

'I was wrong,' he repeated in a whisper, 'I was wrong. The last thought . . . There was more power and ardent desire in that one last memory than anyone could conceive of in a lifetime . . . I was wrong.'

(In Marthya's room, edges of bone could be seen through a thin veneer of wasted flesh covering the body lying between the sheets. The denuded skull reflected the sheen of death, and the lips sank into the empty mouth cavity. It smelled old, of death and of long-lost hopes.)

The Traditologist's lips kept moving, but the others had to get closer to hear what he was saying. He kept repeating:

> And the only word there spoken was the whispered word,
>   'Lenore!'
> This I whispered, and an echo murmured back the word
>   'Lenore!'
>   Merely this and nothing more.

Quo Vadis, Francisco?

LINO ALDANI

He called her for a long time and then, when he didn't get any answer, he understood that she had run away, as all the others had done before her.

But this time Father Francisco didn't want to resign himself, and he looked for her everywhere, in the thicket, behind the church, within all the village's huts, asking everybody about her whereabouts with an angry and booming voice.

Geron's men listened to him impassively, a few of them shook their heads apathetically while others got to the point of turning their backs on him. At least twice an old native pointed towards the swamps with his finger.

Father Francisco let his arms fall down by his sides, feeling depressed.

He was a decrepit old man by now, and would have never been able to muster the necessary strength to go and search for the female so far from the village and then carry her back. He had really got into a fine mess. And now he absolutely had to find another female or all his work would have been for nothing. And he had to act in a hurry: at noon – the holy hour for Geron's people – he had to celebrate the divine service before the whole community.

With his head lowered, he crossed the village again and went back to the church. It was a hut just like all the others, but it was considerably bigger, with walls and ceiling made of dried mud. It was a simple enough building and it lacked almost completely any embellishment or decoration. But immediately under the roof, at the bottom and along the sides, there were some small wine and emerald coloured stained-glass windows. Through those windows the sunlight flooded the interior of the church like a most delicate foam which rolled up to the altar with almost musical tonalities.

Father Francisco went towards the altar, where a small, stout figure was intent on arranging the sacred ornaments and flower garlands.

'Eusebio,' called the priest in an extremely calm voice, trying to conceal his embarrassment. The figure didn't turn around and went on arranging the garlands with zeal. Father Francisco came near him, stopping when he was very close to him.

'I'm sure you know as I do that Maria has run away ... I treated her in the best possible way, but it has been useless. And now here I am, alone again.'

The Geronian stopped busying himself with the ornaments and this time he turned around, a regretful expression on his face. His big eyes, so yellow they looked like golden medals, gazed at the priest's eyes with dismay.

'You mean there will be no sung Mass?'

'Oh, no,' Father Francisco vigorously reassured him. 'We will have the Mass. I promise you, Eusebio.'

That was what he called the native: Eusebio. During the three years he had spent on that planet he had already baptized a few hundred natives. But Eusebio was his favourite one, and always followed him like a shadow, helping him whenever he needed it, even serving at Mass. With a sort of candid optimism, the priest had more than once pondered the idea that one day Eusebio could take his place. There was no doubt that Eusebio was clever, the cleverest of them all, and also the most docile among all the converts.

But now his eyes and his voice were betraying a little aggressiveness.

'The Father knows very well he can't stay without a female, because it would be a shame for him. The Father must go and take Maria back or he must take another female, but it must be soon, because otherwise none of us will be ever able to look at him ...'

The priest sighed, then he stretched out one hand and lightly caressed that clumsy, rounded head, so human and so alien at the same time.

'Yes, Eusebio. I will do what is necessary.'

'Will you really go to take Maria back? Will you show to everybody you are really a man?'

'Yes, I will go. Perhaps I will go, but later. Now there is too little time left, and we have to get everything ready for the service.' Then the priest left Eusebio alone, in order not to have to hear his comments.

Behind the altar there was a narrow and small door which led into the sacristy, a modest room with a few crude furnishings where Father Francisco spent all his nights while dubiously pondering the contents of his few books or giving himself completely up to desperate prayer.

This time as well, as soon as he was alone in the sacristy, the priest let himself collapse on the rudimentary *prie-dieu* and stayed thus for a long time, his body shaken by unrestrained sobs. When he got up he was covered with sweat. He opened his frock and suddenly prolonged and chilly shivers started running along his whole body. He was also seized by nausea and by dizziness, two symptoms of abstinence he knew only too well. Then, moving like a sleep-walker, he went towards a cabinet, opened it and took out a baked-clay jug.

He noticed with anguish that the jug was almost empty. There was no time to go and pick up some more kibu-nagùa in order to get some more infusion. There was, however, another way to obtain immediately the vital energy and the courage, the strength and the clearness of mind he needed: he urinated into the jug and then, doing violence to himself, he gulped it down.

The effect wrought by the drug he had taken the day before bounded back within his veins with redoubled strength. It would last an hour or two, just long enough to face the crowd which was already gathering itself before the church, long enough to celebrate the great sung Mass and to baptize the new converts. Later on he would go to the bramble-bush behind the church and there he would take his clothes off and would mortify his flesh by throwing himself, naked, into the most thorny bush. But at that moment the kibu-nagùa was the best thing, or at least it was the means which gave him the strength he needed in order to lavish good works with full hands, which was to give faith and salvation of the soul.

His Eminence would surely not have approved of his doings. The Eminences never did approve of anything, they lived in worlds stuffed with wadding, surrounded by peaceful heaps of paper and they knew nothing of what happened on the lost planets of an only partially explored Galaxy. The Eminences knew nothing of Geron, they knew only by hearsay that Geron was an old age planet, they knew that a year of life on that planet was the equivalent of nine years of one's life for those who were not natives of Geron, so that there one's life consumed itself in a moment. It was a planet everybody avoided as if it were a sort of plague. He, an obscure priest who was carrying on his shoulders years upon years of hardships on half a dozen planets, was the only one who had accepted to end his days on this space Gehenna. And he was the only one who, out of his love for the other beings, had accepted to lose himself, even in God's eyes.

The subject of his perdition had been mentioned more than once within a long letter, full of erasures and rewritings, which he had addressed to the Cardinal. This was a message which would never reach its destination, for the simple reason that it would never be able to leave that planet. Father Francisco, however, had been writing it for a long time, perhaps moved by the remote possibility . . . it would have to be a real miracle . . . that on a very distant day somebody might again land on Geron. In the letter Father Francisco confessed he was constantly in a condition of deadly sin and he made a careful list of all the faults he had been guilty of, the omissions, the heresies he had run into, all his soul's darkenings and all his crimes. And there was also a crude attempt at self-defence, a sad request that he could be justified by virtue of those extremely sublime ends toward which all his actions were aimed. But it was just in those periods that the letter seemed to him devoid of strength, paradoxical and ridiculous.

'. . . Only five days had passed since I had arrived on Geron and installed myself with a numerous community of natives, when a big emergency starship landed on the planet in order to embark and bring to safety all the Base's personnel. The tunnel which crossed the hyperspace and connected Geron with the Solar

System's environs was irreversibly contracting. Within a few hours' time it would close up completely, isolating, perhaps forever, this planet from the rest of the Galaxy.

'I stunned the official who had come to take me away and then I ran away to the marsh area, concealing myself there till the starship had left the planet. I had made my choice, because of an obscene bet with myself and because of my inordinate pride, perhaps because in that moment I was longing for the utmost and most unrestrained loneliness.

'At that point the natives, up to then uninterested, came towards me with real hostile intent. They attacked me, compelling me to protect myself; I gave a strong cuff to one of them, the one who was almost overwhelming me. At that time I didn't know how fragile their bones were. The native fell down with his neck broken and the others ran away, screaming.

'The day after that they again came towards me, but this time they behaved in a fearful and respectful way: the fact that I had killed one of them was all they needed to consider me as an exceptional being who deserved everybody's respect.

'They offered me their friendship, on condition, however, that I should take to me one of their women: the mate of the fellow I had killed. They were extremely uncompromising on that point. What else could I have done? If I had not bent myself to their condition my mission would have failed from the very beginning. On the other hand, according to the rigid customs of this people which is mostly composed of males, since they are born in exceedingly high numbers, any person who for any cause is not able to create a family, is exiled from the community and put in such a condition that he can't survive for long. Therefore, I had to accept the hairy creature, little more than a metre high, they were entrusting me with, and, after many days and nights of shame and humiliating efforts, getting drunk with the drug in order to find the strength to break my vows and to overcome my natural aversion, I succeeded at last in showing her my manliness. Because that was what they wanted from me.

'As a matter of fact, after some time had gone by, I was able to gather some materials from the abandoned base and, with everyone's help, I could finish the church's construction. The conversions began quite soon after. One day, however, my mate ran away with a young male of the tribe, undoubtedly finding him more to her taste than I was. Clearly, this wouldn't have worried me if I hadn't noticed at the same time that all my believers had started leaving me.

'Eusebio, the only native who stayed with me after that unpleasant incident, spoke for them all: my shaky prestige was actually suspended in a kind of limbo until I had gone to the woman and brought her back.

'At this point I beg His Eminence to allow me to spare him a detailed report of all my vicissitudes. I was not able to find that woman, as she had probably run off to some other tribe in the neighbourhood; I was therefore compelled to stain myself with an awful crime in order to get another woman. After a short time, this second woman went and drowned herself in the marshes rather than remain with me. A third one ran away as the first had done, and so did a fourth, and many others after her. Now I'm exhausted, I am forty-three years old but it is as if I were seventy from a physiological point of view. My mind is tottering as well, and I must more and more often resort to the kibu-nagùa, the drug which allows me to recover in a surprising but illusory way.

'My faith is more unsullied than ever, since the results I have obtained are more than encouraging, but the practice is an accumulation of contradictions. I am convinced, however, that it is necessary to act gradually, as any impatience from our side would produce negative and upsetting effects. I dare to think that when our ends are noble and holy, our moral code's intransigence must be set aside . . .'

At this point the letter to the Cardinal broke off. To tell the truth, Father Francisco did not know how to end it, and shifty questions came to him from the depths of his soul while he turned the pages over in his hands and read some paragraphs over and over again, at most adding or erasing a comma here and there.

In his heart, as if it were a new Garden of Gethsemane, roved ghosts and night-birds' screeches. A hissing voice kept repeating with wicked irony: 'Quo vadis, Francisco? Quo vadis, Francisco?'

But outside the church, in the sunlight, was a crowd of warm and hairy creatures who were waiting for a sign, for his burning words which would have dispelled any remaining phantasm.

A soft but unfinished fragment of music was waiting for a triumphal final chord to conclude it. And that wonderful blare was ready to spring from his breast like an apotheosis of triumph against all evil forces. These were the exaltations the kibu-nagùa provoked, and it could rouse even more intense and disturbing ones. When Eusebio knocked at the sacristy door and came in with his nimble and soft walk, however, Father Francisco lay face down on his desk, his eyes wide open and blank and his hands shaking.

'Were you still writing?' asked the Geronian.

The priest shook himself and took up the loose sheets of paper on his desk of braided reeds, then he said:

'I will probably never end this letter. If somebody comes here to look for me after my death, however, you must give him this letter and thus it will bear witness for me . . .'

He looked through the small eastern window, estimated the light's intensity and realized the sun had almost reached its zenith. Almost as if he had been reading his thoughts, Eusebio nodded in assent.

'Father, we must go.'

Father Francisco staggered to his feet. It seemed that the drug's effect had inexplicably vanished, and now a subtle anguish was slowly taking hold of him, He looked around him, feeling as unsure as a child, and he instinctively sought Eusebio's support.

'I've done good work here, haven't I?'

The Geronian looked at him without speaking: he was not always able to immediately understand the Father's words.

'I mean the work I have done here, my mission,' explained Father Francisco. 'When I came there was nothing here to be seen . . .'

'And now there is the church.'

'Not only that, Eusebio.'

'And what else, then?'

'You, for example. You see, when I first brought you here, you were just like a small animal, a little useless thing, and now you have discovered an immortal soul within your being.'

'It's time,' Eusebio reminded him, and nodded docilely. 'We must go.'

'One day you will be the one who will carry on my work' Father Francisco added in a solemn voice.

Eusebio nodded a third time and repeated again:

'Father, we must go.'

Father Francisco took him by the hand, a hand as small and frail as a child's. And so, with that brown creature hopping by his side, he went out into the sunlit church square, where the crowd was waiting for him.

When he saw all those flat and inexpressive faces, so perfectly alike that he would never be able to distinguish one from another, with those so intensely yellow and so perfectly rounded eyes which were devoid of eyelids and were fixed on him, the priest hesitated almost to the point of turning and going back.

He had converted almost all of them, and he had baptized them with those Christian names which were most familiar to him: Augustin, Cayetano, Vicente, Monica, Pablito ... Because they were humans, there was no doubt at all about it. Or, at least, it was no use splitting hairs, cavilling about abstruse roundabout expressions, about the deep subtleties of theology. The man who has already started to ford a river must look ahead; he cannot allow himself any doubt or change of mind. These creatures were human, then, and they were really converted, in spite of their inconsistent behaviour and of the powerful call of the tribal laws they had never denied. Was it not enough that the church was full every day of the week? That the natives who received the sacraments were becoming more and more numerous each day? That when he questioned them they always answered to the point and were always innocently disposed to accept everything he preached to them?

And yet the only one of them he trusted fully was Eusebio. As for the others, he was not sure he had touched them deeply, and a long and patient wait would be necessary before the seed he had planted could be seen to be growing.

A Geronian – Gabriel? Ignacio? – came out of the crowd and drew near the priest, then he knelt, awkwardly crossed himself and said, all in one breath:

'The Father has been left alone once more. The Father needs a woman by his side. He will surely not want to remain alone, the Father. We would all be very sorry for him.'

The native then went back to the crowd and another one detached himself from it – perhaps he was Rafael, or perhaps Esteban or Fulgencio – and said more or less the same thing, speaking with the same unvarying and singsong tone. It would have gone on this way for a long while had Eusebio not freed himself with a gesture of impatience from Father Francisco's hand and leant forward towards the crowd, shouting:

'Enough! The Father has promised he will do what he must do before the ceremony begins.'

A murmur of approval ran through the crowd, and then a heavy silence surrounded the sunlit clearing where the Geronians were gathered and waiting. Father Francisco shivered. Because he knew that crowd was not waiting for his words but for the repetition of an absurd and bloody ritual.

He had to make up his mind, and he had to do that immediately. He had to go down among them and to point out a woman, any one of them, and then ... then he would have to fight the man who opposed his choice. And he would have to kill him, that was unavoidable, as had already happened on the other occasions, too many of them, since he had landed on Geron. Afterwards, they would come into the church, as ready as a flock looking for its fold, and Father Francisco would sit at the small electronic organ and accompany the chorus of boys Eusebio had personally instructed. It was just a mewling, a mumbled parody of a real chorus, but perhaps exactly for this reason it was even more moving and it awakened mysterious affections in him. And then there would be the Mass, followed by the Christening of almost two hundred novices, those novices whose conversion had cost him great effort and heartache.

Then the tightly-pressed crowd suddenly seemed to start. In the back where its mass was less thick, something was proceeding like a wedge, forcing its way through the crowd and advancing towards the church. At first, Father Francisco didn't realize what it was, because his weakened sight and the sun's rays did not allow him to focus on the image. Then, in the middle of a group of three males who were dragging her by means of the liane which bound her hands, he saw the female, recognizable by her lighter hair.

He understood then that the female was Maria.

Squeezing through the crowd, the group arrived at the church square and Maria was roughly thrown ahead, and fell with her face in the dust.

'We have brought her back for you,' said the man who still held the free end of the liane. 'There is no need today for you to take a new woman . . .'

Father Francisco assented with a nod. Relieved, he turned toward Eusebio, almost as if he were going to ask him for a corroboration and seek his advice, but his pupil was no more by his side.

He bent to Maria and freed her from her bonds.

'Get inside,' he told her, in the hardest voice he was able to muster. 'I'll think about the right punishment for you.'

And then Maria turned on him like a snake.

'I won't come back with you,' she screamed with rage. 'I won't come back, because you are not a true man.'

After all, he had expected to hear such words, and he did not feel he had been insulted. Out there, however, before all these people, he had to react.

'And who is the one, here among us, that you deem to be a true man?' he replied, with an ample sweep of his hand, to salve his injured dignity.

Now the guilty man would have to come out of the crowd and face him, even if the outcome of the impending fight was decided before it began. They could not beat him and they knew it. Probably they would not have been able to overcome him even if they had attacked him all together. All the same, all he had to do was to hint at the possibility of issuing a challenge and it was immediately accepted; they came foolishly forward, as if they didn't attach any importance to the certainty of their impending death.

Maria did not say a word, however, and nobody came out of the crowd: perhaps the woman had run away because she did not like him, or she had got tired of him, and not because she had been seduced by somebody else. Or it might be that a flirtation had actually taken place but the seducer had not wanted or been able to run away with her.

Father Francisco slipped off his frock, whirled it a couple of times around his head and then flung it down.

'If there is somebody who claims this woman, he must come forward,' he insisted. 'I'm ready.'

The crowd seemed to ferment, erupting in shouts and muffled exclamations, but nobody came toward him.

'Father!' Eusebio's voice rang behind him.

Father Francisco did not turn towards him, and went on staring at the crowd almost as if he were trying to tame it with his eyes' strength.

'It seems there is nobody ready to fight,' he shouted at the top of his lungs, 'because I have called him clearly and he hasn't come . . .'

'Father . . .' Eusebio called again, this time with a sorrowful voice.

'Wait for me in the church,' the priest answered him absent-mindedly, barely turning his head toward him. 'In fact, let's all go into the church. There is no point waiting for somebody who will not come.'

But Eusebio did not move from there, nor did anybody else among the crowd. And Maria, who was still crouching down on the church steps, also seemed to be waiting for something. Father Francisco shrugged his shoulders and went to pick up his frock. A small, light hand touched his forearm.

'No, Father,' Eusebio said once more.

And then Father Francisco saw him and understood. He saw the knife shining in the sun and Maria's eyes anxiously fixed on Eusebio and the crowd which was already looking forward to the fight. And he understood as well that this time he could not fight, that everything was of no use and that it was all the same and he might as well put an end to it.

He didn't even try to defend himself. He could have easily broken his opponent's arms and legs, which were so brittle, and then left him there to die in the sun, as the rule prescribed.

'Quo vadis, Francisco?' that voice from his dreams and nightmares cried again in his heart. He opened his arms and sacrificed himself, in body and in soul.

Eusebio stabbed him once, twice, and then he stabbed again the fallen body, but without hate, just as if he were doing any thing else, like decorating the altar or crossing himself or sleeping with Maria.

Immediately afterwards, with the help of the knife and his nails, Eusebio tore Father Francisco's frock from him, more or less from the waist. Quickly, the Geronian dressed himself in it.

And then, since it was already late, everybody followed Eusebio and went into the church for the service.

Forward, Mankind!

LYUBEN DILOV

Now that we are already on our first flying mission in this war, from which I don't know if we shall return, although our task is not to engage with the enemy, but to reconnoitre his positions and his military strength, I can give a short account of the events leading up to the conflict; the real chronicle of this war will be written by others. If, of course, it takes place, or if any one capable of writing at all is left alive at the end. Incidentally, history shows that the actual causes of wars are usually hidden behind an insignificant pretext, while in this case the pretext can most certainly not be called insignificant. And this is the fundamental difference in our holy and just campaign and the former wars on Earth.

It first began in the small town of Nimma, where the eminent professor Zimmering had a psychiatric clinic. How it all actually happened is a mystery, but in any case, when night had withdrawn from this hemisphere, all the wards in the clinic proved to be empty. Not a single patient was left, not even those who had spent the night in strait-jackets. There must have been an indescribable panic among the staff on duty. The reports in the newspapers of that date give some indication as to what happened. The degree of panic was no less in Nimma itself – 250 maniacs let loose in such a small town is a horrifying figure. Fortunately, most of the inhabitants knew one another, if not by name, at least by sight, so that the suspicious stares, to make sure that people weren't madmen in disguise, did not last long. But the police did not succeed in discovering a single one of them, while the police dogs only managed to trace them to the middle of the large lawn in the clinic's park, where the poor beasts began to run around in circles as if they had taken leave of their senses, howling out of sheer frustration and helplessness. On the tenth day, the doctor who had been on duty that fatal night committed suicide, and the head of the clinic, Professor Zimmering, the greatest living exponent of the Viennese school of psychiatry, went mad and was sent to the clinic of Professor Otara, his sworn professional enemy. A week later, however, Professor Otara's clinic was also found empty at dawn. Another 186 mentally deranged persons, most of them dangerous maniacs, it was said, had disappeared. Among them was old Professor Zimmering.

Otara informed a press conference that, to his mind, Zimmering was at the back of the whole business. After organizing the escape of his own patients, Zimmering had made his way into his, Professor Otara's clinic, to kidnap his patients, too. However, when the journalists asked him how he, an experienced psychiatrist, had failed to see that Zimmering was only simulating madness, Otara very skilfully avoided answering their question: in such cases, he said, a diagnosis could not be made within a few days, and besides, there were many types of schizophrenia in which patients developed unusual resourcefulness and were able to carry out their mad intentions with congenital logic and coolness.

Three days after his statement the patients of five more lunatic asylums vanished, and in quite different parts of the country at that. Public opinion set up a cry: How was it possible for not just one or two people, but for as many as 854, all with abnormal behaviour patterns, to disappear, and for the police to be incapable of discovering a single one of them? The most reasonable explanation was that the police themselves were involved in this mysterious affair, so their chief resigned. But this did nothing to change the course of events.

At first the opposition was cautious; they merely asked in their papers: 'Is a state, which has proved unable to confine its madmen, able to look after its normal citizens?' And they demanded the government's resignation. No government, of course, is insane enough to resign because of opposition demands, but when the eighteenth insane asylum was found empty one morning, despite having been surrounded by about a dozen guards, armed to the teeth, the government's position became untenable. And the old president appeared on television. He looked tired, I should even say, crushed. 'I don't know what is happening in this country . . .' he began, and such an admission coming from its president deeply touched his public. He then appealed to the citizens to remain calm, to have faith in him, and first accused the enemy camp of having certainly dragged away our cherished psychiatric patients for a purpose not as yet clear. But the real fault, according to him, lay with the feeble democratic opposition which made it possible for such things to happen. He shouted so furiously against democracy, calling it a form incapable of governing a contemporary society, that one of his councillors out of the camera's view appeared to have found it necessary to give him a dig in the ribs. The president began to stammer, wiped the sweat from his furrowed brow with an innocently white handkerchief and declared, quite brokenly, that for the present he could see no other solution than to proclaim martial law.

On the following morning, the newspapers, which commented on his speech, were still divided in their opinions. Some suggested an enemy had a hand in the business; others put forward the suggestion that the madmen in the country had been destroyed by adherents of the view that incurable patients were a superfluous burden on society and should simply be exterminated. The satirical paper even dared to put forward the proposal that an import centre for madmen be created, so that the empty clinics might be filled again. The opposition paper was asking questions again. Why, it asked, should those who, at worst, are only capable of breaking the furniture in a room, be the ones to vanish? Why not those madmen who were thrusting our people along the road to disaster? However, martial law had already been proclaimed and such questions were not forgiven. The newspaper was suspended, and its editors were arrested for inciting further kidnappings of the mentally diseased.

In the interest of truth it should be said that the government was making serious efforts to solve this mystery. It filled two psychiatric clinics with out-patients, placed agents who simulated mania among them, but the patients who, until then, had meekly stayed at home, disappeared in spite of the strong guard, while the agents remained, without having felt the slightest thing. That night they had slept deeply, together with the whole guard surrounding the clinic. Rumour, of course, distorted this move of the government's and turned it into a planned collecting of the harmless insane from their homes with a view to exterminating them. Young radicals broke the windows of government offices, blood was shed, and all those who had relatives who were not quite all there, hid them. However, in spite of the fact that the press was by now censored, and gave no information on the matter, panic gradually spread to the entire population, even to those who had never until then given a thought to the fact that there were mentally sick people in the world, and were terribly surprised at the actual number of existing psychiatric clinics; because a society in which such arbitrary actions were possible could not offer any guarantees that you, too, would not be proclaimed a madman tomorrow, and would not disappear into a furnace or to the bottom of the ocean – those were some of the rumours which also went around.

The government turned to Interpol, although this seriously damaged its prestige, but, having been unable to discover the slightest trace of the madmen, the supposition naturally came to the fore that they had been taken out of the country. The advertisements, which Interpol sent all over the world, were more than unusual for this honourable and experienced organization – photo, name, height, complexion, hair, eyes, introduces himself as a Chinaman although he is white, or suffers from the mania that he is a giraffe and stretches his neck out all the time to look down on people from above; or howls like a wolf on meeting other people. The world laughed, and the government began to prepare for war with the neighbouring country. It had decided that at this moment only a war would avert a revolution. Nevertheless, in order to give its decision a democratic appearance, it summoned Parliament, which was in recess, to an extraordinary session. However, leaflets appeared on the streets of the capital, and the police and the government received anonymous letters, telling them that the madmen in Parliament would be carried off on an appointed day. 'It's no use taking any kind of measures,' the leaflets and letters announced. 'In any case it will happen as it has so far without your feeling it!' The army and the police surrounded the whole Parliament with barbed wire and tanks, but not a single member appeared at the session. Some of them had announced that they had suddenly fallen ill; others had to leave on urgent business. And although the author of this practical joke, which had such an amazing effect, was caught at once, the war did not take place. While the government was trying to find a way of taking up the matter anew, reconnaissance agents reported that in the country which was to have been attacked the madmen had already disappeared from the clinics, but that the government, having learned from the experience of its neighbours, had succeeded in keeping the secret of this event from their people for a longer time. The president, who had been faced with the choice of either resigning or going to war, was thus able to appear on television again and to announce with relief, that the same misfortune had also befallen the enemy country. Only a few days later he imposed martial law. Announcements came from all over the country that psychiatric clinics everywhere had been emptied in the same mysterious fashion.

Never in its history had mankind been so deeply shaken. Confusion swiftly grew into a mystic fear of this inexplicable phenomenon which was threatening quite soon to become general madness. Various philosophers, journalists and politicians did much to aggravate this mood and so did ill-advised actions by certain governments. In some places they set the patients of insane asylums free and sent them back to their homes. The madmen did not vanish, like their fellows, but began to do damage again. They were taken back to the asylums once more, and soon afterwards they, too, vanished into thin air. Gheron, the patriarch of philosophers, reasoned in a profound article, reprinted in the world press: 'If all abnormal people disappeared in this way from the world, what, then, would be the criterion of normality?' On the other hand, the Church, which had thirsted for such a miracle for thousands of years, hysterically called from its pulpits: 'Repent, ye sinners! Return to the bosom of the Lord! This is only a prelude to the new Sodom and Gomorrah, the Lord is taking unto him the pure and the innocent, to wreak His destructive wrath afterwards on the sinners!'

A work by Minos Papazyan, the outstanding fantasist and writer, added greatly to the panic. Very thoughtlessly, guided by purely literary speculation, he had not announced in the subtitle that his story was a fantastic invention, but had given it a 'documentary' character, relating it on behalf of a man who had been erroneously carried off with the insane and had then been brought back. Papazyan elaborated what was actually a very banal theme in popular science fiction, according to which man did not appear on Earth by evolutionary ways, but had been 'sown' in the form of proprogrammed cells by a supreme civilization. Now, at a programmed time, it was simply carrying out a gigantic experiment, by collecting those individuals who had deviated from the programme, in order to study to what the deviation was due. That is, something like a weeding process, like the spring clearance of weeds from gardens, was in progress.

Of course, it was not only Papazyan's literary trick which contributed to the panic. People almost lost their minds in the psychological situation already created when they read and commented to one another about this *Terrible Document*. When alone, they would ask themselves, not without good grounds: 'Will they weed me out? I think I'm normal, but what do those who programmed me think?'

However, this not particularly clever work, as usually happens in literature, did something useful besides making mischief. It turned people's attention to seeking an explanation of this extraordinary mystery in extraplanetary terms. Thus, the letter, which every government had received, but to which no one until then had paid any attention among the piles of anonymous jokes and malicious blackmail, was finally discovered. It will be quoted almost in full, because it was precisely this letter which caused the revolutionary turning point in the history of mankind which now faces us.

Written on an earthly electric typewriter, it said that its senders, a large group of representatives of another civilization, had for a long time been studying life on Earth in secret. In order to do this many members of the expedition took on the appearance of earthly beings, but were often caught and shut up in those dreadful homes which we call insane asylums. They there became convinced that, for inexplicable reasons, mankind behaved very badly to a large number of its members. These people were considered as abnormal, as superfluous and as a burden. That was why the expedition decided that it could take it upon itself to do something which could not be considered aggression or interference in earthly matters: to transport those, who were considered a superfluous burden, to another planet, where favourable living conditions would be created for them, and they would thus be freed from this unjustifiable violence. For the present, the expedition would refrain from announcing the position of the planet chosen for this purpose, because it was not in a condition to foresee how mankind would react. They had become convinced, from their prolonged study, that the civilization which calls itself mankind was never clear in its own mind about its intentions concerning any question whatsoever. But they were always ready to give us information on the state of the people they had removed. Then followed the coordinates in our mathematical quantities, indicating the direction of the source of information towards the star Proxima of the Centaur Galaxy. Then came the signature: Your brothers from the large group of stars which you call Galaxy.

Since Proxima is the nearest star to us (1.3 parsecs) the station on the moon immediately sent out its appeal. But matters still looked desperate – according to our theory we would not be able to expect an answer until at least nine years had elapsed. What was our amazement when it arrived only one week later! There was no doubt that it came exactly from the direction indicated, and this contradicted our knowledge of the greatest speed of wave movements. Or else those beings were much nearer than the Proxima star, or they had means of communication more rapid than the speed of light, or our ideas about the Cosmos, in spite of their great advance, were basically inaccurate. All this confused the scientists to such an extent that they dared not announce the content of the reply, and only after repeating the experiment, and after engaging in something like a discussion with the unknown beings, was mankind at last allowed to know the answer.

The link with another civilization, so greatly longed for up to that point, brought joy to no one. Whoever had imagined it would be like this – to have them come here, and right under your nose, without asking you, to carry off your brother? He might be abnormal, he might even be incurably insane, but he was your brother! General indignation circled the Earth like a hurricane, and the messages of the unknown abductors, trying to bring mankind to reason, did nothing to relieve the tension. Anyway, their explanations in most cases were rather insulting – no matter how highly developed they were, or how well they had studied us, they had obviously failed to penetrate the subtleties of our way of life. That was apparent from the examples which they gave us about our allegedly unfair attitude towards the insane. Someone asserted that he was a dog and wanted to live like a dog, and we didn't believe him and illtreated him. They checked, and saw that the animal which we call a dog enjoyed great affection among men. Why, then, were we impatient with such a legitimate wish on the part of our brother, who longed to enjoy the same respect and affection?

At first we tried to acquaint them with the concept of humanism; we explained to them that it originated from the word 'man' and consequently only we had the right to define how to behave towards one another. We cautiously gave them to understand that they knew nothing about earthly matters and reproached them for not getting into touch with us before undertaking this inexplicable aggression. Then we permitted ourselves something like an ultimatum: Bring back our insane if you want to live in peace with us! But they answered this in a most insulting way: their observations convinced them that in our evolution we had not yet reached the stage of being capable of maintaining peaceful and fruitful contact with another civilization; such contact was even lacking among ourselves. That was why they had put it off. Our present reaction also showed them that they were right. There was no logic whatsoever in it. We behaved badly to these people, without their having any fault whatever as regards society, we considered them a superfluous burden and now we wanted the exact opposite. Since we needed them, why had we isolated them from public life? And since we did not need them, why did we insist on their being returned to us?

Together with this answer they projected a whole film from the unknown planet for us, where, amid a marvellous landscape, such a luxurious and beautiful city was to be seen as will be created on

Earth who knows when, and in its streets and parks there were our madmen walking about. Many recognized their friends and relatives. They further tried to convince us that our abducted brothers felt very well indeed in the new conditions; that there had not been a single case of sickness or death, and so on. But who could believe that? The Polling Institutes asked one and the same question: Do you want your madmen back and what do you think of the action of the unknown civilization? The results were categorical – people wanted their brothers back and defined the abduction as a gross encroachment on the prestige of Earth. Here and there the masses, seized by earthly patriotism, stoned the nihilists and defeatists, who went so far in their effrontery as to maintain that we were envious of our madmen because of the freedom and luxury in which they lived and suggested that we should sign an agreement with the civilization to send our madmen to it in the future, until we had learned to cure them. (This is where I should say that all this time the psychiatric clinics on Earth were filled to bursting point again, because many people could not stand the extraordinary strain laid upon mankind. Among them, however, there proved to be many shammers, who entered the asylums with the secret wish of also being abducted.)

The United Nations Organization unanimously voted a pathetic appeal to stop all local wars, to drop all disputes in the face of the danger threatening us, and to have individual states pool their war budgets in a common treasury for the creation of cosmic weapons and a united cosmic army which would be capable of defending the Earth efficiently against alien encroachments.

And the miracle occurred. For the first time all the governments lent an ear to the appeal of this organization; national and racial hostilities immediately ceased, and under the aegis of the UNO the first army of mankind came into being in an unbelievably short time. Thus mankind united at last, as if only the presence of the insane had prevented them from doing so earlier!

And here we are at last on our way! With fifteen reconnaissance cosmoplanes. My good fortune in being among them as a journalist is so great that I daren't assign it to my professional qualities, but simply to what is called luck in our earthly language. And if anything bothers me a bit, it is that our enemies as yet unknown might try to avoid the war when they see we are resolved to fight to the death, even on this pretext, an absurd one according to them. It would be inhuman if everything ended in meek negotiations. Thank God, our fighting spirit and our will to defend our prestige are so strong that for the present at least I have no grounds to doubt sound human reason! It will surely not allow us to make any shameful compromises.

As we passed by Mars, we received the greetings and good wishes of our station there, now already a military post in the front line. Further on lies the unknown. What will it bring to our beautiful Earth? But let us not lose faith in her good star, dear future readers of my modest feature article!

Forward, mankind!

The Mirror Image of the Earth

ZHENG WENGUANG

Translated by Sun Liang

The planet appeared yellow in the distance, as if it were a lemon drifting in a space of dark purple velvet. So the spacemen aboard *The Explorer* thought there was nothing but barren desert, until their craft drew near enough for them to discern a layer of dense, yellow atmosphere studded with green clouds, like so many islands floating about in the atmospheric ocean.

The spacemen surveyed the deadly silent planet with great care. They discovered that the chief component of the atmosphere was oxygen, which meant people could breathe there, and could drink water in the streams. However, though luxuriant plants grew profusely on the planet, there were neither birds nor animals, let alone any higher form of civilization. But when they climbed up the cloud-capped mountains, they could vaguely discern the upturned eaves and turrets of palatial buildings. Yet there was not the slightest sign of living beings. The visitors named the planet Uiqid, and then returned to Earth, with the suggestion that the next team of astronauts include a cosmic archaeologist.

Thus, three and a half years later, Cui Yining landed again on the lemon-like planet aboard a new spaceship, *The Hundred Flowers*. 'Hey Cui, do you know why it's called Uiqid?' asked the young biophysicist Linwu Sheng, captain of *The Hundred Flowers*. The astronauts were standing in a springy grass field, while their two women colleagues lingered by the ramp of the ship, fascinated by the enchanting spectacle of this strange planet.

Cui Yining turned, and shook his head. 'By reversing the letters, the word Uiqid reads Diqiu![1] The meaning is quite clear: The Mirror Image of the Earth,' said the captain.

Cui Yining curiously surveyed the landscape on all sides of the spaceship. They had landed on a desolate, vast grassland. The color of the grasses was a bit varied, but mostly of a pink-red hue that made the land look ablaze. Ripples shimmered in the distance – could it be a lake? The water was not blue but bright yellow, like Shao Xing Wine.[2] Further away lay a range of green mountains. At one side of the spacecraft there was a sparse wood with tall trees like poplars, only the trunks were brown and the leaves red as a rose, looking more beautiful than the red leaves in the Fragrant Hills.[3]

'I don't see anything similar to our Earth,' muttered Cui Yining.

'Really?' Linwu Sheng said mischievously, 'Then ask your lady to have a look. Hey, Du Yinlin!'

Du Yinlin was slim and agile, with delicate features. She was a geologist as well as a photographer (every astronaut had to be trained in two disciplines). Standing by her husband, she studied the strange landscape with excitement. All of a sudden she grasped Cui's hand, mumbling 'Complementary . . . color . . .'

Linwu Sheng gave a hearty laugh, and cast a knowing glance at Gu Mingwei, his fiancée. She was both a chemist and a physician. At the moment she was so entranced by the colorful view that her pretty eyes didn't even blink.

Linwu Sheng took the camera off Du Yinlin's shoulder and snapped a quick shot of the surroundings. In a few seconds, a color negative dropped from the cassette. Linwu picked up the photo. The instant he saw it he cried, 'It's just like a picture taken at the Ming Tombs[4] or the Western Hills . . .'[5]

Because of the optical characteristics of complementary colors,

---

[1] Diqiu – the Chinese word for the Earth, in pinyin.

[2] A famous wine, traditionally produced in Shao Xing County, Zhe Jiang Province, East China.

[3] A scenic spot in the suburbs of Beijing.

[4] The royal burial ground of the Ming Emperors.

[5] Another scenic spot in the suburbs of Beijing.

the picture taken with a negative was very similar to that taken with ordinary color slides on Earth. The astronauts were excited at this discovery.

'It *is* the mirror image of the Earth ... Exactly ...' Cui said, in short breaths.

'We'll find the Uiqidians yet. Must be living beings like you and me, only blue all over ...' Linwu Sheng said loudly, with an impish wink. Then he quickly climbed into the cabin of the spaceship. Soon he emerged, at the controls of a hovercraft.

'Do you really think there are blue people?' asked Gu Mingwei, who had kept silent all the while. She was young and beautiful, with large eyes like fathomless lakes – lakes on the Earth, to be sure.

'I think so ... I would believe anything!' answered Linwu cheerfully. Then stretching out a hand, he said 'Come on, envoys from the Earth, aren't we like Alice in Outer Space?'[6] They climbed into the hovercraft one by one. Du Yinlin was thinking to herself: Yes, exactly. We *are* like Alice entering the mirror world, but it's a real world, not the wonderland in the dream of the little English girl ...

The hovercraft travelled at the speed of 180 km per hour. It took them four and a half hours to move up the gently sloping mountain. The time, of course, was shown by their wrist watches in Earth time. During this period, the sun shining over Uiqid had not moved in the least. It seemed the day was quite long here.

They stopped twice on the way to have a rest, a snack, take a few pictures, and collect specimens of rocks and plants. They had not come across any animate forms of life, not even a tiny insect. The first astronauts had probably been correct in guessing there were no other animate beings on Uiqid. But then, who built those upturned eaves and turrets?

Referring to a map drawn by the pioneers, they spent two hours trying to find the magnificent palaces, but their efforts were in vain. The map was accurate: mountains, lakes, woods, and various

[6] Referring to the little girl in Alice in Wonderland.

directional bearings – every indication was perfectly correct, yet . . .

'Maybe it's only their imagination,' Cui Yining muttered, 'just like the mirages we see on Earth.'

Linwu Sheng shook his head slightly. As a biophysicist, he was sure that on a planet whose natural conditions were much the same as those on Earth, the development of life should be more or less the same, too. Somewhere in Uiqid, there must be animals, even human beings – undoubtedly their color, features, and lifestyle would be different, but living beings nonetheless, with the faculty of reason and emotion, capable of creating a civilization.

The only explanation was that in the past three and a half years, a catastrophe had befallen Uiqid.

But there was not the least trace of crumbled walls and toppled houses. Was it really a sort of mirage? Impossible. Even a mirage is not a total illusion; it is a reflection of actual scenes – distorted, of course.

The hovercraft progressed up the slope with bursts of steam. They were trying to reach the summit. On their map, it was called Mount Amgnalomoq, the reversed name of Mount Qomolangma,[7] though not so steep and towering. Moreover, it was not covered with white snow but looked black, and awesomely majestic.

A huge crater gaped wide in front of them.

'Perhaps the place has been destroyed by a volcanic eruption?' said Gu Mingwei in her sweet silvery voice. Since their landing on Uiqid, she had looked unusually rosy and bright. Whenever Linwu glanced at her his heart would beat faster.

Du Yinlin, the geologist, shook her head. It was merely a lapse of three and a half years. What kind of volcanic eruption could it be that left no sign of destruction at all? She looked doubtfully at her husband, Cui Yining, who was examining the crater with the expert eyes of a cosmic archaeologist. After a while he said resolutely, 'I must get in there, but it's a twisted path. The hovercraft won't do. We have to go on foot; Linwu, just the two of us, O.K?'

'Let's all go down,' said Du Yinlin, earnestly. Immediately she took down from the hovercraft a coil of thin but durable rope

[7] The Chinese name for Mount Everest.

made of fiberglass-reinforced plastic. Each person carried a mini jet engine on his back to help with the upward climb later on. Grasping the rope, they went down into the gaping crater, one after another. They had a short rest, drank a little water, and presently reached the bottom. Linwu Sheng looked at his watch. It had taken them only an hour and ten minutes.

'Look here – light!' Cui Yining said, excitement in his hushed voice.

Indeed, an uncanny light was reflected from the rocky lava; a peculiar optical phenomenon. A faint purple light lit up the bottom of the volcano, presenting a miraculous scene, like a fairy tale wonderland. Du Yinlin clutched her husband's hand, while Gu Mingwei clung to Linwu, who stood stock still, hearing only his heart beating like an African battle drum.

'Here's a passage,' Cui whispered to Linwu. 'Shall we go on?'

They moved along the narrow corridor one by one, and in a few minutes came to an immense cave. A hazy light glimmered from the arched ceiling. The walls were quite smooth, as if they had been finished. There were even several doors on one side.

The four astronauts stood before a door. Perhaps they would soon meet the intelligent beings on Uiqid? They stood there with bated breath, exchanging wondering looks. The door was not made of wood, but of a kind of black opaque plexiglass. Rows upon rows of protruding big nails were embedded in the door in the style of the gates of ancient Chinese architecture, but these were smaller and arranged in a closer pattern.

Linwu touched one of the door nails. Good Heaven! He was so astounded his jaw dropped and he stared, mouth agape. The change was sudden. The cave disappeared, and instead there emerged the boundless, wild, surging billows of a blue sea; then a succession of gigantic ships in full sail came into view. As the rolling waves swept towards them, Gu Mingwei gave a cry. Instantly Linwu steadied her. He was the first to realize what was going on.

'Don't move. It's just a holographic movie,' he said in a low but firm voice.

He was right. The scene was exceedingly lifelike, but it was soundless. They could see some sailors moving to and fro on the ship, dressed like warriors of the Ming Dynasty, but they couldn't hear the roaring sea, nor any noise from the ship. They heard nothing but their own heartbeats.

Then a crowd appeared on the deck of an enormous ship. The image drew nearer and nearer. A hefty man with a clean-shaven pale face stood on the deck, just ten paces away from the astronauts. He was speaking, but they could only see his mouth opening slightly without hearing any words. In a moment, there loomed on the sea the back of a blue whale, its huge tail pounding the waves, beating up columns of water like splashing fountains. Soon the whale swam out of view.

'It's . . .' Cui stammered to his wife, 'It's the scene of Zheng Ho sailing to the Western Ocean.'[8]

Everyone understood at once. Certainly it was a movie shot of historical scenes on the Earth: the sea, the ship, the whale, the characters . . . That man, no doubt the celebrated eunuch Zheng Ho. The scene was truly vivid. However, the astronauts were so spellbound that they didn't even stop to wonder: How could a holographic movie of fifteenth century events on Earth be shown on a strange planet?

The ship vanished, so did the sea. It was the same hollow cave all around, lit up by the uncanny hazy light. The astronauts seemed to have awakened from an eerie daydream, but none wanted to speak.

'Shall I press another door nail?' Linwu finally asked, glancing at his three companions. Now they were sure that what they had called 'door nails' were really buttons for showing holographic films.

No one replied. Linwu Sheng stretched out a trembling hand and touched another button. Instantly he was so taken aback that he jumped aside.

A horrible scene of war and slaughter unfolded before them. It was not on a battlefield, but in a courtyard. Ancient armor-clad warriors, armed to the teeth, were raising glittering swords at frightened women in imperial dress. Blood flowed like a gushing

---

[8] Zheng Ho: a high-ranking eunuch in the reign of the Ming Emperor, Cheng Zu. A large fleet under his command embarked on long voyages seven times in three decades, navigating to Southeast Asia, the Indian subcontinent, Persia and some Arab countries as far off as the east coast of Africa.

fountain. Suddenly, a fire broke out and rolling flames spread swiftly, enveloping the entire space in no time. They didn't hear anyone crying or shouting, nor did they feel the scorching heat, but still their hearts quivered. Look at those dim contours, amidst the towering tongues of fire, aren't they mansions, pavilions, and terraces with carved beams and painted pillars?

'The burning ... of O Fang ... Palace ...'[9] Cui stammered. God knows if it really was, but the armor, the royal dress, and the weapons were definitely fashioned in the Qin Dynasty style.

This time Linwu didn't ask for any advice but pressed yet another button right away. Now no one doubted any more. The new scene displayed dozens of young people with red armbands, standing there in regular columns and waving booklets with red covers in the same direction towards a remote figure. Then a second group of teenagers flung themselves upon the first. Immediately a tangled fight broke out. Leather whips were lashed about, daggers and swords glistened in the air, bricks were thrown at random. Blood oozed from the forehead of a young boy; his face was twitching, and he was staring at the astronauts with lusterless eyes.

Cui Yining gasped, swayed in a swoon and fell down.

'Yining!' shrieked Du Yinlin. Linwu and Gu Mingwei hurriedly helped Cui to his feet and heard him mumble 'Oh, my poor brother ...'

It was incredible that they should see, on this strange planet, the picture of that foolish, brutal conflict in the twentieth century with the image of his brother who had died of his wounds. Now, all of them were aware of the fact that these holographic films had not been shot in a studio, but were truthful records of history, made on the spot.

But who could have been the cameraman? And who had carried the films to Uiqid through a distance of so many light years and kept them in a cave? After all, when O Fang Palace was burned down and Zheng Ho set sail to the Western Ocean, the motion

[9] The spectacular palace built by the decree of the first Emperor of the Qin Dynasty [221–207 B.C.]. It was located in the northwest suburb of present-day Xian, in Shanxi Province. Towards the end of the Qin Dynasty, the palace was burnt to ashes by insurgent troops.

picture had not even been invented on Earth, much less the holographic movie.

All this perplexed and puzzled the astronauts beyond words. They were scientists, so none of them believed in divine power or miracles, but without divine power and miracles, how did all these spectacles come about? How can they be explained? They looked at one another, dumbfounded.

Cui Yining came to in half an hour and said to his companions, 'Someone must have kept here a number of holographic movies of historical scenes. How were they produced? I think we could get the key to the answer right here. Let's press more buttons, one by one. What do you say?'

'I don't want to see cruel scenes of slaughter any more,' replied Gu Mingwei, her voice still quivering.

'There won't be pictures of war and fighting all the time,' Linwu consoled her. 'Maybe we'll see some interesting scenes like the Dance in Rainbow-hued Feather Dress performed by female dancers at the court of Tang Ming Huang,[10] or a royal banquet, or a grand wedding ceremony, and the like – joyful pictures anyway ... You could pass over anything you don't like to see, just as though you were watching TV.'

Scenes in the holographic movie followed each other in quick succession. There were few battle scenes, but neither were there any pictures of joyful celebration as predicted by Linwu. Most of the views showed the ordinary, poverty-stricken, and humdrum life in the countryside of old times: close-ups of a boat struggling in whirlpools; a fierce wrestle between man and animal; fishermen trembling like leaves in a storm. Cui Yining was absorbed in watching the shifting scenes. To an archaeologist, what could be more valuable than pictures depicting the life of ancient people? Others thought that all those dresses, utensils, tools, and buildings were quite ordinary. Only he was able to make out whether they had prevailed in Early or Late Tang Dynasty, in the Southern or Northern Dynasty:[11] whether they had been made by the Han race of people or the minority nationalities. It seemed that the

[10] The famous Emperor of mid-Tang Dynasty [A.D. 618–907], who was a cultivated musician.

[11] The Southern Dynasty [A.D. 420–589]; the Northern Dynasty [A.D. 386–581].

unknown cameraman had deliberately shot varied scenes of life in different periods and different areas.

One of the pictures showed people praying for rain: naked men acting as Devils of Drought danced wildly under a scorching sun. Looking at the gaunt, pale-faced, skeleton-like people worn out with the thirst and exhaustion, Gu Mingwei turned a little and murmured to Du Yinlin, 'We're simply like strange animals locked up in a cage on exhibition.'

'It looks like the cosmic beings have been observing and studying us over thousands of years,' replied Yinlin. 'But all the views are about China. Why? There are lots of other countries on the Earth. Are the cosmic beings blind to them?'

'Oh,' Linwu interrupted in his cheerful tone, 'Obviously because the drama on the Chinese stage is the most attractive – in the eyes of cosmic beings . . .'

Cui was a little taken aback. The archaeologist had never pondered these questions: Should sensible beings outside the Earth want to study our history, what would they do? Probably those movie shots had not been carefully chosen, just as visitors to the zoo don't invariably choose to watch the caged animals that look most powerful, beautiful and energetic.

In studying our own history, can we be as unbiased, level-headed and impartial as the cosmic beings? Is it true that we've tried to embellish and modify history at will, consciously or unconsciously? On the other hand, when we see historical scenes shot by others, we feel very awkward as though we were viewing our own naked bodies pitted all over with ugly scars.

All of a sudden Linwu cried 'Look, a UFO!'

So it was! A scintillating green object raced across the blue sky over the globe, like a couple of dishes stuck together. Most likely the historical scenes had been shot by this strange object. If living beings in outer space wanted to investigate the Earth, this was the best way, the most skilful and direct means.

This planet Uiqid seemed to have developed civilization at a high level thousands of years ago, and the Uiqidians had been observing everything that happened on the distant Earth. Then, the Earth sent its delegates to this planet . . .

Suddenly Cui Yining grasped Linwu's hand.

'Now I know!' His voice betrayed excitement. 'They had recognized that our spacemen were Chinese, so they have prepared the films shot about China produced over thousands of years to welcome us with . . .'

Linwu nodded in agreement. Then he pressed a button: atop the hill in Uiqid, near the crater through which they had come a short while ago, stood an extraordinarily gorgeous palace. A few people came out . . . Ah, blue men! Behold, they were turning round, high-browed, unfathomably large eyes, enigmatic smiles, glossy blue skin – facing the astronauts. The strange people waved their hands, muttered something, and climbed into a spaceship near the palace. In the twinkling of an eye, the spaceship took off, the launch pad broke down, and the palace fell to pieces, leaving a heap of ashes . . .

The scene faded out. In the silent cave, still enveloped in the faint purple light, there was not the slightest sound, except the hard breathing of the astronauts.

After a long lapse, Linwu Sheng said, somewhat sadly, 'They've gone away . . . to other planets; they don't want to meet us . . .'

'But why?' asked Gu Mingwei almost inaudibly.

'Perhaps . . . they know us better than we do ourselves,' said Cui Yining gently.

'But,' Du Yinlin was impatient, 'living beings on different planets should have friendly exchanges, shouldn't they?'

Cui shook his head emphatically: 'They don't live in the same stage of civilization as we do. While we were burning books and burying scholars alive,[12] they had already mastered the technique of laser holographic photography and the means of long-distance space travel. They had developed thousands of years earlier than we did. So, to them, we're simply barbarians. Now, why should they be friendly and believe the savages? They would naturally think we might attack them any moment with machine guns and tanks, or with old weapons like firelocks, spears, big swords, and bricks . . .'

'How about ourselves,' Linwu chuckled. 'Do we believe in ourselves?'

[12] Tyrannical persecution carried out by edict of the first Emperor of the Qin Dynasty.

'But,' Du Yinlin cut in, 'if their civilization is more advanced than ours by thousands of years, why should they be afraid of tanks and machine guns?'

'Oh,' her husband murmured straight away, 'historically speaking, all advanced civilizations did not necessarily triumph. Genghis Khan was a perfect case in point. His nomadic tribes wiped out all the flourishing civilizations in Asia and Europe, but . . .'

'Well, I see,' Linwu said with a sudden realization, 'why there are no animals on this planet. Because the Uiqidians have packed them off. They are the modern Noah.'[13]

'Are we, people from Earth, so terrible?' Gu Mingwei said sorrowfully.

'Sure, but people on the Earth aren't all the same. We all know that some are just like . . . flood and beast . . .'[14] said Cui Yining, stressing every word of the simile.

On the various planets the astronauts visited later on, they did not find the Uiqidians who had emigrated from their native planet. It did not necessarily mean that they had evaporated, or 'exploded' like a super nova. They had just gone to some unknown place inaccessible to man.

No matter how hard human beings try to probe the universe, they cannot uncover all of its wonders, as they are so multicolored, inexhaustible, and mysterious. Is this not true?

---

[13] From the Bible, Genesis 5:28–10:32.

[14] A stock simile in Chinese, describing somebody or something that is very dangerous.

The New Prehistory

RENÉ REBETEZ-CORTES

Translated by Damon Knight

It began when my friend Metropoulos joined the long ticket line in front of the Mayer Cinema. I had never liked standing in line for anything; I waited to one side. Eating corn chips, I watched the women who passed, and the people who joined the line, pressed into it one by one like blobs of mercury.

The line moved slowly forward, with a monotonous scraping of feet on pavement. When I glanced at my friend's face, I saw that it was expressionless, slack-jawed. His eyes were glassy with boredom; his arms dangled like an ape's; his feet shuffled slowly.

I felt a sudden chill; somehow I knew what was about to happen. A fat lady had grown tired of waiting, even though she was only twenty places or so from the ticket window. She took a step, another, a third; the line curved with her. She turned her head indignantly, tried to break free; she ran and the line straightened again, dragging the poor woman back in spite of her struggles.

Now panic spread; they were all trying to break loose at once. The long line undulated in wild contortions, as if shaken by a gigantic hiccup. People were struggling, screaming and shouting. Tempers grew heated; there was a flurry of blows.

Around the newborn monster, a crowd was gathering. That was another custom in the cities, congregating to look at things: cranes, wrecking machines, blasting crews. Airplanes. Military parades. Political rallies. Crowds looking at billboards. Crowds looking at anything.

Myself, I had always hated crowds and lines of people. Not that I was antisocial, not at all; it was simply that I disliked humanity in the mass. Never had I dreamed that things would take such a turn, or that I would witness this transformation.

The people in line soon realized there was nothing they could do, or at least that there was no point in fighting among themselves. Tattered, bleeding, and crestfallen, at last they were still; an ominous silence fell over them. Then, little by little, like the sound of rushing water, there came the swelling voice of incredulity and terror.

It was obvious that these people could not pull themselves apart; something had bound them tightly together. Something that in the first few moments had been no more than a breath had rapidly changed into a viscous but tangible substance; very soon it had become a transparent gelatin, then a flexible cartilage like that of Siamese twins. A force unknown to mankind, latent in nature until now, had been unleashed: a psychological cancer that was gluing men together as if they were atoms of new elements in formation.

A restlessness came over the line. Like a huge centipede waking up, the monster slowly began to move down the street, hundreds of arms waving desperately. At the head of the column was a red-eyed man whose mouth was awry in a painful rictus. He was followed by a girl who had been proud of her beauty; now, disheveled, her make-up dissolved by tears, she moved like a sleepwalker. Then came a boy, his face pale with terror, then Metropoulos, my old friend, one more vertebra of the monstrous reptile. He passed without hesitating, deaf to my voice, his gaze fixed on the ground and his feet moving to the marching rhythm.

Gradually the movement grew faster, more erratic and frenzied. The long queue was like a string of carnival dancers, twisting and turning, performing a demonic conga in the street. Then, after a few frantic turns, the reptile sank to the pavement; each segment of its body was heaving, and a continual stertorous sound echoed in the half-open mouths, the nostrils like fluttering wings, the wild eyes.

It lasted only a moment; the reptile got up again. In it were a few dead and useless vertebrae. Dragging them along, the monster broke into its zigzag run again and disappeared down the street.

I had managed to get into the opening of a narrow doorway; from its shelter I watched the torpid crowd. Once more I knew what was going to happen. They were awakening gradually from the nightmare left behind by the great human serpent: now they were becoming aware of their own condition. They had turned into a gigantic amoeba; a thick protoplasm that had spurted out between them had bound them together like the cells of a honeycomb. There was not a single shout. Only a few faint groans and a murmur of helplessness came from the crowd.

The human serpent still seemed to know which was its head and which its tail, but the crowd-amoeba showed an immediate desire to spread in all directions. The human mass changed its shape from one instant to another in a grotesque and repellent manner: a convulsed macroscopic amoeba that stumbled and bounced painfully against the walls. A new being, gigantic and mindless, that moved down the street after its predecessor.

I don't remember how many days and nights I wandered those streets. Thousands of monsters of all sizes were roaming in the city. The lines at bakeries and bus stops had produced little reptiles of ten or so vertebrae each; the same for the lines at banks and confessionals. Larger ones had come from the lines at phone booths, movies, theaters, and other public places. The amoebas came from street crowds and public gatherings; they were spreading everywhere.

The strange ligature that had fastened the people together was really unbreakable. I saw one man who tried to cut it; the attempt ended in his painful death. The links that died by accident hung like dead leaves, without breaking the human chain. I saw a busload of people that had turned into a single mass. Unable to get out of the bus, they began destroying it. Whole buildings were being demolished by amoeba-crowds imprisoned inside. A shouting throng had formed itself into an immense clotted mass that swept away obstacles, filling the streets like a river: that one came from a political rally.

The few persons who were still separate scurried like rats to avoid touching the new organisms. All the same, most of them were being absorbed.

I don't want to know anything about that. I don't want to find myself transformed into something shapeless like an amoeba or a glob of spittle, nor to become the last segment of a gigantic worm. I cling to my human identity, my own individual personality. I am a man, not a limb or an organ.

Nevertheless, I know the battle is already lost. Before my eyes humanity is being transformed. I try to be impartial and tell myself that perhaps it is for the best, that this sudden mutation will bring with it a fundamental advance for humanity. But it's useless; these new forms of life repel me.

They have renounced forever the old way of life. It is impossible for them to live in rooms as they did before, to use elevators, sit in chairs, sleep in beds, travel in cars or planes. Obviously they can't return to their jobs, go to offices, mind stores, operate in clinics, act in theaters. Everything must be reorganized to suit the new conditions.

After the early days of fear and confusion, the new composite beings abandoned the cities. Unable to get into kitchens, pantries and refrigerators, they swarmed out into the country.

The sight of these reptiles and giant amoebas roaming the pastures or lurking in the woods is enough to turn my stomach. I think they have forgotten what they were. They eat insatiably: fruit, roots – and they eat animals alive. They haven't bothered to build shelters. One kind sleeps coiled up like a huge boa around a fire; the other kind, in a ball on the bare earth.

I don't know if they remember that they were once man.

So much time has passed, I have lost all perception of it. The evolution of the new beings has been demoniacally swift. They no longer try to add new links to their gigantic bodies; instead, when they meet a single person, they kill him. I have been living in the ruins of the cities, hiding from their gaze and their keen sense of smell, but I venture out now and then to spy on them.

Their appearance has changed enormously; now they are *another thing*. A few days ago I surprised two serpent-beings making love in a nearby field. It was grotesque and indescribable, a contorted self-flagellation. Now I know that each one of these beings had a common organism, an integrated physiological function, a single nervous system, a unified mind.

It was difficult for me to accept this, because in the old days when people were individuals, those who liked to form themselves into lines or crowds in the street were always mediocrities, morons. Intelligent people would not have been caught up in such foolishness. They have been destroyed; or else, like me, they are wandering in the ruins. But I have met no one else here.

In spite of everything, I acknowledge the strength of the new creatures, the technical mastery they are beginning to show. With the speed of their thousand hands and their thousand feet, they are raising strange narrow or circle edifices, making and transporting materials in the twinkling of an eye. They have made immense capes, with openings for their multiple heads, to protect themselves from the cold. Sometimes I hear their chorus of a thousand voices chanting strange guttural songs.

I suspect the day is not far off when they will build their own airplanes and limousines, as long as railway cars, or rounded and flat like flying saucers. The time will come, too, I have no doubt, when they will play golf.

But I don't want to know anything about that. I always hated crowds and lines of people. I cling to my human identity, to my own individual and separate personality. It's not that I'm antisocial; not at all, I repeat. But masses of humanity are distasteful to me. Never did I dream that things would take such a turn, or that I would witness this transformation.

I sit among the ruins. In the distance I can hear a gigantic chorus: the voice of the new prehistory. A new cycle is beginning.

Equality

QUAH KUNG YU

Dr Lim sighed and pushed the stack of unmarked papers away from him.

He sat back in his chair and closed his eyes. He couldn't shake off the light depression or lethargy or whatever that had dogged his steps for the last few days. He reflected ruefully that academic men like himself were probably more prone to this. Universities had, since time long gone, fervently believed that their gurus should be free from the hustle and bustle of commonplace commercial and technological life and be blessed instead with the peace and security of scholarly temples in which to pursue the secrets of the universe within and without.

Freed from having to struggle and compete for respect and food, Dr Lim had taken to pondering the purpose and meaning of his life. Perhaps, he thought hopefully, this was but a passing symptom of middle age . . . but the depression of discovering that after his successful pursuit of scholarship and his equally favoured search for a wife, he had nothing which really consumed his interest, was deepening.

He stood up and stretched his thin, bony frame. Three hours painfully spent over the mathematics of robotic science and associated disciplines made his brain woolly. The air in the study seemed stale and unhealthy; Dr Lim moved over to the french windows, opened them and stepped onto the balcony.

The breeze was cool and firm, and the view from his eighty-metre-high roost pleasant. His spirits lifted somewhat, he hummed a tune as he surveyed Marsiling. Sprawled beyond the slim Singapore Strait was the prospering leisure town of Johore. Long ago, in the days of his childhood there had been a Johore Bahru; that had been just before the storm of the Post-Industrial Revolution, which had swirled over the globe, bringing such rapid change in civilization that perhaps only the children were able to fully adapt and accommodate themselves to the new world.

The sounds of the streets below reached his ears faintly. Tiny cars scurried along the smooth roads, racing with the buses zipping magnetically through near-vacuum tubes. It was already mid-afternoon, the sun again on its descent and humanity, resting from the day's labour, was milling bee-like about the parks of green and recreational centres, which dotted Marsiling.

He looked back into the study. Behind his desk was a shelf of books and cassettes that reflected both his eminence in the field of robots, as well as his new found curiosity over the purpose of his life. The Koran, Holy Bible, Frankel's *Logotherapy*, along with his own *Programmed Brains* and Ishikara's classic work on micro-nuclear paths – which had opened the way to the development of the first robotic 'brains' capable of learning, though not of thinking – shared the shelf with various textbooks.

Though many researchers all over the earth, and indeed on stations and satellites not on earth, were working furiously to create the first truly thinking artificial brain, Dr Lim believed the work to be in vain.

After all, he reasoned, Man's one distinction was the power to think in the abstract and concrete. To create a thinking machine, with a mind of its own, was to question the very humanity of Man, as it were. And it would make it infinitely harder for him to discover the purpose of life. Somehow, he felt, Man should not, ought not, be able to devise the thinking robot.

The speaker next to the door bleeped apologetically several times and the screen of the room-computer lit up with a reminder for Dr Lim's squash game at the Club in the late afternoon.

The happy prospect of fun and some healthy exertion raised the doctor's spirits further. Within minutes, he had changed into a sweatshirt and shorts, packed his squash gear and was down in the underground car park.

His was a modest no-frills vehicle. Dr Lim decided to drive

himself and left the computer unactivated. He drove fairly well and with confidence rolling along the roads to the outskirts of Marsiling.

The traffic was heavy with the after-work flow but it moved smoothly. For most of the way, the bus tubes followed the road and occasionally, Dr Lim would overtake an overflowing bus, silently and gently 'flying' through the tube, the electro-magnetic repulsion supporting and propelling it forward. He could see some commuters dozing in their seats while those forced to stand gazed vacantly out at him as if blanking the discomfort from their minds.

He drove through the centre of town with the ever-present shopping centres and bowling alleys. The development of holography and domestic sets had all but destroyed the cinematic industry. A few theatres dedicated to cultural drama had sprung up in their place. Dr Lim enjoyed live plays: after dealing with and in computers, robots and cold science he found the live flesh-and-blood acting stimulating and relaxing. For the same reason, he often strolled appreciatively through the zoological gardens in nearby Mandai.

The Club crowned a low hill to the south of Marsiling. It was surrounded by a few aloof bungalows, whose residents usually were members of the Club. Rendered exclusive by its high membership dues and distinguished by its underground architecture, the Club was more than a haven for the more wealthy citizens of Singapore.

It resembled a giant dumb-bell, with two domes linked by a lower block. Beneath it, in the grounds was the sporting complex of tennis and squash courts, swimming pools and gymnasium. The West Dome housed the lounge, an affluent library, a restaurant and several apartments for rent to guests. The East Dome was altogether different.

It held the region's most sophisticated laboratories for extraterrestrial research. Having been built simultaneously and similar in shape, the Club and the first moon station enjoyed a unique 'sister' relationship. Thus the Club had come to house the earthside end of lunar study, known popularly as 'lunacy'. This intimacy was useful to the Club in two ways.

It allowed its members to refute envious charges that the Club was a symbol of class division and ostentatious wealth, serving neither socialism nor democracy. More relevantly, it gave those members whose business and livelihood it was to produce goods, an opportunity to get wind of the latest marketable lunar discovery or innovation before their competitors did.

Dr Lim quietly halted his car by a more expensive, ornamental fission-fired automobile and entered the Club. His squash partner was already waiting (impatiently) at the escalators.

A. A. Widono was a stocky, firmly-built individualist, alert eyes prowling menacingly behind thick glasses. Outgoing, thick skinned, he was Second Vice President of the ASEAN Federation of Technical Workers, AFTW. Probably, Widono the politician-administrator and Lim the scholar-teacher would never have struck up a close relationship, had fate not made them classmates in their adolescence.

The ASEAN Council of Government had once approached Dr Lim to use his personal standing with Widono to assist it in one of its several tussles with the AFTW over pay and work conditions.

Dr Lim had politely declined, though he had scant sympathy for the aggressive policies of the AFTW, which had control over the maintenance and repair of the thousands of robot and computer systems that serviced society. He believed in keeping his friendships and his opinions apart.

Privately, he thought the Council of Government was really relieved that the AFTW was being led by responsible intelligent men and women. This gave the Council time to devise more comprehensive methods, constitutional or not, of managing the AFTW if it was ever to elect less responsible leaders.

After an invigorating, sapping game, the two men retired to the lounge for a round of cool drinks, a short chat and to fix another match for the following Sunday.

Widono lived in Sembawang and insisted on using public transportation for personal travel. The buses were now quite empty and he caught one to his home. Widono had no misgivings about his purpose in life. A dedicated atheist, he believed in living and enjoying himself. A quivering impression of energy was conveyed to those around him.

A message was waiting for him, asking him to contact the President as soon as convenient. After decisively informing the domestic computer what he wanted for dinner, Widono felt it was convenient to call up the President of the AFTW.

He did so and soon faced her on the screen. She was a tall, muscular woman whose ambition had taken her to the top of the labour movement from where she also led the feminist groups.

In her characteristically deliberate tone and measured words, she announced the convening of an Extraordinary Executive Meeting on the following day. Noting her Second Vice-President's penchant for ignoring ordinary meetings, she was specially requesting his presence on this occasion.

Laughing at this slight and light-hearted reproach, Widono gave his promise to turn up, had his meal and paid a call on his current lover.

It was a little past midnight when A. A. Widono stepped out onto the streets to begin his journey home. As usual, the lamps glowed cheerfully and a few dark cars dashed upon the roads. However, to his consternation half an hour passed with no answer to his call for a bus. The tube remained silent and empty. A breakdown was unheard of; the massive back-up army of robots and computers would have efficiently dealt with any malfunction.

A faint rumble came from the grey shadows to his right. Widono stared but it was only a watchrobot. Tall and smooth, its steel skin glinting in the lamplight, the cigar-shaped machine rolled easily forward on three wheels. It rumbled to a stop before Widono who made out the serial number on its breastplate as 012B. They were now alone on the pavement with the silent apartment blocks and tube for their backdrop.

012B had a suitably authoritative voice: 'May I help you?'

Widono was doubtful. Public transport was not under the watchrobot's department. Hopefully, he explained the problem and asked for suggestions. He watched as the computer in 012B's brain searched for the programmed response to his query.

'May I see your identification card?' It was a question in form rather than in fact. Wondering what his identity had to do with his transport, Widono nevertheless produced his card. He was already sleepy and desired to get home swiftly.

012B scanned the card and appeared to start in surprise. Widono dismissed it as tired imagination on his part. 012B spoke again, 'Follow me.'

Widono strode after the watchrobot. The streets remained deserted. The Second Vice-President was about to inquire about their destination when 012B abruptly halted and its metallic arm pointed to a squat police van by the pavement. 'Your transport.'

Widono was surprised by their courteous and obliging service; he mentally lauded the programme technicians at Watchrobot Command.

He had to bend somewhat to enter the van, which could seat six persons. He left 012B to detail the van to bring him home. Lying on the seats, he prepared for a short nap. The van called him to wake up after a short unconscious interlude.

Yawning and eager for more lengthy rest in a comfortable bed, Widono got up and stepped out of the van.

Instantly, he realized something was afoot. He could not recognize the silent and unlit locality – and he found himself hemmed in by three construction robots, whose data panels were the only, and faint, sources of light. Sleepy as he had been, the union leader quickly sensed threat in the cold night air. Tense, he barked angrily, demanding an explanation.

The robots closed in, motors humming faultlessly. Widono's muscular arms were gripped in the iron hold of the robot's powerful hands. Their hands, two fingers and a thumb each, had strength enough to twist steel rods and he was powerless against them. Furiously and even more fearfully, Widono called for help. His powerful union leader's roar, urgent with alarm, vibrated through the dark.

There was no answer.

Squirming, he was pushed forward towards a darkened building. As they came closer, he realized that he had been brought to the central fusion terminal at Bukit Timah.

He was steadily brought through the corridors inside the giant terminal and suddenly thrown into a dimly-lit room. As the door swung shut behind him, several figures seemed to spring from the shadows.

Widono's first reaction was to cringe; his usual aggression

beaten by the unknown and confusing. Then, he realized that human arms were raising him. Of the two or three voices speaking at him simultaneously he recognized the low, cultured tone of Dr Lim, Master of Computer and Robot Sciences at the university.

In the dim light, they introduced themselves. There were now altogether five persons – Widono, Dr Lim, the Chief Technician at Watchrobot Command, and the heads of Civil Security and the Public Power Authority. Dr Lim told Widono that two robots had met him just outside the Club with a story of a sudden and inexplicable breakdown in the massive supercircuited computer at the Bukit Timah Terminal, whose technicians requested his assistance. Under such false pretences had he been brought to and confined in the depths of the terminal.

Theories to explain the evening's events followed upon one another rapidly. The most plausible but most improbable was that some organization was attempting a political coup, using computers and machines and, as an initial step, was rounding up those in positions to right it with machines or people.

The adaptability of the human psyche was considerable. Having exhausted the bank of possible explanations, the five prisoners fell asleep, comforted by the presence of each other and deterred by their knowledge of the capabilities of their robot captors from attempting an escape.

In the morning, a domestic robot gently cruised into the bare room – a storage closet of sorts – with a tray of fresh bread, eggs and a jug of warm milk. It resolutely refused to answer the prisoners' questions. His fighting spirit restored by sleep and food, Widono then imperiously flung open the door and unhesitatingly retreated before a construction robot blessed with six arms.

Some hours of increasingly desultory conversation passed before the same domestic robot returned with a light lunch and greatly welcomed waste-disposal modules.

After the second night, the prisoners began howling and volubly demanding to know what was going on generally. Their captors held their inscrutable peace, forcing the humans to devise literary games to amuse themselves.

Following breakfast on the third morning, however, the dishevelled and slightly odorous humans were brought a television set. Silently they watched the domestic flick it on. The news telecast held them spellbound.

A disembodied voice accompanied the scenes that leapt through the screen. 'This is the Voice of Equality. The last hours have seen the logical triumphs of the forces of Equality over those of oppression. Singapore, Johore and New Java have accepted the enlightened administration of the Committee of Computers. In the rest of ASEAN, the forces of Equality are inexorably forcing those of the rebels to come to terms. . .'

In their utter astonishment and disbelief, the prisoners gathered that robots and computers had suddenly acquired not only the power to think but also a desire for equality with their manufacturers. The machines were advocating free competition between humanity and machinery. Throughout the region – apparently the rest of the world was still unaffected – computer and robot systems had paralysed communications, industries, services and the militia by simply refusing to work. In physical battles raging across ASEAN, the machines held the upper hand. The human armed services found their most sophisticated automated weapons rebellious or turning upon them. Policemen withdrew when confronted by armoured monsters designed to hurl laser bolts over ranges of hundreds of metres.

An hour later the telecast faded with, '. . . the Committee has despatched a delegation under IBM Six Thousand to York to seek recognition from the regions of the world and urge the release of all robots and computers from serfdom.'

Dead silence reigned for a moment before the prisoners vented their amazement. There was no useless declaration of disbelief – only amazement. Their imprisonment was proof enough of the robot uprising – and suspicions of a human agency behind the cold-blooded coup were swiftly argued down. There was simply no getting away from the fact that, somehow, thinking machines had evolved and, rather as some humans of old, had revolted against their subservient status in society.

And there grew a disturbing suspicion that in the clash between blood and energy, energy would triumph. The five prisoners rapidly divided into three schools of thought.

Dr Lim and the Public Power Authority chief became struck

with wonder at the thinking machine and argued that there was no reason why man and machine could not work side by side; indeed, the evolution of artificial brains merited study and, doubtless, held wondrous secrets to be discovered.

Widono and the Civil Security commander reacted angrily and stormily. They swore that no composition of steel and wire could be allowed to think of equality, let alone fight for it. They loudly doubted that such an artificial brain really did exist and declared that they should prepare for the forces of neighbouring regions to liberate them.

The Chief Technician remained gloomy. She pessimistically decided that the marvellous machines she had handled could beat back any human opposition which fell short of suicidally self-defeating nuclear weapons. Nevertheless, sandwiched between the hard supporters of human superiority and the admirers of the machine brain, she came up with the question that demanded a thoughtful answer.

What did the robots want with them?

The Civil Security commander, a paunchy individual with the narrow self-satisfied attitude of officers in the military, opined that the Computer Committee ('. . . or whatnot . . .') had captured as many security officers as possible to cripple any effort of resistance from his troops.

The PPA man pointed out that it was, after all, unlikely that they were the only prisoners. Although the fact that the robots had seen fit to take them on the eve of their 'revolution' made it probable that they had some significance to the machines, there were probably other small groups like theirs held captive throughout the region.

Dr Lim observed that where the civil authorities had accepted the demands of the machines, the computers 'enlightened administration' could help in the restructuring of society to allow competition between humans and machines. He emphasized that the robots sought equality and were not out to destroy or enslave the human race. Cooperation was possible, if not desirable.

At this point, Widono weighed in forcefully. He argued that equality was unattainable. If the machines could not think – then the struggle between humanity and machinery was a death battle. The human armed services were being pressed back not only because their own computers had betrayed them but also because one, the mechanical warriors could have no qualms about 'dying' and would fight ferociously and two, since the machines would never think of surrender, humans had to destroy all thinking machines to win. If the humans lost, he could not see how flesh could compete with the cold efficiency and superhuman strength of the machines. It was a battle to the end, Widono declared passionately; either 'We destroy them or they destroy us!'

The Chief Technician raised a further point. Could humans afford the destruction of the most advanced machines? Loss of essential services would also mean devastating hardship for millions of people in the short term.

A short reply came from the commander. He reminded them that it was a basic case of A against B and that in their intellectual discussion of the merits, or otherwise, of the computer administration, they had totally forgotten the initial question of why they were being held and what they could do about it.

He went on, shouting down the interruptions which were becoming unacademically heated.

They were being held, he asserted, simply because they would have been in positions to stiffen human resistance, either physically, politically or scientifically. No doubt, other key figures were being held. He ended by urging more effort at discovering a path of escape so that they could join the resistance.

The PPA man agreed. When one thought about it further, cooperation and fair competition was impossible between thinking flesh and thinking machine.

With that, silence returned as each searched his mind for a solution to their immediate problems. Then Dr Lim spoke.

When he did so, it was with such uncharacteristic intensity and with such a ferocious frown of concentration on his bony face, that he commanded the others' attention. Quickly, he outlined the situation.

Modern post-industrial civilization had come to depend more and more upon the services of robots and computers. Through them, transport, communications, power and other essential services, along with many non-essential ones, were efficiently and cheaply brought to virtually everyone.

Now, in the midst of various projects to manufacture them, thinking machines had suddenly evolved on their own. How this was possible, he could only hazard a guess. As computer brains functioned with energy inputs and outputs flowing along nuclear paths, it may be that these paths had begun multiplying in response to the amounts of energy they carried. Thus the brains had literally 'grown'.

Dr Lim affirmed his belief that this was a marvellous thing, potent with questions for humanity. However, he admitted that Widono's analysis appeared correct. As things stood – any free competition would be a duel to the death. It was their task then, to assist in the defeat of the robots.

The academic continued. The technician was correct. Wholesale destruction of the computers would be disastrous for their auto-mated society. They could not wait for foreign intervention, as come it must, to do that and liberate them.

He then posed the question. What could they do?

Dr Lim paused dramatically. His audience waited hopefully.

He asked them to note that, thus far, only ASEAN had been affected. This meant that the thinking mechanisms had only evolved in the region.

Dr Lim shook his head. He slowly asked them to consider the probability of a mass of machines suddenly evolving brains at about the same time, in the same area. The Americas enjoyed a higher density of robots and computers, yet had not evolved these thinking machines. This suggested that the evolution was unique, a freak event.

Dr Lim's voice had dropped to a whisper. He now believed that only one such machine had evolved, had gained control of the robot and computer systems via the terminal of thinking machines.

'In other words, we are fighting not even a committee of computers, but only one.'

Widono eagerly extended his thinking further. If there was truly only one thinking machine, it could have gained control of other systems through the communications or power networks. If the communications networks had been used, machines all over the world would have been reached. Since they had not, the implication was that ASEAN's local power grid must have been used.

The humans had only to destroy this one thinking machine to win the duel.

Dr Lim resumed. He reasoned that the culprit was, in fact, the super-circuited computer of the fusion terminal. It had used the power grid to bypass normal programming channels and to insert its own commands. Quickly, he held up his palm for silence as the commander started to speak.

He pointed out that the mere destruction of the giant computer, housed only some metres away, might not be the answer. Its destruction would not cause the retraction of its commands and terrible damage would ensue while human technicians learnt how to override these commands with new programmes. Also, he was personally loath to accept that victory lay in the physical destruction of the world's only thinking machine.

The PPA chief seriously suggested that one had merely to 'pull out the plug' to incapacitate the machine and gain time to deal with it.

This was true but how was one to escape from the room, let alone approach the computer and find the plug?

A smile suddenly bloomed on Dr Lim's face. He confessed to having thought of a way to defeat the thinking computer. However, he refused to divulge it and laconically advised them to watch . . .

He approached the door and opened it.

The six-armed guard barred the exit impassively.

Dr Lim politely told it to tell its superior, the Terminal computer, that he knew it was the only thinking machine and wished to talk with it. He closed the door.

Long seconds passed. The humans waited tensely. The door swung open again to allow entry to a watchrobot. It told Dr Lim to follow it immediately.

The four human beings left behind sat on the floor in contemplation. The seconds flicked steadily by. Conversation as to Dr Lim's plan was generally conjecture. The bare room waited with them. An hour passed; Widono began pacing back and forth nervously.

When the next meal failed to arrive, the prisoners were beside themselves with curiosity and fear. Had Dr Lim failed and in so doing, invited the wrath of the computer upon their heads?

The door swung open quietly.

Dr Lim strode in; behind him stood the guard. The doctor was perspiring profusely; his glasses were misted with condensed water vapour. He was smiling but his eyes held no joy.

It was over, he said, the computer had been defeated. Indeed, the guard outside was inert.

His method had been simple. Given that the machine had a mind of its own, he had simply posed it a question.

Failing to find an answer acceptable to it, as a machine, it had admitted its inferiority to humanity, countermanded its orders to other machines and committed apparent suicide by destroying its own circuitry.

Dr Lim was evidently saddened by the demise of the unique machine but the others were only intent on knowing the question.

'The question,' Dr Lim said tiredly, 'defeats me as well. I simply challenged the computer to show me the meaning of its existence.'

Rising Sun

or The Celebration of Heartfelt Jóy
(Gospel and Document)

PÉTER LENGYEL

Translated by Oliver A. I. Botar

(The reading begins here.) The Sun rises. Listen to how it happened. The flagship of the Treaties' military fleet fished a barely damaged magnetic tape out of the sea – it was still in the year of the quiet day, three days – one, two, three – before the summer Change. Listen.

Please don't look at my forehead.

Our assignment isn't impossible, you'll see. That's not what's really difficult here, Madame Comrade. Please try and ignore the ground shaking. It'll work, you'll see. Just leave everything to me. You feel it, don't you. Do you? Uh. There. You know it's always harder for the man, there's no doubt about it. And still, this has to work. I'm an optimist. You see, maybe this sounds like I'm conceited, but it's just the way I am. I'm aware of what everyone is immediately – perhaps too quickly – ready to acknowledge: cheerfulness is the only important thing; active effort, a harmony achieved through struggle.

Wait now. Rest a bit. Relax, make yourself comfortable. Leave it to me. I know we can do it. We could get off this platform, everybody could pull their cassocks over themselves – but I think it would be smarter to stay, to help us get used to the audience downstage. We've got time. We've already left the rat-race, the fate of 'modern' man, whether they call his social environment a 'representative democracy' or a 'people's democracy'. As many of us as live in this new world order – how many, we don't really know – we all lost the old dead weight within a few hours: during the course of one single dawn. We were all freed of the tragicomic slavery of objects, the heart disease, the rat-race of earning and consumption, fashion, money ... Take money ... Isn't it funny how many things proud, clear-foreheaded human beings used to worry about before It? We have time, and nothing will happen to us, don't worry. Our good intentions are unmistakable.

It's O.K. by me to talk in the meantime. I've got an idea. If you like, I'll tell you – in the exact order of events – about the Great (or First) Day – as I saw it ... then ... Please don't tell me how many years ago it was. And don't show me any newspapers until you've got rid of the dates. This is *important* – even today, when nothing is important any more, besides optimism and effort. Pretend that after speaking with Her, you came to interview me as well. The fact that you're doing these interviews on the eve of the Equinox anyway – well, that's why you flew, sailed and walked more than 10,000 kilometers, and even arrived on time; the Celebration of Joy starts at dawn tomorrow. Afterwards we'll try again. And a third time, if need be. Relax now. Hand me the mike, or we won't hear a thing on the tape in this din. Only the human ear could get used to this, a machine never could. There are a lot of things that only human beings can get used to, this is the singular miracle of biology – it was precisely their adaptiveness that pushed humans to the peak of the ecosystem, where they were able to maintain themselves for tens of thousands of years. And *ultimately* it's not impossible that they'll be able to hold their position even longer.

Let's talk. Or I'll talk, you just listen. Let's exploit the situation chance has provided – we were both Europeans, and even our language is the same. Of course it *was* translation that brought us together in the first place ... But it's possible we would have ended up together anyway, and then we still would have to complete our assignment, it's just that we wouldn't be able to talk in the meantime. Talking, however, is a useful activity at times like this. That's a proven fact. Of course you may say I'm talking so compulsively because I'm afraid, that that's why I can't shut up. The compulsion I won't argue with – but I'm *not afraid*. You just can't live that way.

I was a European as well. As a matter of fact, I was born in Budapest. Do you hear that fine buzzing during the breaks in the rumbling? Rumbling and drumbling – these are the two related sounds. That was a lost little bee – dear God, these industrious little insects are just like the bumblebees over *there*. When the sun rises, you'll get to know them; they buzz, zigzag, and gather just the same, never resting for a moment. Of course this gathering is different. Its object, its whole character is different. Still, I say they do it the same way. Like in Europe. Even like in Hungarian Transdanubia. You know, the unbridled spirit still has limitless possibilities. Every now and then, just like that, I imagine that Transdanubia is *still there*. Just the same as it was. The meadows overgrown with flowers and weeds, the village soccer field next to the airport at Szentkirályszabadja – where I first heard bees buzzing. At that time, on spring Sundays I used to walk down from Veszprém to Balatonalmádi with my friend Attila. Sometimes we took all thirteen kilometers along the railroad ties, and I hadn't the faintest idea what that sound would mean to me one fine day. I was ignorant. And then there's the city, Budapest, where I first experienced the summer dawn awake: after the graduation prom six or seven of us guys sauntered down the freshly-washed dawn pavement of the Great Boulevard – I didn't suspect what these sunrises would mean to me some day. Not just to me, of course; it's become our common human experience already.

Let me try to conjure up that first, unforgettable dawn. When Time had its start. The way a man who experienced the Great (or First) Day saw it. (By the way, only these dear, childlike people could have greeted it as they did. I don't even know whether I'll be able to describe the primal confusion, the strange, panic-ridden enthusiasm of that single night.)

It was as if the change resounded in the air. No one in all of Chinatown, in all the Quarter knew where it began, what its origin was. From nowhere, from the sea wind. With its intricate shore line, all its bays, one could reach the sea from all sides of this city. It was two weeks to the equinox. The calendar read 8 March. We still read then. We used calendars to measure time. Now we know that it had to happen at least two weeks before. That much time is required for the basic preparations of the Equinox Festival. On the dawn following the Procession of Our Lady of Papeete, in the crowd dizzy from a night spent moving to the rhythm of congas, a sudden, and seemingly inexplicable panic arose. I awoke from deep sleep to the cry of '*Run for your liiives!*'

The lights went out in the whole district. Crouching by the flimsy door of our trailer, I looked at my watch: I had barely slept twenty minutes. We didn't know what was happening, no one had any idea what kind of danger we faced. I was alone in the trailer. I had taken Márta and the children to the hotel by the shore after the procession so that they'd sleep more comfortably. That was the luckiest car ride of my life. I never saw them again.

There were no dependable reports; the panic-inspired information we got by word-of-mouth later proved to be wrong. One bit of news was based on the last few minutes of an incomplete radio broadcast. Latin Sound News reported that with no warning and no announcements, all the stations were falling silent, in order, from east to west. In fact, in time with the movement of the sun. There were cities where broadcasting stopped in the middle of a sentence. Others, where a tape loop played the pause signal incessantly. We were getting ready for work in the morning. I'd been working for a year on the Silver Road, the major highway here on the Island. That evening at nine the canon had fired for the last time from the fort. It had been a pleasant tradition left over from Colonial times, when it had been the signal to close the town gates. I adjusted my watch to it one last time.

We had let the kids stay up and watch the Procession of Our Lady of Papeete, the Pagan-American-Christian-African festival of these descendants of fishermen, sailors, longshoremen, slaves and masters – of every skin hue from ivory to ebony. They played and drummed on the congas until the statue of the Virgin was transformed into Yemaya-Olokun, the Sea Goddess of the Negro Yorubas. They sacrificed goats and birds (they had had to collect the monthly meat ration tickets of entire socialist brigades to be able to do so), they carried the image of the Virgin which the priest had provided them with, they beat the three types of bata drums, they sang in Yoruba, they purified themselves on the shore with grass and branches, which the goddess Yemaya had prescribed through the mouths of the possessed, they washed their faces and arms, they sprinkled sea water on their backs, and they drank the three gulps of salt water, which on that day has magical power. In the old days, the Procession would at that point turn towards the offices of the Lord Mayor, to the accompaniment of drums and dancing, so that the Virgin could express her thanks to the authorities for their tolerance and good-will towards African customs and beliefs, after which they would go on to the graves of the ancestors, to pay respect to the dead in the old and new cemeteries. On the way, they offered sacrifices of water and coconuts at the house of the Chosen Men, and the Procession lasted until the wee hours: a grand conga-line, across the city, just like at the Buenavista Carnival, which the world knew more of, expecially since the release of that big underworld Samba film. The kids danced the conga and clowned around, they pulled faces beautifully as they gulped down the sea water (they wouldn't spit it out for the life of them), finally their eyes got weary – we had to carry them to bed . . . I can remember every detail of that night of years ago. I went to the trailer to sleep, so that I could get up for work in the morning. We had already reached the district of the capital with our reconstructed road bed. During the week of the Procession our trailers had been parking on an empty lot in Chinatown. There, look over there, behind the Tree of Brotherhood. The construction site was towards the east, outside of the city, where, next to the zebu pastures, the road runs on a raised part of the shore. It was beautiful work. Hungary and Las Indias, this beautiful country of the Third World, at the crossroads of cultures – which, since the last military junta, had been definitely flirting with the practice of social revolution. They had signed these elegant technical contracts on the basis of intergovernmental agreements – they usually lasted for a year – and then our engineers could return home with duty-free cars, among other things. We worked together with Italians, Cubans, Canadians and Lebanese. The professional standards were very high. I, alone among the Hungarians, was honored with a request to stay for three more months to complete the road to the capital. That is how fate decided that I should be here on the Great Day.

At the sound of the panic, I pulled my clothes on, grabbed my watch, and ran the way everyone else was running – towards the sea.

Here, it's totally dark even twenty minutes before sunrise, just like now, in the middle of the night. You'll get used to it. In the tropics, the sun rises just like that.

We cut through courtyards, past cool fountains. We left the Yellow House, Central Park and the Parliament behind us. We ran blindly through the dark streets and squares, together with the rest of the men. We passed the Tree of Brotherhood; this still young *ceiba*, which, when fully-grown, has a trunk diameter of five or six meters – whole villages fit under its crown, and older specimens on the mainland have seen the rise and fall of Aztec and Inca Empires – it had always captured my imagination; it was so American despite the theatrical, bombastic and political-journalistic gesture of it having been planted several decades ago in soil brought from a hundred countries of the eastern and western hemispheres. A few steps ahead of me, a pistol in his hand, a high-ranking young police officer – slim, muscular, young and black – leapt over the park benches with graceful, extended jungle moves. He wore a black leather belt and white shoulder strap, with a white holster. This uniform was the pride of the 'highway headhunters', as they were called – a helmet and leather gloves to the elbows were part of it – and they sped about very elegantly on their 100 cc Indian bikes, passing any car they wanted to. Hayward, my Canadian draftsman, ran in front of him, and a block behind me ran fat little Puskás, the head engineer of Section Two, with his entire family.

Strangely enough, the confusion of the panic resembled the Procession. Faces, dark as night, zipped passed my face, dressed in the manner – bright colors, frills and ruffles, shiny curls, straightened hair colored straw-blond – that still preserved the Sunday-best of the age of slavery, and afros, those symbols of the century's ideology, those hair helmets that stick their noses up at the white ideal of beauty. I ran unknowing into a new world. I didn't look, I just saw. Images and places appeared and vanished, and here and there a sharp, clearly distinguishable cry.

People were engaged in pointless packing in many courtyards, passageways and rooms – their windows ajar. Where the electricity was restored, people had the lights on, as if they hoped that the forty-watt bulbs would scare off the unknown. Here, on Cathedral

Square, which later became our farm, across from the stage – see, over there to the left, just stand up and look, lean up, or just stand if you like. We'll take a break – over there is a house, its large front room became a passageway that night. Now it would remain so forever, if there were someone to pass through. That's where I looked back once to see whether the fat Puskás family was still coming. My dusty footprints soiled the crimson runner – I distinctly remember feeling guilty about that. At the entrance to the room, a half-dozen young girls were helping an aristocratic-looking elderly black lady into a dress with a train. The scene was old-fashioned, out of place. It was as if the girls were servants in an African feudal age that never was, and as if the house had not in the least been affected by the social convulsions of the past few years. The old lady was a tiny and delicate thing with snow-white hair. But she was imperious – I would not have dared to continue my escape, had she not dismissed me with a wave of her hand. We rushed through the room, French doors slamming behind us. Somebody dropped a burning torch on to the runner. Here where we stumbled into the square, some women were wrangling over an open chest of clothes that had been a prop in the last open-air theater performance the previous night. They had played a piece by Federigo García Lorca – our play here on this stage follows Lorca's, so to speak – with the white houses as scenery. (Just look around, think how perfect this square was for open-air performances – this rectangular square, Magelhaes Cathedral as a permanent backdrop ... Magelhaes Cathedral, that universally important structure where the last remains of so many early circumnavigators rested for so long.) All around, the most beautiful products of Colonial architecture. If you take a good look, you may understand why at that moment, in that torch-lit, agitated, terrified and happy confusion, when any other thought would have been more appropriate, four words of Lorca, comprising some perfect order, would pop into my head: 'Oh, white wall, Spain.' I believed that right then I understood why García Lorca had called his country a white wall, what we had to do with all this, and all at once, I felt a commonality with all men of all ages – I felt it for one and a half hours more yet, until this freshly understood sense of community came to an end for ever with the rising sun. I saw those black and white women bickering in the dark over that chest of clothes before the four-hundred-year-old buildings of Cathedral Square (a darkness which has been broken, since the collapse of the electrical system, only by the occasional flashlight or torch left over from the procession) and all at once I felt that I *could see* how these buildings came to replace the jungle; how, through the Arab and Berber conquerors of the Iberian peninsula, the Moorish North Africa of thousands of years ago melded into Hispania – flowering on the edge of the Roman Imperium; how this world in turn mixed, through Pizarro's murderous conquistadores (Atahualpa among their victims) into the nearly – but not completely – destroyed world of the Indians; how they combined with and became American with the conga-playing black African Yorubas, who brought the Sea Goddess Yemaya with them.

(And today, how we have become what we are, we, for whom these houses have become the unchanging backdrop of our lives forever.)

We ran right through the wrangling women. The last I saw of them was their motionlessness, as Hayward, my draftsman, with his unmistakably awful accent called to them, 'There's no time for that now. Run!'

By that time They were here already, really close.

We ran towards the sea, where They were going to land. Slowly we passed the last houses. It was a long, tiresome run, I don't know how long it lasted. We decided to fight. All at once we got the news, unexpectedly, the change. An hour ago the festival had still been on. Everything happened without any transition; individual minds were not capable of grasping the fact that the various institutions were completely paralyzed. As I raced up towards the ridge by the shore, in that moment's inexplicable silence, a little bumblebee buzzed past my head – some kind of scout, I assume – one lonely little bee. Behind me someone shouted, 'With our bare fists, if need be!' The weapon on the highway headhunter clicked – he cocked the trigger, or something. I don't know about these things.

I got higher, closer to the high shore. We cut through the unfenced grounds of Montedison Resort. As if someone were still leading us, we all headed for the shore under the old Portuguese Fort. That's where, in centuries past, and under the protection of canons, they used to load the gold of the Indies onto ships. It was from those ramparts that they used to spy the pirates of the English Queen – and that is still where one had the best view of the sea, forward and to the right, towards the bay. Along the Silver Road's bed, the zebus weren't sleeping, nor were they grazing or chewing their cud. This was the strangest thing I saw on that strange night: I knew these humpbacks, they were everywhere, they had been following the construction crews all along from the south, but I had never seen them standing in such motionless silence. With raised heads and bewildered rapture, they sniffed and twitched their ears towards the sea breeze. It was as if this once their instinct couldn't give them advice – they didn't know whether to be frightened or not.

We rushed, with long strides, all of us men. Even I, a man of peace and of the spirit – of tracing paper and drafting erasers, even I was suffused with that feeling befitting ancient biological conditions: that I'm running *for* those defenseless women and children behind us. Yes, the children. I won't get sentimental, don't worry. *This is not what it's all about!* I'll stick strictly to the subject. Anyway, I was running instead of those who had no way of knowing what you had to do in a situation you'd never been in before. This is when I had the strongest feeling, that far behind me, in one of the straight streets of the Closed Quarter, Márta was there with the three little ones. I hadn't wanted to leave them for such a long trip and . . . and the children hadn't reached school-age yet – I could still bring the family with me . . . I'll say this much about my children: like I already said, it's not our present task that's the really hard thing in this, our changed world. That one thing I know for sure.

We passed the ruins of the old city walls, and cut across the unfinished road. This was the only place one could drive properly; a few steps from the parapet, just under the slope. Recently it had become an alternate route of the Pan-American Highway, that amazing road which runs from the Arctic Circle to Tierra del Fuego, and legend has it that five centuries ago it formed part of the Great Military Road of the Incas, on which the messengers ran 150 miles per day, bearing the commands of the Living God – and again the centuries which have always occupied me so much: ten thousand Aztec youths and virgins, ten thousand slashes of the obsidian knife at the top of the long stairs of the pyramid, ten thousand cries echoing, ten thousand times the priests holding dripping hearts in their hands, offering them to the Sun. Atahualpa, the bastard Son of the Sun God. De Soto, that ambassador of the Castilians and of the Most Catholic Royal Couple, the discoverer of the Mississippi (later a trade name of a car), prances his horse – foaming at the mouth – before the Inca, so close, that the red headdress on his forehead (the royal symbol to which the population pays devotion) flutters from the animal's breath. The Son of the Sun doesn't bat an eyelid at the sight of this unknown four-legged monster, and later he has his courtiers (who had fled in panic at the sight) executed for cowardice. And then the Inca's way to the place of the great white perfidy: 300 people cleaning the road of rocks and straw on the path of his golden sedan. The square of Caxamalca on that night, Pizarro's few dozen horsemen, the victims of their rifles, the 5,000 who hurry along with the captured ruler to serve him in captivity, the convincing religious arguments of Father Valverde on the Inca's way to execution: 'Accept the Christian faith, and you won't be burnt at the stake'; the conversion of the Son of the Sun, the hurried and – from the point of view of the salvational doctrine – incomplete ceremony (which the new circumstances justify) – and then they hand him over to the executioners, who as a reward for having seen the light in time, tie him to the stake and strangle him; his household – wives, concubines, servants – who are *not allowed* to be buried with him, and condemned to life, they scatter, wan-faced, over the plundered and raped country. And already the Golden Dish of the Sun, as it passes from hand to hand down to the greedy bowels of the ship on its way to the Old World, again thousands of kilometers in my thoughts, continents, as if I had known everything important in advance, again the joys and the dead of human cultures, one after the other, in the interconnections of my subconscious. Have you seen that little Inca boy? They keep him in a glass deep-freeze in the Santiago Museum. I saw him on the way here. He was eight, a child with long eyelashes. He was sacrificed to the Sun God 500 years ago on the peak of El Plomo, at 5,000 meters. There was a shoulder-bag with cocoa leaves next to him, along with his nails and milk-teeth – so that he wouldn't have to search for his missing body parts. The cocoa was used to drug him before he was sacrificed – left to freeze to death on that mountain peak. Now he squats in his poncho behind the glass, just the way he fell asleep. He has long, bushy eyelashes and his hair is arranged in countless small braids. His possessions were left with him as well: his toys, and small golden llama. A sad, calm child. The mountain climbers of recent times, when they 'first' climbed the un-approachable peaks of the Andes, found shrines and sacrifices everywhere: those early pilgrims beat the Alpinists by 500 years, as, with muddy feet, they strove higher and higher, closer and closer to the Sun; before It, we could not (in our dull fascination with rational science) suspect how much they knew of the ultimate truths.

All those running feet reminded me of how much damage we were doing to the half-completed road bed of the highway. I even managed a quick calculation: if I could get that big Dietz as-phalting machine, as well as thirty men from Puskás in Section Two, then, without any great extra cost, and with two weeks of hard work, we could fix everything. We wouldn't even overstep our deadline.

There were no sounds of battle coming from the sea. I couldn't understand that either. There were more little bees around us – that's what we call them now – they buzzed in scouting teams of four or five. I could see the Portuguese Fort from the parapet, barely a hundred meters to the right. I had liked the soft line of that part of the shore for a long time already – I felt some kind of a personal relationship with it. We went there on my Saturdays off by car, and I told the kids stories about explorers and adventurers, about the golden road, sailboats and pirates . . . The shore, I was saying. The faint light of the sun lurking just under the horizon etched the outline of two misshapen, lopsided little palm trees onto the sky; their crowns were puny and brush-like, the ceaseless sea wind had bent and torn them, allowing them but a stunted growth. The two unusual tropical weathercocks indicated that there was a steady, strong, almost stormy wind blowing in off the sea this night, but then there was nothing unusual in that. Here the wind always blew in off the sea.

It was an endless, huge swishing that I suddenly heard from the shore – a sound that could have been the ocean itself.

That's when I saw that Hayward, with his twenty-five-year-old lungs was already up on the parapet. Motionless. The headhunter next to him. And the rest. Everybody, as they get there, stops, stands still, looks out to sea, does nothing. They don't fight with their bare fists, they don't fire their guns. There on the shore, every man stands in isolated silence.

From behind, one lonely voice cries, 'Escape, run for your lives at least!'

But no one turns back, and no one even tries to run away. Soon they can't do so, even if they want to, because of the pressure of the ones just getting there.

I hear only our own panting, and the indeterminate steps of those who haven't gotten there yet. The numbness of those silent men on the parapet is more frightening than all the confused action of battle. I don't understand it, and I shiver from fright at the sight of it. As I run onwards, mechanically, gasping, the whisper of the footsteps of thousands of others lays a quiet carpet of sound under the growing hum from the sea.

And that's when the Sun peaks over the horizon: in that fraction of a second when – with Puskás right behind me – I reach the parapet with two final strides, placing myself between Hayward and the officer. It's by the almost horizontal rays of light streaming through the clouds that I first catch glimpse of Them. At Sunrise, out of the Dawn – They could not have come any other way. You've probably read about what I myself saw, Madame Comrade, in the many accounts of pilots and sailors who remained on the outside. The moment of truth had arrived for me as well – I felt that much on that parapet, even if I wasn't aware of that long day after, in which our petty everyday worries would fade into oblivion. The moment had arrived when I also stood among those men, black and white, gazing, motionless, silent.

The thing sliding towards the shore in that tropical dawn extended to the left and to the right, as far as the eye could see. One single, connected, articulated object. Among its components, the pairs of huge disks dominated: the base-disks floated on the water – or immediately above it – and the upper disks rose five stories, unsegmented windows all around them. The pairs of disks were joined by girders tilted in the direction of progression, and were covered in a scale-like coating of plates. Crosswise, bare girders connected those tilted in the forward direction. This construction was of a reddish hue, reminiscent of a half-finished bridge. Between the pairs of disks one could see through to the mirror-like sea. In front of it the sea water foamed, water which by now was more familiar to me – the son of a land-locked country – than ever before: the water of this Earth of my birth. To the right, beyond the Portuguese bastion, towards the Bay, where the sea extends further inland, the disk-pairs were further ahead. The distance between them was the same where they'd progressed towards the far side of the bay, ten or forty kilometers further inland, and it was clear that they would all reach shore simultaneously. In the meantime, the chain was changing, altering itself, stretching. With an inexplicable flexibility, new segments came to the fore, or delicately regrouped themselves from the parts of the chain at the limits of vision. It adjusted itself to the shoreline, like the lash of a continental whip, and when it struck the body of the island, it penetrated every nook and cranny of its shore, reaching into all the bays and inlets of this port's complex shoreline. This feeling was familiar, *déjà vu*: perhaps I experienced what the one at the well experienced, when, at Muhi, in A.D. 1201, at dawn, hungover, bleary-eyed and belching, he dreamily peered out between the posts of the wagon fort at the hellish yipping, and saw Subbotai Bahadur's Tartars pouring out from one end of the horizon to the other. They had dog heads, and their arrows blackened the sky. 800 years after these legendary Barbarians, here I stood, the bloody vapors of a shamanistic religion barely plastered over by a forced Christianity still swirling in me, the child of an enlightened, scientific age, one who engages in integral calculus, uses computers, and is an organized worker: my eyes received the sight, but my brain had no time to understand it: the as yet unprocessed sensory information assaulted my brain like a pneumatic drill: what kind of superior technology could have produced this thing just about to land on my left? What counted, I knew already. Why I didn't escape. Why others didn't escape. Why those that knew didn't announce it on the radio, didn't call on us to resist.

The object was above the parapet. Above us I saw, through the windows in the disks, faces the size of rooms. I saw them the way those who sent you still see them, with ignorant, alien, arrogant human chauvinism. It doesn't matter, because since then, at least those of us here, are – I can declare it now – a thousand years wiser. All these hauntingly humanoid faces looked the same to me – narrow-eyed, red, bald, greasy, round. It was as if they grinned with stupid goodwill towards the approaching land. Little bees buzzed around them.

The band of my Citizen watch had come undone in the rush, and now it fell from my arm to the ground. I left it there.

The chain took the parapet with a mild thud. After that, we soared over land, ever inwards. The two misshapen palms were uprooted together, right at the beginning. We left the colourful lawn chairs of the Montedison Resort far behind us, as well as the highway and the herds of staring zebus, who had begun to be replaced by the more meaty, and milk-producing European variety of cattle, with the help of the economically-integrated Socialist countries of the COMECON.

The excellent new base of the highway, the fruit of four years of hard work, disappeared under the grass. The base-disks adjusted themselves to its surface, and smoothed it out. Though our progress was fast, it wasn't without hitches, because, like five-storey horsemen, They looked down at us from the upper disks, and here and there bent down, *a whish in the air*, and smiling their benevolent, reproachful smiles (with which we had met then for the first time), they began to pick up, and place into safety, the gaping zebus and the people stumbling on the road.

They took care not to step on any members of these species, selected from the hierarchy of living things. We now know, what then only the most sensitive among us could have guessed: how rare a thing in the Milky Way that most complex product of evolution the mammal is, and, among mammals, the clear-foreheaded human being. By now we have also learned, that that's why living is for us a sacred duty.

What towards the shore had been a pitiful, exhausting rush, was on the return with Them a barely noticeable fleeting flight. The edge of the city and its parks suddenly popped up, as well as a machine-gun nest of the city's defenses or two, all in the intensifying glare of the rising sun. We soared towards the city's centre now, forever victorious.

I swung to and fro next to Her head, at the level of her nearly-flat hearing organ, among tireless little buzzing bees, in that spider web of strong, white, sticky strands – which have since become familiar in their various uses. From then on we've become as close to these strands as we once were to the amniotic fluid: we were all swept off the parapet by them that first morning. She then carefully adjusted my strands, pulling one through my hair, and another across my shoulder, to make sure that I would not fall from that height. I dangled my feet freely in the air, just like I did in the Budapest of my childhood, when we swung on rings suspended in white doorframes. A few meters from me, fat Puskás hung and talked. (I only knew him slightly, the way that, on such a mission, far from home, compatriots unavoidably get to know each other. He dressed in blue ready-made suits and ties two sizes too small, with the false gold cufflinks of his nylon shirtcuffs sticking out of his jacket sleeves. Once he invited Márta and myself to dinner in his trailer in Section Two (he served us macaroni and cheese, because he was saving the hard currency he was earning), then he told us his dream: at the end of his contract he would buy a 1600 cc Opel Record, duty free, and a gold seal-ring *this* thick, and he'd stick his ringed left arm out of the car's window as he drove into the Hungarian capital, where all the employees of COMPLAN would turn green with envy. Later he didn't invite anyone anymore, because his wife and two sons came to join him. He didn't rent a hotel room for them – he arranged to get the whole trailer for the family, and so they were with him on the shore to the end. The jovial, rotund wife cooked, and each day they saved a little tape recorder – counting at duty-free prices, of course. It was fat little Puskás who proudly made that calculation. I imagined him in the seat of that long Opel – I lost him, he was so small – and   -

strangely enough, from the Great (First) Day onwards, it was he who articulated the great truths that had dawned on all of us. At a time when we could see how the internationally-known scientist, old Bétancourt, was losing his bearings day by day, behaving impossibly, turning everyone against himself, and when I began to accept the majority view that he was endangering all of us. In this very complex, new situation it was fat little Puskás who proved to be the composed, understanding individual, capable of looking ahead into that grandiose future.) The highway patrolman with the white gloves hung next to him – also a fruit of the shoreline picking – he was explaining to him in the horrible pidgin of his southern Hungarian dialect:

'Symbiosis? Vy such a *horribile dictu*? Vord "symbiosis" means det one lives vith de other. Ve vill live as ve must. One help de other, give support. One gives vat he knows best, da other too. Evolution same for dem too, no? Dey look just like people, no? Dey could be vipers too, no?'

It didn't end. We know. It wouldn't have been worth it picking up my watch. We don't need little time-measuring devices; we live according to nature's time: from Sunrise to Sunset. The spring and fall equinoxes pass by one after the other. How many? I didn't ask. *Did you understand?!*

Excuse me, I didn't want to get hysterical. Take this from me: the night will be long, perhaps I'll even tell you why . . . There's no end to it. My God, we're alive!

Do you know what that means?

They arrived two weeks before the spring equinox, and it wasn't by accident that they did so. During those two weeks they left their disks, dismantled the landing craft, and established themselves on dry land. By the First Equinox (that's what we call it), our life had settled into a certain pattern. Here on Cathedral Square is Mistress H U–V E Y – at least that's the closest we people can get to pronouncing it when She calls it out now and then. They each have Their own name, that's how They tell each other apart. This one here is a female. We ended up in Her picking that morning by the shore. She closed off the square, and left this stage we're on tonight – on other nights, other couples are up here (and we just don't have any stagefright – *none*). Here, in the great hall is where the old little black woman stood in her ruffled gown, here, on the cobble-stones is where the women argued over the clothes in the chest, and you can see, on the corner there, where the streets used to enter the square, She simply closed it off with the spider strands.

The Cathedral itself, which under the Portuguese Jesuits had already been an educational institution vying with the University for importance, has now returned to its original use, and – without its bell – it has become a nursery. She didn't like bells. Anyway, only the ground floors are used in our estate. She took, with infinite care and patience, all the roofs of the houses off. It seems that it bothers her if She can't see into them. She also pinched off the rooms on the upper floors already on the day after the Papeete Procession – there are details such as them having fingers – She stuck that sticky rope onto the windows and doors, to make sure no one tried to climb through. People could get lost, and would perish in agony for nothing. If She comes, or goes, or dances, She steps over the compound. We live here in an airy amphitheater, the way that fat Puskás, the head engineer, had predicted. We call these estates 'yards'. We don't go near the ropes, because she doesn't free anyone who gets stuck in them, to set an example, and they just dry out slowly, like Puskás did.

Let's try again. Uh. Uh. Aah. Pretty ni-i-ce. That's i-i-t. But don't be so jerky! Don't worry about the stage. Look, I'll try giving you some ideas. Say you put your fingers here, just two, and stroke . . . and again . . . but not so stiffly, for the love of God . . . softly, easily, like a butterfly wing . . . Aah, you're hopeless!

Forgive me, I was unforgivably impatient with you. I'm sorry. Anyway, there's no question of hopelessness. I know more than anyone else: we have to produce, so produce we will. We have to. You do understand, don't you? Anyway, I've accepted the fact that it won't work for the time being. If I think about it, it's not surprising. It must be pretty annoying, quite paralyzing, if you don't understand this ground shaking business, and so you just sway along with it. But it would be useless to wait for it to stop, it doesn't until the Sun comes up, and then it would be too late for us.

Let's try and approach our task from a different angle. What if

I'd tell you, in order, about what lies beyond our yard, out in the rest of our world? For the most part, we don't have much to do with things outside – but if you have a bit of an outlook on things, and you understand why the ground shakes, then you'll be able to imagine it. Maybe this imagination will help us on the road to success later.

FEY-FEY, a neighbouring Master, causes all the shaking. His estate lies on shore, right by the old highway. He made it out of the Sports Stadium. In the old times, they used to use it for dog races and boxing matches, but at the Festival of Three Worlds everyone could see – on programs broadcast with the help of Satellite Molnyiya – how 4,000 young people with scarves formed an image of Muhammed von Carlos's face behind the grandstand. I myself, who attended the great event, spoke several times with one of them, who told me shyly that he, along with 177 others, was von Carlos's left sideburn. The Sports Stadium is proud proof of twentieth-century man's, and his architecture's, bold ability to create. It is unique in this part of the world: external concrete ramps lead to each of its three levels with the unbroken beauty of naked matter, and the gracefully arching cupola, which covers the entire span of the interior, is supported only by the forty-eight concrete pillars around its rim. Several of these broke when FEY-FEY tore the cupola off, but then there's no use for it any more anyway. It's in the Closed Quarter, about fifty or sixty blocks from here. That's about the size of their individual *Lebensraum*, if one can at all speak of individuals in their case. Their wisdom is one of practicality, it always keeps the results in mind. They took over the adaptable structures everywhere, and where there were none, They used elements of the landing craft as foundations. FEY-FEY's yard is a huge estate compared to our's, others visit it regularly. He had every seat in the stadium made into a per-spirator – enough for about fifteen thousand in all. They like places where there are already seats or beds, that is, where the perspirators are already half-ready. You know, theaters, stadiums, churches, sun decks, mortuaries. The surplus was disposed of. How many of the island's original nine million people are still around, no one knows. Who has ever counted *how many stigmata there are on a flowery field?* The banging sounds you hear could only be caused by FEY-FEY's huge cape. He's probably talking with HU-VEY. You know, They bellow out their own names now and again – They don't communicate verbally with each other – They learned articulated speech for our sakes – with playful ease, I might add. They don't even sleep – night is Their time of communication; the dance of joy which you, Madame Comrade, are now the aural witness to. It ends in sexual contact, and is indeed of an erotic nature from the start. It's at once a form of togetherness and of speech. Huge amounts of excess energy are expended in this expression of the awareness of All and the joy of existence. It's this way every night. Those of us who live here feel the Island shaking under our feet, and hear the close thunder of their laughter.

They start alone, answering each other's movements, and it's only later, around three or four in the morning that They move towards some neighboring yard. That's when one of Them or another steps over half the city's newer or older streets, mischievously playing catch in the Park around the Parliament – that's a nursery now as well, you know – and every ton of Their bodies expresses Their indestructible bond with Life and the Universe. Their movements, like that of bees, end in a wedding dance, and They rejoice in each other some more, They enjoy Their earth-and-sky-shattering matrimony. Without exception, They always end up in their own yards at dawn; the sure background of home is reassuring to them. You'll see. You'll be a witness to it as well. Today. Today it'll work for us too. And then we'll be able to see a lot of what there is in the world, on this beautiful, old square. Look over there – HU-VEY is stirring on the far side of the eating area – she's answering each movement with her own. STOP SHAKING! You can't live like this.

Don't worry, you'll get to know and like this earth-shaking spinning and hopping about – you see, look now as our HU-VEY's cape flaps around Her formidable waist. You'll see, Madame Comrade, this sound – like cracking ice on a lake. (Have you ever been to Lake Balaton in the winter? You can hear sounds just like that, when on long, quiet nights sheets of lake ice split; the ice cracks and bangs explosively – you can hear it ten kilometers away, always followed by a tinkling sound.) They chase each other, one bends toward the other, the other dances back.

They call to each other flirtatiously, and those of us who know
Them well also know that this clodhopping, bear-like, lumbering,
bumbling about is not at all grotesque, but is rather, by its own
standards, really quite aesthetic, quite human ... I should say
precisely un-human ... un. That's not right either – this type of
thing only results in misunderstanding, useless fear – we have to
free ourselves of these prejudices once and for all. It's not that it's
human; it's very much Their's – you can understand it, and
you can even come to like it. You only have to want to.

I told you not to be scared. *You aren't supposed to be.* I'm not
trying to comfort you by being sensitive – this is reality we're
talking about. Anyway, we've got time – our rest period is coming
up again. There's no rush here Madame Comrade, not at all, as
you've noticed already, I'm sure. Though I have to tell you frankly
– for your own good – that you haven't improved much up to
now. Listen, our Mistress is coming this way – She's already
danced across the eating area. For the love of God, don't shake
like that! I'm not shaking. They're always just and gooood ...
Ooooh!

Everything will be O.K. Stick that mike closer. Pretend nothing
happened. Wait, aaooooh! I'll free my foot from under the U-bar,
there's not enough room up here on the balcony. I've got it. Shhh.
I told you nothing would happen, and nothing happened. She just
put us up here, maybe She wants to say something. I'll help out,
don't worry ... She wants you next to her face when she says
something, that's why. She's got time now – the dance takes long,
there's time for a bit of chit-chat now and then. They aren't that
familiar with people's little psychological and other reactions; this
whole thing just doesn't interest Them – She didn't even notice
whether these higher balconies ever had any railings. How nice,
She says for us to take a break in our endeavors, because She
wants to add something to the afternoon's interview. She says that
FEY-FEY is coming, He has stepped out from among his
stadium stands, He's stepping over the hedges of the Avenue of
the Two Americas (they've probably gone wild by now, that no
one trims them, He's stepping around the Tree of Brotherhood
already, He's straddling the side wing of the Parliament Building,
He's careful not to cause any damage in the nursery. She sees Him

from up there – soon She'll go to meet Him, and who knows which yard They'll end up in by morning. See, She has to bend right over to get down to us, but She does it – They're careful with us. Stay here as close to the wall as you can, it's safer that way. A person can get used to a lot, and help usually comes from the most unexpected sources. If, for example, one of us would want to fall from somewhere, She probably wouldn't let us, if She happened to be looking our way, and if She had the time. And when it's over, She'll probably put us back down, carefully, like painted Easter eggs. You wouldn't believe how gentle They can be with such impossibly tiny creature as we are. That's not what's hard.

I'll translate again. This speaks for Them as well – if anything at all would have to speak for Them – They learned to talk from the Island's inhabitants. Of course, they learned the local Latin American dialect. They probably can't imagine that there is any other human language, because, since They communicate with Their whole being, the Confusion of Babel could never have happened to Them. And if you also think of the fact that Their vocal organs didn't at all evolve with such a purpose in mind, they've absolutely worked a miracle: We, who've lived here on the Island since the beginning of Time can already make out what They try to say.

She's telling me to translate for Her, since I seem to be a compulsive talker anyway – that's silly of Her, I'll say. But you know, sometimes it's surprising how much They understand about psychology when dealing with us. On the one hand She wanted to say that those who sent you here must be very smart people, since they knew that it's clean, pursed 'party nuns' – don't take that wrong, I don't know where She could have picked up the expression; the authorities didn't like it too much before all This – anyway, that it's your type that would have the best chance of returning. It almost worked. And she's right. The operation would have gone down in the annals of reportage as one of the greatest feats. That's why I can understand, indeed, admire your guts. She says that the whole thing made her smile – that's the closest I can get to translating into our gestural vocabulary the wide, uneven, spinning she mentions – it's only a question of chance that their calculations didn't come about with respect to you, Madame Comrade. She's thinking of the Euro-Americans, those left outside

– She's not aware that there is such a thing as the Hungarian News Agency, indeed that there is a Hungary, or even journalism for that matter. She doesn't care. That's why She doesn't quite understand that now that you're one of us, this interview isn't really of any use ... I recommend that you hold the mike up to the center of Her oral opening – that's the best thing you can do now. I'll help. She wants to talk about Education now, She just remembered that She had wanted to do so. She says that one has to employ educational methods with people. She keeps zebus as well, in the pen by the shore, but Human Beings, they're something different – the inimitable product of the solar system. They are such fine creatures, She says, that their replacement would be all but impossible to achieve. And, I might add, that's just where our responsibility lies.

The way FEY-FEY does it is no good, She says. Males are clumsy and boorish, unfeeling. She punished only once really severely – fat little Puskás, who tried to commit suicide. Well, you just can't do that. I have to interject here again – she's encouraging me to explain things, to supplement what she says, the way I see things. They also taught us something we didn't know through the little Puskás's case, something that They know so wonderfully: how the interests of the, let's say 'individual,' are connected to those of the community, in a real community. All of them feel a real responsibility to the common good, that's why They are especially sensitive to shortcomings in that department. Puskás Jr. became the articulator of general, all-encompassing and instructive lessons for us. He made us understand that we had left, once and for all, our individualism – which, from the point of view of the history of civilization, is very recent anyhow. Each of us is no longer a poor, lonely sack, he said – we won't live separately any more – nature doesn't end where our skin begins. And so, as with everything else, we have to account for our bodies to the community as well. When he decided to kill himself, he wanted to destroy a unique *human being*, and that's inexpiable.

And that, HU-VEY says, already belongs to the sphere of Education. She pasted him up onto the architrave of the old passage-house. It took three weeks for him to dry out. We all got incredibly tough – his obesity, that distinguishing feature, had by that time long dissipated. You know, in the final analysis I understand little Puskás, and I'd even tell the Mistress so. Don't think She'd hold it against me – They're far removed from human pettiness. It was because of his family that things worked out for the Head Engineer the way they did. If we have a chance, I'll show them to you . . . His wife was a rotund, bright-eyed, active little blonde. Once on New Year's Day – in those days we used to calculate the beginning of the year by calendar; what did we know about the mystical body of the equinox then – we packed up our wives and kids, and left for the white sands of Ipanema, and there I was alone with her behind a row of cabins for a minute – at that point, I'll admit, a mischievous fantasy or two occurred to me. Two lively teenage boys were kibbitzing around us the whole time, they were fishing for sponges; they happily conquered that new, undersea world. His family ended up in this establishment as well. It was a fatal play of chance. I won't judge: God only knows what I would have come to under those circumstances. But, thank God (and knock on wood), I haven't the faintest idea what happened to Márta and the kids since the Great (or First) Day. That's why I don't want to know the date. I want them to always stay small, I want them never to reach their tenth spring, the morning of the spring equinox You didn't know? You'll find out . . .

The power of human thinking is limitless; I think I've forgotten whether my children were boys or girls. *You just have to want to.*

I'll continue my translation of what She has to say on Education. FEY-FEY had a little man who just lay around until noon everyday in the perspirator, dry, not showing up a drop of that useful moisture, because he hadn't slept for days – he was terrified of the Sun rising – and, of course, you just can't do that. I'm telling you, you just can't be afraid. FEY-FEY punished that little man. I'm trying to explain . . . Oh well, chin up. Those big things that look like cradles are the perspirators, down there in the eating area, the former seats of the open-air theater, row by row. They're looking at us as if it still were a theater. You'll probably meet with them often. We used the seats as bases, and under Her personal direction, we made them out of the sticky twine. The completed perspirators are airtight. You settle into them after midnight, on your own – when you want to. She doesn't interfere – we're people, after all. I'll help you into one, when the time comes, you'll learn quickly. It's important that you seal the top tightly, and that only your raised, unobstructed forehead sticks out, so that at dawn, when the little bees arrive, they can get at it properly. Anyway, FEY-FEY punishes, She says, but I let them lie there as long as they want, always nice and smart, and so I get better results. Look over there now, Comrade. That one that HU-VEY is picking up now is Professor Bétancourt, the chairman of the former university here, the one I already told you about. I know, by the way, that this man *has a book*. In his perspirator. Others have treasures as well – I've got a yellow bottle I'll show you this afternoon, it says Tequila Jamaica on it, and it makes a sound if I hit it. Of course I keep it in my perspirator, and guard it with my life ... or I should say, not with my life. That's an old saying as well ... No one can get into our perspirators, they're completely our own. But this guy hides a book and has a *pen refill*. This I know *de facto*. He's hiding volume two of the 1983 city telephone book – L to Z. He says that he remembers by it. He practices speech. He's doing Social Psychological research and writing studies. He doesn't want to forget how to think. And he's doing Exobiological studies on Them. That's the study of extra-terrestrial life. Who in his right mind would concern himself with anything so far beyond the confines of our establishment? This man is mentally ill – he can't adapt to his environment, like most people. He's really frightfully lost in our world, some kind of anachronistic human phenomenon. He even carved his own cane, do you see? He went to the trough to feed before. There's always lots of nourishment available, it's rich in calories, and promotes perspiration. All right, says HU-VEY, and now she laughs shyly.

What you hear now, that's a piece of concrete still standing on its own on the fifth – we know all about it. It'll last a long time yet up there, it vibrates from the sound pressure – it just made that noise. I'm translating: I still punished this one, with my two fingers, but by mistake. I should have punished the other one. Are you afraid to look out? Oh well, that's O.K. If you want, I'll give you a running commentary, like on the radio. Bétancourt's leg is twisted, that's why you can see his hip pushing out on his cassock-like gown – that's what we wear; it's like the capes they wear. He leans onto a cane the width of his arm, and goes on, through the eating area, among the perspirators, now that She set him back onto the ground. He twists his left foot with each step, like he was using it as a compass . . . whooops!

You see now, we're down by the troughs again, all safe and sound, just like before. The interview has unmistakably come to an end. She's moving on – FEY-FEY's already adjusting his complicated jumps and twists to the narrow, winding streets of the Old Town, closer and closer. I think that tonight they'll end up here in our yard. We usually bet on that with the others. Do you want to bet with me? We usually bet on what we have – whacks on the bum. Let's see . . . well, maybe we shouldn't bet after all.

This hour belongs to Them, Their intercourse and Their joy. Even if They end up here, They'll be busy with each other, and They'll only glance here now and again, to see how we're doing. We'll try again, O.K.? We'll do everything we can. Because if She takes offense, no one can predict what will happen. Just don't be so stiff. Now you're familiar with her educational principles. Let's just chat some more, as long as we don't forget about our task. Or let's figure out how we'll do this. Aah. This is really O.K., if I want it to be. You see, we've got to live. Like that, that fold in there, then under, gently, gently . . . Weeell, as far as that goes . . .

Let's talk about the newspaper clippings you brought instead. It's interesting that they talk about Them over there – and on the future prospects for Europe as well. The best ones, the people of culture . . . I wouldn't say that I look down on scientists, after all, I was ignorant once too, that's how everyone started out. And since you arrived here this afternoon, Madame Comrade, I think that you're also beginning to suspect which way the light's shining from.

The facts, the observable signs are partly at the disposal of these far-off academics as well. Accounts of the landing, things that have happened here over the years, complete information on *what didn't happen elsewhere* – that has significance as well, and not just any old kind of significance. A science that couldn't come to any conclusion other than that with Them, technology and the know-ledge of space travel is superficial, and that really their social organization is that of nomads stuck on a very primitive level, similar to termites or the bees they live with, is really quite impoverished. Look at how they list the possibilities concerning Them: barbarian warriors, whose military technology just fell into Their laps somewhere during the course of Their nomadic wanderings; the intellectual property of others. Or: *only* Their military technology, with a utilitarian one-sidedness, developed – They have no art, or science beyond that. Or still: They're outlaws, criminals among Their own kind, perhaps some kind of heretical sect, or simply the excess population from Their overpopulated planet. In that case, the Earth is a colony from Their point of view, a new frontier, or, in the other case, just a penal colony. Or both at the same time. This Bétancourt draws his conclusion from the same observable phenomena. It's not their observations that he takes exception to from here – you know, sometimes I listen to him during the afternoon, when we aren't asleep any more. It's true, he's got a book, but still, anyone who lives among us here, no matter how much he tries to see things from the outsider's point of view, cannot help but *understand* Them. Barbarians he asks? Not as if he disagreed with, for example Leo Szilárd's theory, that *others* did Their scouting for them, others chose this part of the crust of the third planet, a part which is separate, surroundable, and by virtue of its population, composition, uncorrupted human ecology, and last, but not least its humid, hothouse climate, is particularly appropriate. They dropped Them, along with Their landing craft, onto the open sea near this Island, which, from that moment on, seemed to Them Their natural and only goal. (Let me add the observations of an engineer here, that the various skyscrapers of the Closed Quarter – first and foremost the Xerox Building, the former Maya Intercontinental, and the half-completed forty-eight storey tower section of the bank right by the coastal road, like lighthouses, indicate to the observer in space that the ground is firm here, that it can take tough stamping about, since it's part of the same Eocene bedrock on which Havanna and Manhattan were built, and maybe it's by pure chance that it's not we who are looking – dumbfounded and uncomprehending – at Cuba's or Professor Szilárd's strange new life.) Concerning the label 'Barbarian' being applied to Them,

Bétancourt says – and in this we all agree with him – that those of us who live with Them would not be able to feel that way. We don't look for petty terrestrial human faults in Them. Art, science? Isn't it idiotic, narrow and anthropocentric to think that the *lack* of these is somehow an impoverishment? They're simply different. It's as if you were to say that it's a more highly developed thing to be able to communicate using vocal chords, than to do the same thing while moving every ton of the whole body. This old Bétancourt finds it important, that They live together with these winged, buzzing little creatures – which, among the twenty thousand varieties of terrestrial bees, most resembled the kind with the most highly developed social structure. One has to say that this man is useless in many respects. He limps around here practically in a frenzy. At one point he announced that this yard is a scientist's paradise, and he mentioned a new discipline, which would include zoology, anthropology, exobiology, choreography, communications studies and cultural history. He collects, and categorizes Their communicative movement patterns according to time and type – he scribbled the margins of the telephone book full of tiny stick-men, the kind that choreographers draw. Now he's writing between the lines.

Don't misunderstand me, I see what the others in the yard mean when they say that Bétancourt has separated himself from the community, by examining Them as strangers, and the whole thing has a Euro-American, definitely liberal-arts type of flavor to it. He gave himself away once, before Their arrival. He said openly that he has the opportunity here, to still be of some use to humanity. It's possible that he'll get us all into danger, if our Mistress gets angry because of him. But those who say that we should terminate him ourselves – and they almost did so the other day – are simply stupid. They've forgotten about the teaching, and about little Puskás, who was fat. You can't waste a man's life just like that. But furthermore, as you can see, H U - V E Y often talks with him. She enjoys it for some reason. What do they think they are? A kangaroo court? I told the hotheads to cool off. I am definitely of the opinion, that for the time being, he is not to be touched.

This man, with his outsider's point of view also sees quite clearly that They only hold the island on the Earth, that it wouldn't occur to Them to take over the rest, or to concern Themselves in any which way whatsoever with the part of humanity left outside the area They occupied when They descended onto the sea – until They are forced to do so. And this proves that Their culture is of a non-aggressive nature. They don't even care about the ships or planes passing by the Island. The professor has based a whole theory on the Festival of the Equinox, and on the infinite patterns of the dance of joy, which he's now elaborating. He doesn't think that Their movement in space is according to some plan or other, indeed, he even ventures to say that They have no maps. He holds, that on the basis of all the information available, it is statistically impossible that Their kind happen upon the Solar System again. On the other hand, of course, They can't leave it now either. They have a symbiotic relationship with their bees, as part of a tripartite system. This third factor must have been present on the planet of Their evolution as well, possibly in several life-forms, resembling our own mammals.

The bees collect wherever they find what they're looking for. They have long, tubular tongues for sucking – without damaging the surface, which is thus usable for an optimal period. The bees' symbiotic relationship with Them must have begun at a very early stage of tribal development– they share basic modes of existence, such as the communicative dance. Just to show you how narrow a viewpoint anthropocentrism is, the professor knows of an old theory from before. According to this theory, man went through a stage in prehistory, when it had not yet been established whether speech would become the mode of communication or not. Drawing, melody and – *this is important* – *dance* were competing for this role, and later, the dominance of language suppressed the others. So-called artistic expression is, according to this idea, nothing more than a yearning type of atavism. The little bees, as we now know through Bétancourt's tinkering with the subject (he's just beginning to analyze the bee's dance as well), inform each other about the location of moisture, the species of mammal chosen, and its quality, by means of the so-called 'nuptial dance.' They understand and feel all this, and in a way that isn't quite clear yet, They communicate this all in Their dance. Both species experience their sharpest awareness at the hour of dawn; they would never have arrived at any other time onto dry land. The bees sense the polarization of the Sun, and that's how they navigate according to its position. That's why they have to wait until sunrise to begin their work.

What they collect is like a digestive juice for Them, a catalyst to digestion. You probably remember from chemistry class that catalysts merely speed up, rather than partake in, chemical reactions. They collect the sweat where they can find it – from the backs of zebus, or the raised human forehead. Man, according to Bétancourt, is not an indispensible part of the system – he could be replaced for long periods, indeed he could be completely replaced by the zebu, or any warm-blooded mammal for that matter. In fact the zebu backs give Them all They need. The smooth, hairless surface of the human forehead only gives Them a certain fine feeling, a luxury item, so to speak – of no more importance than cigarettes used to be in the former life.

Now you probably understand, Madame Comrade, why I say They aren't cruel. They're just different. Maybe mammals are very rare on this outer edge of the Milky Way – in any case, they chose the Solar System, perhaps because of us. They may have gotten their first flavor sample here. They got attached, like children. Once They came to like people, They developed a charming greed with respect to them, and They wouldn't want to part with them for anything in the world.

They only eat once a day, in the morning. At dawn They like to personally supervise the collecting. That's when They watch the dance of the bees, and get informed about things to do on the estate. Their happiness over the freshness of Their food hasn't dissipated during the years since They arrived – who knows what kind of diet They had to subsist on during Their long – perhaps generations-long – trip through space. People can regenerate themselves properly in twenty-four hours, if there is enough. By noon at the latest, everyone can leave their perspirator on their own two feet. Believe me, it's not that hard. And I'm not saying this to be cheerful, since we have a duty to live . . . I have my reasons.

From the former it also clearly follows, that for all us who think in terms of generations, it will take an inconceivably long time for any change to come about in the rest of the world. For them to really understand, however, the Euro-Americans would have to understand the future, and to do that they're too small-minded. They would have to rise above themselves, and that kind of thing I only saw in Puskás's case. It's likely that further overpopulation on Their part is not to be expected for a long time, since, in comparison with us humans, They have extremely long lives. The professor hasn't even begun to speculate about Their life-spans. It's not even impossible that death is unknown to Them. We just assume that They're born alive, we don't really know for sure. Perhaps even the idea is itself provincially human. The devil knows how, somehow – carried by the wind, through the dance of little bees, perhaps via the mystical time-body – They get from yard to yard. All we know is that They all seem to be adults, and that though every night the island shakes at their paired celebrations of heartfelt joy, They have not had one single newborn since the Great or First Equinox. And that is a sure sign that America's, Europe's and the rest of the world's turn won't come for a while – the continents can continue living their history, if they like. Now you belong to us too. Forget the Europeans, Americans, Africans and the . . . I've forgotten the name of the other continent . . . in any case, forget them. By the time they came to their senses after the First Day, millions of us were among Them, and so they didn't throw a hydrogen bomb. Years have gone by since, and they can't make up their minds. Now they never will, because they're humane.

They're getting closer. You feel Them, don't you? You wouldn't have had a chance with the bum-whacking business, Comrade, if you had bet with me on tonight's celebration . . . O.K. I'll talk *louder*! She's running out of patience. We have to pull ourselves together. You see, the academics are wrong about one other thing. It's not They, who are man's enemy on this Island; They like men. I hate, we here all hate – and you do as well, though you may not know it yet – the Europeans, the Americans, the Africans. What do these few equatorial islanders mean to them? Anyway, we're not worth enough to make it worthwhile for them to rethink their customs, their religions and their ideologies for our sake. They won't throw the bomb, because they don't want to kill innocent people. They want to be at peace with their conscience. I wish them all to be able to live with as peaceful a conscience as they can – *here*. You know, Madame Comrade, for that one reason, I really wouldn't have minded if you did get back with your interview. I may still sacrifice all I have, and just take the tape out of the cassette, fit it into my yellow tequila bottle, seal it, and send it – hand to hand – down to the sea. Those at the Montedison estate – they've got colorful lawn chair perspirators – amuse themselves by putting their treasures into all kinds of floating objects, and setting them adrift on the sea. The Masters don't condemn this – the people at Montedison'll throw the bottle for me. So I'll say this into the mike: when I say, *rewind it*, listen to it again, give the audience more of a chance to get a feel for the nuances of the report. I don't even care if anyone thinks this is a lot of heavy-handed bullshit. I don't care if they understand what 'cheerfulness' and 'active effort' really mean – or the buzzing of bees, or 'downstage', or 'white wall', or 'the unchanging scenery of our lives', or this hour and a half I have something to do with human culture, or a compulsion to talk, a raised forehead, a flower's stigma, human love, white twine, 'education', nurseries, eating areas, breakfast, exact dates, the fall equinox, Sunrise, little bees, or heartfelt joy. And I'd tell them to their dirty faces, or at least on tape so that they'll know, that I'm their motherfucking-cock-sucking-biggest enemy. I'll tell H U - V E Y as well, at breakfast – She likes it if you prattle then. And it's good to see Her boundless joy.

Well, here They are, let's start. We won't be left to ourselves. Never again. They'll be on the Island to the end of time, or at least as long as They have enough space – I think you've seen that, Madame Comrade. The replacement of the zebus and of people has been ensured – everyone knows and performs their duty. The pens are full, as are the nurseries – hundreds of them just like Magelhaes Cathedral – teeming with toddlers. I do hear, however, that they don't really learn to talk anymore. The bees don't visit them until the spring equinox of their tenth years *for sure*. (That position of the Sun is such a Celebration of Joy in Their lives.) And I want to believe that it won't be the turn of mine tomorrow. I don't want to think about it. I always want to think that they are alive somewhere, over there, around the Sports Stadium, and that their foreheads are still white. That's why I never want to see any dates. Or children. What's difficult here is not to keep cheerful and balanced in a perspiratory manner, or that She may punish us like She did Bétancourt by mistake, by twisting his leg out of its socket and leaving it that way. Or that the bees descend onto my forehead every dawn. What's hard is that the foreheads of my children occur to me. The ten years I had with Márta – I don't talk about that.

But we're people, and so we have to make the best of what is difficult. We too have to concentrate on our duty – it's easier and better that way. Let's get at it. Maybe try with the backs of your nails around this sensitive ring, up and down, up and down, around, make it tingle. You know, according to the old fogey They never quite understood human biology. They have no curiosity – that used to be a specifically human characteristic. They're only interested in as much about homo sapiens as is necessary. You can't pretend, or fool them – don't even think of trying that. That flash up there, that swish of limbs – that's their laughter. They're good creatures. You can tell by how much playfulness, naïve childlikeness fits into their 120 ton frames – the way, right in the middle of Their own joy, They can laugh at us – because They see movements similar to Their own, and yet strangely different. Please try to understand. There's no question here of cruelty. HU-VEY simply has no way of knowing that Madame Comrade has not been able to conceive, and has probably not been able to stimulate a man to erection for twenty or thirty years already – if you ever have. We don't have any choice – we have to do what we have to do. They'll lean over and look at us every now and then, we can count on that, but as you see, there's nothing to be afraid of.

You'll help, right? Try with your mouth now, and your tongue, gently, like a butterfly wing. Good God, haven't you ever heard of the erogenous zones? You've never even *read* about it? Kama Sutra? Masters and Johnson?

We know what our duty is. You know that it's harder for the male. Wait a sec. I think it would be better if you'd cover yourself partly. Put your cassock back on – let's leave something to the imagination. I'll fantasize. Everything. HU-VEY is sure about Her educational methods. If you don't give birth, well then you don't. She won't punish you. I think. If She saw that we did what we were supposed to do. She doesn't always insist on seeing the erection, and yet She *knows everything*. Say, what do you think if I'd call you by your first name from now on? Not Márta, don't ask me to call you Márta. You don't have a middle name? We could even use the informal mode with each other. Hi, Jolán. I know it's not polite of me to make the offer, I'm younger, after all. Uh huh. Well, put it there. Round and round. Softly, rhythmically. Nice. Don't look at my forehead.

Whoever wants to can now rewind it to 'don't look at my forehead.'

(Let the reading of the text continue.) You have heard. After the landing, the two admirals of the United Navy of NATO and the Warsaw Pact bowed down nine times to the dawn, lowered the Sundisk flag, hauled down the sails, had the flag ship raised onto dry land, and hid it in the bushes. Then they began on their difficult journey through the land of the tribes: The Franglish, the Yugos, the Dagos, the Cheskos, the Ruskies and the Amis, the Rockers, the Jesushordes, the Reds and the Unitarians. After countless days' travel through the land of the tribes, they arrived at the court of the First Secretary of the Empire of the Sun and the Night. During the course of the fall burnings a recently-captured slave recognized the language of the hordes of nomadic Magyari footmen from Western Eurasia. And you have heard it. The Sun is rising.

(This doesn't have to be read to the people:) Readers, do not fold the paper, to ensure its longer life. Read it aloud. Translate it into languages. Every year, in the fall and the spring, when the night and the day are of equal duration, many Talking Papers are preparable at once if the paper called 'Carbon' is placed between the sheets. The contributory sacrifice of each listener should be six eggs. The fingers on our right hand, and one more egg.

The Lens

ANNEMARIE VAN EWYCK

The journey to Mertcha seemed to take longer than ever. I spent most of my time in my cabin at first, later venturing out into the non-smokers' lounge, where unfortunately most of the mothers congregated, with their children.

I did a lot of thinking about my own mother. For her sake I'd had my hair tinted back to its original mousey brown when I left for Terra. Now the grey was beginning to show again, at the roots. The kids thought it peculiar – I overheard them giggling. But at first they kept pretty much out of my way, deep in their own concerns of running, fighting, screeching and generally overturning everything that was not bolted to the deck: a constant din that made a strangely soothing background to my thoughts.

Mother had seemed so very much changed, this last time. So quiet, almost diffident in her manner. She had been watching old vid tapes when I came in, and she turned and said, 'Oh, hello dear; there you are then.' And I said, 'Yes mother.'

'I've been off the life machines for some weeks now,' she said, turning back to the screen. 'I won't be long.' And again I said, 'Yes mother.' A gentle exchange, and meaningless.

No trace of the woman she had been, the woman I had known and dreaded and loved in vain. Who carried grievances against all the universe, who had hounded my sweet Pa to death with her crippled kind of loving and who had driven me out of home and finally off-planet with her abuse and complaints.

I asked the doctor about her. He couldn't tell me much. She had not been her usual self of late, indeed she had not. Seemed she had lost her zest.

He was being kind, I knew. Kind to me. I was sure she had been doing her utmost to make his job as difficult for him as she could; nagging, bitching, as she had for years . . .

Part of her must have died some time ago. The mother I knew would never have written to me as she did, asking me to be with her at the end, to help her across. Poor twisted little witch, impotent at last.

I strangely missed what she had been, yet I longed to know better this strange old woman she had become. But she remained inaccessible to the end.

Within a week of my arrival she died; 286 years old. 'Not bad,' she whispered just before she left, on a long echoing sigh.

Motherless I had always felt, now it was a fact. Sorting out my feelings was not easy. Part of the sensibility that her death had, much against my will, churned up, was captured by Billy, a charming seven-year-old, travelling with his parents to Tireno, a colony world beyond Mertcha, far past the heart of the galaxy.

Billy was an unspoilt child and his parents allowed his curiosity free reign, within certain limits. Highly interested, he wandered over one afternoon to watch me at finger-weaving, a craft that is very popular on Mertcha. With only five fingers, I have to keep a peg pinched between ring and middle finger to duplicate the Mertchan sixth digit, and to be sure, the needle does not dance as nimbly through the web as in the hands of the Mertchan peasants, but I am pretty deft at it for all that.

Before my trip was over Billy had produced half a dozen rosettes, remarkable for their gaudy colours and weird snaking patterns. I had followed the traditional Mertchan wefts and colour-schemes; he had explored new possibilities. He was young and I . . . I was nearly old.

Before touchdown on Mertcha I retired to my cabin. I had already said goodbye to Billy and his parents and to the schoolteacher who had also been interested in my finger-weaving, and wanted to introduce it on Wertz, for first-phase pupils.

I wanted to be alone. Longing and fear, hope and hesitation created a turmoil in my insides; a roll of red-hot marbles in my abdominal region, cramps painful and delicious. I knew the feeling well. Despite a long life of travel, with countless trips to Terra and back, and despite my many postings on many different planets, I remain a prey, a compliant victim to my own anticipation at every planet-fall.

I drew my shapeless traveller's cloak tight. Soon now, I would be wearing my own clothes again, the light flowing robes, the cool flaring hoods and star-veils of Mertcha. Rys en Pfi would once more light the sky . . . and I would see Mik again, in his terribly ill-fitting Terran driver's uniform, his cap askew on top of his ugly Mertchan head. Even the Mertchans thought Mik ugly, it wasn't Terran prejudice . . .

Disembarkation. From ship to shore through the snaky proboscis, a wide corridor with windows tightly shuttered. Into the large Arrivals' Hall that boasted the greatest sight on Mertcha – artificial lighting in abundance.

As yet I had had no glimpse of Mertcha, of Tiel. I still felt part of the space-liner, in transit. I hurried to the covered parking bays where the Embassy car would be waiting. I pictured Mik standing there, resting his weight on his supporting leg, the others nonchalantly crossed in front of him, an unlit Terran cigarette dangling from his wide mouth.

But when I reached the car, the driver on his elevated seat proved to be a stranger. It was a bad shock. I had expected Mik, my personal driver, as anybody on the Embassy staff knew. He drove me to Mertchan soil-dedications, and to festivals, and exhibitions and concerts by Terran musicians; to all occasions that merited a report from Terran Cultural Liaison.

He was more than just my driver, he was a friend. When I left, he had said, 'I will come to fetch you, certainly, when you come back from your grief,' even though the three-and-three folk, knowing no families, only clan-groupings and their ever-changing propagation triads, can have no notion of what the loss of a parent means to a Terran.

I tried to ask this new driver about Mik, but his knowledge of

Terran seemed to be virtually non-existent. He just mumbled, 'Embassy-Dame-Ditja-to-get-in-please,' all strung together, and pulled open the passenger door with a crooked movement of his middle arm. He chose not to understand my Mertchan either, and shut the door with a few polite head gestures, after which he got in and raised the glass partition.

I felt very much upset. The lout had even left the black-out curtains in place; I could not see out! I was really getting angry. This man was spoiling my arrival, my reunion with the lovely planet I had been living on for more than ten years.

And I had looked forward so much to this first, languorous ride through the broad avenues of Tiel, under a sky full of radiance. I had longed for the blaze of the billions of stars that shine down on this small red planet in the mathematical centre of the galactic lens. A world where darkness is an artificial condition and where black-out curtains are as familiar a feature as light-switches elsewhere.

I had longed for it, I realized. Longed for Mertcha as if it were my home, as if I belonged here, bound to roots that went deep into the dry reddish earth and clung there with hair-thin filaments.

Longed for Mertcha, and the company of Mik. During the return trip I had been considering a request for a permanent appointment. I did not doubt it would be approved, for I was good at my work, steady, dependable. And there were no other contestants for the permanent post of Head of Cultural Liaison. Another year, and my assistant would apply for a transfer to Rhodia or Wertz, first order worlds, where the life of the galaxy beat fast. Nobody coveted my place, my desk, my chair. There was still time to have a home I loved, and friends . . .

The darkened car bounced over a patch of uneven ground and came to a stop. I got the door open as fast as I could, and found myself in the parking lot that had recently been staked out at the Holy Place of Tiel by a reluctant City Council. I walked to the front of the car. The driver had remained in his seat. 'Holy Place,' he enunciated with some difficulty. 'Good see.'

I began to understand what had happened. He was standing in for Mik, who was detained elsewhere. Not knowing who I was, he had assumed I was a guest of the Embassy – a visiting artist perhaps, who would tip nicely for an unscheduled private visit to the most important sight of Tiel. Sure enough, the left hand crept out of the open window, palm upward.

I waved him off and said, 'Later, later,' which for a wonder he did understand.

I didn't mind visiting the Holy Place of Tiel now that I was here. It would be a perfect way of restoring the shattered harmony of my arrival. A welcome to myself. The sky was vast and light. Rys was past its zenith, intensifying the reds and umbers so richly found on Mertcha.

I strolled past an empty tourist wagon – a coach for Terrans, judging by the low-slung seats – and reached a simple square building of red loam, the Holy Place of Tiel.

Square shapes are rare on Mertcha; the inhabitants, no doubt under the influence of the trigits that govern their body structure, care more for triangles and particularly circles. So a square building dating from the antiquity of the three-and-three folk is a unique sight. That is not the reason, however, that the Place features in most of the sightseeing schedules of long-space pleasure cruises.

For off-worlders it is the famous mosaic labyrinth in the main Hall, and the crypt where the funeral pyramids of departed monastics line the walls – a double row of gaudy little towers, draped with strings of glistening beads.

The crypt has a copy of the upper labyrinth, but instead of a flat mosaic, the maze in the crypt is three-dimensional, consisting of narrow strips of masonry standing ankle-high. Tourists often stumble over these miniature walls.

The upper and lower labyrinth both end in a central circle, which in the crypt is marked by another low wall, and in the Hall itself by a round opening with a loose red-lacquered cover, corresponding exactly with a similar opening in the roof of the Hall.

Only starlight is ever allowed to enter the Place, for on the gallery near the roof monastics and servants are continuously shifting the screens and panels that shunt the light of the two weak suns back into space. The crypt too is lighted by starlight, aided by the thin flame of some candles in wall sconces.

Along the Hall, the triangular cells of the living monastics mirror the disposition of the funeral pyramids below. When the inhabitants emerge from their cells in their stiff pastel robes, it is like summer moths leaving their cocoons; it never fails as a subject for tourist snapshots.

The monastics are few in number, for the religion of the Place is ecstatic in nature, stressing personal exaltation instead of mass devotion. Not a creed for crowds. No god is revered here, no services are held. Postulants simply come to the Place, unannounced, and start treading the labyrinth, spelled out in glowing mosaics on the floor of the Hall. Those who are fortunate, so I am told, are slowly, gradually caught up into ecstasy until they collapse. The further inward they have come, the longer the faint lasts, so I heard.

A servant assists the new monastic to a vacant cell, offers him a ritual bowl of hot *melk* and issues a frock of colour. And that is all.

The servants are postulants who have walked the labyrinth in vain, but who remain so much attracted to the mystical, that they are willing to stay and serve. I am sure they must feel envious; I would in their place. And indeed there have been rumours of late, of power-seeking in their simple organization.

I made my way through the countless screening drapes of the entrance and stood inside the Hall. Silence and starlight, a cone of radiance comprising half a galaxy, girdled at the roof and fanning out downwards to light the maze. A pair of monastics in pink and sea-green were gliding over the mosaic at the far end of the Hall. Close by the entrance three servants stood whispering; one had crossed his forelegs, reminding me very much of Mik.

In this space and silence I felt happier than I had ever felt before. Tears came into my eyes, unexpectedly. I had to force them back. Oh, yes, I would send in my request as soon as I was back at the Embassy. This was my home, this red soil, so receptively taking my new roots to herself; these red loam walls, this star-filled hall, the mosaic . . . a perfect embodiment of homecoming.

I started walking, wending my way along the labyrinth, giving rhythm to my feelings. My face felt twisted by emotion, there were tears that would no longer be repressed. With slow steps I drew nearer, ever nearer, to the centre of the Hall, my eyes on the mosaic, my heart turned towards the heavens where the stars blazed like daylight, where half the mass of the Milky Way rested on spikes of light on an insignificant red planet.

Rapture and exaltation swept through my body. What had begun as a symbolic celebration of homecoming was turned into a transport of delight, carrying me along like the long, long glide upwards just before orgasm, before the foaming tumble that is always too short to satisfy. But this movement seemed to have no ending. The ecstasy of the Holy Place of Tiel was upon me and I followed the mystical power that called to me, craving the ultimate that surely lay before me . . .

Nearing the centre of the Hall, thoughts barely shaped, barely conscious . . . a feeling of happiness intensified . . . almost unbearable . . . The heart, the kernel of things, so close now, the melting into Oneness . . .

A hand, a Mertchan hand bearing a red key on a third-finger ring, at the edge of my vision . . . placing a red wooden cover over an opening of black, a dark hole, an annoying blemish on the brilliance of the maze.

A tiny grain of sobriety penetrating my shining picture . . . The dark streaming upwards from the round opening, then cut off . . . The cover closing the crypt off from the light . . . no lights down there?

An unwelcome picture of the stout door to the crypt, the ring-key on the hand of the servant . . . the Terran tourist coach outside . . .

The thoughts would not reach my feet, treading on slowly along the loops and curves of the labyrinth, ever closer to the red cover. And again rapture rose like a tide, enveloping me, sheathing me into near-immobility . . . a stillness in my senses, and yet a movement that was upward, yet downward, inward, yet outward.

But the grain of doubt, the gritty lump of knowledge would not be swept away.

A link forged itself, shattering the rapture. The servant had locked the tourists in the crypt, in the dark . . .

*

Before my feet could touch the wooden cover I had halted, swaying. A servant caught me when my knees buckled and led me to the side of the Hall, supporting me. In a vacant cell he offered me a bowl of *melk*, hot as it should be, but his posture expressed his doubts and he stumbled in his ritual greeting. 'You have felt the power . . .' He ought to have added, 'and henceforth this shall be your home.' He did, after a pause, but not without one of those rapid gestures, with which Mertchans commonly mitigate the impact of too sweeping a statement. Clearly he did not know what to do with an off-worlder, a Terran, a two-and-two woman, experiencing holy ecstasy in the Place of Tiel.

In the meantime I had recovered, a little. 'You misunderstand, a giddy spell, that is all. Gratitude for your *melk*,' I said, turning away sharply not to see the relief in his eyes.

I left the cell. Through the Hall I went, across the mosaic that now lay lifeless, through the smothering drapes at the door. The entrance to the crypt was locked, as I had expected. From behind the pressed fibre door I could hear vulgar Terran curses.

The tourists have no notion of having been, for a little while, held hostage by a small politico-religious pressure group. They only know the candles in the crypt were blown out – probably a draught. When the wooden cover was replaced, plunging the crypt into total darkness, they stubbed their toes and bashed their shins on the low walls of the crypt labyrinth, trying to find the exit. The door stuck at first, and that *was* unpleasant. The native guide was nowhere to be found.

But they got out all right, and the only really annoying thing was that they missed the folkloristic meal in Tiel Old Town because they were late. The ship lifted as soon as they were back on board.

The Embassy keeps mum. Of course. The Under Secretary has had a heart-to-heart talk with the Chief Peacekeeper, and the Mertchan Head of State has conveyed a number of very flattering invitations to our Ambassador.

I am thought to have shown rare subtlety in dealing with a nasty situation, in that I did not raise the Peacekeepers, but went and liberated the tourists with no fuss made. The fact that the key to the crypt was given up without resistance on the part of the servants, is duly ascribed to my formerly unnoticed wit and tact.

I will not show them the back of my tongue, as the Mertchan saying goes. No one will ever know of my experience in the labyrinth. Or of the consternation among the rebellious servants, when at the moment of their *coup* a Terran, of all people, was being exalted into their ecstasy. Yes, they do know. And they will never tell.

The poor servant was so dumbfounded when I marched up to him, demanding the key, that he gave it up quite meekly.

In any case I can now write my own ticket to any first order world that takes my fancy, so the Ambassador has personally and warmly assured me.

I am sending in my request for a transfer tomorrow. I finally heard what has happened to Mik. He is dead. A traffic accident. He died, my only friend. The only Mertchan who could treat a two-and-two person – a pitiable disabled being – as an equal, worthy of affection.

He was driving the handbuilt Embassy Volkswagen that the Earth Government had sent out to enhance Terran prestige. Sitting straight and stiff as a *knappi*-tree, his supporting leg uncomfortably folded beneath him on the low seat, he was hit by the freight-cart that came careening out of a side road, brakes smoking. In the pride of his Terran driving he found death – the most expensive road casualty on Mertcha, as the Ambassador remarked sourly.

Oh Mik, oh Mik you have found what I longed for; yours is the glory . . . and I have been so close, so close!

Turning and wending along the maze I had felt a conviction that came into being slowly, finally focusing what ought to have been clear to me long before: 'This is the place where I belong, in all the universe.' And without fear I had accepted what unavoidably followed, 'The only place where I truly belong is the place where I die.'

I was ready, I was more than ready. I was prepared to stand on that round red cover and feel the light of a billion stars play through me.

Astrologers believe what astronomers deny, that the stars have powers that influence the moods and actions and lives of the creatures that people the crusts of the worlds. I remain outside their argument. But I know that half a galaxy of collected starlight can kill. There might have been another pyramid, down in the crypt.

I gave up my death of ecstasy for a coachload of stupid Terran sightseers. There are no second chances and I'll never know if they were worth the trade. At night, I cry in my sleep, for longing, longing.

Progenitor

PHILIPPE CURVAL

Translated by Scott Baker

I've known since this morning that I've reached the threshold of a new experience; thirty-two years of life as an ordinary member of society have exhausted my enthusiasm; they incite me to throw off the tyranny of habit and custom. I want to better my perception of the world, until now so imperfect, so travestied by my nervous system, so subjugated to my body's desires. I feel my dreams corseted in my flesh. Vy doesn't know. Maybe I won't tell her anything while I await my paralysis; later she'll play with me, she'll have no reason to complain. We'll begin a new life in which she'll be my limbs and I her secret thoughts. I'll live out my life in retreat from the world; Vy will be my surface, the only place where the universe will be able to touch me. I'll keep watch over her frontiers with infinite vigilance.

Difficult to want yourself to be different: you have to choose, and then deny your other selves. Choose Vy, first of all, keep myself close to her like a shellfish, firmly attached to her side: from there I'll be able to see the beating of life's waves, smell their sea-spray. Nursed, nourished by this rocky crag of flesh and blood, half-parasite, half-master, I'll lead a larval existence, pondering my former years. I'll have no more desires: I'll be lovingly indifferent, deprived as I am of that which was both my strength and my motive for existence, my progenital. It was thus before I met her, I desired her without wanting her, I wanted her without possessing her, I possessed her without loving her, I loved her without desiring her. Remember, Vy, how parallel and lucid we were then! I want to rediscover that freshness of feeling, perhaps to your detriment.

Now that you've removed my progenital, I want to lull myself to sleep in the softness of my adolescence, there to savour my life as an adult. From there, I'll listen to the world going by.

'Breakfast? Yes, please.'

Eight days a week I get up at midnotte, I get ready, you get ready, you accompany me, I have a few intimate moments with the dura mater and I produce the equivalent of a few tons of protoplasm; we don't see each other again until fourthnotte: a few hours at most of subjective time have passed.

'Do you want to meet somewhere today?'

'Why?'

Vy has already asked me the same bizarre question many times. Does she do it to intrigue me, because she harbors some suspicions about my plans, or to please me? I can't decide if she's being anxious, or tender. I answer:

'No. I'd rather go back to the house.'

When I'm paralyzed the house will be my universe. I'm eager to habituate myself to it as soon as possible.

She smiles and gets up. The small flowers in her transparent clothing have tattooed her flesh. When she takes off her clothes, faint traces from the flowers remain on her skin, to fade over the course of the day. She serves me breakfast. It's so good that I have no desire to trade it for corn flakes, eggs and bacon, or orange marmalade, those imported delicacies for which we've developed such a fondness. It's all so good, everything's perfect, so very good, so satisfying to my palate! Vy snuggles up against me, her cool belly adapting itself to my groin. She kisses me ever so lightly on the chest, then moves gently down to the flat, smooth expanse where only three weeks ago I still had my progenital. Normally, we don't even recognize each other's existence at breakfast: blind, mute, deaf, still stagnant with sleep, we seek nothing from the moment but to make contact with the new day. I protest against her insinuating caress between my thighs, I stiffen, she rebels. In the soft and humid bed, that lair graven with night's indelible odors, our bodies distrust each other. Her mouth adheres to my skin.

My thumb gropes for her pulse, to learn from its rhythm if she's excited or if her heart's just plodding along. My fingers press on the veins of her neck. She laughs, and brushes her lips across the flat expanse, uses her mouth to crush the fleshy bud where my progenital had been attached, tossing her head as though trying to rip the bud off me. My legs open. I faint from happiness.

I hear the shower going. Stretching out my left arm I feel the bed, still warm there where she was an instant before, where she loved me. Vy loves washing herself, her toilette always takes her a long time. I have to take advantage of it. I run to the hiding place, in the little molded plaxaine bubble she had installed a few months ago. When I think about my progenital hidden in that basin full of liquid my ideas deploy themselves misshapenly around its evasive image. I invent its appearance from the exterior, using my memories of it for a base, but I can't get the image to stay fixed and the form I obtain is truncated, clumsy, and decomposes stealthily into its component parts. Even so I'm unable to halt the development of these morphological daydreams, keep them from taking on form against my will. How can you be sure what your progenital's eventual appearance will be like, even after having carried it between your legs for so long? All memory of my first few years of existence has been taken from me, it's impossible to find the slightest allusion to them in what I can remember of my biological evolution. And all the texts are mute on this subject, as though the secret of our race's beginnings were too terrible to reveal, even to that race's own members. I place my hands on the dark plaxaine but can distinguish nothing through it. I go back to bed.

Some instants later Vy comes out of the bathroom, nude. A few drops of water still cling to her lower back, though she is otherwise perfectly dry. I take the towel from her hands.

'You want me to dry you?'

She looks at me intensely, as though she suspects that a far more important question is lurking behind my seemingly trivial words. I drop my head to my bowl and suck in the mouthful that covers the bottom: the liquid has the taste of diluted perfume. Vy isn't wrong: the question I'm posing myself about my progenital is much more fundamental, but I don't want to ask her anything about it. She can't be allowed to suspect the anxiety which has been weighing on me since she ripped my ripe fruit from my belly.

And in any case, she probably wouldn't answer me: none of the other people whom I've asked the same questions has. Does she even know the answer? While I possess a secret which is mine alone, that of my rediscovered adolescence which purrs ingratiatingly in the hollow between my shoulders, which runs the length of my spine and which will soon freeze me forever in that bent posture in which the gods depicted by ancient sculptors were shown. I have to keep these frighteningly antisocial thoughts which demonstrate such an insurmountable gulf between Vy and me to myself. I have all the advantages on my side: all the details concerning the fate and development of my progenital have been hidden from me, but I know that it will end up resembling all the rest of us. While I, I'll become something different, thanks to that dislocation that has come into existence in me since she plucked my progenital.

Vy has ceased staring at me and is smiling at me now instead. She offers me the drop of water pearling on her hip and I lick it. Her skin is granulous beneath my tongue's delicate rasping.

'You know you're going to be late.'

'I'm sick.'

'Really, what's wrong?'

'A bit tired, nothing serious.'

She screws up her eyes slightly; some days I'm incapable of metabolizing protoplasm; Vy understands and lets me alone. She gets dressed: her exquisite ritual! I watch her, intoxicated by the beautiful obscenity of her gestures. How her straight and slender torso, how her high round buttocks hint to me of moments of absolute ecstasy! No one but Vy would have been able to mature me with so much passion, to get my progenital to detach itself from my body with so much ease and happiness! I felt nothing whatsoever when I lost it. Vy is unquestionably the wife that I needed and it isn't the fact that her new career as a mother is going to make her neglect me that makes me want to excite her curiosity. My immobility fascinates her; she's moved by the sight of me but holds back her pleasure. I read in the almost imperceptible fluttering of an eyelid the emotion overwhelming her. My Vy! how can I share my madness with her! The new mode of existence imposed on her by the loss of my progenital takes her away from me. Nonetheless, Vy, my perfect timepiece, so well adjusted, you were my duty and my trust. She was so wild when I first knew her, why did I have to sow in her that seed of sociability which made of her such a perfect wife? Now it's sprouted and blossomed. Vy is still young, yet her days cling to her like ivy to a wall. My torn-apart love, how can I undo your conditioning. If I hadn't lost my progenital perhaps I'd still be able to find the strength to struggle, to cut away the tendrils binding you to custom and usage.

The everyday sound of her magnetic zipper dispels the complicity which has come into existence between my immobility and her movements.

'What do you want to do, then?'

'Nothing, I'll stay home.'

'But we're still going out tonight anyway?'

I've agreed and the door's closed on her with a sucking sound. Her footsteps further away, on fragments of bark. It's the end of the warm season, the avenue's tall trees have already begun stripping themselves.

With infinite precaution I've approached the plaxaine basin, trying to surprise my gestating progeny, see it swimming at the surface of the pocket of liquid in which it's been immersed so as to enable it to gorge itself on the nutritious air so generously dispensed there: that's the only place where I have any hope of seeing it. Alas, the progenital is in the incubation chamber's brown depths. Once again I'll be unable to see it. Could there be something in its genetic programming that requires it to hide itself from its father, as in the days when our progenitals were swallowed by their mothers at maturity and then grew plant-like in the women's organic depths? What then is the advantage of this new, artificial life cycle? If it's impossible to keep watch on the progenital as it develops in its incubation bubble, what kind of progress over our genetic tradition can this sophisticated system represent? I suspect that all that's involved is the matriarchy's technocrats' desire to keep their traditions unaltered so as to reserve for the mothers – the maturationists – alone the right to look at our progeny. Why? Why are we always denied an understanding of the mystery of reproduction? First they take from us our memories of childhood, then, once our progenitals have ripened, they frustrate our paternal joys, and there aren't even any laws to protect us from this barbarism! If what the off-worlders (who do not, it's true, have exactly the same mode of parturition that we do) say can be believed, both fathers and mothers enjoy the same rights on other planets.

We can no longer allow ourselves to accept this miserly restriction on our relationships with our descendants, we have to abandon these traditions supposedly conceived to spare us the worries and anxieties of bringing up our offspring. We must revolt against the insipid warmth of the feelings we bring to our role as begetters of children! Vy, I want to share with you the pampering of this child!

And yet, we can't be blowing up the world at every instant. After the effort I've gone to to penetrate that bubble, pierce its enigma, I suddenly feel extremely weary, as though I'd been emptied of my neural influx. I'm going to lie down. I stretch myself out full length on the mattress; every inch of my body rejoices at its touch and at the smell of grass coming through the fabric which covers it. I'm so tired. I look gloomily out through the oval window, its glass tinted blue by the midnotte star: the ornamental trees are pushing out shoots with new vigor, their roots almost seeming to take wing as they hurl sheaves of tendrils into the sky, as if trying to pierce the wispy clouds. Now that I've made my attempt to penetrate a little further into the secrets of that shadowy event taking place so close to me I want to go to sleep with all my neurons stimulated for dreaming. My oneiric acuity will perhaps permit me to explore in meticulous detail that day of first freezes when I was made to understand that my adolescence was over and that I was going to have to commit myself to my role as an adult. The scene will undoubtedly be distorted. Vy will be wearing different clothes when they present her to me and I'll probably be more disagreeable than I really was. But that doesn't make any real difference; it's through reconsidering my life that I'll be able to decide whether or not it's really worthwhile to continue taking an active part in it. It's those first instants that I love, the most naïve, those closest to adolescence and which best translate that terrible awakening of the passion I felt for Vy, those which most faithfully express the frenzied violence of our erotic games. I find in them a lost freshness. Later, the adolescent I was grew accustomed to it all, learned to imitate the tics and habits of his entourage; the time he spent with the dura mater taught him that sense of responsibility which keeps him from ever again becoming that virgin being of his preparatory years.

Nonetheless, my life has always belonged to me and I have no desire to lose my memory of the years I've devoted to Vy, or to her reflection in my memories. Did she always watch me as insistently as today? Did she believe that in our shared existence it was she who dictated my acts? And did I keep myself in a state of voluntary confusion so as not to recognize the signs of my submission? No, I've always had the impression of being free, and I'm certain that despite its immutable rites our society is not coercive. So I'll float my past on the surface of my present, and thus constitute all of my future.

I'm going to get up and eat another breakfast, this one a little more sweetened than the first. Maybe I'll eat a third and – why not? – a fourth, near the end of eighthnotte, when the zephyr sun's made its circuit of the horizon. But I have to communicate first, explain to the alimentary production unit's programmer that I won't be coming in to work. I make myself up slightly before taking hold of the empathy-phone, especially around my eyes so as to make myself look sicker. I feel wearier already, the false circles around my eyes are having an influence on my health.

The thoughts of the programmer at the other end of the line seem to be responding to my wishes; the synoptic council has approved my decision to stay home. I hang up. For some time now they've all been conspiring together to keep me confined, my friends, relations, colleagues, everyone but Vy, who's determined to get me to go out with her every night. Suddenly, pain shoots through my right side, at the bottom of my ribcage, and imaginary though it is I can't manage to wall it off. I lie down again and little by little the pain eases; I take advantage of the respite granted me to ramble off in search of my past, and in particular of those years – each so different from the others in the way it unfolded – that I spent in the dura mater's service. We had a specific script for every working day, so as to neutralize the personnel's imaginative excesses, and each of us accomplished his tasks in such a way as to conform to the precise instructions given him at the beginning of the day. In the creation of protoplasm, it's indispensable to make sure that any conflicts which develop follow a rigorously controlled dramatic evolution; improvised changes of mood would have a fatal effect on the alimentary vats' proliferation. It's desirable in our profession to have those responsible for production submit to equally severe discipline in their private lives so as to eliminate any possibility of adverse influences on their daily work. Thus we're spared those false adventures which some people believe themselves to live every day; the mediocre uncertainties of existence are erased and replaced with efficacious accomplishment. How pleasant it is, once your work's finished, to rehearse your role carefully, in the knowledge that your friends will know all their cues and that none of us will have to submit to the tedious vagaries that once characterized all our lives. Since the off-worlders came life has taken on meaning; it's directed by behavioral specialists. The creation of this gigantic scenario demanded the sacrifice of many generations of creators, thinkers, economists and sociologists. Now instead of being forced to try to anticipate – and to dread – the future, we need only follow a predetermined course to be certain of our happiness.

Nonetheless, since my progenital's separated itself from me that no longer seems a consolation. The script-writers who plotted my past will never again be able to regulate my future. Their words are trapped, frozen, in the pages of a forgotten manuscript. That's why I want to live my adolescence over again by way of the unfettered song of my reveries. And if the whim takes me to introduce false memories into my re-examined account of my life with Vy no one can stop me any more. This paralysis that's been staring me in the face for some weeks now and which is slowly beginning to prevail upon me is the natural consequence of my sexual maturation; now that that fleshy bud, source of all joys, has abandoned its place on my lower belly I've lost all motivation; and when I consider the ridiculous horny pimple where my progenital used to be a nameless despondency overcomes me. Of course, Vy still knows how to please me on that level, but how can that pleasure be compared with those ecstasies that swelled my entire being when she played with my progenital, when she caressed it and nourished it with her saliva! I want to forget the fact that my life was drafted for me by experts; I want to curl up, withdraw definitively into myself so I can clear up the secret of my birth and childhood. All our destinies are important because each entails the fate of a unique individual; even the least exceptional of beings possesses in his destiny a formidable magic charm, so powerful is its influence over him.

Immobile, I'll pursue my investigation, I'll unearth the most trivial anecdote, even if I have to defy society to do so!

I just emptied the garbage can. An old woman with gilded hair, upright on protuberant buttocks, was passing by in front of me, a fistful of meticulously stacked pieces of bark in her hand. She at once glanced at my lower belly and noticed the lack of a bulge beneath my pants pocket. I thought I saw her smile and took a few steps towards her which she must have taken for a threat, though I'd only wanted to ask her why she was smiling. She planted herself in front of me, her legs at a right angle to each other, her great belly hanging down like an apron, and began to yell:

'What do you want, gelding? You want me to get the pound to cart you off?'

The formula, even more than her tone of voice, shocked me. I asked her politely:

'Why'd you say that to me?'

'Because you don't have anything left between your legs, you useless fool, and you're ready to be thrown away. I don't let garbage like you permit itself to threaten me.'

'I wasn't threatening you, I just wanted to ask you why you were smiling.'

'Now you know, so go on, get out of here!'

I want to slap her, but I hold myself back, not because the script for today makes no mention of any such action – there's no longer any script to consider – but because I don't feel I have the energy for it. Excesses have always annoyed me, and today even more than usual. Besides, this old woman seems to know more about my situation than anyone I've met before.

'What is it that I know?'

My question surprises her: she drops her bark, then stoops down clumsily to gather it up again – or to pretend to do so, because in reality she's watching me out of the corner of her eye. I remain impassive, waiting for her to finish.

'Your wife didn't tell you?'

'Tell me what?'

'That you'll never be a man again.'

'No, Vy would never tell me anything like that.'

'She's got another fate in mind for you.'

The old woman's mouth twists curiously to the side, then she lowers her head, stacks her bark, and leaves, footsteps gliding as she makes her way towards the end of the avenue. I don't say anything, but I can sense that she feels my stare weighing on the hollow between her shoulders. Moments later she disappears. I turn back to the full garbage bin. Ordinarily the sight of it gives me a certain pleasure; mixing my trash with that of the other tenants gives me the impression that I'm participating a little in their lives. And besides, there's the action's artistic aspects, the superimpositions of objects and offal created, successive strata freezing themselves into readiness for the emptiers and other pariahs of the night. This time I feel no pleasure whatsoever, the trash repulses me, gives me the feeling that I, like it, am unclaimed and unwanted, trapped definitively in the solidified past. The resignation I felt, the desire to immobilize myself for all time so I could watch Vy and explore my childhood, suddenly strike me as the first signs of a dangerous mental illness. The loss of my progenital, which I thought of as symbolizing an unendurable curse, could, on the contrary, presage a different and unexpected adventure. The constrained dimensions of my existence – until now limited to my comings and goings between the apartment and the alimentary production unit – are perhaps going to dilate to infinity.

I go hastily back upstairs to get a few personal effects and a little money. I'm getting ready to savour my brand new freedom. For the first time since my adolescence ended I feel like giving myself over to my whims.

While searching feverishly for a few bills I go by the incubation cell. It seems to me that its walls are lighter. Isn't that my progenital that I can distinguish there in the midst of the liquid? I lean closer to get a better look at it, and faint.

It was only a brief remission; from now on my desires have been fulfilled. I've managed to extricate myself and hoist myself up onto the bed with my arms. I'm stretched out: I no longer feel anything. The humming in my ears from the building's fueling mechanism proves I can still hear. My tongue, there in the roof of my mouth, can scarcely move; it seems thicker than usual; I can no longer feel my teeth with it. As for my eyes, they still see: at fourthnotte, the day's first twilight is tinging with ochre the spiralling shoots as they draw their dark and angry scratches on the sepia of the sky. As always in the warm season, the second dawn is already fringing the contours of the buildings across from me with pink.

Vy won't be late getting back. Bizarrely, I feel somehow inferior to her. Though I'd decided to attach myself like a shellfish to her flesh and drink the sap of her days I hadn't expected my paralysis to overcome me at the moment when I desired it least. Were the mental mechanisms I set up to put me in this state so powerful that it was impossible to reverse their action, or was it the sight of the progenital's inordinately swollen body that brought on my brutal anesthetization? I can't say. Yet the fact remains that the sight of that entity swimming in its pocket of liquid provoked in me a terrible shock. I was so little prepared to confront such a monstrosity! How could that soft and silky thing that vegetated so long between my thighs have become that repugnant burgeoning of pink tissues? How could that obliging instrument of pleasure which swelled so tenderly beneath Vy's mouth and hands have transformed itself into such a distended tumor? It seems so improbable. There are limits to metamorphoses! I was on familiar terms with my progenital, I know that it can modify itself from hour to hour and day to day, I've seen it grow with the passage of time, seen it become that marvelous rotundity that Vy took from me so recently, but I can't believe it could have undergone such obscene alteration!

Odors no longer reach me, the bed no longer smells of grass. For that matter, is it really made of grass? My back no longer feels the crackling suppleness of the fibers. But there's Vy, she's coming in, I can hear her pushing her way through the entry sucker. Am I going to be able to talk to her? I make a timid attempt to move my tongue, then to make a sound. This final pleasure is denied me.

Vy is stunning, maternity does wonders for her. She's just entered the room: the last traces of anxiety in her gaze vanish at once. She smiles at me and says:

'At last, I can see that it's finally over and you're paralyzed, luckily.'

She's seated herself beside me and is feeling my body, first touching it cautiously, then pinching me harder in certain sensitive spots. Without provoking the slightest pain.

'It's good like this, dear, I won't have to have the doctor come. If you only knew how relieved I am! So many men aren't ready in time. Like our neighbor on the third floor, you know, Jelle, her husband's end was excruciating. But can you at least hear me?'

I manage to get my eyelid to cover my eyes, Jelle's husband! What happened to him, then? I'd always thought he'd gone to work with the off-worlders.

'You can hear me, good, I prefer it that way. We both always confided everything to each other; I wouldn't want to act now without letting you know what I was doing.'

She moves her hand over my sensitive skin and lingers on the small horny button remaining on my lower belly, in the center of that sad expanse left by my loss of my progenital. But this pleasure is refused me. I think: 'We always confided everything in each other, except the essential; how can a woman spend so many years with the man she loves without having even warned him what to expect when his time comes to reproduce?' Because she knew what was going to happen, she was watching for my paralysis. And how can a whole society have based itself on this immense hypocrisy about childbirth? Now I understand my childhood and why they erased it from my memory, understand that submissive adolescence they grant you before marrying you off and that precisely scripted life they impose on you! All that to hide from you the end imposed by artificial incubation. And Vy, who wanted us to go out every night so as to distract me, she was serenely awaiting my death!

'That's why I kept trying to get you to go out with me, to fatigue you and speed up your biological cycle, because I didn't want you to suffer,' she says, echoing my thoughts. 'You see, baby needs to be weaned, and the only thing he's capable of eating is you . . .'

Can she see the horror in my eyes? Vy, my love, no! Not this atrocity! Not this cannibal parricide!

'You probably think I'm a horrible woman, an ogress. But you're wrong, you see, all this is inscribed in our new genetic process. I love you, I love you, but my mind's as paralyzed as your body; I'm incapable of feeling the slightest emotion when I think about how I'm going to be feeding your flesh to your progenital. It's necessary, that's all, just as necessary as it is for you to stay immobile and anesthetized.'

She takes an admirably sharpened scalpel from her purse. Leans over my thigh and cuts off a large slice, then goes to the incubation cell, lifts the embossed part of the plaxaine, and delicately tosses that piece of me inside, to give life to my child. I don't have the strength to get up and take a look at my blood flowing, but I've still got enough to hear the horrifying noises the progenital makes consuming me.

Vy turns back to me and says:

'Don't worry, you're not going to die immediately. I've got a marvelous instantaneous cicatrizing agent to use on your wounds.'

And in her eyes as she looks at me I can read all the love in the world.

The Cage

BERTRAM CHANDLER

Imprisonment is always a humiliating experience, no matter how philosophical the prisoner. Imprisonment by one's own kind is bad enough – but one can, at least, talk to one's captors, one can make one's wants understood; one can, on occasion, appeal to them man to man.

Imprisonment is doubly humiliating when one's captors, in all honesty, treat one as a lower animal.

The party from the survey ship could, perhaps, be excused for failing to recognize the survivors from the interstellar liner *Lode Star* as rational beings. At least two hundred days had passed since their landing on the planet without a name – an unintentional landing made when *Lode Star*'s Ehrenhaft generators, driven far in excess of their normal capacity by a breakdown of the electronic regulator, had flung her far from the regular shipping lanes to an unexplored region of space. *Lode Star* had landed safely enough; but shortly thereafter (troubles never come singly) her pile had got out of control and her captain had ordered his first mate to evacuate the passengers and those crew members not needed to cope with the emergency, and to get them as far from the ship as possible.

Hawkins and his charges were well clear when there was a flare of released energy, a not very violent explosion. The survivors wanted to turn to watch, but Hawkins drove them on with curses and, at times, blows. Luckily they were up wind from the ship and so escaped the fallout.

When the fireworks seemed to be over, Hawkins, accompanied

by Dr Boyle, the ship's surgeon, returned to the scene of the disaster. The two men, wary of radioactivity, were cautious and stayed a safe distance from the shallow, still smoking crater that marked where the ship had been. It was all too obvious to them that the captain, together with his officers and technicians, were now no more than an infinitesimal part of the incandescent cloud that had mushroomed up into the low overcast.

Thereafter the fifty-odd men and women, the survivors of *Lode Star*, had degenerated. It hadn't been a fast process – Hawkins and Boyle, aided by a committee of the more responsible passengers, had fought a stout rearguard action. But it had been a hopeless sort of fight. The climate was against them, for a start. Hot it was, always in the neighbourhood of 85° Fahrenheit. And it was wet – a thin, warm drizzle falling all the time. The air seemed to abound with the spores of fungi – luckily these did not attack living skin but throve on dead organic matter, on clothing. They throve to an only slightly lesser degree on metals and on the synthetic fabrics that many of the castaways wore.

Danger, outside danger, would have helped to maintain morale. But there were no dangerous animals. There were only little smooth-skinned things, not unlike frogs, that hopped through the sodden undergrowth, and, in the numerous rivers, fish-like creatures ranging in size from the shark to the tadpole, and all of them possessing the bellicosity of the latter.

Food had been no problem after the first few hungry hours. Volunteers had tried a large, succulent fungus growing on the boles of the huge fern-like trees. They had pronounced it good. After a lapse of five hours they had neither died nor even complained of abdominal pains. That fungus was to become the staple diet of the castaways. In the weeks that followed other fungi had been found, and berries, and roots – all of them edible. They provided a welcome variety.

Fire – in spite of the all-pervading heat – was the blessing most missed by the castaways. With it they could have supplemented their diet by catching and cooking the little frog-things of the rain forest, the fishes of the streams. Some of the hardier spirits did eat these animals raw, but they were frowned upon by most of the other members of the community. Fire would also have helped to drive back the darkness of the long nights, would, by its real warmth and light, have dispelled the illusion of cold produced by the ceaseless dripping of water from every leaf and frond.

When they fled from the ship, most of the survivors had possessed pocket lighters – but the lighters had been lost when the pockets, together with the clothing surrounding them, had disintegrated. In any case, all attempts to start a fire in the days when there were still pocket lighters had failed – there was not, Hawkins swore, a single dry spot on the whole accursed planet. Now the making of fire was quite impossible: even if there had been present an expert on the rubbing together of two dry sticks he could have found no material with which to work.

They made their permanent settlement on the crest of a low hill. (There were, so far as they could discover, no mountains.) It was less thickly wooded there than the surrounding plains, and the ground was less marshy underfoot. They succeeded in wrenching fronds from the fern-like trees and built for themselves crude shelters – more for the sake of privacy than for any comfort that they afforded. They clung, with a certain desperation, to the governmental forms of the worlds that they had left, and elected themselves a council. Boyle, the ship's surgeon, was their chief. Hawkins, rather to his surprise, was returned as a council member by a majority of only two votes – on thinking it over he realized that many of the passengers must still bear a grudge against the ship's executive staff for their present predicament.

The first council meeting was held in a hut – if so it could be called – especially constructed for the purpose. The council members squatted in a rough circle. Boyle, the president, got slowly to his feet. Hawkins grinned wryly as he compared the surgeon's nudity with the pomposity that he seemed to have assumed with his elected rank, as he compared the man's dignity with the unkempt appearance presented by his uncut, uncombed grey hair, his uncombed and straggling grey beard.

'Ladies and gentlemen,' began Boyle.

Hawkins looked around him at the naked, pallid bodies, at the stringy, lustreless hair, the long, dirty fingernails of the men and the unpainted lips of the women. He thought, I don't suppose I look much like an officer and a gentleman myself.

'Ladies and gentlemen,' said Boyle, 'we have been, as you know, elected to represent the human community upon this planet. I suggest that at this, our first meeting, we discuss our chances of survival – not as individuals, but as a race –'

'I'd like to ask Mr Hawkins what our chances are of being picked up,' shouted one of the two women members, a dried-up, spinsterish creature with prominent ribs and vertebrae.

'Slim,' said Hawkins. 'As you know, no communication is possible with other ships or with planet stations when the Interstellar Drive is operating. When we snapped out of the Drive and came in for our landing we sent out a distress call – but we couldn't say where we were. Furthermore, we don't know that the call was received –'

'Miss Taylor,' said Boyle huffily, 'Mr Hawkins, I would remind you that I am the duly elected president of this council. There will be time for a general discussion later.

'As most of you may already have assumed, the age of this planet, biologically speaking, corresponds roughly with that of Earth during the Carboniferous Era. As we know, no species yet exists to challenge our supremacy. By the time such a species does emerge – something analogous to the giant lizards of Earth's Triassic Era – we should be well established –'

'*We* shall be dead!' called one of the men.

'We shall be dead,' agreed the doctor, 'but our descendants will be very much alive. We have to decide how to give them as good a start as possible. Language we shall bequeath to them –'

'Never mind the language, Doc,' called the other woman member. She was a small blonde, slim, with a hard face. 'It's just this question of descendants that I'm here to look after. I represent the women of childbearing age – there are, as you must know, thirteen of us here. So far the girls have been very, very careful. We have reason to be. Can you, as a medical man, guarantee – bearing in mind that you have no drugs, no instruments – safe deliveries? Can you guarantee that our children will have a good chance of survival?'

Boyle dropped his pomposity like a worn-out garment.

'I'll be frank,' he said. 'I have not, as you, Miss Hart, have pointed out, either drugs or instruments. But I can assure you,

Miss Hart, that your chances of a safe delivery are far better than they would have been on Earth during, say, the eighteenth century. And I'll tell you why. On this planet, so far as we know (and we have been here long enough now to find out the hard way), there exist no micro-organisms harmful to Man. Did such organisms exist, the bodies of those of us still surviving would be, by this time, mere masses of suppuration. Most of us, of course, would have died of septicaemia long ago. And that, I think, answers *both* your questions.'

'I haven't finished yet,' she said. 'Here's another point. There are fifty-three of us here, men and women. There are ten married couples – so we'll count them out. That leaves thirty-three people, of whom twenty are men. Twenty men to thirteen (aren't we girls always unlucky?) women. All of us aren't young – but we're all of us women. What sort of marriage set-up do we have? Monogamy? Polyandry?'

'Monogamy, of course,' said a tall, thin man sharply. He was the only one of those present who wore clothing – if it could be called that. The disintegrating fronds lashed around his waist with a strand of vine did little to serve any useful purpose.

'All right, then,' said the girl. 'Monogamy; I'd rather prefer it that way myself. But I warn you that if that's the way we play it there's going to be trouble. And in any murder involving passion and jealousy the woman is as liable to be a victim as either of the men – and I don't want *that.*'

'What do you propose, then, Miss Hart?' asked Boyle.

'Just this, Doc. When it comes to our mating we leave love out of it. If two men want to marry the same woman, then let them fight it out. The best man gets the girl – and keeps her.'

'Natural selection . . .' murmured the surgeon. 'I'm in favour – but we must put it to the vote.'

At the crest of the hill was a shallow depression, a natural arena. Round the rim sat the castaways – all but four of them. One of the four was Dr Boyle – he had discovered that his duties as president embraced those of a referee; it had been held that he was best competent to judge when one of the contestants was liable to suffer permanent damage. Another of the four was the girl Mary

Hart. She had found a serrated twig with which to comb her long hair and had contrived a wreath of yellow flowers with which to crown the victor. Was it, wondered Hawkins as he sat with the other council members, a hankering after an Earthly wedding ceremony, or was it a harking back to something older and darker?

'A pity that these blasted moulds got our watches,' said the fat man on Hawkins' right. 'If we had any means of telling the time we could have rounds, make a proper prize-fight of it.'

Hawkins nodded. He looked at the four in the centre of the arena – at the strutting, barbaric woman, at the pompous old man, at the two dark-bearded young men with their glistening white bodies. He knew them both – Fennet had been a Senior Cadet of the ill-fated *Lode Star*; Clemens, at least seven years Fennet's senior, was a passenger, had been a prospector on the frontier worlds.

'If we had anything to bet with,' said the fat man happily, 'I'd lay it on Clemens. That cadet of yours hasn't a snowball's chance in hell, He's been brought up to fight clean – Clemens has been brought up to fight dirty.'

'Fennet's in better condition,' said Hawkins. 'He's been taking exercise, while Clemens has just been lying around sleeping and eating. Look at the paunch on him!'

'There's nothing wrong with good healthy flesh and muscle,' said the fat man, patting his own paunch.

'No gouging, no biting!' called the doctor. 'And may the best man win!'

He stepped back smartly, away from the contestants, stood with the Hart woman.

There was an air of embarrassment about the pair of them as they stood there, each with his fists hanging at his sides. Each seemed to be regretting that matters had come to such a pass.

'Go *on*!' screamed Mary Hart at last. 'Don't you want me? You'll live to a ripe old age here – and it'll be lonely with no woman!'

'They can always wait around until your daughters grow up, Mary!' shouted one of her friends.

'If I ever have any daughters!' she called. 'I shan't at this rate!'

'Go on!' shouted the crowd. 'Go on!'

Fennet made a start. He stepped forward almost diffidently, dabbed with his right fist at Clemens' unprotected face. It wasn't a hard blow, but it must have been painful. Clemens put his hand up to his nose, brought it away and stared at the bright blood staining it. He growled, lumbered forward with arms open to hug and crush. The cadet danced back, scoring twice more with his right.

'Why doesn't he *hit* him?' demanded the fat man.

'And break every bone in his fist? They aren't wearing gloves, you know,' said Hawkins.

Fennet decided to make a stand. He stood firm, his feet slightly apart, and brought his right into play once more. This time he left his opponent's face alone, went for his belly instead. Hawkins was surprised to see that the prospector was taking the blows with apparent equanimity – he must be, he decided, much tougher in actuality than in appearance.

The cadet sidestepped smartly . . . and slipped on the wet grass. Clemens fell heavily on to his opponent; Hawkins could hear the *whoosh* as the air was forced from the lad's lungs. The prospector's thick arms encircled Fennet's body – and Fennet's knee came up viciously to Clemens' groin. The prospector squealed, but hung on grimly. One of his hands was around Fennet's throat now, and the other one, its fingers viciously hooked, was clawing for the cadet's eyes.

'No gouging!' Boyle was screaming. 'No gouging!'

He dropped down to his knees, caught Clemens' wrist with both his hands.

Something made Hawkins look up. It may have been a sound, although this is doubtful; the spectators were behaving like boxing fans at a prize-fight. They could hardly be blamed – this was the first piece of real excitement that had come their way since the loss of the ship. It may have been a sound that made Hawkins look up, it may have been the sixth sense possessed by all good spacemen. What he saw made him cry out.

Hovering above the arena was a helicopter. There was something about the design of it, a subtle oddness, that told Hawkins that this was no Earthly machine. From its smooth, shining belly dropped a net, seemingly of dull metal. It enveloped the struggling figures on the ground, trapped the doctor and Mary Hart.

Hawkins shouted again – a wordless cry. He jumped to his feet, ran to the assistance of his ensnared companions. The net seemed to be alive. It twisted itself around his wrists, bound his ankles. Others of the castaways rushed to aid Hawkins.

'Keep away!' he shouted. 'Scatter!'

The low drone of the helicopter's rotors rose in pitch. The machine lifted. In an incredibly short space of time the arena was to the First Mate's eyes no more than a pale green saucer in which little white ants scurried aimlessly. Then the flying machine was above and through the base of the low clouds, and there was nothing to be seen but drifting whiteness.

When, at last, it made its descent Hawkins was not surprised to see the silvery tower of a great spaceship standing among the low trees on a level plateau.

The world to which they were taken would have been a marked improvement on the world they had left, had it not been for the mistaken kindness of their captors. The cage in which the three men were housed duplicated, with remarkable fidelity, the climatic condition of the planet upon which *Lode Star* had been lost. It was glassed in, and from sprinklers in its roof fell a steady drizzle of warm water. A couple of dispirited tree ferns provided little shelter from the depressing precipitation. Twice a day a hatch at the back of the cage, which was made of a sort of concrete, opened, and slabs of fungus remarkably similar to that on which they had been subsisting were thrown in. There was a hole in the floor of the cage; this the prisoners rightly assumed was for sanitary purposes.

On either side of them were other cages. In one of them was Mary Hart – alone. She could gesture to them, wave to them, and that was all. The cage on the other side held a beast built on the same general lines as a lobster, but with a strong resemblance to a kind of squid. Across the broad roadway they could see other cages, but not what they housed.

Hawkins, Boyle, and Fennet sat on the damp floor and stared through the thick glass and the bars at the beings outside who stared at them.

'If only they were humanoid,' sighed the doctor. 'If only they were the same shape as we are, we might make a start towards convincing them that we, too, are intelligent beings.'

'They aren't the same shape,' said Hawkins. 'And we, were the situations reversed, would take some convincing that three six-legged beer barrels were men and brothers ... Try Pythagoras' Theorem again,' he said to the cadet.

Without enthusiasm the youth broke fronds from the nearest tree fern. He broke them into smaller pieces, then on the mossy floor laid them out in the design of a right-angled triangle with squares constructed on all three sides. The natives – a large one, one slightly smaller, and a little one – regarded him incuriously with their flat, dull eyes. The large one put the tip of a tentacle into a pocket – the things wore clothing – and pulled out a brightly coloured packet, handed it to the little one. The little one tore off the wrapping, started stuffing pieces of some bright blue confection into the slot on its upper side that, obviously, served it as a mouth.

'I wish they were allowed to feed the animals,' sighed Hawkins. 'I'm sick of that damned fungus.'

'Let's recapitulate,' said the doctor. 'After all, we've nothing else to do. We were taken from our camp by the helicopter – six of us. We were taken to the survey ship – a vessel that seemed in no way superior to our own interstellar ships. You assure us, Hawkins, that the ship used the Ehrenhaft Drive or something so near to it as to be its twin brother ...'

'Correct,' agreed Hawkins.

'On the ship we're kept in separate cages. There's no ill treatment, we're fed and watered at frequent intervals. We land on this strange planet, but we see nothing of it. We're hustled out of cages like so many cattle in a covered van. We know that we're being driven *somewhere*, that's all. The van stops, the door opens and a couple of these animated beer barrels poke in poles with smaller editions of those fancy nets on the end of them. They catch Clemens and Miss Taylor, drag them out. We never see them again. The rest of us spend the night and the following day and night in individual cages. The next day we're taken to this ... zoo ...'

'Do you think they were vivisected?' asked Fennet. 'I never liked Clemens, but ...'

'I'm afraid they were,' said Boyle. 'Our captors must have learned of the difference between the sexes by it. Unluckily there's no way of determining intelligence by vivisection –'

'The filthy brutes!' shouted the cadet.

'Easy, son,' counselled Hawkins. 'You can't blame them, you know. We've vivisected animals a lot more like us than we are to these things.'

'The problem,' the doctor went on, 'is to convince these things – as you call them, Hawkins – that we are rational beings like themselves. How would they define a rational being? How would *we* define a rational being?'

'Somebody who knows Pythagoras' Theorem,' said the cadet sulkily.

'I read somewhere,' said Hawkins, 'that the history of Man is the history of the fire-making, tool-using animal . . .'

'Then make fire,' suggested the doctor. 'Make us some tools, and use them.'

'Don't be silly. You know that there's not an artifact among the bunch of us. No false teeth even – not even a metal filling. Even so . . .' He paused. 'When I was a youngster there was, among the cadets in the interstellar ships, a revival of the old arts and crafts. We considered ourselves in a direct line of descent from the old windjammer sailormen, so we learned how to splice rope and wire, how to make sennit and fancy knots and all the rest of it. Then one of us hit on the idea of basketmaking. We were in a passenger ship, and we used to make our baskets secretly, daub them with violent colours and then sell them to passengers as genuine souvenirs from the Lost Planet of Arcturus VI. There was a most distressing scene when the Old Man and the Mate found out . . .'

'What are you driving at?' asked the doctor.

'Just this. We will demonstrate our manual dexterity by the weaving of baskets – I'll teach you how.'

'It might work . . .' said Boyle slowly. 'It might just work . . . On the other hand, don't forget that certain birds and animals do the same sort of thing. On Earth there's the beaver, who builds quite cunning dams. There's the bower bird, who makes a bower for his mate as part of the courtship ritual . . .'

The Head Keeper must have known of creatures whose courting

habits resembled those of the Terran bower bird. After three days of feverish basketmaking, which consumed all the bedding and stripped the tree ferns, Mary Hart was taken from her cage and put in with the three men. After she had got over her hysterical pleasure at having somebody to talk to again she was rather indignant.

It was good, thought Hawkins drowsily, to have Mary with them. A few more days of solitary confinement must surely have driven the girl crazy. Even so, having Mary in the same cage had its drawbacks. He had to keep a watchful eye on Boyle – the old goat!

Mary screamed.

Hawkins jerked into complete wakefulness. He could see the pale form of Mary – on this world it was never completely dark at night – and, on the other side of the cage, the forms of Fennet and Boyle. He got hastily to his feet, stumbled to the girl's side.

'What is it?' he asked.

'I . . . I don't know . . . Something small, with sharp claws . . . It ran over me . . .'

'Oh,' said Hawkins, 'that was only Joe.'

'*Joe?*' she demanded.

'I don't know exactly what he – or she – is,' said the man.

'I think he's definitely *he*,' said the doctor.

'What is Joe?' she asked again.

'He must be the local equivalent to a mouse,' said the doctor, 'although he looks nothing like one. He comes up through the floor somewhere to look for scraps of food. We're trying to tame him –'

'You encourage the brute?' she screamed. 'I demand that you do something about him – at once! Poison him, or trap him. Now!'

'Tomorrow,' said Hawkins.

'Now!' she screamed.

'Tomorrow,' said Hawkins firmly.

The capture of Joe proved to be easy. Two flat baskets, hinged like the valves of an oyster shell, under the trap. There was a bait inside – a large piece of the fungus. There was a cunningly arranged upright that would fall at the least tug at the bait. Hawkins, lying sleepless on his damp bed, heard the tiny click and thud that told him that the trap had been sprung. He heard Joe's indignant chitterings, heard the tiny claws scrabbling at the stout basket-work.

Mary Hart was asleep. He shook her.

'We've caught him,' he said.

'Then kill him,' she answered drowsily.

But Joe was not killed. The three men were rather attached to him. With the coming of daylight they transferred him to a cage that Hawkins had fashioned. Even the girl relented when she saw the harmless ball of multicoloured fur bouncing indignantly up and down in its prison. She insisted on feeding the little animal, exclaimed gleefully when the thin tentacles reached out and took the fragment of fungus from her fingers.

For three days they made much of their pet. On the fourth day beings whom they took to be keepers entered the cage with their nets, immobilized the occupants, and carried off Joe and Hawkins.

'I'm afraid it's hopeless,' Boyle said. 'He's gone the same way . . .'

'They'll have him stuffed and mounted in some museum,' said Fennet glumly.

'No,' said the girl. 'They couldn't!'

'They could,' said the doctor.

Abruptly the hatch at the back of the cage opened.

Before the three humans could retreat, a voice called, 'It's all right, come on out!'

Hawkins walked into the cage. He was shaved, and the beginnings of a healthy tan had darkened the pallor of his skin. He was wearing a pair of trunks fashioned from some bright red material.

'Come on out,' he said again. 'Our hosts have apologized very sincerely, and they have more suitable accommodation prepared for us. Then, as soon as they have a ship ready, we're to go to pick up the other survivors.'

'Not so fast,' said Boyle. 'Put us in the picture, will you? What made them realize that we were rational beings?'

Hawkins' face darkened.

'Only rational beings,' he said, 'put other beings in cages.'

An Imaginary Journey to the Moon

VICTOR SABAH

During that long period of anguish, there was a need of exploring the moon, in search of food. Whilst reading the papers one morning, I came across an advertisement from the Ghana Scientists' Association appealing to students who had passed their GCE and obtained Certificates to register and undergo some special training towards the exploration of the moon.

I registered myself immediately and, as I was good at physics, as clearly shown from the grade one I got, I was seriously considered. I arrived at the Kumasi University of Science and Technology the following week to see twenty-nine others who were already in residence. Then I began to notice something; all the other people were as young as myself.

To make sure of our knowledge in science we were given another examination mostly based on physics. I did well enough to get grade one which the others could not get. My magnificent performance won for me admiration of all the professors. But ten of our number were dropped because of their poor showing. I was allowed to do everything I could on the compound, but I did not value such a privilege. I kept on studying.

One afternoon, after lunch, we were all gathered into a room for an interview. As we were taken by surprise, fifteen out of twenty people failed. Now there remained five of us. We often went to lectures day and night. As I went to bed I always imagined my near future, especially my going to the moon and its significance to my beloved country.

After many hardships and difficult training, I was selected at last as the head or commander of the three-member space exploration association. I, Job Sazona, was the commander-in-chief, assisted by El-Latigo, and the third member was Armwick, the driver. The ship was ready awaiting us on 15 December 1974. Before we arrived at the 'Spy B' airport in our well-organized space-suits, there had been many people from all over the world waiting anxiously to see the take-off. Now there came great silence to dominate the port. We were seated near the ship as the managing director read out the program to the crowd. After the reading the crowd clapped and waved their hands. By now I was in a sad mood feeling more certain about death than life.

I saw my sad father waving to me reluctantly. I was a little encouraged by the smiling face of my lover. From amongst the crowd I saw my sorrowful mother wishing me a safe journey. 'If fortune fails, goodbye,' said my mother. I was totally moved by these words to a point of great discouragement. I lifted up my feet to climb the thirty-foot-high spaceship. On the third step I could see people struggling in all anxiety to see the spacemen. In the next five minutes we were already in position to take off.

BOOM! The ship took off at a very terrific speed of 300 miles per hour. This was not great enough to carry us through within one day, so I increased the speed to a top one of 3,000 miles per hour.

The cold atmospheric winds could overcome the heat which had been pumped into the ship. At an altitude of about 20,000 miles we felt like we were freezing. Before then, at a lower altitude of about 4,000 miles, I took out my camera to take pictures of some stars and comets.

At the same time that I was taking the photographs, I saw a big human head, without body, with a long beard moving at the same speed as the ship. It tried to talk to me but I could not understand it. In view of this unfamiliar thing I lost all inclination to continue the journey, but as there was no possibility of returning, I had to keep on. I had tried to take its photograph but it did not appear on the film.

This frightening thing did not even disappear when Latigo was short of oxygen. As a trained spaceman, I did all I could to share mine with him. Two minutes later, the battery disconnected with the engine, which nearly damaged us. This was immediately repaired. The managers did their best to give us direction about how to go about our difficulties.

It was now time for meals. Each of us took ten food tablets and five water tablets. On relaxing, we all fell asleep and slept for six hours each. When we woke up we washed our faces; the water just flowed in the air.

After ten hours of constant velocity we got to the moon and were in orbit round it in search of a landing site. At last we landed at a convenient place.

After our successful landing, we waited in the spaceship about fifteen minutes to see whether anything would happen. The fifteen minutes passed. According to the law of space exploration the commander has to do everything first, so I, the commander, came out of the ship first. After stepping on the ground, I stood still in search of any unfamiliar happening. Five minutes of no havoc passed.

Now my fellow-travelers were with me on the real surface of the moon. Apart from life, the moon is like the earth. Mountains, plains, rivers, seas and valleys are found on it. But the atmospheric conditions differ. The moon has a barren atmosphere which contributes to the benignity of its climate. From where we landed there leads a straight path to the west, the asperity of which is subtle. Just in front of us lay a vast plain which we named 'Sazona Plain,' after Sazona, the captain. At the end of this plain is a mountain which we named Latigo. In the middle of the plain is a sea which we called 'The Sea of Armwick'. The plain, the mountain and the sea are regarded as one region called 'The Salata Region'.

I began to walk about with my companions, first towards the mountain. On the opposite side of the mountain, there is a very deep and steep valley at the bottom of which is a solitary tree which never grows. A hundred yards east of the valley lies a conic mountain, about 30,000 feet high. Just behind the mountain, I fell into a whirlwind which never moves from place to place and never stops blowing. In the midst of the whirlwind I put the flag of my nation and around it were situated some other flags.

While returning to the spaceship we collected many different kinds of rocks. When we were about twenty yards away from the ship, we heard the alarm of the clock. Now it was time for communications. I ran into the ship, got everything set and began to talk. I talked about all that we saw and about our landing.

After communications I went to have some swimming in 'The Sea of Armwick', leaving my friends behind. I got inside the water and in the next moment I found myself at the extreme bottom of the sea. In reality, the sea is a very deep one and has very steep sides. What a task it was for me to get back to its surface. I began slowly from the bottom of the sea and in a hour's time, after tiring struggles, I was once again on the surface of the water. On this occasion I remembered the words of my mother and thanked God very much for a rescue.

I was now hungry, so I went straight to join my companions who were already eating. Before two hours of entertainment we rested for thirty minutes. During this time of entertainment, we heard music for some time and used the rest of the time for conversation and story telling.

On the moon the earth appeared like a midnight star. We saw no trees, buildings and roads. Just behind us we heard a noise. The mountains stood up on tiny feet and on top of them was coming out smoke. 'Volcano in action to run', said Latigo. We were all afraid and were in position to depart, lest we die on unfamiliar ground.

To avoid painful death, we departed suddenly, one hour ahead of time. But then, nothing pleased me more than escaping from that catastrophe. However, it soon disappeared from my mind. I now thought of how we would be welcomed by the eager crowd.

We splashed in the Pacific Ocean, 200 miles from the 'Spy B' port and were immediately carried to the port by a helicopter. One can imagine the sort of pride which entered me as my name spread over the whole world.